# Regency

## COLLECTION

VOLUME
—10—

# THE
# *Regency*
## COLLECTION

### VOLUME
### —10—

## Eleanor
by
*Sylvia Andrew*

## Miss Weston's Masquerade
by
*Francesca Shaw*

*MILLS & BOON and MILLS & BOON with the Rose Device
are registered trademarks of the publisher.*

*First published in Great Britain 1999 by
Harlequin Mills & Boon Limited,
Eton House, 18–24 Paradise Road,
Richmond, Surrey, TW9 1SR.*

The Regency Collection © by Harlequin Enterprises II B.V. 1999

The publisher acknowledges the copyright holders of the
individual work as follows:

Eleanor © Sylvia Andrew 1994
Miss Weston's Masquerade © Francesca Shaw 1994

ISBN 0 263 82423 3
106-0002

*Printed and bound in Spain
by Litografia Rosés S.A., Barcelona*

# ELEANOR

by

## Sylvia Andrew

**Dear Reader**

Love, laughter and some tears, drama, a sense of style, a flavour of the language of the period—these are what attract me in writing 'Regency Romances'. And since I am, after all, a woman of the twentieth century, I like the idea that women of that period, unlike their Victorian daughters, were allowed to display spirit and intelligence.

In *Eleanor*, Miss Southeran needs all her spirit and intelligence when she discovers that Mr Jonas Guthrie is more interesting than the aristocrats she meets—if she ever gets the chance to know him!

I hope you enjoy reading about my lovely, spirited heroine as much as I enjoyed writing about her.

Sylvia Andrew

**Sylvia Andrew** taught modern languages for years, ending up as Vice-Principal of a sixth-form college. She lives in Somerset with two cats, a dog, and a husband who has a very necessary sense of humour, and a stern approach to punctuation. Sylvia has one daughter living in London, and they share a lively interest in the theatre. She describes herself as an 'unrepentant romantic'.

**Other titles by the same author:**

Serena
Perdita
A Darling Amazon
Serafina
Francesca
Rosabelle *Volume One*  } The Christmas Belles
Annabelle *Volume Two*

# CHAPTER ONE

ELEANOR had never seen anything so beautiful. The crystal drops in the huge chandelier splintered the flames from its candles into a million points of sparkling light. It was like. . .like fireworks frozen in the air, like all the stars in the Milky Way gathered together. It was worth coming to London just to see this. A fairy-tale enchantment. . .

'Eleanor, my dear, Lady Dorothy and her daughter wish to speak to you!' Eleanor was recalled to a more mundane reality by the sound of her aunt's voice. Without waiting for her niece, Lady Walcot had moved on a few paces in the direction of a dowager with a haughty air and an imposing turban, complete with feathers.

Eleanor gave a small sigh and started to follow, but stopped again when she became aware that a tall, broad-shouldered man with dark, hard features was staring at her from the other side of the room. He would have been an impressive figure in any circumstances, but what made him even more striking was the fact that in this crowded room he was standing quite alone.

As her eye caught his, he raised one eyebrow and smiled ironically. He was laughing at her! Of course, she had been behaving like the country bumpkin her cousins accused her of being, gazing like a moonstruck idiot at the chandelier, but she was not about to be put out of countenance by this creature's boldness! She raised her chin, gave him a cool stare, and then turned away to join her aunt and Lady Dorothy.

After exchanging civilities with Lady Walcot and agreeing, with every sign of pleasure, that the rooms were sadly crowded, Lady Dorothy said with a significant movement of her head, 'I see that he is back in London.'

'He?' said Lady Walcot blankly. Then her puzzled expression changed to one of disapprobation. 'Is he here now?'

'Come, Lady Walcot! You must have noticed him.'

'No, where?'

'Further down on the other side of the room—you passed him as you came in. He is quite on his own, of course. How he has the effrontery to show himself I cannot imagine!' The ladies turned and stared down the room. Eleanor looked too, but more discreetly. The tall man was gazing indifferently at the passing crowd, but when he became conscious of those two icy stares directed down the room at him he bowed ironically. Whatever the gentleman lacked it was not self-assurance, thought Eleanor with some amusement.

'The impertinence!' said Lady Dorothy as she turned back again, outraged. 'But, my dear Lady Walcot, there is worse. Mrs Anstey is here tonight, too. I only hope the poor woman is not brought face to face with him—that would be most unfortunate. In a moment I shall seek her out and warn her.'

'Indeed you must!'

Most of the sense of this conversation was lost on Eleanor, though it was certain that the two ladies were talking of the man who had smiled at her. Her aunt seemed to be genuinely worried by his presence, but beneath her display of righteous indignation Lady Dorothy was relishing the idea of seeking this Mrs Anstey out to warn her. Lady Dorothy had never forgotten that she was the daughter of a duke, and that marrying Edwin Rushton—a mere commoner—in no way diminished her right to order the lives of those around her. When they had last met, Eleanor had thought her an uncharitable busybody, and she now saw that the years did not appear to have mellowed or changed her. She sighed and waited patiently until the lady turned to her.

'Miss Southeran. How nice to see you in London again. Are you here for the season? I believe your mama is not with you?'

'I am a little old for that, Lady Dorothy,' said Eleanor with a polite smile. 'No, I merely came to take part in my cousin Bella's wedding celebrations. But I must go back soon—I have been away too long already. My mother is now something of an invalid, and I worry about her.'

Lady Dorothy's daughter, a pretty, fair-haired girl with doll-like features, cried, 'But how can you bear it, Miss Southeran? To be leaving London just as the season is beginning!'

'Be silent, Maria! Miss Southeran will do as she ought. No doubt she regrets having to leave London at any time, but it is not as if she were a girl in her first season. As I recall, you came out the same year as my Charlotte, did you not?' said Lady Dorothy, turning to Eleanor again with a crocodile smile. 'Let me see, that must have been seven or eight years ago.

How time flies! Has your aunt told you that Charlotte is now the mother of three charming little girls?'

'Indeed she has, ma'am. And how happy Charlotte is in her marriage.'

'It is fortunate. She was always a good, obedient girl, of course, and would never have dreamt of refusing Lord Crawford's offer. Her father and I would not have permitted it. But as it happens the match has turned out very well.' She turned to her youngest daughter. 'I hope you are paying heed, Maria! Miss Southeran here had just the same opportunities as Charlotte, but I am sorry to say that she wasted them all. Indeed your own brother Arthur was quite taken with her for a while. I dare swear she now regrets her foolishness and wishes she too had an establishment and children of her own!'

Eleanor replied calmly, 'If I could have been sure of making your son as happy as Charlotte is in her marriage, I would have accepted his very flattering offer, Lady Dorothy. But I am persuaded that his second choice of partner was a better one for him. As for the rest—you will perhaps remember that I had to leave London halfway through the season, when my brother died. I have not been back between then and now.'

Eleanor's voice might have been calm, but her aunt, observing the faint colour rising in her niece's cheeks, intervened hastily. 'I am sure that no daughter could have been more loving or more dutiful than Eleanor, Lady Dorothy. I have done my best to keep her in London a little longer, even pleaded with her to keep me company for a while now that Bella has left me, but she insists that her mother needs her.'

'I suppose that is understandable—London must seem strangely noisy after so many years in the depths of the country. For myself, I cannot imagine what it would be like to live so far from any really civilised society—very tame, I dare swear. Arthur and his wife live with me, of course, in the centre of town. They are forever entertaining and visiting. But now, if you will forgive me, I really must go in search of Mrs Anstey. Enjoy the rest of your stay, Miss Southeran! Perhaps we shall see you again. Come, Maria.' As Lady Dorothy sailed away with Maria in tow, Eleanor let her breath out in a long sigh.

'I had forgotten how odious that woman is.'

'Eleanor!'

'Well, she is, Aunt Hetty. I am willing to wager that Arthur is as much under her thumb now as he was seven years ago. I pity his poor wife.'

It was clear that Lady Walcot agreed with her niece, but was not about to say so. Instead she changed the subject. 'Would you like me to find you a dancing partner, Eleanor?'

'Do you think you could? At my great age? Lady Dorothy would think it most unlikely.'

'Eleanor, you let your tongue run away with you— you always did. It is not becoming in you to make fun of your elders, and especially not Lady Dorothy. In any case,' she went on, somewhat spoiling her effect, 'you are as handsome now as you ever were, and I am sure I shall have no difficulty at all in finding someone to dance with you.' As they walked up the room she went on, 'But I confess that I wish I could be happier about your future! Since you refuse to stay here in London, I suppose you must look for a husband in

Somerset.' She sounded so doubtful about the idea that Eleanor burst out laughing.

'You are right to rate my chances low, Aunt Hetty! The young men of Somerset have younger, richer game to pursue—when they are not pursuing real game, or shooting pigeons, or. . .or. . .whatever they spend their time doing. Truth to tell, I find them rather boring! But pray do not concern yourself on my account. Mama and I are quite happy together. And you know that I have always loved Stanyards.'

Lady Walcot stopped by a quiet alcove. 'My dear, it isn't enough!' she said earnestly. 'A woman's best chance of security lies in a suitable marriage.'

'Such as one to Arthur Rushton, perhaps?' asked Eleanor with a slight curl of the lip.

'Why not? He is rich—or will be one day. And from what I hear young Mrs Rushton has a handsome allowance and any number of servants to look after her. And she has her children. It is a pity that her nerves do not always permit her to enjoy her advantages. . .'

'You see? No, Aunt Hetty. I think I am happier in my tame country existence than I could ever be in Clara Rushton's place.'

'Happiness is not the sole aim of marriage, Eleanor. Not even the chief aim.'

'Isn't it? I think it is the only one.'

'What nonsense you talk! Pray be serious for one moment! If you would only put yourself into my hands I could almost certainly find you a suitable husband here in London.'

'Well, then, I promise you, when I feel the need of one I shall come to you first of all! But for now I shall look around me and enjoy the spectacle of London society amusing itself. The memory of it will console my tame country evenings.'

Lady Walcot shook her head at her niece's refusal to be serious, but decided to say no more, and they resumed their walk down the room. It was a magnificent apartment, lavishly furnished in red velvet with a richly decorated white and gold ceiling. Eleanor found it slightly overpowering—vulgar even, but dared not say so. The chandelier was lovely, though. She looked up at it as they passed, and nearly walked into her aunt as that lady suddenly stopped. The stranger from the other side of the room was standing in front of them.

'Lady Walcot——' Eleanor's aunt looked coldly at the gentleman but said nothing. He continued, 'We met at my cousin's house in Berkeley Square. My name is Guthrie. I should like to ask your companion to dance with me.'

'Thank you, sir, but my niece does not intend to dance this evening—not at the moment, at least,' said Lady Walcot frostily.

Perhaps the gentlemen saw Eleanor's astonishment, for he made no move to go, but said gently. 'Forgive me, but how can you possibly know? You haven't even asked her.'

'I would not dream of doing so, sir. I know that to have any closer acquaintance with a man such as yourself would be as abhorrent to her as it would to me, or to any woman of principle. And now you must excuse us, if you please. Come, Eleanor!' She took Eleanor's arm and almost dragged her niece away. Eleanor couldn't help casting a glance over her shoulder at the stranger to see his reaction to this massive set-down. He was gazing after them with the same ironical smile on his face. Then he shrugged and walked calmly towards the door to the rooms where the card tables were to be found.

'My dear aunt, you must, you really must explain! I shall explode with curiosity if you do not! Who is this monster called Guthrie? You and Lady Dorothy were talking about him before, were you not? What has he done that puts him so far beyond the pale? Tell me!'

Lady Walcot hesitated, then shook her head. She and Eleanor were sitting at one of a number of small tables which had been placed in the conservatory, and Lord Walcot, who had joined them for supper, was fetching some refreshment.

'That is impossible, Eleanor. The story is not a suitable one, but at the risk of setting your back up I assure you that that man is not a fit acquaintance for you.'

'Oh, come! I am not a simple schoolroom miss. As Lady Dorothy so kindly said, I am well past my first season! I need a better reason than that for not being allowed to dance with him!'

Lady Walcot looked even more determined. 'I am afraid that you must do without one, Eleanor. All I will say is that his treatment of the Anstey family has been wicked.'

'Can you tell me, at least, who these Ansteys are?'

'Mrs Anstey and her younger daughter, Marianne, are sitting over there in the far corner. The poor woman is trying to make herself inconspicuous.'

Eleanor turned her head a fraction and saw a pale,

sweet-faced woman in black, almost hidden by the overhanging branch of a potted palm. Next to her sat a very beautiful girl in a pale blue dress. 'Marianne Anstey is exquisite! She looks like a fairy princess!'

'Absolutely lovely, I agree. They have aroused a great deal of attention since their arrival from America. The girl is certain to make a good marriage, although they are as poor as church mice, and totally dependent on their relatives.'

'What did Mr Guthrie do?'

'I cannot discuss it now—here is your uncle. All you really need to know is that the man is a scoundrel.'

'Who is this scoundrel?' asked Lord Walcot. 'No, let me guess. Jonas Guthrie, without a doubt. Why can't you leave him alone, Hetty? From what he says, Guthrie has decided to leave London soon and retire to the country. And I must say I don't blame him! Lady Dorothy and her cronies——'

'Cronies!'

'I beg your pardon, my dear, I forgot you were one of them—I should have said her friends! You've all been making life impossible for the poor devil with your scandalous stories about the Ansteys—not that he needs anyone's sympathy; he's well able to take care of himself.'

Eleanor, swift to seize her opportunity, asked, 'You do not agree with the stories, then, Uncle?'

'We don't know enough of the matter to judge, my dear. It's possible that Guthrie is a villain—I suspect he's no weakling, and he certainly isn't a fool—but I have found him to be perfectly straightforward in his dealings with me.'

'Are you suggesting that that sweet woman is not

telling the truth when she says that Jonas Guthrie is the cause of all her misfortunes?' asked Lady Walcot, bristling.

'Not at all. I'm certain Mrs Anstey believes every word she tells you. How much she understands of business affairs is another matter. But this is the most idle speculation, and not fit for an evening of enjoyment! Come, Eleanor, if your aunt won't do her duty and find you a partner, I shall dance with you myself.'

Since Lord Walcot was generally considered to be the best performer of the waltz in London, Eleanor rose with alacrity and accompanied her uncle into the ballroom. Though she looked somewhat nervously around her in case Mr Guthrie should be watching, there was no trace of him. He had not, it seemed, found anyone else to dance with. Perhaps he had not tried?

They returned to her uncle's house in South Audley Street that evening without any further mention of Mr Guthrie. But her aunt's somewhat high-handed action had roused Eleanor's spirit and she was determined to find out more about him. She waited until Lady Walcot was in her bedroom and then went along to visit her. They discussed the evening for a moment or two, then Eleanor said, 'About Mr Guthrie, Aunt...?'

'Why are you so fascinated by the subject of Mr Guthrie? I would much rather forget him—he is an unworthy topic of conversation.'

'But you must see that I am consumed with curiosity! Now that we are private, can you not tell me why you refused to let me dance with him, when just a minute before you had said you would find me a partner? I am not Bella, Aunt Hetty. I am not accustomed to being treated like a child.'

Lady Walcot looked in affectionate exasperation at her niece. 'My dear Eleanor, you may be six-and-twenty, but you are still a young, unmarried woman! Oh, I know that you have been more or less in charge of Stanyards ever since you were a girl. I am sure anyone would admire the devoted manner in which you have looked after your mother——'

'There is no cause for admiration there, Aunt Hetty—I adore her!'

'—and managed the Stanyards estate——'

'I adore that, too!'

'Be quiet and let me finish, Eleanor!' said her aunt, smiling. But she quickly grew serious again. 'I have been thinking for some time that I should say something to you, and this seems to be a good occasion. Come and sit by me, my dear.' She thought for a moment, then, taking one of Eleanor's hands in hers, she said carefully, 'The...somewhat unusual circumstances of your upbringing have given you an independence of mind which you do not trouble to hide. And of course this same independence has recently stood you in good stead while you have struggled to keep the Stanyards estate going. But, sadly, it is not generally regarded as a desirable quality in a young woman, and I fear it does not endear you to prospective suitors—nor to society in general.'

'Father always said I should think for myself, Aunt Hetty——'

Lady Walcot gave a small exclamation of impatience and said with sisterly scorn, 'Your father always had his head too high in the clouds to be a judge of anything. I don't suppose it ever occurred to him that that is the last thing to teach a young girl! Neither he nor your mother ever had the slightest idea of what goes on in the real world.'

Eleanor removed her hand. 'We were very happy, all the same.'

'But what now? Here you are—a very pretty girl, but six-and-twenty and no sign of a husband. Why on earth didn't they insist that that brother of yours run the estate if your father didn't wish to? Why leave it to you? It is no occupation for a woman!'

'Since both my father and my brother are now dead, it is difficult for them to reply, Aunt Hetty,' said Eleanor, colouring up. 'I loved my father, and my brother, just as they were. And I love looking after Stanyards—I always have.' She got up and moved away. 'Moreover, I came here to talk about Mr Guthrie, not about the shortcomings of my family.'

Aware that she had overstepped the mark in criticising her brother to his daughter, Lady Walcot accepted Eleanor's reproach with grace. She said gently, 'My dear, I was trying to help you, believe me. I wish you would abandon this interest in Mr Guthrie. It might be well to think over what I have said about your own behaviour, rather than speculating on that of a known scoundrel. I want to see you settled—married, with a future which is secure, not tied to an ailing estate.'

'Ailing, Aunt Hetty? What do you mean? What do you mean by ailing?'

Lady Walcot looked at her niece sympathetically. 'It is time that you faced facts, Eleanor.'

'Stanyards is doing very well, and Mama and I are

perfectly happy to live there together. I do not need a husband!'

'Then there is no more to say—tonight, at least. I hope you will come to see things differently before it is too late, my child. Goodnight, Eleanor. I shall see you tomorrow.' She turned away and rang for her maid.

Eleanor went back to her own room with a distinct feeling of grievance. How dared her aunt suggest that Stanyards' future was not secure? It was true that it was not as prosperous now as it had been in her grandfather's day, but it was still a handsome property. Eleanor dismissed uncomfortable thoughts of damp walls and decaying barns—they would soon be put right, just as soon as there was money for them. Quite soon, in fact.

And how could her aunt accuse her of not attempting to hide the fact that she had opinions of her own? That really wasn't fair! Why, ever since she, Eleanor, had been in London, she had taken great pains to behave as Lady Walcot wished, though it had been far from easy. During interminable calls she had meekly listened to the vapid gossip which passed for conversation in Lady Walcot's circles, had attended innumerable routs and parties at which she had confined her remarks to the conventionally obvious, had danced with young men who, in spite of their town bronze, were as limited in their interests as the young men back home in Somerset. She had begun to doubt that she would ever find anyone interesting in the whole of London! Yet she knew that outside her aunt's narrow acquaintance there was a vast world full of interest and excitement waiting to be explored. It had

all remained frustratingly closed to her. She thought
she had been successful in hiding her impatience. It
now appeared she had not.

Her mind returned to the subject of Mr Guthrie.
What had he done that was so disgraceful? It was
flattering that he had braved an inevitable snub to ask
her to dance, and his boldness had intrigued her. But
her interest in him might have remained slight if her
aunt's refusal to discuss him had not roused her curiosity and a feeling of rebellion at being treated like a
child. She fell asleep with Mr Guthrie's dark features
floating before her eyes. . .

The next morning Eleanor rose at her usual time and,
since she usually kept country hours, this was very
much earlier than the rest of the household. Lady
Walcot had tried in vain to convince her niece that it
was highly unfashionable to be up and active before
midday, but when that had proved impossible her
indulgent uncle had arranged both a horse and a
groom for his niece's use, and Eleanor rode every
morning. At this hour the park was usually pretty
deserted, and the air comparatively fresh, and of all
her activities in London these morning rides were her
favourite. Lord Walcot, who sometimes accompanied
her, was not up so early this morning, and Eleanor
was alone except for her groom. This was a relief, for
she was still wrestling with the spirit of rebellion which
had been roused the night before. She made herself
recall her aunt's many kindnesses, she told herself that
her aunt was wise in the ways of London society, and
she finally reminded herself that she would shortly be
back in Somerset where none of this would matter.

As for Mr Guthrie—she would probably never see him again, and it was better so. She nodded to herself. That was right—she would forget him, remove him from her mind. She urged her horse to a brisker pace and rode forward, aware of a feeling of virtue and common sense. She was therefore slightly disconcerted when Mr Guthrie drew in beside her and raised his hat. He appeared to bear her no ill-will and greeted her cheerfully. 'Good morning, Miss Southeran. I see you are an early riser.'

The colour rose in Eleanor's cheeks as her composure deserted her. 'I am not sure, sir, that my aunt would approve of...of...' Her voice died away as he looked at her with such quizzical amusement in his eyes that she found herself wanting to respond.

'She wouldn't want you even to bid a perfectly respectable acquaintance good morning? I find that hard to believe. Your aunt is a stickler for the rules, I'm sure.' There was a dryness in his voice that roused Eleanor to defence.

'I doubt very much that she would describe you as "perfectly respectable", Mr Guthrie. My aunt may be a stickler, but I have never before heard her speak to anyone as she did to you last night.' She stopped short. She had almost sounded apologetic! She added coolly, 'I am sure she had good reason. Good day, sir.'

'So you're just a doll, a puppet without a mind of her own! When you're told to dance, you dance—oh, yes, I saw you last night! And when you're told not to dance, then you don't. I thought better of you.' Eleanor flushed angrily and moved on. Mr Guthrie moved with her. He said solicitously, 'You should not be riding alone in London, Miss Southeran. It really isn't safe, especially for dolls.'

'I am not alone, Mr Guthrie. I have my groom, as you see. Pray go away!'

'You certainly don't need both of us, I agree.' He turned round in his saddle and called to the groom, who had dropped back a pace or two, 'John! Be a good fellow and take a message to Colonel Marjoribanks at the Barracks. Tell him I've been delayed and will meet him shortly at Tattersall's. Miss Southeran will be quite safe with me—we'll see you at the end of this path in a few minutes. Off you go!'

Eleanor was both surprised and angry to see that John instantly wheeled away. 'How dare he? I think he must have gone mad!'

'No, no, nothing of the sort!' he said soothingly. 'I ride a great deal with your uncle, you see. John knows me well. He knows I am to be trusted, even if certain others. . .' He looked at her again with that quizzical gleam in his eye, and once again she felt a strong wish to respond. He went on, 'But never mind him—I want to talk to you. Are you really a mindless doll? Tell me it isn't so. Tell me my first impression was correct— that you're a young woman with a mind of her own, that you don't judge a man on hearsay and gossip.'

Eleanor made one last attempt to obey her aunt's wishes. 'Mr Guthrie, I know it must seem feeble—as feeble-minded as gazing in such an idiotic manner at the chandelier last night——'

'I didn't find that idiotic! I thought it was enchanting! The look of wonder on your face, the reflections of those crystals in your eyes. I was bewitched!'

This was so totally unexpected that Eleanor gazed at him in surprise.

'Yes, that's something like the look,' he said softly. Eleanor snapped her mouth shut and made an effort to recover herself.

'P-please!' She was annoyed to find herself stammering.

He laughed and said, 'I'm sorry. I didn't mean to put you into such confusion. Forgive me. What were you about to say?'

'What was it. . .? Oh, yes! I believe I am not without a mind of my own. But I do defer to people whose judgement I trust. Tell me, why should I disregard my aunt's opinion of you—which is that you are not a fit companion for me—in order to pay attention to anything you might say? I met you for the first time last night.'

He was silent for a moment, then smiled wryly and said, 'You are right, of course. I seem to have caught the American disease of wanting to hurry things along too swiftly. You need time to get to know me. Well, that can be arranged. But dare I ask you to hold judgement until you do know me better?'

'I fear that may prove difficult. From what I observed last night, my aunt would never allow you to enter her house.'

'I agree with you—nor would most of the others! And I must confess that up to this moment I have not given a dam——'

'Mr Guthrie!'

'A dam, Miss Southeran, is a small Indian coin worth practically nothing.'

Eleanor was not wholly convinced of this, but let it

pass, since her interest had been caught by something else. She asked eagerly, 'Have you been in India? Oh, how fortunate you are! I have always been fascinated by the stories I have heard of it, and of the countries in Asia.'

He smiled at the expression on her face. 'The romantic East? Don't get too carried away, Miss Southeran. There's a wealth of myth and legend about the East, not all confined to its history, literature and art. It's true that when I was young fortunes were there for those prepared to work for them, or, rather, fight for them. But the climate—and the life of most of the people—is very hard.' He looked down at her absorbed face. 'Would you really like to hear more about India? Come for a drive with me this afternoon in the park.' Eleanor hesitated. 'Unless you're afraid, of course.'

'Afraid?'

'Oh, not of me! You have nothing to fear from me. No, of what the tittle-tattling matrons of London might say. Any lady seen with me is automatically deemed to be beyond redemption! It makes for a somewhat isolated life.' When Eleanor still hesitated he said somewhat grimly, 'I see. I am to be condemned without a hearing, even by you.'

'I. . .I. . .' The battle with her conscience was lost. 'What do you drive, Mr Guthrie?'

'I normally drive a curricle. But if you were to consent to a drive with me I would use something more suited to a lady.'

'No! That is not what I want at all! I have always wanted. . .that is, I should like very much. . . Do you have a phaeton—a sporting phaeton, a high one?'

He stared at her, then his hard face broke into a smile. 'A woman of spirit! I knew it! I shall arrange to have one this afternoon—but what will your aunt say?'

'I think my aunt would rather see me in a tumbril than in any vehicle driven by you, Mr Guthrie. But you are right. I am not a doll—nor a child! At what time do you drive in the park?'

'Usually about five.'

'If I happened to be walking there at that time, would you offer to take me up?'

'I should be honoured. At five, then?'

Eleanor took a deep breath and said, 'At five.'

They had reached the end of the path where John was waiting for her. Mr Guthrie raised his hat again, gave a nod to the groom, and rode off in the direction of Knightsbridge. Eleanor returned to South Audley Street, wondering if she had gone mad.

# CHAPTER TWO

By the afternoon she was sure she was mad. Hyde Park was crowded with the *ton* all taking their afternoon airing—walking, riding and driving in every form of vehicle. Gentlemen drove by in their gigs and curricles, ladies displayed their pretty dresses and parasols in open landaulets—the smarter set in handsome barouches—and Eleanor had the feeling that here was a world just waiting to watch her defy it. If she had not given Mr Guthrie her word she would have obeyed her strong inclination to go back to her aunt's house before the fatal hour of five.

However, when the gentleman stopped and offered to take Miss Southeran up, Eleanor interrupted her aunt's refusal, and accepted. In response to Lady Walcot's startled protest, Eleanor said firmly, 'Forgive me, Aunt Hetty. Half an hour only,' and climbed into the phaeton. She ignored the stares directed at her and put on an air of serenity which belied the pounding of her heart as Mr Guthrie drove off.

'Bravely done! Allow me to congratulate you.'

'I am not at all sure it is a matter for congratulation, sir! As you very well know, I run the risk of being sent to Coventry for this venture. However, since I have only a short time left in London I can bear that. Why do people dislike you so?'

'Because they mistakenly believe me to be dishonest and dishonourable.'

28

Eleanor blinked at this forthright statement. 'Have they cause?'

Mr Guthrie paused. At last he said, 'Matters are not always what they seem, Miss Southeran. They think they have cause.'

'You are fencing with me, I think.'

'You are right. Miss Southeran, there are reasons why I cannot be frank in talking of my own affairs. I do not intend to give you tedious half-truths. My hope is rather that if we could get to know each other better you would judge me more kindly than the rest of society does. But now you tell me that you have only a short time left in London?'

'I return home in a week's time.'

'At the very beginning of the season? Do you not regret that?'

'Not in the slightest. I love my home. I cannot wait to see it again.'

'Tell me about it.'

Eleanor never needed much encouragement to speak of Stanyards, and with that and stories of India the half-hour passed swiftly for them both. It was with regret that Eleanor noticed that they were leaving the park and making for South Audley Street.

'Where are you going tonight? Shall I see you there?' asked Mr Guthrie as they drew up at the Walcot house.

'Tonight? I think not. My aunt is taking me to a ball at the French ambassador's.' She paused, but curiosity got the better of her. 'Tell me, how was it that you were at Carlton House last night? I thought all doors in London were closed to you.'

'Not all, Miss Southeran, not all. There are still

some brave souls who ignore Lady Dorothy and the other gorgons. The Prince Regent is one of them. Who knows—perhaps the French ambassador is another? But in case he isn't, shall I see you tomorrow morning?'

'I. . .I am not sure. I still have to make my peace with my aunt.'

'Come! It took a great deal of courage for you to make this afternoon's gesture on behalf of the under-dog. Don't waste it!'

'Very well.' She smiled slightly. 'I'll see what I can do.'

Eleanor entered the house in a defiant mood. Mr Guthrie had proved a most interesting companion and she found it hard to believe he was the scoundrel her aunt had described. She could see, however, that he might not appeal to those who set great store by polished manners and the elegant niceties of polite behaviour, and was surprised that he apparently had the entrée to the Prince Regent's circle. But his abrupt style of address had not offended her, and she had actually found his directness curiously appealing. She felt a strong wish to see him again, and decided that she would do all she could to coax her aunt to agree. Meanwhile she would no doubt be faced with reproaches and some justifiable anger.

Lady Walcot was sitting in the salon on the first floor. When Eleanor walked in she said, 'I am relieved to see you back safely.'

'Aunt Hetty, I was never in any danger!'

'A high-perch phaeton! Driven at such a reckless

pace! It only shows what disregard the man has for any lady's sensibilities——'

'No, Aunt! I asked Mr Guthrie to take me in the phaeton. And we went rather sedately, I thought.' Eleanor got up and went to sit beside her aunt. 'Truly, Aunt Hetty, Mr Guthrie is not the villain you have described. We talked of the most interesting things, and though he is not as polished as some of your acquaintance he was always the gentleman.'

'Really?' Her aunt was still annoyed. 'Allow me to tell you, Eleanor, that you have made a pretty spectacle of yourself this afternoon. What Lady Dorothy will say I cannot bear to think.'

'Pray do not worry yourself over such a trifle! I am not concerned with Lady Dorothy and her tales.'

'But you should be, Eleanor! She is not without influence in London, let me tell you.'

'Not with me, Aunt Hetty.'

Her aunt ignored her. 'I blame myself, of course. I should have remembered how wilful you can be, and told you more about him when you asked. What did he tell you? A pack of lies, no doubt.'

'I don't think so, Aunt. We didn't discuss Mrs Anstey, if that is what you mean.'

'I am not surprised at that—she would be the last person he would mention! Well, Eleanor, you have forced my hand. I shall tell you about Mr Guthrie. It is not an edifying story, as I think you will agree.' Lady Walcot paused, then began, 'Mrs Anstey is a widow. She is an Englishwoman, but she married a man from Boston in America, and lived there for many years. The family was a wealthy one and Mrs Anstey might reasonably have hoped for a comfortable and secure existence. However, some years ago her husband went into partnership in a business venture with the man Guthrie. Guthrie ruined them.'

'In what way?'

Lady Walcot said impatiently, 'How should I know what piece of chicanery was involved? I understand nothing of business or trade. But ruin them he did, and now Mrs Anstey and her daughter haven't a penny to their name. That is your precious Mr Guthrie.'

'How do you know all this, Aunt Hetty?'

'Everyone knows it!'

'Gossip, idle rumours, scandal. I am surprised you give so much credence to them.'

'It was Lady Dorothy who first told me, and she had it from Mrs Anstey herself.'

'But——'

'No, Eleanor, there is no "but"! What is more, I believe there is something else, which I am not at liberty to discuss. But if it is true, then I assure you on my life that the man is a dishonourable villain.'

'Mr Guthrie said people were mistaken in believing that he was dishonourable.'

'And you believed him?' asked Lady Walcot with contempt.

'Why should I not? Have you any proof to the contrary?'

'Eleanor, the proof lies in what we know to be facts! Henry Anstey shot himself because he and his family were bankrupt. The Guthrie creature, who was a full partner in the enterprise, remains a wealthy man. Whatever else may or may not be true, how do you account for that? Besides, Guthrie has never bothered to deny anything that has been said about him.'

'That is hardly proof of guilt! I agree it is tempting to believe Mr Guthrie to be the villain of this particular melodrama—he has all the appearance of one. And lovely Marianne Anstey looks like the very ideal of a damsel in distress. But is it not at least possible that appearances are deceptive?'

'Oh, it is useless to argue with you! It is just as I was saying last night—you are always determined to make up your own mind, determined to ignore the judgement of people who are older and wiser than yourself. And when you embark on one of your crusades you lose all sense of proportion. Now you are about to fling yourself at a known scoundrel. What am I to do?'

Eleanor drew herself up and said with dignity, 'Aunt Hetty, I promise not to fling myself at anyone—least of all a known scoundrel, whoever that is. But, unless you can give me more convincing proof of Mr Guthrie's guilt, I reserve the right to talk to the first man I have met in London whose company I enjoy— apart from that of my uncle. And that's another thing! My uncle is by no means sure of Mr Guthrie's villainy. I would trust his judgement sooner than I would that of Lady Dorothy!'

'Oh, your uncle is a man,' said Lady Walcot somewhat obscurely. She got up and went to the door. Here she stopped and said, 'I haven't finished with you yet, Eleanor. You have asked for proof. I shall see what I can do.' Then she left the room.

Eleanor was left feeling confused and uncertain. It was perfectly possible that Mr Guthrie had roused Lady Dorothy's enmity by nothing more criminal than omitting to give her the deference she imagined due to her rank. But Lady Walcot was another matter. Eleanor had known and loved her father's sister all her life—she could not dismiss her aunt's views on Mr Guthrie so lightly. She sighed.

'Good lord, Eleanor, don't look so glum!' It was her uncle who had just come in. 'Where's your aunt? Been giving you a lecture, has she? I'm not surprised, but don't worry—she'll soon come round again. Cheer up, my dear! Isn't it time you were thinking of your dress and so on for tonight? I'm taking you both to a ball, I believe. As for your aunt, by the time she's decided what she's going to wear, and what jewellery to put with it, she'll have forgotten about this afternoon. Come, let me see you smile, then you can go and pretty yourself up.'

Eleanor got up obediently and went to the door, but there she turned and came back to her uncle. She hesitated a moment, then asked, 'Uncle Charles, what do you think of Mr Guthrie?'

Lord Walcot shook his head in mock-reproof. 'Now, Eleanor, I'm too downy a bird to be caught by a question like that. What you're really asking is whether I agree with your aunt in discouraging you from having much to do with him. You should know better than to ask me what I think. You are in her charge, and I cannot oppose her wishes as far as you are concerned. That would never do.'

'I'm sorry.'

He looked sympathetically at her downcast face, and relented a little. 'He's a difficult fellow to know. A man who keeps his own counsel. Except for the stories about him, I've never had any occasion to

distrust him—in fact, I would say that I quite like him.
But your aunt and the others may well be right, you
know. I believe Mrs Anstey tells a convincing enough
tale, which he has never denied. Give it up, my dear.
You're upsetting your aunt, and to what purpose? In
a few days or so you'll be setting off for Somerset and
you'll probably never see him again.'

Eleanor looked up and said with resolution, 'You're
right, as always, Uncle Charles. I shall be amenable
from now on.'

He laughed and said, 'Not too amenable, Eleanor. I
enjoy our discussions. Don't become like all the rest!'

That evening Eleanor found it impossible to remain
unaffected by the excitement and glamour of a really
large ball. The splendid rooms, lavishly decorated with
artificial fountains and fantastic pyramids, were
impressive by any standards, and the dresses and
jewels of the cream of London society were a rare
sight. Her own dress, though modest in comparison,
suited her very well, she thought. It had been made
originally by the best dressmaker in Taunton, and had
a bodice made of blue-green silk, with a skirt of white
sarsnet. Her aunt had looked at it thoughtfully, pronounced it delightfully simple and had then taken it
away. It had appeared a few days later with an over-
skirt of blue-green gauze, embroidered round the hem
in blue, green and gold, and caught up at the side with
a knot of matching ribbons. Her efforts had turned a
pretty dress from a local dressmaker into a garment
worthy of the highest London circles. The result was
eye-catching and very flattering.

But, lovely as the dresses were, impressive though

the rooms looked, to Eleanor's mind nothing could outshine Marianne Anstey. The fairy princess was stunningly beautiful in a very simple white silk dress. Her pale gold hair was caught back on top with a knot of pale pink roses, and fell in graceful curls to the nape of her neck. More pale pink roses were clustered at her waist, matching the delicate colour in her cheeks. Eleanor, along with many others, could hardly take her eyes off the girl, and no one was surprised when the ambassador kept more important guests waiting while he greeted this exquisite creature.

'The embodiment of every man's dreams, wouldn't you say, Miss Southeran? A lovely damsel in distress, waiting for her knight to rescue her. And what a prize!'

Eleanor turned round with a start to find Mr Guthrie immediately behind her. She looked round for her aunt, but the Walcots were some distance away, having been separated from their niece by the crowd. Mindful of her promise to her uncle, Eleanor said, 'If report is true, her face is her only fortune, sir. The knight in question may not have to rescue her from dragons—only her own, undeserved penury.'

'Yes, of course. I am cast as the dragon in this fairy-tale, "if report is true", is that not so, Miss Southeran? Well, it looks to me,' he swept on without waiting for her reply, 'as if the knight is about to make his appearance. More than a knight—a viscount, no less!'

The French ambassador had finally released Miss Anstey, and she had rejoined the group of fashionably dressed people with whom she had first arrived. Among them was a young man who was now talking most earnestly to her.

'Robert Morrissey, heir to an Irish earldom. A very worthy candidate, don't you agree?'

'Since I know neither the lady nor her knight, I cannot tell, sir,' said Eleanor coolly, disliking the thread of mockery running through Mr Guthrie's words.

'Well, I think it will do very nicely—it will at least relieve the worst of her fond mother's anxieties.' He bowed and disappeared as abruptly as he had come. Eleanor didn't know whether to be angry or pleased, but saw that her aunt and uncle were about to join her again, and was glad that awkward explanations had been avoided. She asked her aunt about the Ansteys' party.

'They are with their cousins, the Verekers—the ones who live in Berkeley Square. And the young man who is paying such particular attention to Marianne Anstey is Lord Morrissey. Would you like to meet them?'

She took Eleanor over to the other side of the room and made the introductions. Mr and Mrs Vereker were an amiable couple, who were clearly enormously proud of their beautiful protégée. Mrs Anstey was soberly dressed and stayed quietly in the background, pleased to let her cousins take charge. Eleanor, who was guiltily aware that she had spent half an hour in the park that afternoon with Mrs Anstey's reported enemy, was prepared for some coolness, but when they were introduced the lady smiled pleasantly enough, if somewhat timidly. Marianne proved to be as amiable as she was beautiful. Her manner was a delightful mixture of modesty and charm, and Lord Morrissey's attentions had brought an appealing flush to her cheeks and a sparkle to her lovely eyes. He was

obviously well on the way to falling in love, and
Eleanor privately agreed with Mr Guthrie's words that
it might do very nicely.

After a few minutes Lord Morrissey made his
excuses and took Miss Anstey off towards the ballroom. A young man Eleanor had met at a previous
party came up and took her off as well, and soon the
ball was well on its way. Though she did not quite
dance every dance, Eleanor was seldom without a
partner, and received a good many compliments on
her appearance. She found herself enjoying the evening. She had just returned from a set of country
dances and was standing with her aunt and uncle when
she saw that the ambassador himself was approaching
them. She stood back modestly in order to allow him
to speak to her uncle, but then saw that Mr Guthrie
was with him. She looked anxiously at her aunt. Lady
Walcot was smiling at the ambassador, and though the
smile faltered a little when she saw his companion she
quickly recovered.

'Lady Walcot, I am enchanted to see you so well,'
said His Excellency. 'I see that you have lost one
daughter only to gain another—and such a pretty one!
*Mademoiselle*?'

Eleanor curtsied low and blushed as the ambassador
took her hand and kissed it. He glanced mischievously
at Mr Guthrie. 'And now, Lady Walcot, I see that
your niece is not dancing at present. That is quite
wrong. May I present Mr Guthrie to you as a most
desirable partner for the young lady?'

Eleanor had difficulty in suppressing a smile. Her
aunt was undoubtedly outraged by a manoeuvre which
made it impossible for her to refuse, but no one could

have guessed it from her demeanour. She smiled graciously, then inclined her head.

'How can anyone refuse you, Ambassador? My niece would be delighted, of course.'

'Excellent! And I shall take you and Lord Walcot to the refreshment tables—I have a champagne there which will please you, I think. Come, my friend Guthrie will take good care of the pretty niece, *n'est-ce pas*, Jonas?'

'Lady Walcot may have every confidence in me, Ambassador,' said Mr Guthrie smoothly, whereupon Lord Walcot made a curious noise which he was able to turn into a cough. Mr Guthrie raised an eyebrow, then turned to Eleanor. 'Miss Southeran?' he said, offering his arm, and Eleanor, with an apologetic glance at her aunt, moved forward. Lady Walcot exchanged a long look with Mr Guthrie and then turned to accompany the ambassador, and Eleanor's uncle, still amused, shook his head and followed his wife.

'That was not well done, sir!' said Eleanor severely as they walked towards the ballroom.

'Not well done? Well, upon my word, I wouldn't know how a man could do it better! To get His Excellency himself to plead my case...what more would you expect? The Prince Regent?'

Half laughing, Eleanor said, 'You know very well what I mean, Mr Guthrie! It was to pay my aunt back for refusing you last night, was it not?'

'You underrate yourself,' he said with a smile. 'There were other merits in the idea.' Then he stopped and said, 'But there's something you should know about me, Miss Southeran. When I play, I don't take chances. I play to win.'

'And the prize in this case? Was it worth calling out such big guns?'

'Well, now,' he said softly, 'it depends on what you mean by the prize. Victory over your aunt? An opportunity to dance with you? Or. . .what?'

Surprised by his tone, Eleanor looked at him, which was a mistake. He was looking down at her with amusement and something more disturbing in his eyes. She said uncertainly, 'If you are trying to flirt with me, Mr Guthrie, I must tell you that I don't appreciate it. I prefer sensible conversation such as we had this afternoon to. . .to silly compliments and empty phrases.'

'I assure you, I was not trying to flirt with you. And if I were capable of flattery—which I am not—I would tell you that you outshine every other woman in the room, that that entrancing dress is a perfect foil for your sea-green witch's eyes, and the dark gold of your hair——'

'Mr Guthrie!'

Undeterred by her angry exclamation, he went on, 'That, lovely though your features are, they are rendered yet more entrancing by your animation, the liveliness of your expression——'

'Mr Guthrie, stop this at once or I shall leave you instantly!'

'But I am not saying such things, Miss Southeran,' he said earnestly. 'They are quite clearly false, the merest flattery. You are pretty enough, but far from being the prettiest woman in the room. Miss Anstey, for instance, is a star!' After a brief pause he added, 'I grant that you're livelier than she is—and much more intelligent.' He gave a delighted laugh at her indignant expression. 'What sensible things shall we talk about, Miss Southeran?'

Eleanor had never known such a man! Never before had she experienced such a mixture of feelings—anger, amusement, puzzlement, sympathy. Never had she felt so alive.

'You shall tell me more about the East. But first we shall enjoy your prize, which,' she said firmly, 'is a dance.'

They didn't talk about the East, but after the dance was over he took her to supper, and they talked of other things. They walked through the crowded rooms and at one point found themselves among the plants in the winter garden, still talking. Eleanor had objected to something disparaging Mr Guthrie had said about life in England, and was arguing her case passionately. But her voice died away as she saw him looking at her as she spoke, his eyes focused on her lips. She was overcome with a feeling of panic and turned away from him. 'We. . .we must go back,' she said nervously. 'My aunt will be looking for me.'

'No, wait a little. How can we talk sensibly out there among all those people——?'

'I cannot stay here—it is most improper. My aunt would be very angry if she saw me.'

'The devil take your aunt!'

'Sir!'

'Oh, I'm sorry, I'm sorry. It's just that I have something I want to say to you, and there never seems to be a suitable moment. I keep putting it off. . .' He gave an exasperated laugh. 'I think I'm afraid!'

'Afraid?' she echoed, looked at him wide-eyed.

'Yes, and when you look at me like that it all goes out of my head. You have a most extraordinary effect on me—like no other I have ever known. How do you do it?'

Eleanor suddenly became aware of the very strange effect this conversation was having on her breathing. 'You are talking nonsense, Mr Guthrie—I must go back,' she said with determination, and started for the entrance to the ballroom.

'Wait! Eleanor——' he called, but stopped abruptly as he saw Lady Walcot standing at the entrance.

'At last I've found you! What on earth do you think you are doing?' Lady Walcot's voice was sharp, and one or two bystanders cast curious glances in her direction. She forced a smile, whispering to her niece, 'Don't bother to tell me. You've been with that man!'

'Aunt Hetty——'

'We'll talk when we get home, Eleanor, not here. Now come with me—several people have been asking to meet you. Ah, Lady Marchant, there you are! We've been looking for you—this is Miss Southeran, my niece. . .'

Eleanor did not see Mr Guthrie again that evening. Her aunt kept her close at her side until the carriages arrived to take them home. But she would not have looked for him in any case. Her feelings were much too confused to face him again so soon. This same confusion of feeling made it difficult for her to discuss the matter with her aunt afterwards, and Lady Walcot, drawing her own conclusions, was most concerned. 'I blame myself,' she said unhappily. 'I should never have agreed to your dancing with him—I know what he is. Heaven knows how he manages it, for he is not at all handsome. But he is a dangerous man, Eleanor. I beg you to forget this attraction he has for you.'

'He. . .he seemed sincere,' said Eleanor hesitantly. 'As if he too felt the same. . .attraction. Could I be so wrong?'

Lady Walcot exclaimed, 'The devil! The scheming, contriving devil! He has bewitched you, Eleanor, just as he bewitched Ev——But no, I mustn't say any more.' She appeared to be debating with herself, and then to reach a conclusion. 'You must go to bed, Eleanor,' she said slowly. 'And in the morning I shall see what I can do.'

Eleanor slept badly that night. She tossed and turned, reliving the moments with Jonas Guthrie, especially the time in the winter garden. One moment she wanted to meet him the next morning, and then, after another debate with herself, she had decided that it would be better if they did not see each other again. Was he a dangerous philanderer—all the more dangerous because he did not appear to be trying to charm? Or was he the straightforward man he appeared to be? And what was it that he had been afraid to tell her? She eventually fell into an uneasy slumber, still debating the question.

She woke late the next morning to find that one question at least had already been decided. It was far too late for a ride in the park. When she eventually came downstairs she found her aunt waiting.

'I have someone I wish you to meet,' she said briskly, 'and we are late. Put your bonnet on and come with me, Eleanor. Don't delay—the carriage is waiting.'

A few minutes later they arrived at a modest house in a street off Cavendish Square. Here they were taken into a small parlour, where a lady was waiting to receive them. It was Mrs Anstey. She greeted Lady Walcot in a soft, well-spoken manner and then turned to Eleanor. 'Miss Southeran, you are very welcome, though I am sorry the occasion is...is such an awkward one...' Mrs Anstey paused and looked to Lady Walcot for help.

'Mrs Anstey has agreed, at my urgent request, to talk to you, Eleanor. I am very obliged to her—the matter is a painful one, as you will see, and I would not have asked her to speak of it had I not been so anxious for you. I am sure you will give her your earnest attention—it concerns Mr Guthrie and his behaviour towards the Anstey family.'

'Surely this isn't necessary, Aunt Hetty——'

'In view of your refusal to accept my word for Mr Guthrie's character, and especially in view of your behaviour last night...'

'I wanted to explain——'

'Forgive me, Eleanor, but Mrs Anstey's time is precious. We must not waste it.'

Good manners silenced Eleanor. She sat chafing under her aunt's disapproval, convinced that this whole visit was an unnecessary exercise. Lady Walcot said, 'Mrs Anstey, would you mind telling my niece how well you know Mr Guthrie?'

'Jonas and I were brought up together, Miss Southeran. His mother was a Vereker, too. That is to say. . .I mean his mother was a Vereker before she was married. As I was.'

'You were sisters?'

'No, no! Oh, dear, how stupid of me. . .Caroline, his mother, was my cousin.'

'From what you have told me,' said Lady Walcot, casting a glance at Eleanor, 'you practically brought him up?'

'Well. . .yes, I suppose so,' said Mrs Anstey uncertainly. 'I was so much older than he was, and he had no mother. . . He was a dear little boy when he came to us.'

'Came to you? In America?' asked Eleanor, somewhat puzzled.

'No, no. This was over thirty years ago—Jonas was a baby. . . I was a girl and still living in England then.' She looked anxiously at Lady Walcot, then said nervously, 'Perhaps I had better explain. You see, Richard Guthrie, Jonas's father, abandoned poor Caroline before Jonas was born. She came back home to have the child, and died soon after. I think it must have been of a broken heart, don't you? Jonas and I . . .we were both orphans living with relatives. We were very close, though I was ten years older.'

'But what happened to his father?' asked Eleanor.

'He was a bad lot, I'm afraid. I think he eventually went into the army and was killed. But Jonas never really knew him. It is surprising. . .' Her voice drifted away.

'He must have felt very alone in the world.'

'Oh, no! He knew he always had me to turn to— until I left England and went to live in America. . .' Mrs Anstey's voice trailed away weakly again, and

Eleanor felt a sudden impatience with her. The woman is a born martyr, she thought, and then reproached herself for her lack of charity.

Lady Walcot said, 'And later, I believe, your husband took Mr Guthrie as a business partner on your recommendation?'

'Well, partly. Jonas left England for India when he was still quite young. I'm not sure how, but he made a fortune out there. Then he came to see me in Boston. He was looking for a suitable investment, and my husband happened to need some new capital for his family concern and...and they helped each other. It worked very well to start with. I was delighted to see him again, and Henry and the girls were all devoted to him. For a while Henry and I even thought that we would be more closely related to Jonas. But then the engagement was broken off...'

'Engagement? Mr Guthrie has been engaged? To Marianne?' asked Eleanor, growing pale.

'No, no. Jonas was engaged to my other daughter. But then it was broken off. And things went wrong after that.'

'What went wrong?'

'Miss Southeran, I am not precisely sure what went amiss. I took no part in the business, of course. But Henry—my husband—and Jonas suddenly seemed to disagree a great deal, and though Mr Oliver did his best to keep the peace there were frequent arguments.'

'Mr Oliver?'

'My husband's other partner. He is now married to Evadne.' Mrs Anstey's hands were twisting in her lap. She said suddenly, 'Oh, Miss Southeran, if you only knew how wicked Jonas Guthrie has been, how like his father!'

The sudden passion in this timid little woman's voice was startling. Eleanor was impressed, and, dreading what more was to come, she asked slowly, 'Why do you say that?'

Mrs Anstey looked uncertainly at Lady Walcot, who leaned forward and said softly, 'Please, if you can, tell her! I give you my word that it will go no further.'

'I. . . I. . .am ashamed to tell you that Jonas Guthrie is the father of my daughter's child!' This was said in a low voice, and at first Eleanor thought she had not heard correctly. She looked blankly at Mrs Anstey, who added in a clearer, louder tone, 'He seduced my daughter Evadne, and gave her a child.'

# CHAPTER THREE

ELEANOR found herself without a word. The morning's revelations had been a shock and she was experiencing great difficulty in retaining her outward appearance of calm. She wanted to leave that neat little room, to refuse to listen to the ugly story which was being unfolded in it. But this was impossible. She must stay.

Mrs Anstey mistook her silence for embarrassment and said nervously, 'I'm sorry—your aunt did ask——'

'In her own words, my niece is not a child, Mrs Anstey! And I wish her to hear everything,' said Lady Walcot grimly.

Eleanor rallied and found her voice. 'But she is married to Mr Oliver?'

Mrs Anstey lowered her head and said, 'Yes. It is shameful, is it not? He...he agreed to marry her in return for a sum of money—paid by Guthrie.'

'Why didn't Mr Guthrie marry her himself? Why didn't your husband insist?'

'By the time her condition was discovered my husband was dead, and we were on the verge of bankruptcy.' Mrs Anstey's voice faded again and Lady Walcot took over the story.

'Mrs Anstey found herself without anyone to advise or help her and the one man who might have been her support proved to be her worst enemy. He refused to marry Miss Anstey—at first he even denied that the child was his! Then, when he was forced to admit

48

the truth, he paid another man to shoulder his responsibilities.'

'How did Mr Oliver come to agree to this dreadful scheme? He was a partner in the firm, too. Why did he not take up your defence?'

'Jonas was. . .was more masterful. He knows how to get people to do as he wishes—I can't explain how,' said Mrs Anstey, 'and Mr Oliver was in severe financial difficulties himself. He had always been fond of Evadne and he was happy to marry her—but without the money it would have been out of the question.'

'It has proved impossible to find out why the firm foundered, Eleanor,' said Lady Walcot. 'The books disappeared after Henry Anstey shot himself. But Mrs Anstey saw them in Guthrie's possession the day before they vanished and she believes he still has them—or has destroyed them. And is it not significant that he seems to have survived the firm's collapse with his own fortune intact?'

'Conscience money,' said Mrs Anstey sadly. 'He paid conscience money. He made a fool of my husband, and a paramour of my daughter, and he thinks that he has solved everything when he buys a husband for Evadne. But how could he do it to us—to Evadne, to me? We loved him! We trusted him!' She shook her head mournfully. 'He was such a dear little boy!'

'Are you absolutely certain that Mr Guthrie is the villain?' Eleanor heard the slightly desperate note in her own voice and tried to speak more calmly. 'It seems so strange. Is there no one else?'

'It was strange, Miss Southeran! At first I refused to believe that he had cheated us, I refused to believe that he could be so wicked—so like his father! I begged, I pleaded with him to explain what had happened.' Mrs Anstey dabbed her eyes with her handkerchief and continued, 'But he pushed me away. He said we could think what we liked, that he had found a husband for Evadne, and enough money to pay for a passage to England for Marianne and me. That should be enough. His manner was so. . .so hard! It was as if he couldn't bear to look at us. . .' She paused, then added, 'The only other person involved was Mr Oliver, who was as poor as we were until Guthrie paid him to. . .to marry Evadne.' She shook her head obstinately. 'In the end he was just like his father. No, Miss Southeran, Jonas Guthrie is the cause of all our troubles. What else can I think?'

'Indeed, what else can anyone think, Eleanor?' said her aunt sternly.

'I. . . I'm not sure. . . He left you entirely without resources?'

'He must have had some vestige of feeling. He paid for our passage to England, he arranged for someone to meet us when we landed and take us to our Vereker cousins in Berkeley Square. They have been very good to us. But we have not spoken to Jonas since we arrived in England. Indeed, we have avoided meeting each other since we came to London, and, though I understand he was a frequent visitor at Berkeley Square before Marianne and I came from America, he has not been there since.' Mrs Anstey blinked down at her hands. 'I. . . I still find it difficult to believe. . .'

She stood up. 'I'm afraid you will have to excuse me. I must go and fetch Marianne from her lesson; she will wonder where I am.' She hesitated and then said timidly, 'Miss Southeran, I agreed to talk to you today

because Lady Walcot has been so very good to
Marianne and me. I do not know what I would have
done without her. Thanks to the help from my cousins
and your aunt's kindness in sponsoring Marianne in
London, I now have hope that one of my daughters at
least will make the marriage she deserves. Lord
Morrissey has been so very attentive. But any scandal. . . I know I can be sure of your discretion.'

'Of course,' said poor Eleanor, pulling herself
together. 'And I see now why my aunt wished me to
hear your story. I am grateful to you for being so
frank with me, Mrs Anstey.'

'I saw it as my duty,' said Mrs Anstey simply.

As they got into the carriage again Eleanor was
conscious that her aunt was waiting for her to say
something. But what was there to say? Mr Guthrie was
a complete villain, it appeared—there was no mistaking
the sincerity of Mrs Anstey's feelings. Before talking
to her Eleanor had thought, hoped even, that the
woman might be a charlatan—it wouldn't be the first
time that a poor widow with a beautiful daughter had
tricked her way into society. But unless Mrs Anstey
was a consummate actress, which Eleanor very much
doubted, she had been telling the truth. This was no
scandalmonger, no vindictive gorgon—this was a
woman patently sincere in her distress and shame. Mrs
Anstey was completely convinced of Guthrie's guilt,
and very unhappy that it was so.

'Well, Eleanor?' said Lady Walcot finally.

'Please, Aunt Hetty, could we wait till we are back
in the house? I feel. . .I feel a little dazed at the
moment. It was a shock.'

'Of course, my child. We'll soon be there, and you shall do just as you wish—talk to me, or spend some time in your room.'

The rest of the journey passed in silence, but this gave Eleanor a chance to recover her equilibrium and she was quite ready to talk to her aunt when they arrived. They went into the little parlour, and here Eleanor sat down, gave a great sigh and said, 'You were right, Aunt Hetty, and I was mistaken. I am sorry to have put you to so much trouble.'

'I am to take it that there will be no further tête-à-têtes in secluded spots with Mr Guthrie?'

'I. . . I cannot imagine why I was so indiscreet.'

'When you are on one of your crusades, Eleanor, there is no knowing what you might do! However, I think this particular crusade is finished, is it not?'

'It is finished, Aunt Hetty.'

Something of her niece's misery must have communicated itself to Lady Walcot, for she gave Eleanor a hug, then got up and said briskly, 'Come, you must now try to put it all behind you. You must enjoy what is left of your time in London. Would you like to rest now, or shall we go shopping? Have you bought a present for your mother yet?'

Eleanor pulled herself firmly together and declared that she was ready to do some shopping. She and Lady Walcot decided that a note should be written to Mr Guthrie which made it clear that she did not wish to see him again. This they did, and once it had been dispatched she felt as if a burden had been lifted from her, though she still felt a secret regret. If Mr Guthrie had been the man she had thought him, she would have enjoyed his company, and fought to maintain her right to it. But as it was she need never have anything more to do with him. She sighed and then consoled herself with the thought that in a few days' time she would be returning to Stanyards. She was looking forward to it more and more.

However, Eleanor was mistaken in thinking that she had finished with Mr Guthrie. She was to meet him again before she left London, and in very odd circumstances.

On the day before her departure she went out for one last ride. Ever since the conversation with Mrs Anstey she had taken to riding at a later hour than before, in order to avoid the embarrassment of meeting Mr Guthrie. Thus far she had been successful. It meant, of course, that she and John had to venture further in order to find less frequented areas of the park, since at the later time more people were abroad. On this occasion they had ridden almost to the western edge, and they were just about to return when they heard a faint groan coming from the bushes at the side of the path. John slid off his horse and went to investigate. He returned, saying urgently, 'It's Mr Guthrie, Miss Southeran. He's lying groaning something horrible! I think 'e must 'ave fallen off 'is 'orse.'

Eleanor dismounted and followed John. Mr Guthrie was apparently in the process of regaining consciousness. He was trying to sit up, then groaning again and holding his head in his hands.

'Fetch help, John. I'll stay here. Do as I say; I shall be perfectly safe. Mr Guthrie needs urgent assistance, and I cannot be sure of finding the shortest way back. Go quickly—you know the way better than I do.'

John hesitated, but saw the sense of what Eleanor had said. He ran to his horse and rode off. Eleanor looked down at Mr Guthrie. He was now lying with his eyes closed. She knelt down beside him. His eyes flew open, and he said, 'What the devil are you doing here? Where's John?'

'He's gone for help.'

'He shouldn't have left you alone. . . Did you see anyone else?'

'Here? I don't think anyone else was here——'

'Of course there was! Why else do you suppose I'm lying flat on my back like this?' His tone was irritable, but that was perhaps understandable. His head was obviously hurting quite badly, and she could see a huge bruise developing over one eye.

'I thought you might have taken a toss. People do,' she said calmly.

'I am not so careless. And "people" don't usually ride into a piece of wire stretched across the path, do they? Look!' He struggled to sit up and pointed at a length of wire lying beside the path. Eleanor got up to examine it. 'I came off when the horse stopped dead. There was someone else here, though—I saw him standing a short way off before I fell. He looked as if he was waiting. . . He started coming towards me—and then the next thing I knew John was there. Confound it, you must have seen him! I wasn't out for more than a minute.'

Eleanor looked nervously about her. 'I'm afraid I didn't see anyone, nor can I see anyone now. Do you think it was footpads, or highwaymen?' Her voice had risen slightly.

'Oh, for God's sake, don't start getting hysterical!

I'm perfectly capable of defending us both, if necessary.' With some difficulty Mr Guthrie drew a pistol out of the capacious pocket of his riding coat.

Eleanor said tartly, 'I have no intention of indulging in hysterics. And if you will permit me to say so, that pistol wasn't of very great help a moment ago—nor is it reassuring to watch you handle it now!'

'Don't talk rubbish. I was off my guard. And you are perfectly safe from it. What is more to the point— have you seen Captain?'

'Captain? Captain who?'

'My horse, my horse! He must be hurt, too. That wire caught him right across his legs.'

'Is that him? Over there?'

'Go and fetch him, there's a good girl. I'll have a look at him.' He started to get up, but stopped on one knee. Eleanor could hear him swearing quietly to himself. She went to help him, but he waved her away impatiently. 'Don't twitter over me! Make yourself useful by getting the horse, woman!'

Eleanor refrained from comment, though there was much that she would have liked to say. The man was clearly in great pain. She went slowly over to Captain. He was in a highly nervous state and it took her some minutes to calm him sufficiently to catch hold of his bridle, which was fortunately still in place. She led him slowly over to Mr Guthrie, who by this time had managed to stand.

'That was very well done,' he said with reluctant approval. 'You have a way with horses as well as with men, that's obvious. Now, Captain, my beauty, what have we here?'

Fortunately the wire had not been well anchored at

one end and had given way before doing the horse any serious damage. By the time John returned with help, Mr Guthrie was leading Captain along the path, exhorting Miss Southeran to ride on without him. She had up to this point ignored him, merely continuing to walk alongside, leading her own bay. In any case, how on earth did he expect her to mount a fully grown horse without the benefit of groom or mounting-block? But when she saw John and the others approaching she breathed a sigh of relief and turned to her companion.

'Goodbye again, Mr Guthrie. I hope you have not suffered any lasting damage.'

'I am obliged to you, Miss Southeran. I think you might have saved my life, albeit unintentionally.' Eleanor looked at him doubtfully, but he was serious.

'If you think so, then I am happy to have been of service.'

'I've missed our rides,' he said abruptly.

Eleanor coloured, but said nothing. He gave a wry smile and went on, 'Well, I look forward to our next meeting—in more auspicious circumstances, I hope!'

'As I think my aunt said in her note, Mr Guthrie, I don't think another meeting is at all likely. I have now heard Mrs Anstey's story, you see—the full one. I shall take pains to avoid you in future.'

'You may try, by all means. Don't count on success, however,' he said coolly. 'I suppose you have no doubts, no uncertainties about my guilt?'

Eleanor felt a sudden flicker of hope.

'Do you. . .do you deny the truth of what she said?'

He hesitated for a moment, then he drawled, 'Since I wasn't there, how can I possibly know what she said?

She may well have been right. In any case, ma'am, why on earth should I deny anything? What business is it of yours, I should like to know?'

Eleanor was so incensed that she almost ran towards John, requesting him to help her to mount. Then she rode off without waiting to hear any more.

Eleanor went on fuming about Mr Guthrie throughout that last day in London—when she wasn't puzzling over the curious circumstances of the morning's meeting. In spite of everything, she still found it very difficult to reconcile the black-hearted villain of Mrs Anstey's tale with the man she had met. Her feelings were so confused that she was heartily glad to be leaving for Somerset the next day. She told herself she would forget everything to do with him once she was back at Stanyards.

On the day of her departure the whole household, including her aunt, rose early to see her off. She was fortunate enough to be able to travel with some friends of Bella's new husband, who lived near Lyme Regis, and who had hired a post-chaise. When they appeared in South Audley Street, Eleanor thanked her uncle, embraced her aunt warmly and prepared to climb into the carriage. Her aunt held her sleeve.

'I have done my best to change you into a conformable young lady, Eleanor, but I cannot pride myself on my success.'

'And I, for one, am glad of it,' said her uncle, embracing his niece.

'Well, there have been times when I could have shaken you for your behaviour—but we shall miss you. Life is never dull when you are there,' said Lady

Walcot, smiling at her niece. 'Remember! When the time comes, you have only to say the word and I shall still spare no effort to find you a suitable husband!'

'Thank you, darling Aunt Hetty! But I'm afraid the task would be too difficult, even for you! Besides, there's too much to do at Stanyards! Come down and see us when you grow tired of the season. I shall miss you both! Goodbye!'

The chaise rolled off, and Eleanor waved until they turned the corner and the Walcots were lost to sight.

The journey passed pleasantly enough—the roads were dry and the weather favourable. But by the end of the second day she was heartily glad to stretch her legs at the posting house in Axminster, say goodbye to her kind friends, and join the carriage from Stanyards which would take her the rest of the way. Within an hour she was at the beginning of the long avenue of chestnuts which led to the house. She was home!

As soon as the carriage drew up at the door, Eleanor jumped out, ran up the low flight of steps and clasped her mother in her arms. After a rapturous greeting, Eleanor stood back and surveyed her. 'I ought to scold you for standing in the evening air,' she said. 'Why didn't you stay inside?'

'Daniel saw the carriage and told us you were coming. I couldn't wait to see you, Nell—and anyway I'm feeling very well at the moment, so you needn't scold me at all! Oh, it's delightful to have you home again! Cousin Louisa has been very kind, but I've missed you a great deal. Come in, come in!'

Eleanor followed her mother across the huge, stone-flagged hall into a room which opened off to the side.

Here the low ceilings, ingle-nooks and casement windows set in thick walls proclaimed the great age of the house. But the log fire in the handsome fireplace and the books and tapestries around the walls gave it an air of warmth and comfort.

'I hope you don't die of a heatstroke, Nell. Cousin Louisa insisted on the fire.'

'Your mother hasn't enough flesh on her bones to keep her warm even on the hottest day of summer! And this room never really gets the chill off it, you know that. I am glad to see you, Eleanor. How was your journey? No, don't start talking before you have some food in you; I dare swear you have had nothing sensible for the past month. I've told Betty to bring a tray and we'll put it on the table by the window—the dining-room is far too damp unless you have a fire there, too, which would be wickedly extravagant.

'Anthea, I've drawn your sofa nearer the fire. It was foolish of you to stand outside in the night air for so long. Eleanor could well have waited another two minutes to see you; you look quite chilled. I'll ask Betty to bring you something warm, too—— Drat the woman, you may wait till Domesday for what you want. I'll just see what she is doing.' Cousin Louisa went bustling out. Her cry of, 'Betty!' echoed through the hall as she went.

'She means well,' said Mrs Southeran with a wry smile.

'I know she does. Has it been very hard?'

'Not at all. But tell me about the journey, and when Cousin Louisa returns you can tell us both about Hetty and Bella and the wedding. Did you like the

Wyndhams? It's a long journey to be cooped up with strangers.'

They spent the rest of the evening exchanging news and gossip. Candles were necessary quite soon, for daylight always faded early in the house, even in summer, and the three ladies sat cosily in the soft light till the tea-tray was brought in. But in all her descriptions of her life in London Eleanor never once mentioned the name of Guthrie.

The following day Eleanor woke early, and wondered for the moment where she was. There was a totally different quality to the air, and in the distance she could hear sounds of the country. She was home! She rose quickly, and quietly took herself out into the early morning sunshine. She had forgotten how lovely Stanyards was. For the next half-hour she wandered over the familiar paths and fields round her home, finding herself at length at the end of the chestnut drive.

'Good marnin', Miss Nell!' It was Daniel driving the cart up from the village. 'Would 'un like a lift up to the house?'

'No, thank you, Daniel—I'm enjoying the walk. The chestnuts look magnificent this year!'

'You be careful of 'un, Miss Nell! There's a good few as needs chopping down, I reckon. You have a look at the branch that's lyin' up by the bend. Nearly got old Betty last week, 'un did. Had to skip a bit, did Bet!' He grinned, showing blackened teeth, and drove on.

Eleanor refused to be daunted. The trees were said to be over a hundred years old—it was natural that they should be feeling their age. But they were beautiful. The early morning breeze caused the leaves to whisper and flutter in the summer air, now revealing tiny glimpses of a pale blue sky or the slanting rays of the morning sun, now closing over her head like a heavy canopy. It had always been airless in the city. Here at Stanyards it was cool and fresh. She felt a sudden uplift of spirits as she realised she really was home! Stanyards was where she wanted to stay for the rest of her life, and if the choice was to be between this house and a husband, then Stanyards was what she would choose. Her aunt was wrong to pity her, for she was a fortunate woman.

But as she reached the bend in the drive she stopped and stared. How could she have missed this last night? A huge branch was leaning drunkenly between two of the trees, just off the drive, its leaves drooping and a great jagged, bleached wound at one end. There were signs that the branch had been dragged a few feet, presumably to keep the drive clear. It was an unwelcome reminder that time was taking its toll of her beloved avenue of trees. Daniel was right—some of them at least would soon have to be chopped down.

She stood staring at the branch for some minutes, her happiness at being home again slowly seeping away, tempered by a small shadow of uncertainty. Stanyards was in desperate need of repair and restoration. It wasn't just the drive—the whole estate needed attention. For a black moment she began to doubt her own strength and determination. For years she had done what she could, jiggling account books, robbing Peter to pay Paul, trying to be in three different places every hour of the working day, but suddenly she was terribly afraid that she was slowly but inexorably losing the battle.

What nonsense! she chided herself. It only needed a little more patience, a touch more perseverance and energy. She was still tired after her long journey, but she would soon find the necessary energy and hope. Things would be better this year, she was sure. She threw back her shoulders and marched on up the drive.

In the afternoon Cousin Louisa returned to her own home, in the next village, and after she had gone Mrs Southeran told Eleanor several times how kind, how good, how very helpful Cousin Louisa had been.

'I'm sure she was, Mama—but why are you protesting so much? I already know how worthy Cousin Louisa is!'

'That's it! She's worthy! Oh, Nell, I have been so bored! And I haven't written a line since you left!'

'Now that is serious. Well, I am back now and you must start immediately—where are your things? I'll fetch them and you shall not leave your sofa until you have written at least ten lines! I shall be neither good nor kind until you comply!'

Mrs Southeran was a poet with quite a reputation in the West Country, and even beyond. She wrote under a pseudonym and few of her neighbours knew of her talent, but writing was as necessary to her as breathing. The news that she had been neglecting it was worrying.

'Don't be too concerned, Nell. It wasn't just because of Cousin Louisa or your absence. I've been doing some serious thinking and have even taken some action. Sit down, my dear. Now that we are alone again, I want to tell you something.'

Her mother's voice was so earnest that Eleanor's heart missed a beat. Had the doctor been making gloomier prognostications again? 'I knew I shouldn't have left you! You're feeling worse?'

'It isn't my health, it's you! I've been worried over you for some time now, and while you've been away I've decided that we must do something about it. Running this house and estate is sapping all your energy...all your youth. Your life is taken up with worry and work and little else——'

'Mama! I have just spent four weeks doing little else but enjoying myself!'

'And when was the last time you left Stanyards before that? Or went to a ball or a party? Wore pretty dresses? You have forgotten, and so have I. Well, it must not continue—and I have taken steps to see that it does not.'

'But I am quite happy living here and running Stanyards! I don't want to change anything—except perhaps to see you in better health again!'

'Stanyards is destroying your youth and looks, Eleanor, and it is taking away my health. I know, I know what you are about to say! Stanyards has been in the Southeran family for four hundred years or more, and is steeped in tradition and history. But Tom's death——' Mrs Southeran's voice faltered.

'Don't, Mama! Don't talk about it! It will make you ill.'

'I must! I have refused to face the consequences for far too long! When Tom was killed, Nell, the family name died out. You are not a man, however much you have played the man's part since Tom died.'

'And before,' muttered Eleanor.

'Yes, and before. It was a matter of regret to all of us that your brother never had your interest in Stanyards.' Mrs Southeran paused again, but this time Eleanor made no effort to speak. How could she say anything, when her feelings were so hopelessly tangled? Even after seven years she still felt love and grief for her handsome, laughing brother, was still angry at the recklessness which had caused his death and still resentful that he had cared so little for his heritage. Tom had only ever taken, never given.

Mrs Southeran looked at Eleanor's stormy face and sighed. But then she continued in a more determined voice, 'When you marry, or die, there will be no more Southerans of Stanyards.'

'What are you trying to say, Mama?'

'Not even you can claim that this house is comfortable to live in. Not in its present state. It is old, dark and damp. And we don't have the resources to change it. I have done what I must.'

Eleanor's throat was dry. She said in a strained voice, 'Mama, what have you done?'

Mrs Southeran looked at her with pity in her eyes. 'You will not like it, Nell, but it was for us both. I seized an opportunity which came out of the blue, and I cannot be sorry. I have sold Stanyards.'

For a moment Eleanor sat in stunned silence. Then she whispered, 'No, no! It's not true!' She threw herself down by her mother's sofa and her breath caught on a sob as she pleaded, 'Tell me it's not true, Mama! You can't have s-sold it!'

Mrs Southeran's face was troubled as she gazed at her daughter. But she said steadily, 'It is true, Eleanor. In two weeks Stanyards will have a new owner.'

'How could you? How could you, Mama? You must cancel the sale at once!'

'I did it for us both, Nell,' repeated Mrs Southeran. 'And I will not change my mind.'

Eleanor got up. Without looking at her mother she said, 'I feel. . .I feel sick, Mama. Excuse me, please.' She ran out of the room.

# CHAPTER FOUR

ELEANOR could never afterwards remember what she did for most of that day. For the first time in many years she had no thought for her mother, nor for the duties which needed her attention. She wandered through fields and woods, over stiles and ditches, unseeing and deaf. It was a miracle that she ended the day unscathed. She finally came to herself on the top of the hill which overlooked Stanyards, and stood there for a long time staring down at her home. At one point she imagined she might take hold of it, and she stretched out towards it, but then she let her arms drop hopelessly to her sides. Stanyards was lost, and she felt as if a stone had settled on her heart. She stood there for a little while longer and then stirred and turned away. Old habits reasserted themselves—she must go back—her mother would be worried about her. Slowly she set off down the hill.

But Eleanor could not bring herself to talk about the coming move, and spent a great deal of the next day going about her ordinary duties in silence. Finally her mother sought her out and took her firmly to task.

'We have much to do, and I cannot do it alone, Eleanor. I know you feel strongly——'

'You are wrong, Mama. I do not feel anything.'

'What nonsense!' Mrs Southeran looked at her daughter's wan cheeks and heavy eyes and said more gently, 'You have suffered a great shock, I know that. But do you think it is easy for me to leave my home?'

'I would not have thought so.'

'Eleanor, my dear, you must know in your heart that we could not have continued as we were!' Mrs Southeran paused, but when Eleanor merely turned away and looked out of the window she sighed. 'Perhaps I should have said that I could not have continued as I was? Perhaps I have made you pay too great a price for my own selfish comfort?'

Eleanor could not hold out against the note of uncertainty in her mother's voice. She ran to her and held her tight. 'Forgive me, Mama! I don't wish to hurt or worry you. It was a shock…but I will honestly try to understand your reasons, and of course I will help. How could I possibly do otherwise?'

'Believe me, Nell, I would not have done it if I had thought for one moment that it was not better for both of us.'

'Yes, yes. Anyway, it is all finished now.' Eleanor paused, and then said more cheerfully, 'I haven't yet asked you where we are going to live. Somewhere near?'

'Somewhere very near,' said her mother with a smile. 'In the Dower House.'

'But that is part of the Stanyards estate!'

'We have a lease on it. It was agreed in the sale.'

Eleanor got up and walked about the room. She was not sure what to think about this. On the one hand she would still be part of Stanyards, still have her friends and the countryside she loved so much within easy reach. On the other, how could she bear to be part of Stanyards and yet not part? She continued to pace the room, conscious of her mother's anxious gaze. The Dower House. Compared with the main house, it was modern and well-equipped—her mother could be very comfortably established there, with her friends also close at hand. She wondered about its state of repair—it had been empty for years. And, though no expense had been spared in building it, its rooms were pretty rather than large. 'What would we do with Father's books? There isn't a room that would hold them in the Dower House.'

'They...they are included in the sale. I expect the new owner will keep them where they are.' Her mother sounded apprehensive, but Eleanor could see the force of this. Her father, and his father and grandfather before him, had all been keen book collectors and one of Stanyard's largest rooms had been made into a handsome library some sixty years before.

'Shall I tell you about Stanyards' new owner?'

'No!' said Eleanor violently. In reply to her mother's look of astonishment, she went on, 'Thank you, but I do not wish to know anything about the man, not even his name. I cannot at the moment tolerate the thought of strangers in what was my home, Mama.'

'But, Nell, you will have to know more! Or are you going to refuse to meet him? That would be extremely difficult—the two houses are within a stone's throw of each other. I assure you he is a man of honour and integrity—he will do well by Stanyards——'

'No, Mama!'

'I cannot allow you to bury your head like this...'

'I know,' said Eleanor nervously, but with determination. 'Please be patient with me. I will come round, you'll see, but I need time. Give me a day or two, then

you may tell me all you wish about the usurper!'
Eleanor gave a slightly tremulous smile as she said
this. Only she knew how much the effort she was
making was costing her. Only for her mother would
Eleanor have made this attempt to reconcile herself to
losing Stanyards.

The Dower House lay a short distance from Stanyards
itself, at the end of a branch from the main drive. It
had been built about a hundred years before for the
widow of an earlier and more prosperous Southeran.
It was on a small scale but very pretty, built of brick,
which was a rare luxury in this stone-based countryside, with a miniature pediment and sash windows.
Behind was a small stable block and a path, decorated
with ornamental urns and benches, which connected it
with the main house. Here Eleanor and her mother
were to live.

Having promised to do all she could, Eleanor threw
herself into preparations for the move. She would
normally have been out and about the estate, catching
up with all the tasks which had fallen to her since the
two men in the family had died. But now she stayed at
home and directed the servants, supervised the packing of china and linen, consulted her mother on what
should go and what should stay, all without once
displaying the slightest interest in Stanyards' new
owner.

Apart from her mother, no one seemed to know
very much about him anyway. The negotiations had
been concluded surprisingly swiftly—few had even
caught a glimpse of the mysterious stranger who had
apparently won Mrs Southeran's trust so easily.

One thing Eleanor could not help noticing. The Dower House was being given a thorough renovation, and its garden, which had become a wilderness, was being restored to flowerbeds and lawns. Even the small stable block, which had been out of use for years, was being made ready for occupation. She could not help knowing that a vast amount of money was being spent on all this refurbishment, and asked her mother about it.

'I cannot tell you!' said her mother with a small twinkle in her eye. 'The new owner is doing it all, and you do not wish to know about him!'

Eleanor was obstinate enough not to ask further. Later, of course, she wished she had.

A day or two before the Southeran's move to the Dower House, Eleanor, who had been inspecting yet more cupboards there, was making her way towards the path back to Stanyards. A large black dog, hardly more than a puppy, bounded round the corner from the stables and greeted her with all the warmth of an old friend. The dog was a complete stranger.

'Down, Becky! Down, I say! You must forgive her, Miss Southeran. She has yet to learn her proper place in life, I'm afraid. Did she frighten you?'

Eleanor had recognised the voice at once, of course. Who could mistake those deep, resonant tones? But she still stared at Mr Guthrie as if he had been conjured up by the devil himself.

'Miss Southeran? Are you all right? Becky hasn't an ounce of harm in her, I assure you.' He sounded concerned, and Eleanor made an effort to find her voice.

'It's not the dog! Why are you here?' she croaked.

'I beg your pardon?'

'Why are you here?' she repeated in a stronger voice.

'No, no, Miss Southeran! Even in the Colonies we know better than that. You must bid me "Good morning", say that it is pleasant to see me and then ask if I had a comfortable journey from London. Only then do you work round, by devious methods, to finding out why I am here. However, I should have thought you would know that.'

Eleanor still had no idea. The thought that Mr Guthrie had sought her out here in Somerset seemed ridiculous—but what else could it be? She must make the position quite clear. Curiously enough, it was his incivility at their last meeting, not his perfidy, which came first to mind.

'Your final words to me when we last met were unpardonably rude. I believe I have already told you once—I have no wish to continue our acquaintance, Mr Guthrie. If you are here to see me, you have wasted your journey.' She started off towards the main house, her dignity somewhat hampered by the dog, who danced around her feet as she went.

He strode after her and caught her arm. 'I suppose you think your lack of civility to me is allowable. That I don't merit any consideration? But that's neither here nor there—what I'd like to know is what the devil you're talking about—coming to see you indeed! As you very well know, I've come down here to take over the estate!'

'Take. . .?' Eleanor sat down rather suddenly on an ornamental bench. 'Take over the estate?' she said slowly. 'Oh, God! *You're* the one who has bought Stanyards?'

He looked at her white face. 'You didn't know, did you?' He sat down beside her and would have taken her hand, but she snatched it away. He sat for a moment watching her as she struggled with this new blow. 'I'm sorry if I gave you a shock,' he said, more gently. 'The negotiations for the house were conducted discreetly—for reasons of my own, I didn't wish the world to know where I was about to live—but why on earth hasn't your mother told you since you came back from London?'

'I wouldn't let her,' said Eleanor, her mind still reeling at the identity of the new owner. 'I didn't wish to know anything about the man who was taking Stanyards away from us.'

Mr Guthrie sighed and stood up again. 'Purchasing it, Miss Southeran. For a fair price. A more than fair price, considering the state it is in.'

Eleanor fired up at this criticism. 'Stanyards is a jewel! More than you could ever have hoped to aspire to!'

'Too good for me, eh?' This time his voice was full of mockery. 'Well, we shall see. Now, since I cannot see this conversation serving any useful purpose, and as I have a thousand other things to do, I hope you will excuse me. Or—would you like me to escort you to the house? I thought not. Your servant, Miss Southeran.' He turned to go.

'Wait!' cried Eleanor. 'These negotiations—did my mother take any advice before selling Stanyards to you?'

'Now what are you suggesting? That I cheated her?'

'She is under one misapprehension at least, Mr Guthrie. She assured me that the new owner of Stanyards was a man of integrity and honour!'

Mr Guthrie stood quite still for a moment. Then he took a deep breath and said softly, 'And you think you can prove differently? Prove, mind you! I warn you, Miss Southeran, if I find you are repeating here in the country the kind of scurrilous gossip which made London happy, I shall take steps to silence you. Good day, ma'am!' He turned swiftly and walked away. After looking doubtfully at Eleanor, Becky trotted after her master.

Eleanor sat looking at his retreating back in a daze. How could it have happened? She had been truly glad to have seen the last of Mr Guthrie in London, for she had not enjoyed the confusion of feeling he had caused her. Now, it seemed, she was to see him every day, to be reminded every day of the unpleasant revelations in the interview with Mrs Anstey. And this was the man her mother trusted absolutely! What was she to do? She was desperate to talk to her mother, but waited until she saw Mr Guthrie's carriage go down the drive towards the village before hurrying up to the main house.

'You should have told me, Mama!' she cried. 'You should have told me that Guthrie was the man who had bought Stanyards!'

'My dear child,' said Mrs Southeran, justifiably perplexed. 'You said quite categorically that you did not wish to know anything about Mr Guthrie! How was I to know that you did not mean it?'

'I did mean it! That is to say, I meant it at the time,

but if had known that this man Guthrie was the new owner I would have wanted to know!'

'Eleanor, I am not sure I perfectly understand you. Did you or did you not say that you wished to hear nothing about the new owner, not even his name? Oh. . .I see! You met Mr Guthrie in London? Is that what you are trying to tell me? You have never mentioned him to me, surely?'

'Yes, I. . . I met him in London. Oh, he's a deceitful wretch! He knew all the time we were talking that he had bought my home, he even asked me about it, yet he never said a word! Why did you sell our home to such a man, Mama?'

'I am convinced he will be good for Stanyards. Nothing you have so far said has changed that opinion.'

'How can you be so blind? He is far from being the honourable man you think him!'

'My dear child, it was perhaps not well done to conceal from you the fact that he had purchased Stanyards, but it was not dishonourable! Mr Guthrie has very good reason to keep his future home a secret from all but a small number of people.'

'But how can you be so sure? Surely this passion for secrecy is, to say the least, suspicious? How long have you known him? A few weeks!'

'I have known Mr Guthrie for most of his life.'

'I beg your pardon, Mama?'

'Perhaps I exaggerate a little. I knew Jonas when he was a boy. Our families lived quite close. I have heard from him occasionally—he wrote when your father died, and then again when Tom was killed. And then, just after you had left for London, he visited me here and made an offer for Stanyards. In all that followed he has behaved impeccably. Oh, he has no time for compliments and courtesies—but he has been very generous. You will not easily persuade me to change my opinion of him, Eleanor!'

Eleanor was in a dilemma, and left her mother without saying any more. For the rest of that day and through much of the night that followed she debated what she ought to do. Finally, though she was desperate to tell her mother the story concerning the Ansteys, she decided for a number of reasons to remain silent. She paid no heed to Guthrie's threat—that alone would not have deterred her. But she had given her word that she would not betray the most damning aspects of the Anstey affair to anyone. And, most important of all, she concluded that, for the moment, no useful purpose could be achieved by revealing the true nature of Stanyards' new owner. The deed was done, Stanyards was sold, and it could only distress and worry her mother to know how grossly she had been deceived, how sadly the boy she had known in her youth had changed.

So she resolved to say nothing, but to keep a close watch on Mr Jonas Guthrie and all his activities in this part of Somerset. She was no timid widow, no delicate eighteen-year-old to be used and brushed aside. Mr Guthrie would find her, Eleanor Southeran, a foe to be reckoned with! And woe betide him if he caused her mother the slightest, the minutest difficulty!

But, far from causing difficulties, Mr Guthrie seemed to be exhibiting every desire to help in any way he could in the weeks that followed. He treated Eleanor with careful courtesy, but he had a special manner, an unceremonious friendliness, for Mrs Southeran, which delighted that lady. It was not long before the Southerans, together with Betty and Daniel, were established in the Dower House, and Mr Guthrie was a frequent visitor. Eleanor made sure she was present whenever anything remotely like business was discussed, but she found little to satisfy her suspicions. And she had to admit that life was very much easier than it had been for years. The Dower House had been built for comfort, and its light, airy rooms were a refreshing change from the dim dampness of Stanyards. As for Mrs Southeran, she seemed to flourish in the new regime, and spent hours at the little desk in her pretty sitting-room composing some very fine poetry.

Eleanor, however, was far from happy. At first there had been plenty to occupy her, for any move involved a great deal of work in the weeks following. But after a while time began to drag. She went for long rides, she visited friends, she invited visitors to call. After years of hard, satisfying work on the estate it all seemed rather trivial. Besides, the ladies of the village, the occupants of the large houses in the neighbourhood—all were unanimous in their praise of Mr Guthrie. Her only allies, if they could be so termed, were the farmers and their wives on the Stanyards estate. These good people rapidly developed a dislike of their new landlord.

Eleanor acted very properly. She listened to what they had to say when they came to see her, or stopped her on her outings, but she refused to comment on what was no longer her business, and advised them to take their complaints to the new master of Stanyards. But in her soul she rejoiced. Here were some people who were not deceived by Mr Guthrie's apparent benevolence. And, though she was careful not to say anything, she was in truth shocked at the ruthlessness he was showing in his dealings with the farmers. They were being subjected to a vigorous inspection of how they ran their farms, to largely unfavourable criticism of their practices, and were made to listen to blistering comments on the state of their farm buildings. This last was so patently unfair that Eleanor felt she had to intervene.

When Mr Guthrie next called, Eleanor met him in the hall and asked him if she might have a private word with him afterwards. He raised one eyebrow and asked mockingly, 'Are you sure that is wise, Miss Southeran? Are you not afraid to be private with such a dishonourable man as myself?'

'I can be brave when the need arises, sir.'

'You have the light of battle in your eye. Something tells me that, whatever it is, it is not to my advantage. Very well, I, too, can be brave when the need arises. Will you walk up the drive with me? There's something I wish you to see.'

Eleanor agreed stiffly, and they went into Mrs Southeran's sitting-room together.

'Good afternoon, Jonas! How very nice to see you and Eleanor talking to each other at last! Is your feud over, then?'

'Feud, Mama? Whatever do you mean?'

'I may be elderly and infirm, Nell, but I am not yet in my dotage. It has been quite obvious to me that you and Mr Guthrie have hardly exchanged two words in all the times you have met here.'

'But your daughter has not missed a word of our conversations, Mrs Southeran, especially when we talk of Stanyards and its affairs. She is the most attentive listener of my acquaintance. How do you go on? You are looking well.'

Eleanor grew pink with confusion. So he had noticed her silent watchfulness?

'I have often thought you would do well to consult Eleanor more often, Jonas. She more than anyone knows about the running of Stanyards. She could be a great help to you.'

Mr Guthrie looked sceptical. 'Perhaps she could,' he said dismissively. 'If she wished. But I prefer to see things as they are, ma'am, and as far as the estate is concerned your daughter wears rose-coloured spectacles.'

'Come, come, Jonas! If you are going to be unkind about Nell, then I shall not invite you here again.'

Eleanor could not keep silent. 'If seeing things as they are means that you threaten to evict people who through no fault of their own are unable to meet your high standards, then I prefer to keep my "rose-coloured spectacles", Mr Guthrie!' she said before she could stop herself.

'Ah! Now we have it! I thought as much—you've been gossiping with Threlfall and the others.'

Eleanor said scornfully, 'I do not "gossip". Nor did I seek them out.'

'But you have been talking to them?'

'And why shouldn't I? I have known them all my

life. They appear to need someone to defend them, Mr Guthrie.'

'Miss Southeran,' said Mr Guthrie in biting tones, 'when I need help in dealing with *my* tenants, *my* labourers and *my* affairs I shall ask for it. Stanyards is no longer your concern. Meanwhile——'

'Stanyards is my concern!' There was sudden silence. Eleanor turned away and went to look out of the window. 'Was my concern,' she said bitterly. 'Oh, why did you have to come here?'

'Eleanor! Jonas! Stop this at once! I will not allow you to talk to each other like this—not in my sitting-room at least. Jonas, I should like you to apologise to Eleanor for your harsh words to her. It was cruel to bait her with talk of Stanyards.'

Guthrie said stiffly, 'I did not intentionally bait her, ma'am.'

'You have upset her, however.'

'I think my very existence upsets your daughter, ma'am, not anything I say.'

'Jonas,' said Mr Southeran in a warning tone.

They both looked at Eleanor's unreceptive back, then Guthrie gave Mrs Southeran a wry smile and went to the window. He said, 'Miss Southeran, I beg pardon for my harsh words. My only excuse is that I have had a hard time of it since I took over the running of the estate. Country folk are very resistant to change.'

Eleanor turned round on him.

'But you——'

'Eleanor! Mr Guthrie has apologised handsomely. Now it is your turn.'

'But——'

Mrs Southeran continued firmly, 'If you *have* been responding to Threlfall's complaints, then Mr Guthrie has good reason to be annoyed. You must not stand between master and man, my dear, however hard it may seem. It is your turn to excuse yourself.'

Eleanor could see that her mother meant what she said.

'It is true that I listened to Threlfall. But I have always—always, Mr Guthrie—told him and the others to speak to you, not to me, about their grievances.'

'This is an explanation, not an apology, Eleanor. You were very rude to Mr Guthrie.'

Eleanor said carefully, 'I am sorry, Mr Guthrie, for . . .saying that I wished you had not come here.' She looked up at him to see how he would take this somewhat double-edged remark and then wished she hadn't. To her annoyance, the quizzical expression on his face once again made her want to laugh.

'Now come and have some tea, both of you,' said Mrs Southeran with a sigh of relief. She had been no more deceived than Guthrie by Eleanor's 'apology', but thought it better to ignore its deliberate ambiguity.

By accident or design, Eleanor was not quite sure which, Mr Guthrie entertained the two ladies over tea with talk of India and his travels there. Eleanor almost forgot her antagonism towards him as she lost herself in the exotic world of the East India Company and the Raj, and her eager questions kept him talking until it was time for him to leave. Her mother watched them both with a small smile on her face.

When Mr Guthrie got up to go Eleanor rose, too. 'Will you excuse me, Mama? Mr Guthrie has something to show me, I believe. Is that so, Mr Guthrie?'

'Er. . .quite so. I shall be delighted.'

'I shan't be long, Mama. Do you need anything before I leave you?'

'No, no, my dear! You go with Jonas.' As they reached the door she added with amusement, 'And try not to quarrel with each other!'

# CHAPTER FIVE

ELEANOR and Mr Guthrie walked for a few moments in silence. As they reached the beginning of the path to Stanyards Mr Guthrie said, 'You wished to say something, Miss Southeran. Was it about Threlfall? I warn you that I will not listen patiently to accusations of injustice.'

'But you have been unjust! Threlfall tells me that you blame him and the others for the state of their buildings. But the buildings are the responsibility of the Stanyards estate, not the farmers. I do not expect you to understand that landowners have responsibilities as well as privileges, Mr Guthrie, but to threaten eviction——'

'You will doubtless be disappointed to hear, Miss Southeran, that I have so far threatened no one with eviction.'

Eleanor stopped dead. 'No one?' He shook his head. 'No one at all?'

'Not one,' he said slowly and emphatically.

'But Threlfall said——'

'Threlfall's capacity for understanding what is said to him is as limited as his capacity for hard work! And in spite of your scorn, Miss Southeran, I do understand my responsibilities—better perhaps than you! All the buildings on the estate, including Stanyards itself, are in a poor state of repair. I intend to put them all into good order again, but it will obviously take time and money. A lot of time and money. No, don't fire up at me. I apportion no blame—I knew when I took it over what it was like, and rather like the idea of the challenge.'

'Challenge?'

'Yes, Miss Southeran. The challenge of making a beautiful, potentially rich house and estate, which through neglect and ignorance has been allowed to fall into ruin——'

'How dare you?'

'For God's sake be realistic, woman! Stanyards could not have survived another two years! Oh, I know everyone tells me what a heroine you've been— the hours you've spent, and the dedication you've shown. I've been told how much everyone loves you, how generous, how kind you are. To what purpose?'

Eleanor cried desperately, 'Stop this! I don't wish to hear any more!' She turned to run down the path again but he caught her back and held her by the arms.

'You started this discussion. You told me what a landowner's duties are. Now you shall hear what I have to say!' He sat her down firmly on the bench near by and stood over her while he went on slowly and clearly, 'Your tenants are a crowd of lazy good-for-nothings who would rather let their farms fall down about their ears than stir themselves. You have tamely accepted their stories of small harvests and poor returns——'

'They weren't stories!'

'Don't interrupt! I agree, they weren't stories. The returns were indeed poor. The farmers could never afford the higher rents the estate needed, so you, and your family before you, never attempted to raise them. But did you never ask why the returns were poor? The land here is some of the richest in the West Country. So why couldn't your farmers—including you and your own employees—make a decent living? Laziness, Miss Southeran! Laziness and mismanagement. Stanyards has been idling along, content with the old ways, the old methods for far too long, and it was about to die, stifled by its own inertia.'

'You're wrong!' cried Eleanor, putting her hands to her ears. 'I won't listen to you. I loved Stanyards, and I wasn't lazy!'

Mr Guthrie squatted down so that his face was on a level with hers. 'No one is suggesting that you were lazy. But how could a young woman—a girl, when you started looking after Stanyards—possibly hope to run an estate like this without help? What made you think you could tell rascals like Threlfall how to run their farms? Your father or your brother, now——'

'Neither my father nor my brother ever showed the slightest interest in running the estate,' said Eleanor, trying hard to keep her lips from trembling.

'Then why the devil didn't you employ a manager?'

'We did. B-but we found him to be dishonest. And . . .and I thought I could take over. . .' Eleanor's feelings overcame her and she got up and turned away from him, unwilling to let him see her tears. 'I was wrong,' she said forlornly. 'All that work, all those years—all wasted.'

'Miss Southeran. . .Eleanor! Please! I didn't mean— — Oh, confound it, I did!' His honesty produced a reluctant laugh, which ended in a sob. He swore softly and then, turning her round again, he gathered her

into his arms and held her tightly. 'Don't cry! Whatever else I meant, I didn't mean to hurt you.'

'Heaven help me, then, if you ever do wish to!' She
looked up at him.

'I. . .I. . .I cannot imagine the occasion arising,' he
said slowly, holding her eyes with his own. Eleanor
was suddenly afraid and made an attempt to set herself
free. 'No, don't go yet. I let you go once before against
my better judgement.'

'In the winter garden. . .'

'I wanted to tell you about Stanyards then, but. . .
but we were interrupted.' His arms were still round
her, holding her fast. 'Don't go!' he said again. 'I
haven't finished. I want to ask if you would help me.'

'In what way?' asked Eleanor, still feeling strangely
breathless.

'I need you. . .' He cleared his throat. 'I need your
help in talking to the people on the estate. So that
they understand what I'm trying to do, and give it a
chance. Believe me, they will all be happier and more
prosperous for it.' He was still holding her.

'I. . . Yes, I think so. But you must explain it to me
first.'

He smiled. 'Of course I will.' He slowly, very slowly,
bent his head and kissed her. Eleanor had never
before experienced the excitement which now filled
her. She found herself returning the kiss, reluctant to
let it end. But then she came to herself and was
shocked at her behaviour. She tried to push him away.

'Mr Guthrie! Sir!'

'Call me Jonas,' he murmured, and kissed her again.

'Mr Guthrie!' She broke away and stood on the

path a few yards away. 'How. . .how dare you kiss me?'

'It was to seal our bargain,' he said, as if that explained it. 'Was it very unpleasant?'

'Yes, of course!' He raised a quizzical eyebrow. 'Well, no,' she replied more honestly. 'But it mustn't be repeated, or I shall have to refuse to see you alone again.'

'That would be a pity,' he murmured, looking at her lips, just as he had in the winter garden.

Eleanor felt her knees go weak, but said firmly, 'I mean it!'

He laughed and said, 'I can see you do. And you are right. It is too soon.' He grew serious again. 'Much too soon. There are matters which have to be cleared up first. I have no right to. . .involve you in my private difficulties.' Then he smiled again and said, 'Are you prepared to come up to the house? I've drawn up plans and suggestions for managing the estate. It's early days yet—they mostly lie in the future, but I thought you might like to see them. It might explain a few things. And. . .I promise to behave.'

Eleanor put her head on one side and studied him. Mrs Anstey's account of his behaviour had been graphic, and his actions a moment or two ago gave absolutely no reason to suppose that he had changed. She would be mad to trust him. 'Yes,' she was astonished to hear herself say. 'Yes, I'd like that.'

They walked up the rest of the path in a slightly guarded silence. Becky met them halfway and greeted them both rapturously.

'Down, Becky! Will you get down, dog?'

Eleanor laughed at her companion's efforts to

restrain Becky. 'The estate may go in fear and trembling of you, Mr Guthrie, but that dog has your measure. What are you going to do with her?'

'She's young yet, but I think she's intelligent. She'll soon learn who is master here. Meanwhile, let her have her fun. I enjoy her spirit,' he said, with a look. Eleanor wanted to object to that look, but decided in the end it was better to ignore the hidden meaning, and she kept silent.

They went into the house, through the hall, which looked much as it had always done, and up the stairs to the room on the first floor which had been made into a library. As they went, Mr Guthrie explained, 'I've started on some of the rooms—there's a lot of damp. This side of the house seems to be worse than the other.' Eleanor nodded without comment. She wasn't yet ready to voice any criticism of Stanyards. He went on, 'I don't know how your mother survived it so long. She isn't strong—she never has been.'

'You knew her before, didn't you?'

'Yes, we lived near one another when I was a child.'

'Does my mother know Mrs Anstey?' They had reached the library. He stopped with his hand on the door-latch.

'Yes,' he said expressionlessly. 'Yes, she does. We all knew each other.' Suddenly the atmosphere was different. The warm feeling of confidence which had been flowing between them vanished as if it had never been, and the chill of the house surrounded them. Eleanor shivered. Could she really trust this man?

'Shall we go in? The plans are in here.' He opened the door and they entered the room.

The room was in darkness, for the heavy tapestry

curtains which covered a series of small windows were still drawn. Mr Guthrie said, 'Stay here by the door. There are things on the floor and you might trip. I'll let some light in.'

She could hear him making his way to the windows as she stood there absorbing the smell of her father's library—a mixture of leather and candles and mustiness, remembered from her earliest childhood. Her father had spent most of his time here, poring over his books. Recent Southerans had all been scholars, preferring the world of their library to the harsh realities of life. They had amassed a wonderful—and very valuable—collection of books from all ages. But, however pressed for money the estate had been, it had never entered Eleanor's mind to suggest that they should sell any books. They were a part of Stanyards itself. Allowing Mr Guthrie to buy them along with the house had merely been her mother's way of keeping the library intact and at Stanyards.

When the first curtains were drawn she could see that the room was being reorganised. The shelves nearest the door, where the most valuable books had been stored, were bare and boxes were stacked on the floor beneath them. She wondered what the new arrangement was to be. But then, as more curtains were drawn and more light was let into the room, she could see that all the shelves were bare and some had been dismantled—indeed, one bookcase lay in jagged pieces in the middle of the room. What was happening here? She took a step forward and nearly fell over one of the boxes. She looked down. This one was already sealed and labelled, and when she examined the label more closely she saw the address of a prominent London dealer in rare books.

The vandal! The treacherous, ruthless vandal! Oh, now she could see how he intended to pay for his improvements! She should have known he wouldn't use any of his own money—the estate must pay for itself; he had said so. And he was now stripping Stanyards of its priceless, irreplaceable library to pay for the repair of a few farm buildings! Her father's and grandfather's treasures, collected and loved for over half a century, were to be shipped off to market like so many cattle? Not if she could help it!

Mr Guthrie drew back the last curtain at the far end of the room, then turned and said, 'I'm sorry about the mess—I had forgotten what a state the room was in when I asked you to inspect the plans. They're here on the table. What is wrong?'

Eleanor's eyes were burning. She was so choked with rage that she could hardly speak.

'I. . .I. . . You. . . My aunt and the rest were right! You are a heartless, dishonourable villain! Commerce and avarice have so corrupted you that you are not fit to live among honest people! I hate you! But you haven't heard the last of this. I won't let you destroy Stanyards as you destroyed the Ansteys. I won't let you ruin Stanyards' library as you ruined Evadne Oliver! I'll fight you every inch of the way, Mr Moneybags Guthrie!' She ran out, sobbing with fury.

Jonas Guthrie had at first listened to Eleanor's tirade with astonishment. What was this girl-woman so furious about now? Then, as the meaning of her words became clear to him, his own face grew dark with anger and he strode to the door, intending to haul her back and make her eat her words. She wouldn't get far before he caught her. But at the door he stopped in disgust. He made no further attempt to follow her, but stood in silence listening to the sound of her fleeing footsteps.

He turned and went slowly back to the centre of the room, staring down at the plans on the table without seeing them. How dared she? How could she be so unjust? Out there on the walk up to the house they had seemed to achieve a sort of understanding—an understanding which promised to help them in the many difficulties which lay ahead. Indeed, he had felt for a moment that there was more than that between them. Much more. But, whatever he had felt, there was obviously no answering feeling in Miss Southeran's soul.

In a sudden gesture of rage, he swept the plans to the floor. So much for help and confidence, damn her! So much for the stupid idea that he could win her over! To hell with her! He would manage without her. With her soft heart and impulsive ways, she would probably have been a liability anyway.

He moved over to the window-seat at the far end of the room and gazed out at the view. To the left was the long drive of chestnuts—he would soon have to do something about those; they were a daily danger. To the right was the Dower House. She'd be back there now, pouring out her heart to her mother. What would be the response? Not that it mattered—Eleanor was so set against him that she wouldn't listen to any defence, however hard Mrs Southeran tried.

His expression lightened briefly as he thought of

Mrs Southeran. There was one person at least who was on his side—a rare feeling these days. All the other women he had met recently condemned him out of hand... It was the Anstey affair, of course. He had hoped that the full story would not become generally known in England—after all, it might not reflect any credit on him, but some of it didn't reflect any credit on Evadne Anstey, either. Evadne Oliver, he supposed he should call her. With a cynical smile he wondered how that marriage was faring. Probably quite well—they were two of a kind. All the same, he would have thought that Evadne's fool of a mother would have been more discreet. He smiled wryly— when had sweet, silly Amelia Vereker ever been discreet?

He couldn't really blame her. All the same, it was a pity. He could have lived down the question of the money—especially as he had seen to it that Amelia and Marianne had got back to England with a secure future. From what he had observed, Marianne would make a good match quite soon. But the seduction of Evadne—that was the story which stuck in their throats. That was the story which had dished him.

He got up again and moved restlessly round the room, and eventually his eye lighted on the sealed box of books. Those books should be sent off to the restorer as soon as possible. He bent down to check the label. 'Wilkes, purveyor of rare books'. Purveyor... Of course! Wilkes was a *seller* of books, as well as a restorer. That was why Eleanor had leapt to such an unflattering conclusion. She hadn't given him much benefit of the doubt. If she had asked, he could have told her why the books were being taken to

Wilkes, why the bookcases were being dismantled.
However much her damned family might have loved
their precious books, they hadn't thought to look after
them properly—or the shelves that housed them. The
room was riddled with worm and damp. He wasn't at
all sure that Wilkes could save some of the volumes
he was sending.

The discovery of the labelled box had cheered him
somewhat. It didn't remove his strong sense of injustice, but it did at least explain why Eleanor had been
quite so vehement. But he wasn't about to go after
her, begging her to listen to the truth about Wilkes'
parcel! Oh, no! If Miss Southeran chose to ignore all
he had done since coming down to Stanyards, and
continued to believe only the worst of him, then it was
not up to him to convince her otherwise. It would in
any case be a waste of effort.

Mr Guthrie returned to the centre of the room,
picked up the plans and put them back on the table. He
stood there for some minutes staring at them, then he
gradually became more absorbed. He pulled up a chair
and sat down. . . It was a considerable time before he
looked up again. Yes, they would work. Stanyards
could become self-supporting quite soon, given reasonably favourable seasons, and the co-operation of the
people concerned. That was where Eleanor might have
helped, had she chosen to. For a short while, a very
short while, he had visualised a time when together
they would create something worth having out of
Stanyards. But her stupid prejudice against him had put
an end to all that.

He looked at the doorway and in his mind's eye he
saw her standing there. How lovely she had looked,

even in her rage—almost as lovely as when he had first seen her in London, the candlelight turning her dark gold hair to flame and her sea-green eyes reflecting the lights of the crystals. When she was angry the eyes darkened to blue...and when she was kissed... This was pathetic! To hell with her! He jumped up impatiently and strode out of the room.

Mr Guthrie was not seen at the Dower House for some time—at least not when Eleanor was there. He would have been surprised to learn, however, that his picture of Eleanor pouring out her troubles to her mother was quite wrong. Eleanor had been too frightened by the turmoil of her feelings to confide immediately in Mrs Southeran. For years it had been her aim to protect her mother from any form of unpleasantness, and her instinct now was to hide what she felt until she was in control of it. So she avoided any lengthy conversations at home and took to riding out more frequently, and further afield. She avoided the people on the estate, too.

She didn't want to have to think about what Guthrie had said on the walk up to the house. Of course she thought about it just the same, most of the time—and about her reactions to him. From the beginning her feelings about Guthrie had always been confused, but now they were chaotic. Her head and her heart were at odds completely—and even her heart was divided. How could she still feel anything for a man who was destroying all she held most dear? What could she do to stop herself? And what could she do to stop him? However hard she racked her brains, she could think of nothing. Thanks to her mother's unaccountable faith in Guthrie, he had absolute control over Stanyards and everything in it. She had never before felt so helpless and so lost.

But eventually the time came when Mrs Southeran thought that Eleanor had been battling alone for long enough. It was early evening and they were enjoying the last of a glorious day's sunshine. Mrs Southeran's *chaise-longue* had been drawn up between the doors on to the terrace, and Eleanor was seated on a low chair outside. She made a very pretty picture, framed against the evening light, with her dark gold curls tumbling down below the wide straw hat, but there was a weary droop to her shoulders and she had spoken very little over the meal they had just finished.

'Eleanor?'

'Yes, Mama? What is it? Would you like me to get you a shawl?'

'No, sit down again! Please. Don't go away—I want to talk to you.'

Eleanor said nervously, 'Isn't it rather late for you to be in the air, Mama? Shall we go in?'

'Ah, don't, my dear! Don't shut me out.'

'I. . . I don't know what you mean.'

'Of course you do. I want to know what is causing you such trouble. Do you miss Stanyards so very much?'

'No, it's not that. It's nothing. . .' Mrs Southeran shook her head slowly at her daughter and Eleanor could hold out no longer. 'Yes, it is! Oh, Mama, it's what is happening to Stanyards! Did you know that Mr Guthrie is selling off Father's library?'

Whatever Mrs Southeran had been expecting, it was not this. 'Selling it off? What nonsense!'

'He is! I saw it—all the books were packed up, and the shelves had been taken down, and——'

'And this is what has been causing you so much anguish? Really, Eleanor, I could be angry with you if I were not so worried! Listen! Mr Guthrie, far from trying to destroy the library, has, with my full knowledge, been doing his best to save it.'

'Save it! How?'

'Some of your father's most valued books are seriously damaged with damp and mould. The room needs a thorough overhaul.'

'And what about the package for Mr Wilkes? Wasn't he one of Father's suppliers? Does he not sell rare books? I tell you I saw it, Mama! Mr Guthrie is selling off Father's library!'

Mrs Southeran's face was serious as she said, 'I am disappointed in you, Eleanor. I had thought you more clear-headed than this. Pray forget your prejudice against Mr Guthrie for one moment, and think over what you have just said. If it were anyone else, would you jump to such a hasty and ill-considered conclusion? I think not. You might remember that Mr Wilkes does not only *sell* books.'

Eleanor stared blankly at her mother and then her eyes widened as she took in what she was saying. 'He restores them. They were being sent off for repair?' Mrs Southeran nodded. There was a short silence and then Eleanor buried her face in her hands and said in a muffled voice, 'Oh, Mama, I've been such a fool! It never entered my head. . . Why didn't I think before I spoke? I said such awful things to him.'

'What did you say?'

'I cannot tell you; I am too ashamed.' She got up

and walked about the terrace restlessly. 'What can I do?'

'The first thing is to see Jonas. You must make your peace with him. Shall I arrange it?'

'No! I cannot face him.'

'Nell, you must. If what you said was so dreadful, then you must offer him an apology. You cannot do anything else. I'm sure he will forgive you.'

'Truly, Mama, what I said was unforgivable. I would much rather not see him again.'

'That is clearly impracticable—unless you leave here forever and go to live with your aunt in London. But I own I should miss you. In those circumstances I might fall out with Mr Guthrie myself.'

Eleanor responded to this small joke with a wan smile. 'You are teasing me into doing as you wish— you know I would never leave you for such a ridiculous reason.' She sighed. 'Can you arrange a meeting? I have not even caught a glimpse of him since that day. I think he must have been avoiding me as much as I have avoided him.'

'I think that is highly likely.' Eleanor gave her mother a suspicious look. 'No, you need not look at me like that. Jonas has been to see me while you have been out, but he has said nothing. I have, of course, drawn my own conclusions. It would have been difficult for me not to suspect that you had fallen out again, but I had no idea it was over such an absurd matter. I'll see if he will come here tomorrow. Would you like me to see him first?'

Eleanor assured her fervently that she would, and Mrs Southeran promised to do her best for her.

\* \* \*

The next afternoon Eleanor stood back from her
bedroom window and watched as Jonas Guthrie came
down the path to the Dower House. The expression
on his face was not particularly agreeable and her
heart sank. She had a sudden feeling of panic at the
thought of facing him—how could he possibly forgive
her?—but she forced herself to be calm. It had to be
done, though in her own mind she was very doubtful
of success. She would not have been reassured, either,
had she heard the conversation between Mr Guthrie
and her mother.

'I am glad you decided to come, Jonas. Eleanor will
be relieved. I think she wishes to say how sorry she is
for her stupid mistake.'

'Really, ma'am? Which one?'

'Has she made so many, Jonas? Surely not. In any
case, you know which one we are speaking of here, of
course. You are merely trying to be difficult, which is
not kind of you.'

'I must confess, ma'am, I do not feel very kindly
disposed towards your daughter.'

'Nor to me?'

His voice grew warmer, though his expression
remained set.

'I always feel kindly disposed to you, Mrs
Southeran.'

'Well, then, for my sake will you see Eleanor and
hear what she has to say? It would be very awkward if
we had to go on as we are, would it not? You cannot
continue avoiding each other forever. It is most difficult. And. . . Eleanor is in some distress.'

'Forgive me if I say that it is no more than she

deserves.' He took a look at his hostess's anxious face.
'It is almost impossible to refuse you anything, as you
are well aware. Very well, I shall see Miss Southeran
and listen to her apology.' His features relaxed into a
faint grin. 'Though if it is at all like her last attempt
I'm not sure it would satisfy me.'

'No, no. The case is quite different. This time she is
honestly repentant. Tell me, Jonas, why did you not
tell her the truth about the books straight away?'

'I was given no opportunity—— No, that's not the
real reason. It's true that I had no opportunity, but I
would not have taken it anyway.' His face darkened
again and he walked away from her to look out of the
window. 'I told you when I first came to Stanyards
earlier this year that there were...difficulties in my
life—that not everyone would regard me with favour,
and that I was not in a position to defend myself.
London was full of scandalous stories about me when
your daughter was there.'

'You assured me that there was nothing in your past
of which you were ashamed. Your word was good
enough for me, Jonas. I knew you.'

'I... I am deeply grateful for your trust, and I swear
I will not betray it—neither with Stanyards, nor with
Eleanor.'

'Ah, there we have the crux of the matter, have we
not? Eleanor.'

'She hasn't the same confidence in my honour. She
has good reason for this—the tales in London were
very convincing, and Lady Walcot warned her against
me. But I had hoped with you down here she would
learn to trust me as you do. It is clear to me that she
never will.'

'Perhaps she needs more time?'

'That may be true, but I doubt it. And I do not intend to justify myself to anyone—least of all to someone who regards anything I do with instant suspicion!'

'Of course, you cannot entirely blame Eleanor, nor the stories in London, for her prejudice against you. It was a great shock to her to find out that her home had been sold over her head—and to you. I was wrong not to consult her beforehand, but I thought at the time it was better to take that decision from her—and it all happened so swiftly! But why didn't you tell her in London about Stanyards?'

'Yes, that was a mistake. I can see that now. But I thought I had good reason. At first, as you know, I didn't wish to publish my future whereabouts. Then . . .to be frank, when your daughter first described her home to me in such loving terms, I couldn't bring myself to tell her that she was going to lose it. After that, the right moment never seemed to come. I suppose I was always afraid of destroying what friendship she had for me. I was deceiving myself, of course. She has none.'

'That must be the first time I have heard you admit either to a mistake or to cowardice! What has happened to you, Jonas?'

'A slight madness, which I now regret.'

After a short pause Mrs Southeran said, 'You are wrong about Eleanor. She is not usually so unreasonable.'

'No? You know her better than I, naturally.'

'Will you see her?'

'Of course,' he said politely.

'And you will be kind to her?'

'That may be more difficult, but I shall try.'

When Eleanor came into the sitting-room, Mr Guthrie was standing with his back to the window, his face in shadow. Her mother gave her an encouraging smile and said, 'Eleanor, Mr Guthrie is here to listen to what you wish to say to him. I think he can see what brought you to misjudge him so badly, and I know he understands how difficult it has been for you to relinquish your claim to the Stanyards estate.

'I am largely to blame for that, of course. I should have consulted you. I hope you will forgive me, my dear, as I am sure Mr Guthrie will forgive you. And now I am going to leave you to sort things out between you. I shall make my peace with you later, my child.' She went out, shutting the door quietly behind her.

# CHAPTER SIX

THERE was an awkward silence in the room after Mrs Southeran had left. In the friendly privacy of her bedchamber Eleanor had practised what she was going to say and it had sounded elegant and appealing. Now she couldn't think how to begin, and the man in front of the window didn't appear to be about to help her. Finally she said, 'I am not sure what I can say to persuade you to forgive me, Mr Guthrie. I wouldn't blame you if you had refused to come.'

'I am not so unreasonable, Miss Southeran. And I am here to listen.' His tone was neutral.

Eleanor took a deep breath and said, 'I am sincerely sorry for my over-hasty judgement of you in the library last week. I was completely in the wrong, and am ashamed of what I said to you.'

'You now believe that Lady Walcot and the others were wrong, too?'

'It is unfair of you to ask me that. How can I possibly know? But I was wrong to accuse you of selling the books, and I do believe that you mean well by Stanyards.'

'This is progress indeed!' Mr Guthrie's voice was still cool.

'What else can I say?'

'It would be foolish to expect more, I agree. Very well, Miss Southeran, we will forget the matter.'

Eleanor felt uncomfortably close to tears. In all her

encounters so far with Mr Guthrie, whether they had been friendly or otherwise, she had been aware of a current of feeling running between them, a kind of extra line of communication. This was now noticeably absent.

'I. . . It is also my opinion that Stanyards will fare better in the future under your management than it has in the recent past.'

'More progress!' A mocking smile accompanied these words.

'And if I can be of any help. . .'

This time his response was swift and decisive. 'Thank you, but I think not. There must be no divided loyalties among the people on the estate.'

'There wouldn't be! If I gave you my help it would be whole-hearted. Do you believe me incapable of loyalty?'

He drawled her words of a few minutes before. 'How can I possibly know?'

She caught her breath. 'You haven't really forgiven me at all, have you?'

A faint pink appeared in his cheeks. 'Miss Southeran, I do not blame you for thinking ill of me, though I had hoped. . . We'll forget that. I suppose I do understand. And in return I hope you will understand why I cannot accept your offer of help. How can you persuade my tenants and workers to have confidence in me, to trust me, when you yourself do not trust me?'

'But I do! Where Stanyards is concerned, that is. Your life before you came here is another matter.'

'Trust, Miss Southeran, is complete or not at all.'

'But how can I trust you completely knowing what I

do about your past—broken-off engagements and. . . and worse?'

'Engagement?' He looked blank. 'What engagement? Oh, yes, of course! My engagement! You need not consider that. It was of no consequence.'

'Perhaps not to you, sir!'

'Nor to the lady concerned, either, I assure you. You may forget my engagement. The rest is different, I agree, and more difficult to explain.' His manner became even cooler. 'Not that I propose to. I accept your apology in the spirit it was given, Miss Southeran. And now I think we should ask your mother to come in to hear that we have made up our differences.'

Eleanor saw that any further attempt to heal the rift between them would be useless. And what more did she want? Mr Guthrie had already done more than she had dared to hope. Her words to him had seemed to her to be unforgivable, and yet he had forgiven them. She could not reasonably expect him to forget her insults so quickly—especially when she was incapable of saying that she trusted him in the same whole-hearted manner as her mother did. But she was filled with a deep regret, all the same, for something that was lost, though she wasn't quite sure what it was.

That night Eleanor found it impossible to sleep. After tossing and turning for what seemed like hours she eventually got up and sat by the window. The night was warm and the stars were bright. She stared up at them as they slowly moved through the sky, and found herself wishing that she had never listened to the wretched Anstey woman! Could she really reconcile the Jonas Guthrie she knew—a man who was prepared to shoulder all the responsibilities of a large estate, who wanted to create, to make up for the neglect of previous generations—with the Jonas Guthrie of Mrs Anstey's account—a heartless monster who had shuffled off his obligations in exchange for a sum of money? Hardly. But, on the other hand, Mr Guthrie had never attempted to deny the story, or justify himself in any way. He had merely demanded that she should trust him—against all the evidence. How could she do that?

Eleanor got up and paced the room. She had liked this man from the first, but what did that mean? What did she know of the wider world—she, who was so inexperienced? Yes, she had felt a sense of kinship with him. But wasn't it just possible that Evadne Anstey had experienced the same delightful sense of kinship, before discovering, too late, that she had been deceiving herself?

Eleanor came to a halt as she remembered Mr Guthrie's view of his engagement. Of no consequence, indeed—the consequences had been dire for poor Evadne Anstey! She turned impatiently. There were so many questions about this man, and no answers.

The debate which had started that night in Eleanor's mind continued throughout the following week. Her instinct was to trust him but, try as she might, she could not simply reject Mrs Anstey's story, nor could she forget Mr Guthrie's careless dismissal of his engagement. Her mother was unable to help her with any facts which might throw light on the question.

'Jonas engaged? Well, I never heard of it, but that is not to say it wasn't so. I don't know all the details of his life in America. I can tell you that he isn't engaged now. As for Amelia—yes, I knew Amelia Vereker when she was a girl. She was a few years younger, so I cannot say I was a bosom friend of hers. She was a pretty little thing.'

'Is she. . .? It may seem a curious thing to ask, Mama, but would you say she was honest?'

'Completely.'

'I see.'

'She wasn't clever enough to be anything else! No, don't look at me like that, Nell! One has to face facts. Amelia Vereker was everything that was amiable and kind, but not at all clever. She had an air of helplessness about her which some found very appealing, though I was not one of them. Henry Anstey apparently fell in love with her at first sight.'

'How did she meet him?'

'She was visiting the London Verekers, and met him at a ball. They were engaged almost immediately and married very soon after that—his time in Europe was limited and he wanted to take her back to America with him. We were surprised at the speed with which it all happened, but her life with the Thomas Verekers had not been particularly happy—she was an orphan, you know. So was Jonas. I think that is why they were so devoted to each other.'

'Did you know Mr Guthrie's mother, too?'

'Caroline Vereker? Oh, yes. Now there was a character!'

'Oh? I am surprised. I had the impression that she was rather like Mrs Anstey?'

'Good lord, no! Whatever gave you that idea?'

'Wasn't she deserted by her husband? And didn't she die soon after?'

'Yes, but not of a broken heart, whatever Amelia may have said! She was a spirited, courageous creature. Absolutely straight, scornful of any weakness or sub-terfuge, but very headstrong. She was probably too headstrong for her husband's taste—he was fond of his own way, too. No one ever knew exactly what hap-pened between the Guthries—certainly not Amelia, who wasn't much more than a child at the time. But Caroline came back to Somerset without her husband, Richard. She had the baby, and then, typically ignoring all advice, went riding too soon afterwards, developed a fever and died. They tried to trace Richard Guthrie but he had vanished. They found out later that he had gone into the army.'

'This is a different picture altogether!'

'Just what I was saying—Amelia Vereker would always tell what she believed to be the truth, but might well not understand the facts.'

'My uncle said much the same thing,' said Eleanor thoughtfully.

'Why on earth was your uncle talking about Amelia Vereker? And, Eleanor, why do you want to know all this history now?'

'When I was in London Mrs Anstey told me some-thing about Mr Guthrie—Jonas Guthrie. If it is true, then he is dishonourable.'

'Eleanor! Are you still trying to prove that Mr Guthrie is a villain? I thought we had finished with all that nonsense!'

'On the contrary, Mama. I am trying to find out if he could possibly be the victim of some kind of plot.'

'I see.' Mrs Southeran thought for a moment, then shook her head. 'Amelia Vereker wouldn't be clever enough to invent a plot. And she certainly wouldn't harm Jonas—she adored him. You cannot have understood her properly, Nell! What did she say about him?'

'I'm afraid I can't tell you. I gave my word.'

'Well, then, I'm afraid we cannot go much further. But I would never have sold Stanyards to Jonas if I had not had absolute confidence in him. Have you never asked him to explain the matter?'

'His "explanation" was that it was none of my concern.'

'Oh, dear! Not very helpful, but very typical! He was always a touch too arrogant for his own good, just like his mother. But wait! When he first came to see me here he did say that he was unpopular in London— presumably because of the stories you heard. He assured me that he was not ashamed of anything he had done——'

'Not ashamed!'

'And if Jonas said that, then there was nothing to be ashamed of, Eleanor,' said her mother firmly. 'The fact that he hasn't defended himself must be because he is protecting someone—and I would say that was Amelia. He was always very protective of her, even though she was some years older.'

'But that just doesn't fit, Mama!' said poor Eleanor. 'It doesn't make sense! Mrs Anstey was one of the people who suffered because of what he did!'

'*Amelia*? That is inconceivable. There must be some mistake.'

They both sat frowning. At last Mrs Southeran said, 'The whole affair is most puzzling and I don't think I can help you any further, Nell. Since I do not know what crime Jonas has been charged with, I cannot produce a defence for him. Except that I trust his word—and so should you.'

But, in spite of her doubts about Mrs Anstey's story, this was not yet enough for Eleanor.

Life continued quietly enough at Stanyards and the Dower House. When Mr Guthrie and Eleanor met they were civil to each other, and if Mrs Southeran was present they even conversed. But there was an invisible veil between them which prevented any real communication, and Eleanor did not know how to get rid of it—even had she wanted to. She tried to behave circumspectly. If, when out riding or walking, she met the tenants and workers on the estate, she took care to confine her interest to questions about their families. But Eleanor could not avoid hearing that Mr Guthrie was pressing on with reforms on the estate, and she could see the farmers slowly beginning to respond—especially when they saw that their landlord's unfavourable comments on their buildings had been followed by practical measures to repair them.

Then one day Eleanor was drawn by the sound of sawing to investigate the drive. She was horrified to see that a team of men were at work cutting down her beloved avenue of chestnut trees. She waved her arms and shouted to them, but they were intent on their work and the sound of the saw drowned her voice. She started to run towards them, but suddenly stopped after a few paces. What was she thinking of, telling the men to stop? But that was just what she must not do— the trees, the drive itself, no longer belonged to her, and she must not interfere.

She stood for a moment in a state of indecision,

battling with a strong desire to tell them to stop all the same. She thought what it would mean to her to lose her trees—their chestnut candles in spring, their stately green canopy in summer, their brightly polished nuts in the autumn—and the thought gave her courage. How dared he remove them?

She turned on her heel and swept up the drive towards the house, intending to challenge Mr Guthrie. But once again she had not gone very far before she came to a halt. Could she be wrong? Was the episode of the library about to be repeated? Were the men perhaps merely removing those trees which were a danger? Perhaps she should find out before storming in on Stanyards' master.

She started back towards the men only to stop yet again when Becky came running out from behind the trees to greet Eleanor with her usual uninhibited enthusiasm.

A man's voice called, 'Becky! Down, girl!' Becky stopped as if pulled on an invisible lead. 'Sit!' With an apologetic look at Eleanor, Becky came no further but sat down where she was. Eleanor looked round and, with dismay, saw Mr Guthrie leaning against one of the trees on the other side of the drive. From his stance, it was obvious that he had been there some minutes.

'Good morning, Miss Southeran,' he called, and came over to join her. She saw that he was regarding her with some amusement.

Eleanor went scarlet as she realised that he must have been observing her stops and starts. He might even have been able to divine the course of her thoughts from them, and had been laughing at her inability to make up her mind. 'Good morning,' she said abruptly, and turned to leave him. Then she turned back again. 'No, I *will* ask you!'

He burst out laughing. 'Good!' he said. 'We have a decision at last.'

'What do you intend to do with the chestnuts?' This came out more truculently than she had intended, and she added in a more conciliatory tone, 'If you don't mind my asking, that is.'

He looked at her speculatively. 'What do you think I intend to do?'

Eleanor felt this was some kind of test. She hesitated before answering and considered the men at their work. Then she turned to him, an expression of uncertainty on her face. She had come to a surprising conclusion. 'I think. . .I think you are trying to preserve what you can of them.'

'Not selling them for their timber?'

'Chestnut timber isn't worth much,' she said absentmindedly. 'No, I don't mean that! I mean, it's true that it isn't worth much, but I don't think you would cut the trees down in order to sell them, anyway. No, I think you are getting rid of the dangerous ones and will try to keep the rest. Is that. . .is that right?' In a way, this was a declaration of some faith on her part, and she waited anxiously for his reply.

'And if I decide that I cannot save any of them? They are all very old.'

Eleanor's answer came swiftly and instinctively. 'I think you will plant new trees.' She had succeeded in surprising him. Indeed, she had surprised herself. He looked down at her with a faint smile.

'Well done! It seems I am making progress—real progress.'

'They won't be the same as the old trees, of course,' said Eleanor, reluctant to concede too much.

'No, indeed they won't. That is why I am keeping as much as possible of the old stock. I shall plant a new line some distance back and, when the last survivors of these stalwarts finally succumb, the young trees will be ready to take over to form a new, wider avenue. But I won't plant horse chestnuts again.'

'Why not?' Eleanor demanded, her hackles rising at any criticism of Stanyards. 'They are beautiful.'

'They don't last long enough.'

'What do you mean? These are over a hundred years old!'

'That is nothing in terms of an estate such as this. I want Stanyards to be beautiful still in two hundred years, Eleanor—and more yet. I shall plant lime trees.'

Eleanor gazed at him in bemusement. Who would have thought that such a visionary dwelt behind those dark, hard features? How far removed was this man from the callous adventurer of Mrs Anstey's tale, and how could she ever reconcile the two?

He grinned at her. 'You are making me feel somewhat like a chandelier, Miss Southeran.'

'A chandel. . . Oh!' Eleanor grew pink and said in confusion, 'Forgive me. I was staring.'

'You were, but I enjoyed it. It is some time since you regarded me with anything but a basilisk glare.'

Eleanor burst out laughing. 'How unkind! And how unjust! I have merely been reflecting your own cockatrice looks at me!'

They laughed together, and then suddenly became serious. He said quietly, 'Shall we try again, Eleanor?'

Eleanor was filled with a sudden exhilaration. 'Yes!' she said shyly. 'Yes, I should like that.'

'Do you approve of my plans for the drive?'

Eleanor was anxious not to assume too much. 'My approval isn't necessary—but I do.' She said with a touch of sadness, 'I knew the chestnuts would have to go soon—I just hate the thought of losing them.'

He smiled at her. 'A woman of spirit and intelligence, and a sentimentalist, too. What a rare mixture you are, Eleanor Southeran!'

'No rarer than you, Jonas Guthrie!' she flashed. 'I find it impossible to fathom you! What has this lover of the countryside, this designer for the future to do with the business cheat—and worse—of Mrs Anstey's tale?' She stopped short, aghast at her own outspokenness. 'I'm sorry,' she faltered. 'I shouldn't have said that. Forgive me.'

Jonas was frowning as Eleanor waited anxiously for him to reply. She cursed her wayward tongue for spoiling what had promised to be a reconciliation. But finally he said, 'No, it is you who should forgive me. Eleanor, there is an explanation for it all, but I cannot give it to you—not yet, at least.'

'Why not?' asked Eleanor, conscious of the importance of this moment.

'Because the happiness of other people—people to whom I owe a great deal—is at stake. In a few weeks' time it might be different, and then, believe me, I shall tell you everything. Are you willing to wait a little? Or must we go back to our former state of armed neutrality?'

'My mother trusts you,' said Eleanor slowly.

'She, too, is a rare woman,' he said with a smile. 'Eleanor, can you not do the same? I won't deny that there are episodes in my past of which I am now ashamed. I've led a hard life, and a dangerous one sometimes, and I cannot pretend that I have always played according to the rules.' He paused, then added, 'And I always play to win. I have said that once before, I believe, but it is true of big things as well as minor ones. If you don't like it, then I am sorry, but there it is.'

She frowned, but once again his honesty disarmed her. 'I'll wait till you can tell me the truth about yourself,' she said impulsively. 'And meanwhile we shall be friends, I think?'

He smiled, and her heart gave a little jump as he took her hand and kissed it, looking all the while into her eyes. His own eyes darkened and, putting his hands on her shoulders, he pulled her towards him. . .

'No!' whispered Eleanor, more feebly than she would have liked. 'No, Jonas. The men. . .they'll see us.'

For a moment he seemed not to pay any attention, but then he gave a deep sigh and released her. 'What is it about you, Eleanor Southeran? From the first moment I saw you looking at that damned chandelier, I've been bewitched. I've never known anything like it! And now. . .I know very well that I must not do or say anything that we might later regret. And to kiss you in full view of my own workmen would be the very height of idiocy! But you have only to look at me with those sea-green eyes and I am lost! Why do you do it to me?'

'I. . .I don't—not deliberately!'

'That's the hell of it,' he groaned. 'You're not even trying!'

Eleanor's lips twitched as she said demurely, 'You are presenting a picture of a siren which I find very difficult to associate with myself! I have never excited such uncontrollable passions in anyone else, sir!'

'Have you ever felt uncontrollable passion, Eleanor?'

She grew serious immediately. 'I. . .I don't think that is a question you have a right to ask. But the answer is no. Not yet.'

'Then don't joke about it! However, my passions are not yet uncontrollable, thank God! I have enough sense left to know that I must make do with your friendship until. . .until certain matters are cleared up. I have no right to ask for more. Will you forgive me for my behaviour just now and be my friend?'

She was puzzled, but said calmly, 'If uncontrollable passion is the only alternative, then I should prefer it.'

'Good!' Then he nodded in the direction of the drive. 'Now, about these trees. . . You were saying how you loved your chestnuts. We'll plant some in the park. Would you like that? I had intended to put a number of specimen trees about the grounds. Why shouldn't there be a humble horse chestnut among the more exotic samples?'

This was an idea which caught Eleanor's imagination immediately. It was a plan she had cherished for some time, but had never had the resources to carry it out. 'What else are you planting? Are you importing any?' she asked eagerly.

'I have some lists at the house—perhaps I could

show them to you? I'll bring them down to the Dower House,' he said deliberately. 'My contacts in India and North America are going to send me some samples— I don't know how many are suited to this climate, of course, and I thought I might engage an expert to advise me. There's a man in Exeter——'

'Mr Lucombe. I have his list.' Eleanor's eyes were glowing with enthusiasm, and Mr Guthrie laughed as she took his arm quite unselfconsciously and started to urge him in the direction of the Dower House. 'You must tell my mother about your plans. She will like them.'

From then on Mr Guthrie was as good as his word, and Eleanor was able to feel completely at her ease with him. Though he showed her in all sorts of ways that he valued her company, he never once overstepped the boundaries of friendship, and she, accepting the limits he had set, had never been so happy in her life. She was once again involved in the work for Stanyards, but, more than that, she was working with someone who shared her interests, whose enthusiasm for Stanyards and its estate rivalled her own.

She learned a great deal, too. Mr Guthrie brought a fresh approach to management of the land, and it was a revelation to her to see the effect his new methods were having on the farming community. Their former attitude of resigned apathy, their previous hostility to the new landlord were swept away by his energy and his eagerness to make a success of the new enterprise, his willingness to listen to any idea which looked as if it might work, his readiness to finance new ventures.

The neighbourhood was finally at one in applauding Mr Guthrie.

It was unfortunate, therefore, that this state of affairs did not last very long. Cousin Louisa brought a foretaste of the coming storm when she arrived at the Dower House one afternoon for tea with the Southerans. Eleanor came in to hear her say, 'Well, of course, Anthea, we were most intrigued. I mean, it isn't often that we have a newcomer in Combe St James—not that she's a newcomer exactly, but. . . Ah, Eleanor, there you are. How do you go on?'

'Well, thank you, Cousin Louisa. I'm sorry I wasn't here when you arrived. How are you?' An account of the state of Cousin Louisa's health followed, to the general effect that she was very well.

'And I have to say, Eleanor, that your mama is blooming! Your company certainly does her good—or is it the move to this house? I was completely astonished to hear about the sale of Stanyards. Why, I said, why didn't Anthea say anything about it while I was staying with her? I could have helped! But there—I know you, my dear. You didn't want to cause me any trouble—as if I would worry about a little extra work!'

She smiled affectionately at Mrs Southeran as she continued, 'Fancy Mr Guthrie turning up like that and offering to buy! It was providential, was it not?' She paused for breath, then said, 'And now his cousins are coming to stay in Combe St James.'

Eleanor caught her breath, and her mother gave her a warning glance. It was not necessary. Very much on her guard, Eleanor asked casually, 'Cousins?'

'Yes, Mrs Anstey and her daughter. She was a

Vereker, and so was his mother, but you know that, of course. Is that not delightful?'

'Delightful,' echoed Eleanor. 'When do they arrive?'

'Oh, any day! Now that the season is over, there is little reason for them to remain in London. They are not, I think, very rich—at least that is what I have been told, and Mrs Desmond is usually right in her information, though where she gets it from is a mystery to me. Did you meet her when you were in London, my dear?'

'Mrs Desmond? I don't think——'

'Dear me, no, Eleanor! Mrs Desmond hasn't left Combe St James for the past twenty years or more. You'd never believe it, for she always appears to know all the London gossip. I think she has a niece who writes to her quite often.' She paused for thought, then added judiciously, 'Well, not perhaps all that often, but two or three times a year. But no, I meant Mrs Anstey. If you do know her it would be pleasant for her if you were to come over to visit soon after she arrives, would it not? She will probably find herself quickly at home—she comes from these parts, they tell me. That would be before I came to Somerset, Anthea, because I don't think William and I ever met her. . .'

'Amelia Vereker left Somerset just before you married my cousin,' said Mrs Southeran, stemming the flow.

'And now she is coming back a widow, to the home of her youth! I did tell you that she is a widow, did I not? Oh, how stupid of me, of course you knew that already, too. Really, you must think me very silly. Oh, how nice! Here is tea!'

After Cousin Louisa's departure the two Southeran ladies sank back in relief. 'Mama, I have never been so full of admiration for you as I am at this moment,' said Eleanor, not altogether joking.

'I'm delighted, of course. Admiration is always welcome to a lady of my advanced years. But why particularly?'

'How you lived with our worthy cousin for six weeks without murdering her I shall never know!'

'Eleanor! She was very kind, and you must not talk so extravagantly. Though I must admit. . .'

They both laughed and then Eleanor grew serious. 'You realise what Mrs Anstey's arrival must mean to Mr Guthrie?'

Her mother said, 'It will certainly be awkward if what you say is true—that Amelia believes she owes her misfortune to him. Though she is surely mistaken.'

'It hardly matters whether she is mistaken or not. If the story told in London gains ground here in Somerset and Jonas still refuses to deny it, then he will be ostracised here, too.'

'Jonas?'

'I mean Mr Guthrie. It is because you always refer to him as Jonas that I forgot.'

'Of course,' her mother murmured, watching with interest as the colour rose in Eleanor's cheeks. 'But I cannot believe that the neighbourhood will pay any attention to such tales. Mr Guthrie—or Jonas, as we call him—has surely gained too much credit in the district.'

'I hope you are right, Mama.'

'Really?' asked her mother, opening her eyes wide.

'Am I to infer that you have had a change of heart about Jonas's behaviour to Amelia Anstey?'

'No! Yes! I don't know!' Eleanor got up and walked round. Then she said more calmly, 'Yes, I do. I am now virtually certain that Mrs Anstey's story—stories—are wrong. I could not be so mistaken in his character. But there *is* a mystery. And Mr Guthrie refuses to help himself or others.'

'Then we must see what we can do,' said her mother briskly. 'I now realise how important it is. Tell me as soon as you hear any news of Amelia Anstey's arrival.'

## CHAPTER SEVEN

THIS news was not long in coming. Just a few days later a note from Cousin Louisa announced that Mrs Anstey had arrived in Combe St James, and had settled in a house in the middle of the village.

> And, whatever one may say, Church Cottage is not a suitable place for dear Mrs Anstey. It is large, but in a very bad state of repair. What a pity she is so poor! I am sure she has an interesting history, she is such a charming lady, but it must be a sad one. The whole neighbourhood feels for her situation. What I find strange is that she was surprised when she heard that Mr Guthrie lived near by. Why didn't she know? She remembers you, Anthea, quite well, and, of course, she met Eleanor very recently. She says she would like to see you both again. Do come and visit me soon, and I will arrange a meeting.

'I think you must have misunderstood what Amelia Anstey told you about Jonas, Eleanor,' said Mrs Southeran. 'You haven't told me what it was, so I am somewhat in the dark, but it cannot have been as serious as you thought. She has quite obviously said nothing to his detriment in Combe St James.'

'Not yet, Mama. Long may it continue so. What she told me condemned him unequivocally—I could not possibly have misunderstood her.'

'Perhaps she has seen how popular he is in the neighbourhood and doesn't wish to discredit him?'

'I sincerely hope so,' said Eleanor soberly. 'Or that she has decided to be more discreet down here than she was in London. But the temptation to indulge herself with a new audience of sympathetic listeners will be very strong—especially as most of them will press her to confide in them. You have only to read Cousin Lousia's letter to see how eager they are to know.' She picked the note up and read it again. 'I wonder what has happened to her daughter? Cousin Louisa doesn't mention her.'

'Why should she?'

'If you had seen Marianne Anstey, Mama, you wouldn't have to ask. She is the loveliest creature I have seen in years.'

'We must respond to Cousin Louisa's note immediately! I am consumed with curiosity about the whole affair!'

Two days later Eleanor and her mother were sitting in Cousin Louisa's overcrowded parlour. Mrs Southeran had been placed in a large armchair with a footstool at her feet and a rug over her knees. She protested in vain that the day was warm and that she was not at all fatigued. Cousin Louisa knew that she was merely being brave, so poor Mrs Southeran sat in discomfort for the rest of the afternoon, unwilling to disabuse her kind hostess.

'I am glad you have arrived so promptly,' Cousin Louisa began, after taking elaborate precautions to see that they were not overheard. 'I must consult you on a most delicate matter before Mrs Anstey comes. Indeed, it is most distressing.'

Mrs Southeran carefully avoided Eleanor's eye and said, 'Dear me, this sounds very ominous. What can it be?'

'Well, it has come to my ears that Mr Guthrie is not all he might appear to be!' She paused dramatically.

'In what way?'

Somewhat disappointed by Mrs Southeran's calm response, Cousin Louisa went on, 'His benevolence appears to be of very recent date—in fact, since he got hold of Stanyards!'

'What are you saying, Louisa? Mr Guthrie did not "get hold of" Stanyards—he bought it in a thoroughly proper manner. More than that, he has been generous throughout.'

'But have you never asked yourself where the money to buy Stanyards came from?'

'I did not consider it my business,' said Mrs Southeran in a warning tone. Cousin Louisa ignored it.

'From what I have heard, he left England nearly twenty years ago with nothing to his name. Where did all this wealth of his come from?'

'Louisa, I have told you, I do not know, nor do I care very much. It is quite simply not our affair. I know he is to be trusted.'

Cousin Louisa looked at her pityingly. 'But then, you have never been very worldly, have you, Anthea? What if I were to tell you that, according to some, Jonas Guthrie has behaved disgracefully?'

'I would say that it is time you stopped shilly-shallying, and told us exactly what is being said and, even more to the point, who is saying it.'

At first Cousin Louisa refused to be specific, but gradually, under Mrs Southeran's relentless questioning, the same story, but with more detail than had been generally current in London, emerged about Jonas Guthrie. Mrs Anstey, it appeared, had been less discreet in Somerset than she had in London—perhaps because Marianne was now safely engaged to be married to her Irish viscount and was spending the summer with his parents in Oxfordshire.

'The whole neighbourhood is buzzing with it, as you can imagine. There are even one or two who remember the Verekers from the old days, though Thomas and his wife have long been gone, of course, and the estate sold. They are very shocked at Guthrie's behaviour.'

'If they remember Amelia Vereker so well, then they will not accept the unsupported word of such a ninnyhammer!' said Mrs Southeran roundly. 'Really, I might well lose my patience with you, Louisa, if you carry on slandering a good man in this way. Has he not been a good landlord since he came? Has he not been thought an asset to our country society?'

'Yes, but that was before—— Ah! Here is Mrs Anstey now—perhaps we can persuade her to tell us herself.'

For the first half-hour the tea party promised to be a success. The two elder lady visitors exchanged happy reminiscences of their youth, with a good many references to people of whom Eleanor had never heard. Neither lady mentioned the name of Jonas Guthrie. Mrs Anstey complimented Mrs Southeran on having such a charmingly lovely daughter, and Mrs Southeran responded by saying that she had heard much about Marianne Anstey's beauty.

'And now I hear that she is to be Viscountess Morrissey, no less. But why is she not with you?'

'Lord Morrissey and his parents were so kind as to invite both Marianne and me for a visit to their estates in Oxfordshire. I spent some time there with Marianne, but then when Lady Dorothy Rushton and a number of other guests arrived I came down here.'

'Leaving Marianne?'

Mrs Anstey looked nervous, and said, 'I. . .I wanted to see my old home again. Marianne is in very good hands. Her future parents-in-law are delighted with her, and she is a great favourite with Lady Dorothy, too. I find it difficult to be in company for very long—my husband's death. . .' Her voice trailed away pathetically and she dabbed her eyes with a tiny handkerchief.

There was a short silence. Then Mrs Southeran said, 'So you came down here. The Vereker lands have been sold, of course. There isn't much of the old place left.'

'No, but that did not surprise me. Sir Thomas always said that he would be the last of the Somerset Verekers.'

'I suppose he was right—though Jonas Guthrie now owns Stanyards, and he is a Vereker on his mother's side.'

There was another silence. Then Mrs Anstey said with some agitation, 'I cannot discuss. . .that man.'

'Why not, Amelia? You were so close in the old days.'

Cousin Louisa made a gesture of protest. Anthea was being a little too outspoken for her taste. Mrs Southeran ignored it and went on, 'Why not, Amelia? And why do you say you cannot discuss him? Who has been telling all these stories I hear about Jonas?'

'They are not stories!' cried Mrs Anstey. 'I wish they were! You of all people should know that, Anthea! You know how much I loved him!'

'And how much he loved you,' said Mrs Southeran firmly. 'I don't believe he would ever do anything to harm you. Jonas is a good man and a good landlord. Why are you doing your best to destroy his credit in the neighbourhood? Why do you wish to ruin him?'

'Because he ruined——' Mrs Anstey caught her lip and hesitated.

'Go on!'

'Because he ruined my husband and my daughter!'

'From what I have heard, he saw to it that you and your daughters were safe and well provided for.'

Mrs Anstey threw Eleanor a speaking glance.

'I have not betrayed your confidence, Mrs Anstey. My mother is basing what she says on what she has heard in the neighbourhood. Have you perhaps confided in others?' Eleanor's voice was cool. She had decided that she still did not much like this woman.

Cousin Louisa intervened. 'I am sure it would be very natural for Mrs Anstey to seek comfort from her new friends.'

'At the expense of old ones?'

At this Mrs Anstey stood up. 'You will have to excuse me—I do not feel very well.' She turned to Mrs Southeran, and said with a semblance of dignity, 'You are wrong to think so harshly of me, Anthea. I did not abandon my old regard for Jonas without a great deal of distress. But I cannot account for the sudden reversal of our fortunes, and the unhappy situation of my daughter Evadne, in any other way.' She had been getting increasingly agitated during this speech, and could hardly pronounce her final words. 'When you eventually come to see that I was right I hope you will apologise to me for your unkindness this afternoon.' With this she hurried out of the room, followed by Cousin Louisa.

The two Southerans eyed one another ruefully. 'Was I so hard? I had forgotten how irritating Amelia Vereker could be. She used to cry a lot as a child. Jonas was always fighting people who had upset her.'

'But she is a very convincing victim, Mama.'

'Yes. But not of Jonas, Eleanor. Never of Jonas—I must talk to him.'

When Mr Guthrie next visited them, Mrs Southeran wasted no time in telling him of her conversation with Amelia Anstey. She finished, 'But you may rest easy, Jonas. I shall not let Amelia get away with what she is saying of you. When she has had time to calm down I shall talk to her again. She was always very biddable.'

His reaction was unexpected. He had listened to her impassively, but now he said, 'I wish you had not done this, Mrs Southeran. Your kindness was. . .misplaced.'

Eleanor and her mother gazed at him in astonishment. Mrs Southeran found her voice and said, 'Am I to understand that you do not care what people are saying of you? If someone does not stop her, Jonas, the rumours will soon become accepted fact. You will

be an outcast—as I understand you were in London.
Is that what you wish?'

'It probably concerns me less than it would you,' he
said with a slight smile. 'But no, it is not what I would
have wanted. Indeed I wish to heaven Amelia Vereker
had not chosen to re-visit the scenes of her childhood.
I thought I was safe down here.'

'Safe?' echoed Eleanor, startled.

He turned to her. 'Safe from her accusations,' he
said smoothly. Then he went on, 'But since she is here,
and has already. . .told her story, then I'm afraid there
is nothing I can do.'

'Nothing! Of course there is——'

'I should have said nothing I wish to do. Nor anything I wish anyone else to do.'

'But Jonas——'

'You will please me best by making no attempt to
persuade Amelia to change her mind. Believe me, it is
better so.'

'In other words,' said Eleanor, unable to stop herself, 'you are saying what you said to me in the park
that morning—that it is none of our concern.'

He hesitated, then said carefully, 'No, I am sorry to
say that that is no longer true. I had hoped——' He
turned away and stared out of the window. Suddenly
he said violently, 'Oh, confound all the Ansteys, and
the whole damnable business! Why couldn't Amelia
have left me in peace down here? I had hoped it
would all eventually be forgotten, that she would go
back to Boston once Marianne was safely married,
and I would be free to live my own life again.'

He turned back to the room. 'Forgive me, Mrs
Southeran, I am not fit for company in my present

mood. But remember what I have said. I do not wish you to pursue the question of Amelia Anstey's stories.'

'Very well, if that is your wish, Jonas,' said Mrs Southeran quietly. 'I will not mention the matter to Amelia again.'

With a regretful look at Eleanor, he went out, leaving two very puzzled ladies behind him. After a while Mrs Southeran said thoughtfully, 'I wonder if we still have the address of your father's Boston correspondent—the gentleman who visited him here that last winter before he died? I think his name was Bitteridge. I must look for it.'

'You're going to write to him about the Ansteys? If you only could, Mama! But you promised not to pursue the matter!'

'You should listen to what I say more carefully, Eleanor. I said I would not mention the matter to Amelia Anstey again. That is not quite the same thing, wouldn't you agree?'

That evening Mrs Southeran and Eleanor spent some time composing a carefully phrased letter to Mr Edmund Bitteridge in Tremont Street, Boston. Mrs Anthea Southeran, widow of the late Charles Southeran, presented her compliments to Mr Bitteridge, and asked if he could help her to find information on a former friend of hers, a certain Amelia Vereker, who had married Henry Anstey of Boston, Massachusetts. The matter was not one of idle curiosity, but might serve to throw light on a difficult situation here in England. Any details he might send would be treated with the utmost confidence.

'That will be enough, Eleanor,' said Mrs Southeran, laying down her pen at last. 'He was a most thorough

man, with a keen interest in his fellow human beings—
most unusual in bibliophiles! Your father hardly
noticed the existence of the rest of the world!'

The effect of Mrs Anstey's stories was curious. In
general they reversed the situation of Mr Guthrie's
first appearance in Stanyards. With the exception of
Eleanor's mother, those who had been his keenest
advocates now regarded him with disfavour. The
Southerans, who had sold their home to him and were
forced to live as his neighbours, became objects of
sympathy. There were some who regarded Mrs
Southeran's staunch support for Mr Guthrie as a brave
attempt to put a good face on a bad situation. Others,
less charitably, saw it as an unworldly widow's foolishness. Evadne Anstey's story soon became common
knowledge, and many whispered their concern lest
Eleanor Southeran should go the same way.

But the farmers, who had at first seen Mr Guthrie
as an ogre and a tyrant, were now firmly behind him.
One or two, Threlfall among them, still resented his
high-handed ways, but most of them saw how the
estate was improving and had become his keen allies.
Mr Guthrie himself was apparently as little affected as
he had ever been by either. Perhaps he spent slightly
more time with the Southerans. He seemed to enjoy
their company, especially as the number of invitations
to the other large houses in the neighbourhood had
dramatically declined—a fact which did not seem to
concern him in the slightest.

The most curious effect of all was on Eleanor. It
might have been supposed that the reminder of Mr
Guthrie's sins, and his subsequent refusal to permit

anyone to attempt to refute Mrs Anstey's tale, would cause her to doubt him even more. But the opposite was the case. Eleanor found herself seeking his company, delighting in his trenchant views and forthright statements, and becoming ever more convinced of his integrity. More than that, she gradually came to the conclusion that his harsh appearance and uncompromising manner concealed a man of feeling.

'Balderdash!' was his instant response when she said something to this effect to him. 'Don't accuse me of anything so mawkish!'

'You may deny it as much as you please, but you will not dissuade me. If nothing else, you have feeling for the land here——'

'Pride of possession—a very different matter.'

'Your expression showed more than pride of possession when you were contemplating this valley a moment ago. Besides, you may well claim pride in possessing the rest of the estate—the farms and fields, the house and its park. But how can anyone claim to possess something as savagely natural as this?' She swept her arm in an arc embracing the bridge on which they had stopped and the steep combe below them. It was the wildest part of the Stanyards estate— the sides of the valley were almost like miniature cliffs, the stream at their foot filled with boulders. Even as she spoke the horses shifted nervously on the wooden planks of the bridge.

'Beautiful and dangerous, I agree. Let's move on to the other side. Captain is not at all sure the bridge is safe.'

'I assure you it is,' said Eleanor as they made their way to the bank. 'This was one of my father's favourite places—wild, lonely and quiet. I expect you would call him a romantic. He didn't bother much with the farms, but he loved this place and made sure he could get to it even when he became infirm. The bridge was built to take a small carriage, let alone two horses! And it is one of the few things which is still in good repair.'

'I know it is. I've had it checked.' He smiled at her look of surprise. 'I like it, too—not, Miss Southeran, *not* that you could call me a romantic!'

'Heaven forfend!' she laughed. 'And if I am honest I will tell you that I know your liking for this spot, especially in the mornings. Whenever I wish to find you I always look for you first here! Did you never find it surprising how often I seemed to come across you?'

'I was too busy being delighted that you had,' he said, smiling down at her.

She went on a little breathlessly, 'But I still think you are not as hard as you would wish me to believe. And I know that you must have some feeling for people as well as the land.'

'Humanity doesn't rate very high in my esteem, Miss Southeran. I've seen too much of it. Oh, I like some individuals—your mother, for one. Indeed, I have great affection for her. And I suppose I have felt something for others in the past.'

'Your fiancée, for example?' This slipped out before Eleanor could stop herself.

'Who?' he asked, with a frown.

She stared at him. 'Upon my word, sir, I find you an enigma! This is the second time you have forgotten that you were ever engaged. Did you really feel so little for her?'

'Ah, yes! You mean Miss Anstey. I suppose I must have felt something, but I really no longer remember. She was very beautiful.' The indifference with which he said this stung Eleanor into further indiscretion.

'Your effect on her was more far-reaching, I believe!'

'What the devil are you talking about?'

'Evadne Anstey—or Oliver, as she is now called.'

He looked at her blankly, then said, 'You see to be misinformed, Miss Southeran. I was never engaged to Evadne Oliver.'

'Not. . .? But. . .I don't understand,' said Eleanor in confusion.

'No, indeed. Why should you?' he said coolly. 'And I am not about to enlighten you—not on the subject of Evadne Oliver, at least. But the Anstey girl I was engaged to was Phoebe, the eldest. You have seen Marianne Anstey—Phoebe is even lovelier.'

Eleanor was still reeling from the shock of finding out that there was yet another Anstey sister, but she rallied at this. 'That is impossible,' she said firmly.

'Believe me, it is true. She is Marianne's equal in beauty in every way, and in addition she has more animation. A very handsome creature.'

'But you were clearly not devastated at her loss. Or is that a brave front?'

'You know very well that I refuse to dissemble, Miss Southeran. Phoebe and I agreed to part because she found someone more suited to her taste. I was surprised, but not unduly put out.' He took a look at the expression of outrage on her face and gave a laugh. 'Come, it was a long time ago and, whatever it might have meant at the time, it means less than nothing now, as you saw. For God's sake, let us forget her.'

Eleanor returned to her former theme. 'But there are people for whom you do feel—quite strongly?'

'Fishing, Eleanor?'

'Of course not! You know that is not what I meant at all! I. . .' She hesitated, then carried on, 'I was thinking of Mrs Anstey. . .and Evadne. But you need not say anything more—I know you wish to keep your own counsel. As you will undoubtedly say, it is none of my concern.' She spurred her horse and rode swiftly to the top of the hill.

He did not follow immediately, but sat in thought for a minute. When he rejoined her she was gazing down over Stanyards. 'I'm sorry,' she said. 'I am wrong to mention such matters. You have said that you cannot discuss them.'

'Eleanor, half the county refuses to receive me. The ladies of the neighbourhood are unanimous in condemning me. My position here in Somerset is every bit as uncomfortable as it was in London. Yet I believe I am right in saying that you and your mother have remained my friends. Why?'

There was a short silence. Then Eleanor said slowly, 'In London you said once that you hoped I would regard you more kindly once I knew you better.' She turned towards him. 'You were right. I do now know you better, and I have learnt to trust you. I'm not asking you to explain anything. I simply want you to know that I. . .that neither my mother nor I believe Mrs Anstey's story. I do not believe that you robbed the Ansteys, and, whatever the nature of your relationship with Evadne Anstey was, I do not believe that you would have abandoned her so heartlessly, not even to marriage with Mr Oliver. I think you might have given him money, but not for. . .not because you were shuffling off an obligation.' She stole a glance at him but his face was turned away.

'Moreover,' she continued, 'we would not be at all surprised to learn that the support the Verekers gave Mrs Anstey in London was subsidised by you. The mystery in all of this is why you have behaved as you have—but I respect your wish to remain silent on that.'

After a pause Mr Guthrie said in a neutral tone, 'I seem to have more feeling than I thought. Shall we go back?'

The summer wore on. For some weeks it rained every day and the country folk murmured about St Swithin and tried to remember how much it had rained on July the fifteenth. The streams and rivers were unusually full for the time of year and in the combe the water churned darkly through the boulders. The Southeran ladies lived a quiet life. The weather made it difficult for Mrs Southeran to go very far, and in any case the neighbourhood's dislike of Mr Guthrie irritated her. As yet no word had come from Mr Bitteridge—another source of dissatisfaction.

Eleanor continued to ride out on the estate. She learned from one of the farmers' wives that Mrs Anstey was in daily expectation of receiving her daughter at last. Eleanor wondered what Marianne Anstey's effect on the neighbourhood would be. Her fragile beauty was sure to arouse admiration, and would no doubt give extra fuel to the antipathy towards Mr Guthrie.

She decided she would make sure he had heard the news, but when she went up to the house she found he was out riding. This didn't deter her. She knew where she would find him—when he was riding for pleasure he nearly always went in the direction of the combe. Without bothering to disturb her mother, she changed and set off in search of him. Before too long she was approaching the bridge—yes, she had been right. He was standing on top of the hill overlooking the valley, and as soon as he saw her he waved. She made for the bridge, and he started hurrying down the slope, waving all the while. He seemed excited, though she was unable to see him very clearly—the sun was in her eyes. No doubt he would tell her what it was when they met.

She urged her horse on over the bridge—the water below was running swiftly between its ugly-looking boulders, and the animal was uneasy. Mr Guthrie had stopped. He seemed to be waiting. Suddenly there was a loud crack followed by a groaning sound. To her horror, she saw the bridge tilt drunkenly downwards. Her horse reared in terror, throwing her as he did so, and the last thing Eleanor remembered was seeing him leap to the bank. Then she felt herself sliding into oblivion. . .

# CHAPTER EIGHT

ELEANOR grew conscious of a buzzing sound near her right ear. She opened her eyes slowly, then shut them again as the light dazzled her. Her head was aching, and she felt stiff and cramped. She shifted cautiously, but something seemed to be holding her down. 'Please,' she murmured. 'Please—I feel sick. Let me up!'

There was no reply. She opened her eyes again, turning her head away from the light. Scarlet berries, a hazy suspicion of yellow, and green—bright, glossy green. Christmas! No, that was nonsense—that wasn't holly. The leaves were long and smooth, falling in a graceful curve. . .hart's tongue, then.

As she watched, a bee flew up out of the centre of the leaves and disappeared from her restricted vision. What were the berries? She twisted round slightly and examined them, screwing her eyes up in an effort to get them into focus. They were still slightly blurred, but she could see that it was the sturdily vivid head of cuckoo-pint. Where on earth was she? And why was she being held down? She closed her eyes again. Memory slowly returned. Mr Guthrie had been on the hill. . . She had been crossing the bridge to meet him. . . There was something she had to tell him. . .

When Eleanor opened her eyes again she felt less sick and her head was feeling better. Where was Mr Guthrie? Why hadn't he come to help her? She struggled to sit up, but it was awkward—she couldn't move her legs. She used her elbows to prop herself up and gasped with dismay at the scene of devastation which met her eye. The bridge had collapsed at one end, though some of the structure was still intact, including the part on which she was lying. The planks which had been the roadway now formed a sloping platform just clear of the waters, which were rushing angrily past underneath. Indeed, she would have been lying actually in the stream but for the small outcrop of rock which diverted it round behind her and which was home to the plants she had observed. What was worse, some of the supports for the bridge, which had broken away after the main platform had fallen, had landed across her legs, and one heavy beam was pinning her down.

In a panic at the restraint, she struggled to release herself, but a sudden, sharp pain caused her to cry out. Something must have damaged her ankle. She lay back again, panting and feeling very dizzy. Mr Guthrie must have gone for help. But why hadn't he stayed to tell her first what he was doing? She wished he were here—it was odd being so alone and so helpless. . . Frightening. . . This must stop! She must pull herself together. He would be back soon. . .

In the Dower House some time later, Mrs Southeran was expressing surprise at seeing Mr Guthrie. 'I thought Eleanor would be with you, Jonas,' she said. 'She went to the house some time ago to look for you. She had something to tell you.'

'I was up at Badgers' Farm. One of the workers has had an accident. She might have stayed to work in the library—she knows I need some help in cataloguing the books. What was it, do you know?'

'Mrs Anstey's daughter is said to be joining her soon. I have to say that I can hardly wait to see this beauty—Marianne, is it not?'

Mr Guthrie's face had clouded over at the news. 'I hope that it is indeed Marianne who is about to stay with her mother, but I doubt it,' he said. 'My information is that she is very happily established with the Morrisseys, and is unlikely to leave them much before her wedding.'

'But the other girl is in America!'

'The other *girls*. Amelia had three daughters. But yes, you're right. The other two stayed behind in America. And I had hoped that they would remain there.'

'One of the two is Evadne Oliver, if you will forgive my mentioning the name. But who is the other?'

'Did Eleanor not tell you about Phoebe? I had thought she would.'

'Eleanor doesn't tell me everything,' said Mrs Southeran with a small smile. 'Would I be shocked if she did?'

'Not as far as her personal well-being is concerned,' Mr Guthrie replied swiftly. 'But, as you know, there are episodes in my life which are of doubtful merit, to say the least. I was certain that she would tell you that I was once engaged to Phoebe Anstey.'

'Some day I hope you will find your way to telling us about your various relationships with the Anstey family, Jonas. They do seem to be a little confused. But I know that day is still in the future—I am not about to tease you.'

'The matter of my engagement is perfectly straightforward. It was a mistake. I came from India to Boston with money enough to establish myself and a desire to settle. It all seemed to fit very well. Phoebe Anstey was not only Amelia's daughter—she was just seventeen years old and the loveliest thing I had seen in many a long year. I was completely dazzled by her.' He paused, smiling at the picture in his mind.

'What happened?'

'What? Oh, it was the usual story. I should have had more sense—I was, after all, nearly thirty! It didn't take long for me to find out that we were totally unsuited, and for a while I was in a real dilemma. But Phoebe met a young sprig—a member of what you might call the Boston aristocracy——'

'I wouldn't be surprised to hear that you had arranged that meeting, Jonas.'

He smiled, but went on without comment. 'He was mad for her, and the upshot was that she asked me to release her. So I did—with great relief. I don't think I can ever have been really in love with her. But, by God, she was a stunner.'

'Are you in love with Eleanor?'

If Eleanor's mother had hoped to surprise an answer out of him with the suddenness of her question she was disappointed. He stood in thought for a moment, then looked at her, still without saying anything.

'I have my responsibilities as Eleanor's mother, Jonas, and you spend a great deal of time with her,' said Mrs Southeran, for once absolutely serious. 'You have assured me that she will come to no harm in your company, and I believe you. But there are dangers other than physical ones in any relationship. Eleanor is still a child in matters of the heart, and I think I am justified in asking you what might seem otherwise an impertinent question.'

'I don't deny your right to ask. You have been more than kind in allowing me to share Eleanor's company, and I. . .I have been grateful for the trust this showed you have in me. I want to be honest with you, even if what I say sounds unworthy of a sensible man. The fact is, I don't know. The feeling I have for her is totally unlike any I have ever experienced before.'

'Not love?'

'I don't think it can be. It's certainly not what I have understood to be love before. I enjoy her company enormously; I enjoy talking to her, seeing things through her eyes, hearing what she has to say. In some ways she's like the best friend a man could have — certainly better than any I have known.'

'Friendship, then?'

'That's not quite it either! There's more to it than that. . . She has this strange effect on me. There have been times when her obstinacy, her impetuosity have infuriated me to such an extent that I've believed I want never to see her again, then I find myself missing her, and I have to seek her out. And sometimes I suddenly find her completely bewitching. It's a damnable way to be.'

'Poor Jonas!' said Mrs Southeran, beginning to smile.

'You may find it amusing, but I certainly do not. A man doesn't reach my age without having met some women — Phoebe Anstey was one of them — whom he thinks he might marry. But there was never any ambiguity about my feelings for them — no half-tones, no

indecision. That's not my way. And after the initial
attraction had worn off I knew pretty soon that I
didn't want any of them—they bored me beyond
measure. But Eleanor... Eleanor doesn't fit! Can you
understand that? Can you make sense of it? I wish I
could.'

Mrs Southeran said again, 'Poor Jonas! But I'm
afraid I can't help you—you'll have to work it out for
yourself. Meanwhile I should like you to make certain
that you do not hurt Eleanor. She's...vulnerable,
whether she realises it or not.' She turned as the maid
came into the room.

'If you please, ma'am, Daniel would like a word
with Mr Guthrie. He's outside.'

'Bring him in, Betty.'

'I...I can't do that, ma'am. He's in the stables with
one of the horses.'

Mr Guthrie rose and, with a word of apology, strode
out of the room. Daniel was in the yard, attempting to
soothe a bay mare.

'What is it, man?'

'Miss Nell's horse, sir—'er come into the yard just a
moment ago. In a rare old state, 'er is. Look at them
reins. I asked Bet to get you to come out 'ere. I didn't
want to upset the mistress.'

'You did right. Go up to the house and tell them to
saddle Captain. Tell the lad to get one or two of the
men from the home farm to join me at the house in
five minutes. Off you go, Daniel—I must have a word
with Mrs Southeran.'

As Mr Guthrie came into the room again Mrs
Southeran stood up. 'It's Eleanor, isn't it? I knew

there was something wrong. She's not in your library, she's missing.'

'What makes you think that?'

'Don't treat me like a fool, Jonas! Why else would Daniel wish to see you outside? He was probably trying to protect me, as you are.'

Mr Guthrie took her hands in a firm grasp. 'She apparently went riding this afternoon. I've asked Daniel to get some of the men, and we're going to look for her. She won't be far—the Stanyards estate is not that vast, and she seldom goes anywhere else. We'll find her.'

He left the room again without another look, and Mrs Southeran sank back on to her sofa, covering her face with her hands. But after a few moments she stood up and calmly went to call Betty.

'Miss Eleanor will perhaps want some attention when she returns, Betty. Make sure her room is ready for her.' Then she went back to stand by the window.

It was getting cold. The sun didn't reach this part of the combe and the spray from the churning water had made her clothes damp. She must have been here for hours! Where was Mr Guthrie? Eleanor began to get worried. She had tried several times to move her legs, or to shift the block of wood which lay on them. But every attempt had ended in failure and an attack of dizziness. What if no one came. . .? That was nonsense! Mr Guthrie had seen her—he had been there on the hill when the bridge collapsed; he had even waved.

She lay back again. She would count to a hundred— perhaps that would calm her. One, two, three. . . The yellow among the hart's tongue ferns was tormentil. A pretty little flower. Four, five, six, seven. . . How could anyone feel as sick as she felt and yet be hungry? It must be getting quite late. Surely her mother would be worried by now? Eight, nine, ten. . . This was ridiculous—she wasn't feeling any calmer, in fact, quite the reverse. In a moment she might do something foolish, like screaming or shouting. How Aunt Hetty would scold if she heard——

Wait! Was that the sound of men's voices? She *would* scream and shout. Lifting herself as upright as possible, she called with all her strength. Her voice sounded pathetically feeble, and the effort caused her to feel dizzy again, but she forced herself to try once more.

'Oh, my God! The bridge! What in the name——? She's here! She's down here! Daniel! Silas! Over here!' Mr Guthrie came sliding down the slope on the far side of the combe. Heedless of rocks and water, he leapt over to the outcrop of rock near her, taking care not to touch the precariously balanced platform on which she lay. 'Eleanor!'

'I thought you'd never come back!' Shivering and trembling, she could hardly get the words out. 'I'm trapped.'

'So I see. No, don't touch that beam, you fool!' This was to Silas, who was trying to lift one of the pieces of wood on top of her legs. 'Can't you see that'll bring the other lot down? Get a block from the pile over there and wedge the others up. Hurry!'

Gingerly he stepped on to the platform and crouched down by Eleanor. He touched her face and Eleanor noticed with surprise that his hand was trembling. 'Are you in pain?'

'My ankle hurts—I think the beam struck it when it fell. But I'm all right otherwise, I think. It's just that I'm trapped. . .'

'I know, I know,' he said. 'It's a devilish feeling. A few minutes—that's all we need. You'll soon be out, my poor girl.' He held Eleanor firmly, and gave directions to the men, but in the end he grew impatient with their struggles to place the block. 'Here, Daniel. You hold Miss Nell! Careful now!' He gave Eleanor's shoulder a slight squeeze, smiling down at her. 'Don't worry. It'll soon be over, my love. Hold her carefully, Daniel, and when I say "Go!" you pull her gently out. Gently, mind!'

He rejected the blocks the men had taken, choosing instead smaller ones. He gradually placed one upon another until the weight was off the beam which was holding Eleanor down. Then he took hold of it. 'Are you ready, Daniel?' Daniel nodded. 'Very gently, remember! Silas, you keep an eye on those blocks! Go!'

With a Herculean effort Mr Guthrie lifted the beam a fraction. Daniel edged Eleanor out, but, though he was as gentle as anyone could have desired, the movement was too much. Eleanor could not hold back a cry of anguish as her foot was dragged free. The platform rocked dangerously as Mr Guthrie swore at Daniel, let the beam down again and came back to crouch at Eleanor's side. 'Steady, my love! We're nearly there. I'll have to lift you in a moment, but I want to feel if there are any broken bones first. Understood?' She nodded, and gentle hands ran over her body. 'I think you're all right, apart from your ankle. Can you sit up?'

Slowly, carefully, Eleanor was carried on to the bank. Here she was set down again, and the men were dispatched to fetch the horses. Because of the loss of the bridge they would have to make a detour to bring them over a causeway further downstream. Soon, Mr Guthrie and Eleanor were alone. He looked with concern at her pale cheeks. 'How can I make you comfortable? Here, I'll put my coat round you. That might stop some of the shivering.'

'But you'll be cold,' protested Eleanor through chattering teeth.

'Nonsense, put it on! May I look at that ankle? I could bind it up so that it can't move so freely. It might save some of the pain.' Though he removed her boot with utmost care, she had to bite her lip to stop herself from crying out again. He worked steadily, keeping his eyes on what he was doing, and when the foot was clear he took off his cravat and wound it carefully round the damaged ankle. Only then did he look up at her face, which was chalk-white. 'Good girl!' he said softly. 'Now we have to wait—and I shall make sure you are warm.'

So saying, he picked her up and settled them both against a boulder, holding her close to him. Cradled in his arms, wrapped in his coat, Eleanor gradually forgot her aching head and throbbing ankle. A feeling of warm contentment overtook her. For the moment she wanted nothing more than to stay there in a half-sleep, listening to the steady beat of his heart. Her eyes closed. . .

'You should have stayed with me,' she murmured.

'I have stayed with you. The horses are being fetched by the men. They won't be long.'

'No, I meant before. You were looking at me when I fell.'

'Where was I?'

She chuckled sleepily. 'On the hill, of course. You waved. I suppose you were in a hurry to fetch help—but I wish you had told me. And it seemed a very long time before you came back.' Her voice faded and she closed her eyes again. 'I'm glad you're here now,' she murmured.

'So am I. Try to rest till the men return.' His voice was calm and deep, and Eleanor gave a little sigh of contentment. But there was a frown on Mr Guthrie's face as he gazed into the growing darkness.

When Mr Guthrie visited Eleanor the next morning he found her on her mother's sofa, her foot in a large bandage, but looking very much her normal self. 'I wish to heaven Daniel would hurry with that crutch, Mama. Can you not find him and tell him so?'

'I am glad to see you, Jonas. This daughter of mine is driving me frantic. Have you seen Daniel on your way here? He is supposed to be fetching a crutch for Eleanor from Dr Smithson, and madam here cannot wait. Not that I shall allow her to use it for a least another day.'

Mr Guthrie smiled at Eleanor's wail of protest. 'How is she? None the worse for her escapade if the strength of her voice is anything to go by.'

'Dr Smithson said that I had had a lucky escape. The ankle is merely sprained—my riding boot protected the foot from worse damage. I shall be perfectly fit to walk with a crutch today, Mama.'

'And what about the rest? He said that one or two

of the smaller bones might possibly be cracked. Eleanor should rest that foot for at least a week, Jonas. But I know she won't, the silly girl.'

'This is a rare situation! I find myself acting the role of peacemaker. If you will lend me your daughter, ma'am, I could do with more help in the library at Stanyards. I haven't time myself to work indoors at the moment—it's a busy time on the estate, as you know. But I'd like someone I can trust to list some books properly before I send them off to London. Wilkes hasn't yet finished with the first lot, but I have now found more which are in need of attention. The listing could easily be done by someone with one foot on a stool, and I could get Silas or one of the others to pack them up. After that is done there's still the cataloguing. What do you think?'

Neither lady was perfectly happy with the arrangement, but it was finally agreed upon as a suitable compromise. It was decided that Eleanor should be conveyed to the library the following afternoon, unless her crutch proved to be more difficult to manage than she thought. For a while it looked as if the whole arrangement would founder on the question of the stairs, but luckily Mrs Southeran recalled that all of Eleanor's needs could be met on the first floor of Stanyards, and if she was carried up at the beginning and down at the end of each session with the books she could manage otherwise with her crutch. Mr Guthrie promised to supply a bell for her to ring for help. The housekeeper or one of the maids would always be on hand.

Eleanor had some questions for Mr Guthrie, but she had to wait. The last thing she wanted to do was to cause her mother any anxiety, and there was a mystery about the accident in the combe which was disquieting. She did manage to say, 'I must thank you, sir, for rescuing me last night. I think you were just in time. I was about to give way to most unheroic tears! Why were you so long?'

'Eleanor! Jonas hurried out and set off to rescue you as soon as Daniel showed him your horse. If it seemed a long time before you were found, then I suppose I am to blame. I told Jonas you were probably in the library, so we didn't at first miss you. How can you be so ungrateful?'

Mr Guthrie was frowning, and Eleanor decided to hold her tongue. She would tackle him later.

The next day at two Eleanor was ceremoniously driven to Stanyards' front door, where the master of the house was waiting to receive her. He lifted her out and set her carefully down, holding her steady until she was handed her crutch by a grinning Daniel. Then he said, 'Let me see you walk.'

'Here?' asked Eleanor, startled.

'It's flat, and relatively smooth. I want to see that you can manage before you go near the first floor.'

'Otherwise?'

'I will send you back to practise some more. Come on, my girl. Off you go!'

On her mettle, Eleanor made her way over the hall to the foot of the stairs, then turned and looked challengingly at him. 'Well?' she said.

'Very good! I'll let you stay.' He swung her into his arms again, and carried her up the stairs, ignoring her protests.

'You shouldn't be doing this! I thought you'd get

Silas or one of the others to take me upstairs. Daniel would help.'

'I wanted to make sure it could be done. Now do be quiet. I can't carry you and talk at the same time. . . How do you like your throne?' He had rigged up a makeshift desk which extended over an armchair and footstool. It stood in one of the window embrasures, so there was plenty of light, and chair and footstool were covered in cushions and shawls. Eleanor laughed when she saw it.

'No maharanee could ask for a better one,' she said gaily.

'Right, then I will leave you. I believe everything is to hand—books, paper, pen and ink, sand, bell. Yes, it's all there. In any case, you can send for anything you need. Work well!'

'Wait!' she cried as he turned to go. 'We must talk about what happened in the combe.'

He came back to her chair, looking almost reluctant. 'I thought you would rather forget it.'

'What nonsense! How could anyone ignore what happened? I think I was lucky to escape with a damaged ankle. I think. . . I think I could have been killed, Jonas.'

He drew in a deep breath. 'Yes;' he said. 'Yes, I realise that. It. . .it was a shock. It made me realise. . .' He turned away from her. After a pause he said, 'I should have made more certain that that bridge was safe.'

There was a significant silence. 'That may be a suitable tale for my mother, Mr Guthrie, but it isn't enough for me. And it isn't worthy of you. You know that the wood in that bridge was sound and the bridge itself perfectly safe—until its supports were sawn through.'

'What rubb——' Mr Guthrie began, but he stopped when he saw Eleanor's expression. He went on, 'I hoped you hadn't noticed—you were injured and only half conscious most of the time. I suppose I should have known better. You don't usually miss much.'

'I may have been out of sorts but my wits were still sound! I know the difference between rotten wood and sawn wood!'

'A most unusual attribute in a lady,' he said with a smile.

'I don't want compliments, Mr Guthrie. I want to know why someone wanted to kill me.' She looked at him and realisation dawned. She said slowly, 'I wasn't the one it was meant for. It was for you!'

'What nonsense!' he said, but Eleanor was not to be put off.

'Someone is trying to kill you,' she said slowly.

'Some gypsy with a grudge——'

'No! The same thing happened in London—that wire. You said at the time that there had been a man. . .watching.' She held his gaze. 'It wasn't you on that hill, was it?'

'I wasn't there, no. Are you sure you saw someone?'

'Of course I am,' she said impatiently. 'But I couldn't say what he looked like. The sun was in my eyes, and I thought it was you. I suppose he must have been fairly tall. He. . .'

'Yes?'

'I have the impression that he favoured one leg slightly. I remember thinking that you must have hurt yourself running down the hill.'

'I see.' A quiet statement, but Eleanor was convinced that her description had meant something to him. He gave a deep sigh, then said, 'I think you'll be safe enough here. Mrs Cartwright is near by and she'll make sure that either Dora or Annie is within call. Silas won't be far away—nor will Daniel if I know him!'

'Surrounded by an army,' she said. 'But what about you?'

'I can't stay. There's a deal of work to be done. That's why you're doing this for me.'

'That isn't what I meant. What about your safety?'

He got up and crouched down beside her chair.

'I can take care of myself—especially as I now know...'

'Know what?'

'Never mind. But I will be careful.' He bent forward and lightly touched her lips with his. 'Since the day before yesterday I know what I wish to live for.'

She held him when he would have moved away. 'Take care! Please take care.'

He looked down at her troubled face, then put his hands round it and suddenly kissed her again, with more feeling. Eleanor clung to his arms, murmuring his name. Passion suddenly flared up between them, a dangerously exciting whirlwind, as, still holding her face in trembling hands, he kissed her again and again. Eleanor had never before been in the grip of such a strong emotion, and afterwards she was to remember with shame that she had not been the first to call a halt. He pulled away and stood looking at her flushed cheeks and trembling lips. 'I...I'm sorry, Eleanor,' he said. 'I forgot myself. I shouldn't have done that.

Please forgive me. Try not to let it make a difference
to our friendship, I beg you. That. . .is all I can offer
you at the moment. Can you forgive me? Forget it,
even?'

Eleanor nodded. She could not have spoken if her
life had depended on it. He waited a little longer, then
gave her a wry smile and went. She heard him calling
to Annie to make sure that Miss Southeran had everything she needed.

Eleanor sat for some minutes waiting for the wild
beating of her heart to slow down. Then she shook her
head and tried to get on with her work. But Mr
Guthrie's face kept coming between her eyes and the
books, and when she found herself making the same
mistake for the fourth time in succession she put down
her pen and sat back to think.

She rather thought she had just tasted 'uncontrollable passion'. Mr Guthrie had been right that day in
the drive—it was certainly not something to make jokes
about. The loss of all thought, all self-control . . . She
hid her face in her hands. After a while she grew calmer
and sat staring out at the view. Had Evadne Anstey
experienced the same uncontrollable passion. . .? It
would explain a lot. But what had happened after the
passion was spent? Why had the affair ended the way it
had?

Eleanor uttered an impatient exclamation and took
herself to task. She would not allow herself to speculate, or become jealous. Friendship was what he
offered, in spite of that moment of madness. She must
be content with that. 'All I can offer you at the
moment', he had said. Did that mean. . .? No, she
would not speculate! She bent over her work again.

But it was no use. She had put one problem to the back of her mind only to have another take its place. She was full of apprehension. There was no doubt that Jonas Guthrie's life was in danger, and she was certain he knew who was threatening it. He had known as soon as she had told him about the limp. He had not been surprised—it was as if he had been waiting for confirmation, hoping even for something different. The information had not been welcome—there had been anger behind that quiet acceptance. She tried to comfort herself with the thought that he would stand a better chance of protecting himself now that he knew where the threat lay.

At four o'clock she gave up trying to work and sent for Silas. She hopped downstairs with his help and waited in the sunshine while he fetched the little carriage her father had used about the estate. She was glad not to have to face Mr Guthrie again that day—she was sure she could show him a calm demeanour, suitable for friends, when they next met, but an extra day would make it more secure.

Her mother was delighted to see her back so soon, and attributed Eleanor's wan looks and subdued manner to her experiences on the bridge. 'You will spend the rest of the evening on the sofa, my love.'

'But I do not wish to usurp your sofa, Mama! You need it more than I.'

'Do you know, Eleanor, I feel so much better now that we live here? I think I must have been suffering from the damp of Stanyards for years without realising it. No, my dear, your need is greater than mine. I knew you were over-eager to be on your feet again. Come, I shall get Betty to arrange the sofa near my desk and we can share the lamplight. Would you like to hear what I have written today?'

The peaceful atmosphere of her mother's sitting-room, the soft cadence of her mother's voice and the comforting light of the lamp did much to calm Eleanor's agitated mind. The violent emotion which had flared between herself and Mr Guthrie that afternoon had taken its toll, but it now seemed to belong to another world, insubstantial, like a dream. It was even more difficult to imagine that threats of danger and death could be real.

# CHAPTER NINE

WHEN Mr Guthrie called on them quite early the next day Eleanor discovered that she was not yet capable of facing him as calmly as she would have wished. She found him gazing at her with a smile in his eyes which raised a faint staining of colour in her pale cheeks. But when he then announced that he was paying a visit to London, she was startled into protest. 'What about all the work on the estate? You said it could not wait.'

'I know, Miss Southeran, it is very awkward. But it can't be helped. The matter is urgent. You, of course, will be able to continue with your work in the library — at least, I hope you will?'

'Not for a day or two, Jonas,' said Mrs Southeran in a voice which admitted no opposition. 'Eleanor was quite knocked up when she came back yesterday. She must rest a little longer. The work surely isn't that urgent?'

'Of course not, ma'am.' He turned back to Eleanor, his face full of concern. 'I'm sorry to hear you are not well. Even sorrier if I was to blame in any way. That is the last thing I would wish, I assure you. You must rest as long as you need, Miss Southeran, but when you do return I think I can promise you a comparatively peaceful time. Then when matters are clearer we can sort things out a little more. Are you content with that?'

'I think so,' replied Eleanor, managing a smile. 'Are you. . .are you planning to stay in London for long?'

'I hope not. But I will remain there until the matter is settled, and I'm not sure how long that will take.' He turned to Mrs Southeran. 'I shall let you know if I can. Now I shall have to leave you. Er. . .I have taken the liberty of telling my household that you are nominally in charge of the house and estate while I am away. Do you mind? The men know what to do, and there shouldn't be any difficulties.'

Mrs Southeran assured him that she was perfectly ready to step in, adding with a twinkle in her eye, 'And Eleanor, as you know, is always ready to take charge of Stanyards estate. I dare swear she will wish you to prolong your stay in London till Christmas.'

'Mama! That is not so!'

'Your mother knows that—she is teasing you. But I will call her bluff, Miss Southeran, and tell you that you are free to take charge whenever you wish. We have worked together long enough for me to have absolute confidence in your judgement.'

Mr Guthrie could not have paid Eleanor a compliment which pleased her more. It did a little to leaven the shock of his departure.

There was no opportunity for them to talk in private—nor would Eleanor have sought one. But she spent some time after he had gone touching her hand where had kissed it in farewell. Had he taken just a little longer than was conventional on such occasions? Or was she deceiving herself?

Mr Guthrie had taken no pains to conceal the fact that he was leaving for London. The whole county seemed to know—or so it seemed to Eleanor. She didn't know which she disliked more—the commiserations from those who thought she would miss him, or the congratulations from those who believed that the ladies in the Dower House would be happier without him. Of course there were others who ascribed Mr Guthrie's sudden removal to London to the arrival in Somerset of not one but two of Mrs Anstey's daughters.

The neighbourhood had been agog to see for itself the much famed beauty of Marianne Anstey. After all, though practically penniless herself, she had captured the heart of one of London's most eligible bachelors. And when, the day after Mr Guthrie's departure, a handsome chaise drew up outside Church Cottage, those who were fortunate enough to be near by were not disappointed. Out stepped an exquisite vision dressed all in white—from her French silk bonnet with its flourish of ostrich plumes, down to the white leather slippers on her tiny feet. Face and hair were hidden by the bonnet, but the lady's figure was gracefully elegant, and her voice musical. She was accompanied by two grooms, her maidservant, and another lady, dressed more soberly in grey. It was a long time since Combe St James had seen such an elegant equipage, such an impressive retinue, and there was some speculation as to whether Miss Marianne had already married her viscount. But in that case where was her husband?

Quiet Mrs Anstey was showered with invitations, many of which she had to refuse. The newcomers were not seen in public for some days—it was said that they had found the exertions of the journey too much, and were resting. Confused reports began to circulate, centring on the identity of the lady in grey. At first she

was generally thought to be a companion for
Marianne. Then it was said that Mrs Phoebe Gardiner,
Mrs Anstey's eldest daughter, who had recently been
widowed, had travelled with her sister. Then Mrs
Desmond told Cousin Louisa she had it on the best
authority that Evadne Oliver had come to see her
mother. Which sister was the lady who had travelled
with Marianne Anstey? Combe St James had to possess its soul in patience and wait for the ladies—and
the truth—to emerge.

Eleanor had been surprised to find how much she
missed Mr Guthrie, and it took some determination to
ignore the ache in her heart, to put a swift end to
occasional bouts of daydreaming, and to concentrate
on the work in the library. Her foot had now nearly
recovered, but Dr Smithson had advised her to continue to rest it, so even the solace of riding round the
estate was denied her. Mrs Southeran was immersed
in her writing. She was absorbed in an assignment for
a prestigious literary review, and had little time for
neighbourhood gossip.

So the two Southerans, living as they did some way
from the village, were spared most of Combe St James'
excitement about Mrs Anstey's visitors. In any case,
their known support for Mr Guthrie made their
position uncertain. But when Eleanor heard the
debate about the second visitor, she was consumed
with curiosity. Evadne or Phoebe—she would find
either of them interesting and wished she could meet
whichever one it was. In the event, she was one of the
first to find out.

About ten days after Mr Guthrie's departure
Eleanor was working as usual on the catalogue when

a movement behind her caused her to turn round. At first sight she thought Marianne Anstey was standing in the doorway, but she quickly decided that she was mistaken. There was a self-possession, an awareness of her own charms about the figure in the doorway which was alien to Marianne's modest, slightly hesitant demeanour. This was no girl, this was a mature, self-confident young woman.

Eleanor started to get up, but the desk hampered her movements. 'Please don't!' said the woman in the doorway, and she came into the room. 'Don't let me interrupt you—it's unusual to see a female doing the work of a secretary. Are you a relation of Jonas's?'

'My name is Southeran. Eleanor Southeran.'

The Southeran name clearly meant nothing to the visitor. 'Are you his housekeeper? Though it's unusual work for. . . Oh, forgive me. You are perhaps—er—his guest? A dear friend, perhaps?'

This time Eleanor succeeded in standing. She said with all the dignity she could muster, 'My family owned the Stanyards estate, including a library of rare books, before Mr Guthrie bought it earlier this year. I have offered to catalogue the books for him.'

One finely arched eyebrow was raised in surprise. 'That seems very obliging of you. I'm afraid I would find such work terribly dull. But you must excuse my remark of a moment ago. I was trying to place you, and I'm afraid that I made a. . .a *faux pas*. One never knows, does one?'

Eleanor ignored the slightly ambiguous remark and said politely, 'You must in turn forgive me. I am afraid I don't know your name, though I think you must be Marianne Anstey's sister—you are very like her in looks. I am surprised that the housekeeper didn't announce you—she is normally the soul of propriety.'

'I am Phoebe Gardiner, and you are right—I am one of Marianne's sisters. And I'm afraid I didn't see anyone when I came in. The door downstairs was open, so I simply walked up. I knew Jonas wouldn't mind, and I wanted to see him.'

'I'm afraid he isn't here.'

'So I observe. Will he be long? Or don't you know?'

'He is in London.'

A small frown, quickly erased, wrinkled the perfection of Phoebe's brow. 'How tiresome.' She came in and wandered round the room, lifting her skirt and stepping delicately, like a cat. 'How dusty it is in here!'

'Libraries often are!' said Eleanor drily.

Phoebe came to a halt by the window at the end of the room. 'Where do you live?'

'I am surprised that it should interest you, Mrs Gardiner. But I live in the Dower House on the estate. You can see it from that window.' Phoebe looked out at the handsome building a little distance away. She came towards Eleanor, who was standing stiffly by her chair.

'I've made you angry,' she said, charmingly rueful. 'I'd forgotten my manners—in America we tend to be less formal, you see. Forgive me, Miss Southeran. Please?' This was accompanied by a delightful smile, a smile which Eleanor found impossible to resist.

She said in a warmer tone, 'Would you like to sit, Mrs Gardiner? The chair next to mine is reasonably free of dust, I think. Or would you prefer to——?'

'No, I'd like to sit next to you.' She took one of her gloves off and dusted the seat of the chair, then sat down carefully, arranging her dress as she did so. 'You have no idea what a nuisance it is always to have to wear white, Miss Southeran. The slightest speck of dirt shows so! Some days I change five or six times—seven, even!'

'I'll send for some tea,' said Eleanor, picking up her bell. 'Or would you prefer some lemonade?'

'Lemonade would be perfectly lovely—I never drink tea; it's bad for the complexion. Thank you.'

'Why must you always wear white?' asked Eleanor, settling herself in her chair again once the refreshments had been served.

Phoebe opened her eyes wide and said, 'Why, Miss Southeran, because I'm in mourning, of course. I lost my dearest husband not a year ago. And no one could expect me to wear black all the time—or even at all. It simply washes me out. No, I prefer to mourn Gilbert in purest white. He always liked me in white—or blue. Perhaps I could wear blue sometimes? What do you think?'

Eleanor began to enjoy herself. She was not really sure whether her extraordinary visitor meant what she said, or was asking her to share in a huge joke. One thing was certain: Phoebe did not seem to be unduly saddened by her husband's demise.

'If you don't think me impertinent, Mrs Gardiner, I would say that you would look ravishing in whatever colour you chose to wear.' Her visitor flushed with delight at this perfectly genuine compliment, but she shuddered when Eleanor added, 'Black or possibly purple or grey are more usually considered to be mourning colours in England.'

'It is quite out of the question,' Phoebe said with

determination, 'that I should ever be seen in purple or grey. No one who knows me could possibly ask it. No, I shall have to stay with white. Does Jonas help you when you are working here?'

'Mr Guthrie is seldom in the house. He spends most of his time out of doors—there's a great deal to do.'

'And he enjoys doing it. He hasn't changed,' said Phoebe. 'Do you know, Miss Southeran, Jonas Guthrie was one of the richest men in Boston, but he was never content to behave like a gentleman?'

'Whatever do you mean?' asked Eleanor, startled into disapproval.

'Oh, goodness, gracious, I've upset you again! Please don't misunderstand me! He was always perfectly proper. I only meant that he was never content to sit back and enjoy himself. He always had to be busy, always having ideas. Quite exhausting. We were engaged once, Jonas and I, you know.'

'Really?' murmured Eleanor.

'Yes.' Mrs Gardiner smiled reminiscently. 'I was just seventeen, a mere child. He said he was dazzled by me. That was his very word, Miss Southeran. "Dazzled".'

'That is hardly surprising, Mrs Gardiner.'

'You are kind to say so. Marianne is generally held to be the family beauty now. What a match she has made! If only. . .'

The tiny frown returned and disappeared again. 'But there! She deserves it—she is a gem.' There was a short silence.

'You were talking of your engagement to Mr Guthrie?' said Eleanor, trying hard not to sound as if the matter was of any personal interest.

'Oh, yes! I was painfully young, of course. Far too young to appreciate Jonas's real worth. When I met Gilbert—Mr Gardiner—he seemed to be so much gentler, so much easier to talk to. He liked me as I was, too, whereas Jonas was always trying to make me into something different. So I asked to be released from our engagement. It was a big mistake.'

'The engagement?'

'No! Asking Jonas to release me. He was so very gallant about it, too. He must have suffered, Miss Southeran, but I was too young to notice. It would be different now.'

'But what about your husband, Mr Gardiner? Were you not, after all, happy with him?'

'I was *very* happy with him,' said Mrs Gardiner, opening gentian-blue eyes wide again. 'But he was in a stupid street accident and died before we had any children.'

'How. . .how sad,' said Eleanor, feeling the response to be inadequate, but at a loss to think of anything more suitable.

'Yes, it was. If he had lived a little longer, or if we had had an heir to the Gardiner fortune, I shouldn't be forced to live on a widow's jointure—the merest pittance, Miss Southeran. Gilbert never had any money of his own, you see. His father made us an allowance.'

Eleanor looked at the Parisian bonnet, the fashionable dress and the fine white kid of Phoebe's shoes and concluded that the pittance couldn't be all that meagre. But she decided to say nothing. Her visitor seemed to feel that Eleanor's silence expressed disapproval.

'I hope you don't think me disloyal to my darling Gilbert's memory—I was truly very upset by his death.' She took out a minute lace handkerchief and dabbed at her eyes. Eleanor had a sudden picture of Mrs Anstey making much the same gesture at their first meeting. She was thinking that perhaps Phoebe Gardiner was not so very different from her mother when, with a lightning change of mood, Phoebe said briskly, 'But you should not allow me to run on in this fashion, Miss Southeran. I have decided that the future is what I must think of now—I must put the sad past behind me.' She smiled bravely and went on, 'When will Jonas return from London, do you know?' thus making it quite clear where she thought her future might lie.

'I'm afraid I have no idea,' said Eleanor politely.

'It's very vexing. I could have stayed on with my cousins and seen Jonas at the same time. London is sadly empty of people of consequence, but there were one or two. . .' She sat in thought for a moment and then said with decision, 'I shall stay a little longer in Somerset in case he returns, and then I shall go back to Berkeley Square.' She gave Eleanor another of her enchanting smiles. 'May I call on you at your home?'

'I am sure that my mother would be delighted to make your acquaintance.' This was no less than the truth. Eleanor was quite certain that her mother would never forgive her if she was deprived of meeting this fascinating creature. 'Er. . .would Mrs Anstey like to accompany you? Or is there someone else—your companion, perhaps?'

'My companion? Oh, you mean Mrs Oliver, my sister? I shall ask them, of course, but I doubt they will come. To tell truth, I am really quite concerned about them, Miss Southeran. My mother is fast becoming a recluse, and Evadne is little better.'

A certain delicacy prevented Eleanor from suggesting a reason for Evadne Oliver's desire for seclusion. But the thought that the key to the whole mystery of Mr Guthrie's involvement with the Anstey family might be residing in Church Cottage, Combe St James was irresistibly intriguing. However, since it was impossible to ask Phoebe to be as frank about her sister's situation as she had been about her own, Eleanor decided to let matters take their course.

'Then do try to persuade them to come,' was all she replied.

They decided on a date and a time and Phoebe then shook out her skirts energetically, looked with distaste at the marks on her gloves, and left.

Once again Eleanor abandoned her work in order to think of Jonas Guthrie. What would these arrivals mean to him? Phoebe made no secret of the fact that she intended to rectify the mistake she had made in her youth. Would Jonas be dazzled once again? On the whole, Eleanor thought it unlikely. She felt she knew the man sufficiently well to doubt that such a shallow, self-centred nature would attract him, any more than it had in the past.

But who could say? Phoebe Gardiner's beauty, her enchanting smile, might charm anyone into forgetting her shortcomings. She would certainly make a fitting jewel in a rich man's crown. Was that what Jonas might decide? Eleanor grew cold at the thought. But what right had she, Eleanor, to expect anything? Jonas Guthrie had never given her any unequivocal reason

to hope, only hints. Friendship was what he had
offered her—'for the moment'. What *had* he meant by
that?

In London the subject of Eleanor's thoughts attacked
the business on hand with his usual brisk energy. Some
of what he did was what might have been expected of
a prosperous man of affairs. He sought out acquaintances at the Foreign Office, he consulted lawyers and
visited his bank, he sent off detailed messages to
Boston—all this he did quite openly, with the air of a
man who knew exactly what he was doing and why.

But some of his other activities were distinctly
strange. He seemed to be conscious of this fact, for he
took some pains to keep them out of the public eye.
One could not blame him for this, for it was hardly
the thing for a respectable man of business to spend
time in the less salubrious quarters of London, making
enquiries in disreputable inns and taverns, and talking to some very questionable characters—obviously
seafaring men—on the wharves and docksides of
London. Moreover his constant companion on these
expeditions was a man whose appearance and accom-
plishments would clearly be more suited to a dockside
fight than to a soirée or a rout party.

Mr Guthrie eventually seemed satisfied with his
labours and returned to his cousins' house in Berkeley
Square to await results. Meanwhile he was visited here
by agents and architects—he was clearly intending to
buy a house in London, and the few members of
society left in the capital in September started to
speculate on the name of the lady he was intending
to invite to share it.

He also seemed to have developed a taste for gambling, winning and losing considerable sums at Brooks, Whites and other, less reputable gambling hells in Pall Mall. It was interesting that though, of course, his erstwhile companion in the darker quarters of London was not to be seen in such elevated company, he was never very far away when Mr Guthrie finally emerged from these pleasure spots.

Eventually Mr Guthrie's patience was rewarded.

'Oliver, my dear fellow!' he said one evening to one of his fellow gamblers, clapping him on the back.

Nathaniel Oliver, a handsome, dark-haired man of middle height, turned swiftly round. 'Oh—er—it's you, Guthrie. Good evening to you.'

'What a fortunate chance that we've met! Come and join me in a glass of wine, Oliver, and you can give me all your news. Come, I insist.' Mr Guthrie took Mr Oliver's arm and led him firmly to a small table in one of the alcoves. Here he ordered a bottle of Burgundy and poured a generously filled glass for his guest and himself.

Mr Oliver seemed to gain some comfort from the wine. 'I didn't expect to see you in London, Guthrie,' he said, sitting back in a more relaxed attitude.

'Didn't you, my dear chap?' said Mr Guthrie genially. 'A pleasant surprise for both of us, then. I quite thought you were in Somerset.'

'Somerset? Why?' said Mr Oliver sharply.

'To be with your wife. What else? From what I hear, she's visiting Amelia in Combe St James. Am I right?'

'Yes, of course. I shall be joining her in a few days.'

'And meanwhile you're enjoying the fleshpots

before returning to the bosom of your family. I quite understand. How are they?'

'Who?'

'Why, your wife and the little fellow.'

'They're well,' said Mr Oliver shortly. 'But we've left the boy behind in Boston with his nurse. It's too far to bring him to England, and he isn't strong.'

'So I had heard.'

'You've heard? How?'

'I keep in touch. After all, it's natural I should take an interest in the child, wouldn't you say? But you're not drinking, my dear fellow.' He poured another generous glass. 'You seem on edge, Oliver. Are you waiting for someone? Christopher Digby, perhaps?'

'Christopher?'

Mr Guthrie leant forward, his voice full of concern. 'That's the third or fourth time you've repeated what I've said, Oliver. Are you suffering a little in your hearing? You should get it seen to—before it is too late.'

'There's nothing wrong with my hearing,' said Mr Oliver coldly. 'Or with my memory, either, so don't try threatening me. I believe we made a bargain in Boston.'

'We did indeed. Recently I've been wondering whether you remember the terms.'

Mr Oliver leaned back and said, 'I don't know what you mean, Guthrie. What the devil are you talking about? I've kept my side of it. I married Evadne, and I've kept silent on. . .certain matters. That hasn't changed.'

Mr Guthrie was nodding. 'And in return I paid you a sum of money—quite a large sum. And more was settled on Evadne and the child. Do you remember what I said at the time?'

'No, I don't. But I dare swear you are about to tell me.'

Mr Guthrie leaned forward till his face was close to Mr Oliver's. 'I said that I wasn't a man who submitted easily to blackmail; that on this occasion you had me in a cleft stick where I was forced to go along with it, but that didn't make me like it.'

Mr Oliver said, with a mocking smile, 'My dear fellow, do forgive me! But where is all this leading? I wasn't interested in your feelings at the time, and am even less so now.'

'I said, Oliver, that if you did anything more, if that wasn't the end of the matter, one payment, one agreement, then the bargain was null and void.'

'I still don't see. . .?'

'I was willing to give you my reputation along with the money. I am not willing to give you my life.'

'Your life? You must be mad! What would I want with your life?' Mr Oliver had gone slightly pale, but he was still apparently at ease. 'We have never liked each other, Guthrie, but this is going beyond what is tolerable. What are you accusing me of?'

'Greed. Folly.'

'Folly?'

'It was foolish to persuade Christopher to come down to Somerset. It must have been against his better judgement. Did he tell you that I warned him after the first attempt on my life here in London what would happen if he tried again?'

'I don't know what you're talking about.'

'Then I am sorry for you. The game is over, Oliver.

Take Evadne back to Boston and patch up what you can.'

Mr Oliver got up and walked away, giving Mr Guthrie a malevolent look as he went. At the door he was met by a tall, young-looking man, handsome and well-built, whose only physical flaw seemed to be a very slight limp... Mr Oliver took his arm and they hurried away, deep in conversation.

In the early hours of the morning there was a slight disturbance outside the small inn where Mr Oliver was staying—not enough to disturb the guests, certainly not Mr Oliver. Some seafaring gentlemen seemed to have drunk a trifle too much—indeed one of their band could hardly walk. They were making their way back to their ship—an East Indiaman, bound for Madras.

His work in London done, Mr Guthrie came back to Stanyards on a golden day early in September. The chestnut trees in the drive were heavy with fruit and their leaves were starting to turn. Gaps in their ranks reminded him that there was still a deal to do here at Stanyards. He breathed a deep sigh of satisfaction—a challenge was what he had asked for, and so far his work at Stanyards had been richly rewarding. There were glimpses through the trees of fields of pale gold corn, some already harvested. It had been a good year for the farms, and next year and the one after that would be even better, he was sure.

A flight of swallows swooped and wheeled over-head—they would soon make their long journey south. He was sorry to see them go, but they would be back

next spring. He himself had no desire to leave
Somerset again for any length of time. Occasional
visits to London, perhaps—it was as well to keep one's
hand in, so to speak. But voyages further afield, to
America or India—those belonged to the past.

His lawyers and bankers in London had reminded
him what a very rich man he was. His friends at the
Foreign Office had made it clear that he could, if he
wished, be a man of consequence, a friend of princes,
could own a mansion in London and an imposing
country seat, complete with an army of servants and
hangers-on. A title was not out of the question.

But that was not what he wanted. Apart from a
relatively small house near Grosvenor Square for
occasional visits to London, the simple life he lived
here at Stanyards would suit him very well. He would
engage more servants—he had neglected the household side of affairs in favour of the estate—but his
wife would be able to advise him on what was needed.
His wife. That had a good sound to it. And if things
went as planned he would be able to start acquiring a
wife very soon.

He drew up at the front steps of Stanyards, where
Silas was waiting to take the horses and Mrs Cartwright
was ready to welcome him back. There was none of
the impassive, well-trained servant about Silas. His
weatherbeaten face was covered in a huge smile of
welcome. Even Mrs Cartwright, a woman of superior
education and training, was permitting herself a discreet smile.

'Good day to you, Mrs Cartwright. How do you go
on? And Silas—you're looking well. Give the horses a
good watering and feed. I was so anxious to be home

that I've driven them a little hard. Now, Mrs Cartwright, how are things at Stanyards?'

'Pretty fair, sir. The men have been doing the rooms upstairs. I'm afraid there's a bit of a mess. Would you like something to eat after your journey?'

'No, I ate on the way. Is Miss Southeran still at work in the library?'

'She has been, sir. But yesterday and today she has been out riding round the estate again. Dr Smithson says her foot is cured.'

'That's good news! Tell Silas I'd like Captain brought round in half an hour, would you?' said Mr Guthrie. 'And I'd like a can of hot water in my room as soon as possible—I need to tidy up. I suppose the room is free?'

'The men finished in there yesterday, sir. But you're surely not going out again after your journey?'

'I cannot wait to see what's been happening in my absence, Mrs Cartwright. Hurry up with that water!'

# CHAPTER TEN

ELEANOR had finished her tour of the estate and was at the combe. This was her second visit back to the scene of the accident. She had ridden over the day before, but her horse had balked every time she had attempted to cross the bridge. She should have insisted, and, failing that, she should have led Shanty across. But she had felt the same reluctance as the horse to set foot on the structure, even though she had been assured by the estate carpenters that it was completely safe again. So, ashamed of her fears of the day before, she was here to try again.

'Come, Shanty, we shall go together. That's right, straight on now. . .'

But the horse, sensing Eleanor's own feelings perhaps, stopped short where the plank roadway began. 'Shanty!' Eleanor dismounted and started to soothe the animal, to coax it on to the bridge. She was still engaged in doing this when Mr Guthrie rode up. He stopped and dismounted some distance away when he saw what was going on. Slowly, calmly, Eleanor urged Shanty forward. But, sensing Captain's presence, Shanty turned to see the newcomers. Eleanor gave an exasperated sigh and looked to see who had interrupted her efforts.

'Jonas!' Her frown instantly changed into an expression of joy and, heedless of all the rules of proper behaviour for a young lady, she dropped

Shanty's rein and ran towards him. She was caught in his outstretched arms. 'You're back!' she said. 'Oh, what a stupid thing to say—of course you are; you wouldn't be here otherwise.'

When he raised an eyebrow and smiled down at her she grinned and said, 'You needn't look at me like that, Jonas; I know I'm babbling. It's the shock. We didn't expect you so soon.'

'I know I said I would let your mother know—but it seemed simpler to come myself. How are you? I see the ankle is better.'

Eleanor suddenly became aware that she was still clasped tightly in Mr Guthrie's arms and made to free herself. 'My ankle is perfectly cured. But you must let me go, Jonas,' she said nervously. 'It won't do!'

'Well, there's ingratitude! I catch you to prevent us both from being knocked over, hold you merely till you get your balance, and now you accuse me of. . .what, Eleanor?'

'Both of us suffer from lack of any sense of what is proper! I ought to be ashamed of myself. . . You took me by surprise, that is all.'

'I must surprise you more often,' he said, again with his particular, quizzical smile. 'But since you mention propriety. . .' He let her go. 'What were you doing with Shanty? Is she refusing the bridge?'

Eleanor explained her problem to him, including the fact that she was sure the horse could sense her own fear.

'Come, we shall walk across together first, and then we shall lead both horses over. Give me your hand— if that won't offend your belated sense of propriety.'

Holding her hand in his warm, firm grip, he took

her confidently across to the other side. Here he stopped and said, 'Well?'

'No shivers at all. Thank you.'

'Now for the horses. I'll go first with Captain. The lady will follow, don't you think?'

'In these circumstances, perhaps. I would not always agree, Mr Guthrie!'

'Concentrate on your horse, Eleanor. We shall fight other battles elsewhere.'

On the other side they let the horses loose to graze, and he stood for a moment looking at her. 'Hmm—a touch pale, now that the shock of seeing me has worn off. Have you been cooped up in the library for too long?'

'I suppose that is it. The records are almost finished.'

'Come, sit down here. I want to talk to you.' They settled themselves on a huge boulder near by. 'Do you remember when we were last here? This is the very rock I leant against, I believe. I have never admired you more than that night. You were wet, cold, and in pain. But you were so brave.'

'I don't remember being brave,' said Eleanor with a shudder. 'Towards the end, before you came, I remember being distinctly frightened. I thought it was you on the hillside, you see, and expected you to come to the rescue almost at once. It seemed like eternity before you did come. Jonas, you know who the man on the hillside was, don't you?'

'Yes,' he said grimly. 'Yes, I do. But you needn't be afraid he'll come back. I've dealt with him.'

A cold shiver went down Eleanor's spine at the tone of Mr Guthrie's voice. She asked hesitantly, 'Why did he want to kill you?'

'It's a long story, Eleanor, and not a pleasant one. I might tell you some other time, but not here and now. Not when I've just come back to you and Stanyards.'

Eleanor gave a little nod. She said, 'And then afterwards—after you had found me here—I remember that you made me so comfortable with your coat and...the rest. I'm afraid it was less pleasant for you—this rock is very hard!'

'I was so...immeasurably glad to find you that I would cheerfully have put up with much worse. I shall never forget my first sight of you—lying there with that great beam across you. The only thing that kept me from complete panic was that I had heard you shout just a minute before.'

'You, nearly in a panic? I don't believe it!'

'You may do so. I've never known anything like it.'

They gazed at one another and suddenly they were in each other's arms, holding one another so tightly that Eleanor could hardly breathe. Mr Guthrie was murmuring her name, his voice trembling and hoarse. Then he released her slightly, but only in order to lift her face to his and cover her mouth with kisses. Eleanor thought vaguely, Uncontrollable passion—that's what this is. Now I know, before she was swept into a vortex of emotion in which she would willingly have drowned.

After some minutes he held her away from him and smiled at her again. Then he suddenly frowned and said, 'Your lips are bruised. I'm sorry. Does it hurt?'

'No,' said Eleanor dreamily. 'And I wouldn't mind it if it did.'

He laughed delightedly. 'You're completely bewitching!' He caught her in his arms again and hugged her to him. Then he said firmly, 'But I mustn't hurt you any more. We must go back while we are still able to be sensible. I promised your mother. . .'

She looked up at him with a little question in her eyes. He groaned and said, 'Eleanor, I cannot say what I want to say to you until I have removed the shadows from my name and my life. Our lives. It shouldn't be long now. Will you wait?'

'I'll try,' said Eleanor with a sigh. 'If I must. But it's very hard.'

'I know,' he said. 'Believe me, Eleanor, I know very well. But it is essential.' He got up and began to walk towards the horses, which had wandered a little distance away. 'We must concentrate on other matters. Tell me about Stanyards.'

When Eleanor had caught up with him she said, 'There is something I want to ask you. When I went round the estate yesterday I heard something that I think must be wrong. The farmers are saying that you have given Threlfall notice to quit his farm by Michaelmas. Surely that isn't so?'

'It is. I told him before I left for London. He hasn't been making trouble, has he?'

'But his family has been on that farm for generations!'

'Well, I don't know about his forebears, but Threlfall is a poor farmer and a bad tenant. The estate will be well shot of him.'

'You can't throw him out! He has a wife and children.'

'From what I hear they'd be better off without him, too. He's a drunkard and a bully.'

'Jonas, I can't believe I'm hearing what my ears tell

me. Everyone now says what a good landlord you are. Why are you acting so ruthlessly?'

'Firstly because I am a good landlord, and cannot stand by while a good farm is neglected and unproductive. The whole estate suffers when one of its farms lies covered in weeds. And secondly, because I *am* ruthless. I've told you that before. When I see something that needs to be done, I do it.'

'You play to win. You said so in London soon after we met. But I thought. . . Please don't do this, Jonas! Not here at Stanyards.'

'Threlfall has had more warnings than I have ever given anyone before. Don't look at me like that, Eleanor! I am not altogether without a heart. Threlfall won't be completely homeless; I have set aside a cottage near the village for him and his family. He can do as he wishes—stay there, or if he chooses he can seek work elsewhere. I would be glad to see the back of him, and so, I suspect, would his wife.' He looked at Eleanor's downcast face. 'Don't let your heart rule your judgement, Eleanor. I thought you had outgrown that.'

'And I thought. . .' she said miserably.

'What? That, because of my feeling for you and your family, you could persuade me to do something that I know is wrong? No, that is not my way. I have fallen into that trap once before, and I won't let it happen again. Threlfall will go.'

Eleanor had been pale, but now she flushed in anger. She said sharply, 'Then since you have clearly made up your mind there is nothing more to be said. Forgive me for interfering. And now I have things to do—I must go back.'

She waited in silence while he helped her mount, rode off over the bridge without even noticing she was doing so, and galloped off. Mr Guthrie followed her with a face of thunder.

Eleanor now had Dr Smithson's permission to ride as much as she chose. She used her new freedom to go about the estate and learn more of the Threlfall affair. To her surprise, the farmers, even those who had been Threlfall's friends, were solidly in favour of his dismissal. In the days when everyone had done much as they pleased on their farms, Threlfall had been a leader. He had persuaded them that an easy life was better than a rich one, that to do the minimum required to keep the land marginally productive was better than to slave away—his words—to enrich the landlords.

But now his day was over. Mr Guthrie's coming had changed the spirit of the place and the farmers on Stanyards lands had come alive, were eager to work to profit both the landlord and themselves. Threlfall had failed to change with the others. He had always been ready to bluster, quick to feel aggrieved. Now he had made himself unpopular with everyone, including his long-suffering wife.

All this did not at first reconcile Eleanor to Mr Guthrie's action. Her crusading spirit, dormant under the happy time she had recently enjoyed on Stanyards, now came to life. She went to see Threlfall, and listened to his ramblings. She rode about his farm and saw the state it was in for herself. She discussed with him what could be done about it—without success, it might be said. In the end she found she had merely

encouraged Threlfall to feel even more aggrieved at
the high-handed action of the new landlord. He was
now even more convinced that things would have
turned out very differently under the old regime.
Eleanor had to admit failure. The general view was
that the master had acted very properly, generously
even, in providing the Threlfall family with a home—
and she was forced to agree.

She was now faced with the difficulty of conveying
this change of heart to Mr Guthrie. She had not seen
him since their quarrel at the combe—she had avoided
meeting him. That quarrel. Such a short time before it
they had been lost to the world in each other's arms—
why had she even mentioned the name of Threlfall?
They had been so close, and were now so far apart—
and she knew that the bitterness between them when
they parted had been caused by her lack of understanding, her lack of faith.

How could she best put things right between them?
The memory of previous apologies kept intruding as
she wrestled with the problem. But surely things were
different now? Then she had merely been the daughter of an old friend. But now. . . Mr Guthrie might not
have said in so many words that he was in love with
her, but it had been implicit in all he had said and
done. Yes, it would be different. She would just have
to find the right occasion.

Meanwhile Combe St James was once again excited
by the arrival of yet another visitor at Mrs Anstey's
house. Another elegant chaise had brought a visitor to
Church Cottage—this time a handsome, polished man

of fashion, and in a very short time it had been established that this was Mrs Oliver's husband.

Unlike his wife and mother-in-law, Mr Oliver positively revelled in meeting people. Though one or two sticklers at first looked askance at a man who had agreed to such a curious start to his marriage, they were soon disarmed by Mr Oliver's obvious devotion to his wife, and his impeccable manners to everyone. What a contrast he was to Mr Guthrie, who, even at the height of his popularity, had occasionally offended with his blunt way of speaking and his lack of ceremony!

Yes, it was soon decided that, in spite of being an American, Mr Oliver was a true gentleman, a distinct asset to the neighbourhood, and he was welcomed wherever he went.

The ladies in the Dower House were kept informed of these developments by Cousin Louisa, who was among Mr Oliver's greatest admirers.

'Such distinguished manners! He has put many a lady's heart in a flutter, in spite of being married! But, though he talks to us all charmingly, he has no eyes for anyone but that dowdy wife of his. We cannot really understand it. Especially as his sister-in-law is so absolutely beautiful. One would have thought... But there's no accounting for taste.'

'I cannot wait to meet him, Louisa,' said Mrs Southeran. 'And the Anstey sisters, too. But am I wrong? Wasn't there a child in all this unhappy story?'

'Oh, it is so sad! The little boy is not strong. His parents thought it better to leave him at home in Boston with his nurse. I am sure Mrs Oliver must miss him.'

'Then why did they leave him? Why are they here?'

Mrs Southeran's voice was mild, but there was a slight element of censure in it that Cousin Louisa hastened to dispel.

'Mr Oliver says that he had to come over to Europe on business this year, and his wife decided that she would like to see her mother and sister Marianne. They had heard what a great success Marianne was in London. It wasn't until they got here that they learned she was actually engaged to be married. I expect they will stay for the wedding. As will Mrs Gardiner.'

'I have invited Mrs Gardiner to visit us here the day after tomorrow. Perhaps I will include Mr and Mrs Oliver in the invitation. Would your man take a note round to Church Cottage for me, Louisa?'

'Certainly. I am sure you will not be disappointed, Anthea. Such a handsome man. So charming!'

'I already find Mr Oliver a fascinating character, Louisa. I am quite sure I shall not be disappointed.'

The note was duly written and handed to Cousin Louisa for delivery to the Ansteys. As a matter of form Mrs Anstey was included, though neither Eleanor nor her mother expected to see the lady.

Eleanor was still trying to find an opportunity to make her apology to Mr Guthrie, but he had been busy with a backlog of work after his absence in London, and had not been seen in the Dower House. Then she heard that he had been to Exeter to see Mr Lucombe, the tree nurseryman, and it was difficult to suppress a feeling of hurt that he had not told her he was going. She was feeling altogether low, and the prospect of some interesting visitors was welcome—they might take her mind off her troubles for a while. She made one last attempt to see Mr Guthrie before they came. She rode over to the combe, hoping she might find him there.

Mr Guthrie was nowhere to be seen but somebody else was there—a well-dressed man of medium height, dark and quite handsome. He was standing on the bank by the bridge, gazing down into the water below. Eleanor pulled up her horse a little distance away from him. The man was a complete stranger.

'Good morning!' he called.

'Good morning. I don't think I know you, do I?' said Eleanor warily. She didn't enjoy meeting strangers in this particular spot.

He made no attempt to come nearer, but said, 'You must be Miss Southeran. I'm Nathaniel Oliver. I'm staying at present with a friend of yours—my mother-in-law, Mrs Anstey.'

'You are a long way from Combe St James, Mr Oliver.'

'I know. I came to see Jonas, but they couldn't find him. They said he might be here.'

'How did you find your way? It's quite a distance from the house.'

'Indeed it is,' he replied with a charming smile. 'And even further when you lose your way as often as I did! Don't be afraid, Miss Southeran. I'm perfectly respectable. I'm a friend of your cousin Louisa.'

Eleanor was reassured. She dismounted and led Shanty down to the riverbank. 'How do you do?' she said. 'Have you seen Jo—Mr Guthrie?'

'No. I thought I would wait a little longer, then I shall give up for today. My wife will be wondering where I have got to. I am delighted to meet you at last, Miss Southeran. I have heard a great deal about you.'

'Really, sir?' said Eleanor, with a cool smile. 'Well, I will not ask you from whom or to what effect, in case your reply is not what I would wish to hear.'

He looked gallant, and said that her anxieties were quite out of place. 'But I was sorry to hear of your accident, Miss Southeran.'

'Who told you of my accident?' asked Eleanor sharply, her suspicions returning.

'Why, your cousin Louisa has told everyone in Combe St James about your narrow escape. You don't appear to have suffered any lasting damage, if I may say so. It was here, wasn't it?'

Eleanor admitted stiffly that this was so. She was not quite sure why this man was so interested in the matter, and was reluctant to discuss it with him.

He disarmed her suspicions almost immediately by saying sympathetically, 'But I can see that the memory is not a pleasant one, so we won't talk about it. Shall we ride back together, Miss Southeran? I would be glad to have a guide.'

On the way back he talked amusingly of his experiences in Combe St James. He kept Eleanor entertained, for, though his stories were witty, they were never unkind, and they revealed a surprising insight into the ways of a small country village. By the time they had reached the Dower House Eleanor was in perfect charity with him.

'Goodbye, Mr Oliver—for the moment. I believe you are paying us a visit tomorrow with your wife and sister-in-law.'

'*Au revoir*, Miss Southeran. I am looking forward to it.'

He rode off, and Eleanor watched him go. So that was the famous Mr Oliver, who had married for money. Or had he? He had certainly talked of his wife with great affection. What would she be like?

When the two Anstey sisters walked into Mrs Southeran's sitting-room, no greater contrast could have been imagined. Phoebe was dazzling in a bonnet of white crape, and a white mull muslin dress which was delicately tucked and frilled. Eleanor gave a fleeting thought to the poor maidservant who had to iron such confections—six of them a day! But she was amused to see that, perhaps in deference to public opinion, Phoebe had a floating lavender-grey scarf draped round her shoulders. She greeted Eleanor warmly and expressed delight at seeing her again.

Evadne was soberly dressed in a dun-coloured round gown with few trimmings. Her bonnet was of black straw, with a small feather to one side. Though her features were not unattractive, they lacked her sister's colour and animation. Her eyes were greenish-grey, and her cheeks pale and slightly sallow. Her expression was composed, guarded even, and she waited quietly in the background until Mrs Southeran invited her to come over and be introduced. Phoebe was already sitting next to her hostess, her white dress making a striking contrast with the blue velvet of the sofa.

Mr Oliver's manners were indeed charming. He waited till Mrs Southeran had finished greeting his wife and sister-in-law, then stepped forward and bowed over her hand. He complimented her on her roses, which could be seen through the open windows, and waited till she had finished her short conversation with him before moving to Eleanor and saying with a twinkle in his eye, 'Now, Miss Southeran, may I claim to have been officially introduced to you? Or shall I ask your mother to perform that office?'

Eleanor smiled and said, 'I think we may dispense with that last touch of formality, sir. But I have yet to meet your wife. Would you present me to her?'

They went over to the sofa and Eleanor at last found herself face to face with the woman who had caused so much trouble for Jonas. At first sight this was not a face to 'launch a thousand ships'—Evadne's sister was much more likely to start a conflict for her favours. But Mr Oliver seemed devoted. He was very protective of her and hovered over her after he had performed the introduction, looking on while she responded to Eleanor's conversation, encouraging her to say more. Evadne's voice was a surprise. It was deep and low, and had a distinctive, attractively husky note. She seemed reticent, but after a while Eleanor became convinced that this was not the result of shyness, but rather a deliberate withholding of personality. A most intriguing woman, in spite of her colourless manner.

Meanwhile Phoebe was enchanting Mrs Southeran. 'Do you really think this shawl suits me? I have never worn grey before, Mrs Southeran. Grey is not a colour that suits me. Mr Gardiner would not have liked it, I am sure, but he is no longer with us, and I wouldn't like people to think that I lacked respect for his memory. When one is in mourning one must not think of one's looks, don't you agree? Do I look hideous?'

'Mrs Gardiner, I assure you, you look delightful. The lilac shadows in that scarf deserve a poem all to themselves.'

'Oh,' said Phoebe, growing pink. 'How kind of you! When will you write it—the poem, I mean? I should dearly love to have a poem about me! Several of my admirers have said they wished to write one, but they never have.'

Mrs Southeran was fortunately saved from reply by the entry of Mr Guthrie. As Betty explained afterwards, she was so used to seeing him that she never thought for one moment that her mistress would not wish to receive him, and he, as was his custom, strode in without ceremony. He stopped short when he saw who the visitors were.

Mrs Southeran, who was an accomplished hostess, would not have chosen to mix such an unfortunate selection of people, but she faced the inevitable with grace. In fact, the situation appealed to her puckish sense of humour and, as a keen observer of the human race, she was more than somewhat intrigued to see how they would all behave.

'Jonas! How kind of you to call! I...I believe you already know my visitors.'

'Good afternoon, Mrs Southeran. Yes, I believe I do. Very well, in fact.' He bowed to each in turn. 'Phoebe... Evadne... Oliver...' His face was still unsmiling as he turned to greet Eleanor, and she felt her heart sink. She had hoped he would have softened towards her—it would have made things so much easier. But perhaps he might grow kinder during the course of the afternoon—and, in any case, this was clearly not the occasion to attempt to say anything at all about their differences.

Phoebe rose from the sofa in one swift, graceful movement and took Mr Guthrie's arm. She said gaily, 'You must all excuse me. I have so much to say to Jonas, and have been waiting an age to see him.' She led him over to the window-seat and sat down, patting the seat beside her with a smile of invitation. 'When did you return from London, Jonas? Did you hurry back when you heard I was here?'

'Not. . .not exactly,' he replied, and Eleanor suffered a pang as she saw him give Phoebe his special, quizzical smile as he joined her on the seat.

'Oh, Jonas, I have missed you so. Poor Gilbert is dead, you know. . .'

The rest of the party were forgotten by at least one of the two on the window-seat as Phoebe proceeded to entrance Mr Guthrie—or so it seemed to Eleanor. Mrs Southeran, unperturbed by Phoebe's ruthless lack of manners, which she quite rightly thought was totally characteristic, turned to her other guests. They were soon immersed in a discussion about Marianne Anstey's wedding, which was due to take place in a very short time.

'Will your mama be able to travel so far? I have heard she is not very well,' said Mrs Southeran to Evadne.

'Mama will certainly wish to be present. She is very proud of Marianne. As we all are,' she added, but her voice was devoid of feeling.

There was a pause. Mr Oliver's eyes had been fixed on Phoebe and Mr Guthrie, but he now suddenly recollected himself and said, 'Forgive me, my thoughts were wandering. Of course Mrs Anstey will be well enough. We might all go—what do you think, my love?'

'I am not sure Mama would wish for that,' replied his wife.

'Of course she would! And you shall have a pretty dress and a new bonnet.' Mr Oliver turned with a smile to Mrs Southeran. 'You may find it hard to believe, Mrs Southeran, but I have great difficulty in persuading my wife to buy pretty clothes. I think it must be her only fault.'

'If that is Mrs Oliver's only shortcoming, then you are a fortunate man. Not many husbands would complain of such a fault, sir! But tell me, how long will your business keep you in England, Mr Oliver?' said Mrs Southeran. 'I can imagine that you must also be quite anxious to return to Boston.' The Olivers looked blank. She went on, 'Your little son. I am sure you must both be missing him.'

In the circumstances this was an unfortunate remark, but Eleanor was never quite sure afterwards whether her mother had made it deliberately or not. Evadne went paler than ever, and Mr Oliver looked embarrassed. He said finally, 'We miss him of course. But he is well cared for in Boston. I am hoping to return quite soon, Mrs Southeran, but I am not quite sure when. We may yet see Marianne married.' His eye rested on Mr Guthrie, still deep in conversation with Phoebe, and he smiled at Evadne. 'Quite soon,' he repeated, as if to reassure her.

Mr Guthrie rose and came over to the little group round Mrs Southeran's sofa. 'Forgive me. I have been catching up on Phoebe's news. It is sad about Gilbert Gardiner. How are you, Evadne?'

There was no sign of consciousness in either face. 'Well, thank you,' was the brief reply. The group lapsed into silence until Mrs Southeran made some remark about the glorious weather Somerset was enjoying, and how fortunate the visitors were. Mr Oliver took up the conversational gambit and went on to amuse his hostess with a description of the scenery he had admired as he had wandered, lost, the day before.

'Then I met your lovely daughter, ma'am, and was rescued. A reversal of roles, wouldn't you say? The Beast saved by Beauty?'

'Where was this, Oliver?' asked Mr Guthrie abruptly.

'Some valley or other. I believe it was where Miss Southeran had her accident.'

Phoebe Gardiner said, 'You've had an accident, Miss Southeran? So that was why your foot was bandaged up when I saw you in the library? I was quite worried about it, but I didn't like to ask what was wrong. Gilbert had an uncle who suffered dreadfully with gout, but he used to get ridiculously angry if anyone mentioned it.'

'I think my daughter is safe from gout, Mrs Gardiner,' said Mrs Southeran solemnly. 'We have never had any in the family, and Eleanor is very abstemious.'

Mr Guthrie gave a curious choking sound, which he turned into a cough, and Eleanor said hastily, 'It was kind of you to worry, but, as you see, it is perfectly cured now. Tell me, are you planning to make any excursions while you are here? Lyme Regis is very pretty.'

# CHAPTER ELEVEN

THINKING it over afterwards, Eleanor realised that apart from that one question the only exchange between the two men had taken place shortly before Mr Guthrie left.

'Guthrie, I need a word with you. When may I call?'

'There are workmen all over my house at the moment, but I should think the library would be free. How about tomorrow at noon? You are not working at the moment, are you, Miss Southeran?'

Eleanor had shaken her head, cleared her throat and said, 'No. Indeed, I have almost finished, Mr Guthrie. A day or two longer, and then I will not trouble you any more. Tomorrow's work can easily be left to another time.'

She had done her best to keep her voice calm, but a slight tremble at the end had betrayed her anxiety, at least to Mr Guthrie. His expression had softened and he'd said, 'I am sorry not to have seen you these past days. I think we, too, have things to discuss. May I see you tomorrow afternoon?' He'd turned to Mr Oliver. 'I don't think our talk will take very long, do you?'

Mr Oliver had not replied immediately. He'd looked first at Eleanor, then at Phoebe, then back at Eleanor again. There had been a look of speculation in his eye, as if he was making an assessment. Eleanor had suddenly no longer liked him quite so much. She'd turned her head away and looked instead at Mr Guthrie.

'What? Oh, no!' said Mr Oliver. 'It won't take long at all, but it is urgent. I should prefer to see you today if that is possible. I want to ask you about some property of mine.' Something in Mr Oliver's voice caused Eleanor to hold her breath. She saw that Mr Guthrie was smiling. But it was a very different smile from the one he had employed to Phoebe Gardiner.

'Tonight, then. At eight. I shall forward to it. Mrs Southeran, I must thank you for inviting me in to such an...interesting occasion.' His voice was solemn but there was an undercurrent of laughter in it, which made Mrs Southeran smile.

'You are, as always, welcome, Jonas.'

This provoked another sharp look from Mr Oliver.

'Jonas, you cannot be going! I haven't talked to you nearly long enough.' Phoebe Gardiner followed Mr Guthrie to the door and put her hand on his arm. She gave him a look from her gentian eyes and pouted prettily. 'Don't go yet. Please?'

'You are an outrageous minx, Phoebe,' he said, looking at her indulgently. 'I am sorry to observe that time has not taught you how to behave.'

'I always like it when you tease me, Jonas. But you know that I never stand on ceremony with you. And I am sure Mrs Southeran understands——' this was said with a brilliant smile at her hostess '—what it is like to meet an old friend—a very old friend—in a strange country. Now I wish you to be serious. If you cannot stay now, we must meet another time. When are you going to call on me? Soon, I hope?'

'Will the day after tomorrow suit? I should like to see your mother again, too.'

It was evident that this did not suit Mrs Gardiner at

all—she had clearly had something more intimate in mind—but Mr Guthrie overrode her protests and took his leave of them all.

After the other visitors had departed a few minutes later, Mrs Southeran collapsed into her sofa and gave way to her amusement. 'You warned me about Phoebe Gardiner, Nell, though you really didn't do her justice. But you were right in one thing—there is something very taking about her, in spite of her total self-absorption. There's no malice in Phoebe Gardiner. I am not at all sure I could say the same of her sister. There's a deep one. I wonder what the Olivers are up to?'

Eleanor did not ask her mother what she meant. She, too, had been aware of the undertones. And what was the exact relationship betwen Mr Guthrie and Mr Oliver? Not a friendly one. The smile Jonas had given Mr Oliver just before he left had made her blood run cold. . .

The same smile was on Mr Guthrie's face that evening when the two men were left alone. Mr Oliver had walked in behind the housekeeper to find his host sitting at a table, on which stood a handsome colza lamp. The pool of light was directed on to some papers which were spread out before him, and the upper half of Mr Guthrie's face was in shadow. After seeing that the tray with wine and biscuits was to hand, Mrs Cartwright left the room, closing the heavy door quietly behind her.

The ladies of Combe St James would not have recognised their charming favourite in the man who now stood facing Jonas Guthrie. His face was hard and watchful and his hands clenched and unclenched as he waited impatiently for the housekeeper to leave. His manners had lost some of their charm, too.

'Where is he?' he asked as soon as they were alone.

'No, no. Let me offer you a glass of wine first, Oliver. And do sit down.'

'Damn you, what have you done with him?'

'Sit down, Oliver! And take this glass of wine. You might need it.'

Mr Oliver sat down and drained the glass in one long draught. 'Damn you, now will you tell me where he is?'

'I take it you mean Christopher Digby? You would scarcely show this degree of concern for anyone else — not even Evadne. But I see you have finished your wine. Allow me.' Mr Guthrie poured another glass.

Mr Oliver sat staring at his host. 'You're playing a dangerous game, Guthrie. I hope you haven't forgotten what I could do if I chose.'

'No, I haven't forgotten.'

'I'll do it, too, if you don't tell me what you've done with Christopher. Or do you think to hold me to ransom?'

'No,' said Mr Guthrie, his lip curling, but his voice still calm. 'I don't deal in ransoms, any more than I deal in blackmail. I leave that to people of your kidney.'

Mr Oliver got up and leaned over the desk. 'In that case, my high-minded friend, you'd better do as I ask. Perhaps you don't believe I'll do what I say?'

'Sit down, Oliver! I do believe that you would make public the facts about Henry Anstey's misdeeds, in spite of the bargain we made at the time in Boston. But I also think that you might find the impact of your tales would not be as great as you once thought. Henry Anstey has been dead these two years now. There's a new generation of politicians and businessmen in Boston. They're not going to make a fuss about a dead man's peccadilloes.' He smiled cynically. 'They're too busy covering up their own!'

'What about Amelia? You were so devoted to her—how will she feel? And Marianne?'

'I'm sorry about Amelia. I would have preferred her not to know the truth about Henry, but I have now come to believe that she will recover in time. Marianne? I think Marianne's position is sufficiently secure to survive any slight scandal you might cause. It's a long way from London to Boston, and there's an even greater divide between her future world and yours. She is already part of the Morrissey's circle and they will protect their own. No, I don't think you can blight her young life now.' Mr Guthrie got up. 'So. I am no longer as ready as I once was to jump to your whip, Oliver.'

'Henry Anstey was still a criminal. He embezzled the state and he borrowed money he had no right to from his clients. I still think I could create enough of a scandal to make you all rue the day.'

'God's teeth, man, what do you think I've been doing for the last two years? The money Henry stole—you observe that I am not afraid to use the correct word—has been repaid, the contracts he sold have been destroyed! Did you imagine that I would be content to live my life under the heel of a blackmailer forever? No, Oliver, believe me, there's not much evidence to uphold any accusations you choose to make.'

It was clear that Mr Oliver had suffered a shock. 'You cunning devil, Guthrie,' he said slowly. 'You never intended from the beginning to keep to our bargain!'

'Oh, indeed I did! I have! I kept silent when people whispered that I was a villain and a rake. I paid and paid, but allowed the world to think that I had ruined the Ansteys with my own greed. I had other sources of wealth with which to survive the disaster, and I flattered myself that I could eventually outlive the gossip. Indeed, I was on the way to doing it, at least with people whose opinion I most value.

'Yes, Oliver, I was prepared to let you and Evadne get away with your tricks. It was the price you forced me to pay for Amelia's peace of mind, and Marianne's future. But I would have been a fool not to use the time since then to ensure that I could be free of you when I wished.' He gazed sombrely into his glass.

'But then you decided that you wanted more,' he went on. 'God knows how, but you found out that Amelia would inherit what was left of my fortune if I died. So you decided that I would be better dead. Was Evadne in on that, too? You surely cannot have supposed that I would suffer Christopher's attempts to murder me and do nothing about it? My willingness to do anything to save Amelia and Marianne two years ago gave you a false impression. You must have thought me a mindless idiot!'

'What have you done with Christopher?'

'I warned Christopher. I don't usually give people a second chance.'

'You've killed him!' said Oliver, his voice rising.

'I would have, if it had been necessary. Though he

wouldn't have deserved it—he's a poor thing. Your tool, as well as your catamite.'

'*What* have you *done* with him?'

'I'm afraid you've lost him, Oliver, perhaps forever. I've shipped him out to Madras—that should keep him out of the way for a while. I shouldn't be surprised if he stays. A handsome lad like Christopher, with Christopher's propensities, could well find a rich patron out there.'

Mr Oliver thrust his chair back and leapt up. 'You ...you fiend, Guthrie!' he shouted. 'I'll kill you for this!'

He drew a wicked-looking stiletto out of his pocket and launched himself at his enemy without thought, without caution. Mr Guthrie caught Oliver's arm with ease and twisted it back till the knife was wrested from him. Then he forced Oliver to his knees, and, still holding him in an iron grip, he said softly, 'Go back to America, Oliver, and take Evadne with you. For Amelia's sake, I won't pursue this, but I don't want to see either of you any more. Now leave me, you scum.' He flung Oliver away from him, and the man lay abjectly on the floor, moaning Christopher's name.

'Get up!'

Oliver pulled himself together and got up.

'There's just one more thing, my friend,' said Mr Guthrie, with a grim smile. 'In case you still have any lingering ambition, I should tell you that I've changed my lawyers and my will. You won't gain by my death, Oliver.'

'I know why you're doing this, Guthrie.' Oliver's voice was low, but it shook with the intensity of his feelings. 'You're planning to marry. I've heard the rumours in London. That's why you're so eager to clear your name, and that's why you've changed your will. And why. . .' He stopped as his feelings overcame him. 'And why you've taken Christopher from me. But I swear, Guthrie, by God I swear, I will make you sorry for it.' His voice rose, and his face, usually so pale, was suffused with blood. 'You will suffer as you are making me suffer. Take what care you like of your wife-to-be, Guthrie. Once I am certain who she is, I shall see that you never marry her!'

He tore out of the room and down the stairs. Mr Guthrie listened as Oliver's horse galloped away as if chased by the hounds of hell. He stood for some time, lost in his thoughts, and, from the look on his face, they were disquieting. Then he cursed, flung himself into the chair by the table, and poured himself a generous glass of brandy.

The knowledge that she was to see Jonas the next day, that she would have her chance to explain how far she had changed her mind, kept Eleanor awake half the night. She tossed and turned, planning what she would say, rearranging this, rejecting that, until she eventually fell into an uneasy sleep. But when she woke again it was still early. She decided to get up—a walk might clear her mind. The early morning mist was still lying on the fields, but the sun would soon disperse it. It was going to be a beautiful day.

Her heart lifted and she was suddenly quite certain that it would be all right. Jonas would forgive her, and then they would carry on as before until such time as he could, in his own words, say what he really wanted to say. She was practically certain she knew what that would be. She had had little experience of such things, it was true, but surely he couldn't have held her as he had, kissed her as he had, spoken as he had, without loving her!

She wandered down the covered path towards the main house. This was where he had first kissed her. Their argument that day, too, had started when she had tried to defend Threlfall. That had been a mistake, as well. Jonas had been angry, and she had been so unhappy when all her work on Stanyards estate had seemed to be worth nothing. He had tried to comfort her, but his own honesty had got in the way.

She smiled at the thought. It was so very Jonas-like, that inability to fudge, to lie, even when it was to his advantage to do so. And then he had kissed her. . . What a stormy relationship theirs had been! Almost immediately after that, when everything had seemed to be going so well, she had accused him of trying to sell her father's books. Well, at least all that was over. Whatever happened when she met Jonas, she was sure now that she could trust him.

Eleanor turned back towards the Dower House. It was too early to call on Jonas, and yet the afternoon seemed an eternity away. But just as she came into the courtyard he appeared round the corner, much as he had done the first time she had seen him here at Stanyards. He even had Becky with him. There was a frown on his face, and he was so preoccupied that he did not at first see her.

'Jonas! Down, Becky! Jonas, I'm so glad you're here. It seemed an age till this afternoon.'

'Eleanor—I. . .I. . . What are you doing up so early? I didn't expect to see you.'

'What are you doing here? You look as if you are inspecting the Dower House. You are not thinking of altering it, are you? My mother likes it just as it is.'

'No, I. . .I was wondering how safe it was.'

'*Safe*? Of course it is safe!'

'Yes, of course. But I think I'll have the men look at it, all the same.' Eleanor decided not to pursue the matter. She didn't want to start her apology with a disagreement. He went on, 'How can I help you?' His voice, which till now had been perfectly normal, had suddenly become cool. He was clearly remembering their quarrel. Eleanor hastened to put things right.

'I want to apologise, to ask you to forgive me yet again, Jonas. I was wrong about Threlfall.'

'Yes, he's a nasty piece of work. But I suppose it was natural you should want to see things for yourself.' He still sounded distant. She had hurt him more than she had thought by her lack of confidence.

'No, I should have known that you would not take such a drastic decision without very good cause.' Eleanor smiled ruefully at him. 'I never seem to learn, do I?'

Jonas looked at her almost as if she were a stranger. His mind seemed to be elsewhere and it was a minute before he spoke. 'No,' he said finally. 'No, you don't seem to learn. It's a pity. I'm sorry, you'll have to excuse me—I have things to do. I must get back.' He took a few steps, the stopped and turned. 'I forgot. I have to go to Badgers Farm this afternoon, so I shan't be in. Did you wish to see me about anything else?'

'No,' said Eleanor numbly.

'Right. Come, Becky!' He gave her a nod and strode up the path to Stanyards without looking at her again.

Eleanor was stunned. What had happened to the man she thought she knew? This behaviour was ungenerous, to say the least, and to stride away like that, without giving her any chance to respond, to protest... Was what she had done so awful that he couldn't face her? But he hadn't seemed to feel that the day before at her mother's gathering. He had been cool at first, but towards the end she had been quite optimistic.

She swallowed hard—in a moment she would disgrace herself by bursting into tears. She must get back to her room.

'Marnin', Miss Nell! It's going ter be a fine old day again.'

'Oh, good morning, Daniel,' said Eleanor with commendable self-discipline. 'Yes, it will...it will be lovely, I think.'

'I saw Mrs Gardiner yesterday. The others had told me 'bout 'er, but my, 'er's a beauty!'

'She's lovely,' Eleanor agreed.

Something in her voice must have warned Daniel that his Miss Nell wasn't feeling very happy. He came closer and said kindly, 'Not a patch on you, though. Why, there bain't a soul on the estate that don't think you're the prettiest girl in Somerset.'

Eleanor laughed tremulously and said, 'Thank you! It isn't true, but it's kind of you to say so, and I'm flattered.'

Daniel was still anxious to comfort. 'And folks like working for you. They do say that Mrs Gardiner is fearsome hard on that poor maid of hers.'

'Come, Daniel, you know we mustn't gossip about Mrs Gardiner.'

'Oh, I'm not one for gossip, Miss Nell. I leave that to the wimmin!' He grinned and went off to the stables.

Eleanor was left with her own thoughts again. Phoebe Gardiner was not only lovely, she was also determined to win Jonas Guthrie again. And, from what she had observed yesterday, Jonas still had a great deal of affection for her. Was that why he had been so cool this morning? No, she would not believe that to be the case. Jonas was not so fickle that he would turn to a newcomer after being so close to Eleanor. But she isn't a newcomer, her private devil whispered. He was once engaged to her, remember?

She shook her head impatiently in an effort to clear her thoughts. Jonas Guthrie was a man of honour. She must hold on to that fact. He would not have all but declared himself to her, Eleanor, if he had had any doubts or reservations. She had hurt him—worse than she had thought—and it was going to take time for him to recover. Meanwhile she must act as naturally as possible until he did.

It was easy to come to a sensible conclusion. It was much harder to act accordingly, especially for one of Eleanor's impetuous temper. Several times during the course of the day she decided that the situation was absurd, that she must seek Jonas out, tell him how much his good opinion meant to her, plead with him for understanding and sympathy. But his manner that morning had been so brusque, so forbidding, that she was afraid of another rebuff.

She would have confided in her mother, but Mrs Southeran was finishing the project for her literary review, and Eleanor did not want to distract her. Things would come right eventually, she was sure. She must just have patience and trust to her instinct that time would cure the rift between herself and Jonas.

She confined herself to tasks about the Dower House, thus avoiding the risk of meeting him either on the estate or in his library. But after a day or two of this she decided that she could reasonably set about finishing the catalogue, and went up to Stanyards.

Eleanor had found a number of problems in cataloguing the books, and these she had till now put aside. She decided that she would sort them out today before going any further. In order to do this she would have to search through her father's archives, many of which were still stored in his safe-room at Stanyards. Not many non-family members knew of this room, and she was certain that no one had discovered it, even during the recent renovations.

During the middle ages Stanyards had been a fortified manor. Later generations had added to the house, but when religious and political loyalties had come to be a source of trouble part of the original defensive wall had been turned into a hiding place for people in danger—priests, soldiers, even rebellious members of the family. This little room now served as a strong-room. It lay at the far end of the library, and was reached through what appeared to be part of the window embrasure. This gave accesss to a long stone screen passage which opened out into a tiny room in the thickness of the corner wall. The room itself was entirely of stone, lit and ventilated by a narrow slit which was so arranged as to be invisible from the ground outside.

After extracting the documents she wanted out of the chest in which they were stored, Eleanor spread them out and studied them. She was so completely absorbed in the papers that she was at first only dimly aware of voices. One curious feature of this room was that, unless the door to it was firmly shut, conversations taking place in the library were clearly audible there. Eleanor listened for a moment—a woman's voice. Annie or Dora? They must be cleaning the library, and she tried to remember whether she had left anything on the table. No, she had come straight into the safe-room before starting anything else. That was good—she could stay here until they left. The older servants might suspect the existence of a secret room, but none of them knew exactly where its entrance was, and Eleanor didn't wish to reveal it.

She had been very careless. Not only had she forgotten to follow her usual practice of locking the library door before using the safe-room, she had even left the door in the window embrasure slightly ajar. She would just have to hope that the servants didn't notice it. She went back to her papers, but something about the timbre of the voice in the library caught her attention. It wasn't Annie, or Dora. That voice belonged to Evadne Oliver!

There was a short silence, then Eleanor heard Jonas say, 'All the same, Evadne, I think it neither wise nor even desirable that you should come here. Hasn't your husband yet given you an account of our conversation the other night?'

'Nathaniel doesn't tell me everything, Jonas.'

'My impression is, however, that you are usually in his confidence. You were certainly both in league when you blackmailed me into giving you a handsome sum of money. Why did you do it, Evadne?'

Eleanor was in a dilemma. This was clearly an intensely private conversation, and she should not be listening to it, however involuntarily. But what was she to do? To reveal herself now would betray the secret of this room, not only to Stanyards' new owner, who might reasonably expect to be told, but also to this woman, a stranger. Besides, it was already too late to avoid embarrassment on all sides. She would have to keep silent. Evadne was speaking.

'You know why. I was desperate. Father was dead, and none of us had any money—except you.'

'But had you no compunction about what you were threatening? No concern for your mother's feelings? Or Marianne's?'

The beautiful voice was now full of scorn. 'You never really understood, did you, Jonas? I had— indeed I *have* no compunction about any of it. I despised all of them. My father was a cheat and a liar, my mother a silly woman afraid of everything—even life itself—and my sisters. . .ah, my sisters! They were beautiful.' The manner in which Evadne pronounced this last word made it sound obscene.

There was distaste in Jonas's voice as he said, 'You were cleverer than any of them. Was that not enough?'

'Enough? No, it wasn't anything like enough. You are a man, Jonas. It is not demanded of men that they should be beautiful. Clever? Yes. Strong? Yes. Well-mannered? Perhaps. But a woman—she is nothing if she is not beautiful.

'As a child I would always behave better than Phoebe, but Phoebe was the one who was taken before the guests, and petted, and made much of. I knew my tables long before she mastered them, but it was Phoebe of whom everyone spoke with pride. And then there was Marianne. A beautiful, amiable doll, the image of my elder sister, but so good! All the world loved Marianne! Why should I feel sorry for them?'

'This jealousy wasn't necessary, Evadne. You were witty, amusing, clever... I always enjoyed your company.'

'It was Phoebe you asked to marry you, Jonas! It was Marianne's fate you were concerned with, not mine!'

There was a silence in the room. Eleanor held her breath. She was learning at last about the Ansteys and their relationship with Jonas Guthrie, and, though it was not in a manner she would have wished, she could not now have stopped listening if her life had depended on it.

'What about Oliver?' said Jonas slowly. 'What part did he play in all this?'

'I thought Nathaniel Oliver was offering me what no one else had offered before. To come first in his attentions. To be important to him. I couldn't resist it.'

'You didn't know about Christopher?'

Eleanor heard a rustle of movement. When Evadne spoke again her voice was clearer—she must be standing next to the window.

'I thought Chistopher was simply the son of an old friend. It...it was a shock when I found out what the relationship really was. Nathaniel had never given me any reason to suppose that he was interested in men as well as women.'

Jonas drew in his breath through his teeth, and his voice was, for the first time, more sympathetic. 'I'm sorry. It must have been very hard.'

There was sudden passion in Evadne's voice. 'Don't pity me, Jonas Guthrie! I need no one's pity, least of all yours! It turned out much better than one might have expected. We have a delightful *ménage à trois*. Nathaniel admires me enormously—I am so much cleverer than he. It's one way of being needed.'

'But you don't have a *ménage à quatre*.'

'What do you mean?'

'The baby, Evadne. What about the baby?'

There was another silence. When Evadne spoke it was once again in her normal manner, devoid of feeling. 'I think you know about the baby. Don't you, Jonas?'

'Yes.'

'I thought so. It was never strong, and it didn't survive the first winter. We decided not to tell you—instead we used the money you settled on it for ourselves. We needed it more than you. Are you angry, Jonas?'

'No; why should I be angry? It's no more than I would have expected. What does make me angry is the way you speak of the child. "It" wasn't strong, "it" didn't survive—did the baby mean so little to you? "It" was a human being. A boy.'

'From the moment it was born we knew it wouldn't live for long. I wouldn't let myself be fond of it. And Nathaniel wasn't interested in it at all,' she said indifferently. 'But this isn't leading us anywhere, Jonas. I've come today for a purpose.'

'Which is?'

'To warn you.'

'Warn me? Why would you wish to do that?'

'I don't know what passed between you and Nathaniel the other night. I do know that he intends you no good.'

'I told him that I had put a stop to Christopher's attempts to kill me by shipping him off to India.'

'So that's why he was in such a rage! Jonas, he will kill you himself for this!'

'I doubt it. Nathaniel Oliver hasn't the stomach to do anything so risky himself. But you've come here to warn me. How very kind of you, Evadne!'

'I still have some feeling for you——'

'Spare me that, my dear. You've never felt anything for anyone except yourself. In your own way you are every bit as ruthlessly self-absorbed as Phoebe. You are here for your own purposes—whatever they are.'

'If you will pay no heed for yourself, then I want you to warn Eleanor Southeran.'

Eleanor almost dropped the papers she was holding. What on earth did Evadne mean?

'Miss Southeran? What about?'

'I think you love her—and Nathaniel will try to hurt you through her.'

'That would be his way,' said Jonas contemptuously. 'Having failed twice to have me killed, he might just get up enough courage to attack a woman. But why should he think it would hurt me particularly? Miss Southeran is a charming girl—young woman, I suppose I should say, for she's past the age of being a girl. But, apart from being the daughter of an old friend, she means nothing to me.'

# CHAPTER TWELVE

ELEANOR had to put a hand to her mouth to stifle a protest when she heard these words. She stood, unable to believe them, sure it was a mistake. She must have misheard. She must! But Evadne was speaking. Eleanor strained to listen.

'He has heard that you are planning to marry, and he believes you mean to marry Miss Southeran.'

'You mean he's been picking up gossip where he can and has put two and two together to make seventeen!' said Jonas with scorn. 'It's true that when I was in London I looked at houses there with a view to acquiring one, and that gave rise to rumours that I intended to marry. But I assure you—and him—that, if I did marry, I would look for someone who would suit the life I intend to lead, not a pretty little country girl!

'I'll be frank with you, Evadne—there's no reason you shouldn't know; it'll be public knowledge shortly—I've been offered a title. And now that I'm free of your family's affairs there's no reason why I shouldn't accept it. I've a fancy to become a great lord. Can you imagine Miss Southeran as a great lady? I can't.'

'People say that you've been seen in her company a great deal. . .'

'Well, where's the harm in that? A man seeks his amusement where he can, and, believe me, there aren't many alternatives down here. She has helped me to while away the odd hour. Besides, it was very useful—I learned a lot about the estate from her. Has Eleanor Southeran been claiming that there's more to it than that? I'm sorry for her if she has, but I've never given her the slightest reason to suppose I was serious.'

'I see... What about Phoebe? You were serious about her once.'

'Ah, Phoebe! She's more the thing. I can imagine her in society, can't you? And she and Marianne would make as lovely a pair of viscountesses as you could wish to see. But there again, as you reminded me just before, Phoebe hasn't a great deal to offer a man other than her beauty. No, if I were to marry—I say, *if*—I think I would look for someone suitable in next year's crop of débutantes. I may be a little old, and my looks won't win me a bride, but my wealth will. Oliver may threaten, but we both know he wants to return to Boston. He'll give up in time. I don't mind waiting—I have no special candidate in mind.' He chuckled. 'I'll enjoy inspecting the field.'

Eleanor sat like a stone in the room. It seemed to have become icy. The hateful voice went on, 'What's the matter? I know what it is—you are wishing you were free. It's a pity you're not, Evadne. I'm beginning to think I picked the wrong sister all those years ago. But you never gave any sign...'

'If I were free...?'

'No.' Jonas's voice was full of regret. 'It wouldn't do, my dear. Much as I'm intrigued at the thought of having you, I'm not going to jeopardise my future by marrying a divorced woman—nor a widow. But I won't deny that I'd like Oliver out of the way—in

Boston. If you could persuade him to return, there might be something in it for you. . .'

Evadne's voice was colourless again. 'I'll see what I can do. Goodbye, Jonas.'

Eleanor heard Evadne's footsteps fade and then the sound of a door closing. There was a sudden release of breath from Jonas Guthrie and she heard him slump into a chair. She could hardly bear the thought of being so close to him. She wanted to get away, right away, never see him again. But she sat there like a statue, not thinking, trying not to feel, waiting for him to leave the library.

Eventually he got up. She heard him opening and shutting some drawers and then the door to the library slammed again. He was gone. Like a mechanical doll Eleanor put her papers away—she did not know when she would be back to deal with them, perhaps not ever. . . Then she edged her way along the passage and cautiously peered out. The library was, as she had expected, empty. When she heard the sound of a horse outside she looked out of the window—he was riding away along the lane towards Badgers. Swiftly Eleanor walked out of the library, out of Stanyards, and out of Jonas Guthrie's life.

When Eleanor had learned that Stanyards was lost to her she had roamed the estate all day in an effort to rid herself of the pain. This course was not possible now—there was the danger that she might inadvertently come across its owner, and that thought made her feel physically ill. Instead she went to earth. She walked as unseeing, as heedless as that first time, but with the clear purpose of seeking the refuge of the

Dower House. No one saw her, no one stopped her and once she reached her bedchamber there she sat huddled in a chair for hours.

Towards evening Betty came into the room and stopped short when she saw her. 'Miss Nell! Whatever are you doing there? I thought you were out!'

Eleanor turned her head away to the window. 'I. . . I didn't feel well. . .'

'Indeed you don't! You're cold as ice!' exclaimed Betty, feeling Eleanor's hands. 'Come, Miss Nell, let me get you into bed.' She bustled about, calling on one of the maids to warm the sheets, and sending another to make a hot drink. By this time reaction was causing Eleanor to shiver, and Betty was convinced that she had caught a feverish cold. 'You shouldn't have done all that visiting on the farms, Miss Nell. There's a lot of sickness about down there. Let's hope it is a cold, and not something worse!'

By this time Mrs Southeran had been told, and, ignoring Betty's protests about the risk, she came hurrying into Eleanor's room.

'What nonsense! As if I should not wish to see for myself what is wrong! Eleanor, my dear child!'

While Betty scolded and Mrs Southeran talked of sending someone for Dr Smithson, Eleanor lay passive and silent in her bed, wishing they would go away. Eventually the two women decided that Eleanor should be made as comfortable as possible for the present and that Dr Smithson should be summoned if she grew worse the next day. Betty fussed about for a minute or two longer, then left Mrs Southeran in charge. There was silence in the little room.

After a while Mrs Southeran said tentatively, 'Nell?

Are you awake?' Eleanor slowly turned her head towards her mother, who was sitting in a chair by the bed with a shaded lamp on the table next to her. 'Does it hurt? Does your head ache?'

Eleanor looked at her mother's anxious face and whispered, 'No. Not my head. Try not to worry, Mama. I'm not ill, truly. I'll...I'll be all right tomorrow.'

'Something has happened, hasn't it? No, don't turn your head away again. I won't pry.'

'Perhaps I'll tell you tomorrow. I can't just now. I think I'd like to sleep.' Mrs Southeran nodded, and got up and kissed her.

'Call me if you need me, my darling. I'll see you in the morning.' They both knew that Eleanor was not likely to sleep, but rather that she wanted to be alone. 'Do you wish me to leave the lamp?'

'No—you take it.'

Mrs Southeran went out quietly, leaving the door open a crack lest her daughter should call, and the room was in darkness.

Eleanor lay dry-eyed, staring at the shaft of moonlight which came through the curtains. If asked she would have said afterwards that her mind had been empty throughout the night—she was certainly not conscious of thought. But the next morning she found she had made a decision.

Mrs Southeran was seated at the breakfast table when Eleanor walked in. 'Good morning, Mama,' she said, kissing her mother. 'I hope you slept well? As you see, your anxieties were unnecessary last night. I am

perfectly well again this morning. No fever, no aches
and pains!'

Mrs Southeran looked at her daughter's hollow eyes
and pale cheeks, at the evidence of the control she
was exercising in her trembling hands and set mouth,
and said gently, 'I'm glad. Will you have some
breakfast?'

'Of course!' Smiling brightly, Eleanor sat down. 'I
would like to talk to you, Mama.' Mrs Southeran
looked up sharply, but it was clear that Eleanor was
not about to say anything about her distress of the
night before. She went on, 'You remember Aunt
Hetty wrote the other day to say that she and my
uncle were back in London? I think I should like to
visit them again. Would you object? I am sure Cousin
Louisa would be ready to stay with you here.'

The fleeting expression of dismay on Mrs
Southeran's face was quickly replaced with a smile. 'I
think that is an excellent idea! I expect Hetty is
missing Bella still, and would like your company. She
probably wishes to carry on improving you, Nell, or
die in the attempt! And as for me, I really do not need
Louisa. I am so much better now that I think I should
prefer to be on my own. How long would you wish to
be in London?'

Eleanor caught the wistful note in her mother's
voice, and came over to kneel down beside her. 'Not
very long. Two weeks? Three at the most. I. . .' Her
voice showed signs of strain. 'I must get away, Mama.'

'It's Jonas, isn't it, Nell?'

'Yes,' said Eleanor briefly. 'But I cannot talk about
it. And you must not worry, Mama—no lasting dam-

age has been done. But I need some time to come to terms with it.'

'Well, then, you must go as soon as possible! I have a little money saved. You shall travel in comfort!'

A letter to Lady Walcot was dispatched immediately, but, having seen her daughter's impatience to be away, Mrs Southeran decided that it was unnecessary to wait for a reply—they both knew what it would be. Within three days of the scene in the library Eleanor was on her way to London. Mrs Southeran had a word with Betty, and soon it became known about the neighbourhood that Miss Southeran had gone to London on an errand of mercy. When she had heard that her aunt was confined to her bed, and that Bella, Lady Walcot's daughter, was still away, Miss Southeran had volunteered to look after her. In this way, any possible curiosity about Eleanor's sudden departure was satisfied. But Mrs Southeran did not leave it at that. Jonas Guthrie was invited to the Dower House the day after Eleanor had left.

'I am glad you've come, Jonas,' said Mrs Southeran as her visitor came in. 'I wondered a little whether you would.'

'Of course I would come, when you send such an intriguing invitation. I am not used to such formality from you. How are you? And...and how is Eleanor?'

'You know she has gone to London?'

'Yes, I had heard. Lady Walcot is ill, I hear. I'm sorry.'

'Sorry that my sister-in-law is ill, or sorry that Eleanor is not here?'

His face closed up. 'That is a strange question, Mrs Southeran.'

'And I want an honest answer, Jonas.' There was a pause during which Jonas Guthrie stared moodily at his hostess. 'Well?'

'I have to admit that I am glad Eleanor is not here for the moment.'

'Why?'

'I'm not sure I am prepared to tell you.'

'If you value my friendship, if you wish to retain the confidence I have always shown in you, you will tell me, Jonas,' said Mrs Southeran steadily. 'You have made my daughter unhappier than she has ever been in her life, and I wish to know why.'

'We...we had a disagreement—a trivial one, you would say.'

'About something on the estate? Threlfall, perhaps?'

'What else would we quarrel about?' he said, with an involuntary laugh. 'It's the only thing we differ on. And you cannot say it hasn't happened before.'

'Exactly! But in this case it is more than that. What have you said to her?'

'I?' he asked, startled. 'Why, nothing.'

'Jonas, stop playing with me. I am deadly serious.'

'And so am I, by God,' he said with feeling.

'Then you will tell me why you have made Eleanor so unhappy, when you once promised me that you would not. And I trusted you.'

Jonas looked at his hostess doubtfully, then seemed to come to some conclusion. 'I have always confided in you. May I confide in you this time with an assurance that you will tell no one—no one at all, not even Eleanor—what I say?'

'If it is important to Eleanor's happiness, then yes, you have my word. I will tell no one.'

'It may be important to Eleanor's. . .safety. What would you say if I told you that any interest I show in her puts her at risk?'

Mrs Southeran stared at him. 'I'd say you were moonstruck! What on earth are you talking about?'

'Nathaniel Oliver. I think he is mad, but I dare not ignore what he said. He thinks he can best punish me for something I have done to him by. . .hurting anyone I hold dear.'

'Nathaniel Oliver said this?' asked Mrs Southeran incredulously. 'I could imagine it of his wife, perhaps, but not of that milksop!'

'Believe me, I think it is wise to take him seriously for the moment. I am hoping he will eventually give up and go back to Boston, and I have done my best to see that he does, but until then I dare not provoke his malice. And consequently I have used the excuse of our quarrel to avoid Eleanor's company.'

'And do you hold Eleanor dear? I know I have asked you this before, but things have advanced since then, have they not?'

He turned round and said fiercely, 'Not even to you will I say anything of my feelings! When the time comes I shall make them clear to the world, including the peron they most affect, but until Oliver is safely out of the country the only course is for them to remain unknown. Eleanor is safe in London. Let her stay there for a while.'

'Very well. But I still do not understand, Jonas. When she left she was. . .not just unhappy. She was devastated. Are you sure there has been nothing more than a certain coolness between you?'

'Quite certain.'

'Then someone else must have said something to her. I wonder who it was. . .?'

'Mrs Southeran, I beg of you, do nothing to make my interest in Eleanor apparent. Or hers in me.'

'No, I see that I mustn't. But I must write to her— oh, don't worry! I shall not tell her of Oliver's threats.'

'Can I ask you not even to mention my name? Oliver is like a cat—he scents things out. I would trust no one to conceal things from him.'

'May I not even tell her that you are not as indifferent as she apparently thinks?'

'For God's sake, do not! I cannot over-emphasise the danger.'

Mrs Southeran looked at him wide-eyed. 'You really *are* afraid of him, aren't you, Jonas? Then I will do as you say.'

He went to the door, but stopped there and said with uncharacteristic hesitation, 'If you hear from Eleanor, could you. . .will you let me know—in confidence— how she is?'

'Yes, I will. Now go and get rid of Mr Oliver as quickly as you can.'

But after a while it seemed that Mr Oliver had decided to abandon his vendetta for the time being. Mrs Anstey and Phoebe were to travel to Oxfordshire for Marianne's wedding, and Mr and Mrs Oliver decided to accompany them. When Jonas gave this news to Mrs Southeran she thought for a moment, then said, 'But I cannot see that this changes the

situation as far as you and Mr Oliver are concerned—
unless he returns to Boston direct from the wedding?'

'No, he will not do that. I keep a very careful check
on the gentleman's actions, and the Olivers have left a
good number of their possessions at Church Cottage.
They will be back. But at least they will be occupied
for a while, enjoying themsleves in Oxfordshire—the
wedding might have been held in London!'

'That would have been worrying, I agree. I do not
like to think of Mr Oliver near Eleanor. Thank God
he isn't! But, tell me, is it true that Phoebe Gardiner
is also going with her mother? That is surely a sudden
decision—the last time I spoke to her she seemed set
on staying in Somerset.' When Jonas looked slightly
uncomfortable, she went on, 'Am I to take it she is
abandoning her pursuit of you, Jonas?'

'Let us say, rather, that when I mentioned one or
two very eligible gentlemen who were certain to be at
Marianne's wedding she decided her duty lay with her
family. I do not think she will return to Combe St
James. But I am glad to say that we parted friends.'

'I must make sure I see her before she leaves. I have
written a little poem for her—knowing her has given
me so much pleasure, I could do no less!'

Mrs Anstey, Mrs Gardiner and the Olivers set off in
state with the good wishes and admiration of the
neighbourhood, and after they had gone life in and
around Combe St James resumed its normal, unevent-
ful course. However, in picturing the Olivers safe in
Oxfordshire, Mrs Southeran and Jonas were deceiving
themselves. It was true that this was what the Olivers
had originally intended, but there was a change of

plan after the first day of their journey. It resulted from a conversation between man and wife in the Woolpack Inn at Trowbridge, where they spent the night.

'Phoebe is quite cast down, Nathaniel.'

'Really, my dear? Why?'

'It has become clear to her that she will not entice Jonas into her net again. She did not say so in so many words, but it is evident that he is no longer attracted to her—if he ever was.'

'Are you sure, Evadne? Perhaps he is feigning indifference to put us off?'

'No, I do not think so. There must be someone else. Yet I thought he was convincing about the Southeran girl.'

'Then perhaps what he told you was true—he intends to catch one of next year's fillies?'

'It's possible. Though. . .'

'What?'

'Well, why did Miss Southeran disappear so quickly to London?'

'Her aunt is ill.'

'Do you believe it? Might Jonas not have seen to it that she was sent out of the way? It is a possibility.'

There was a silence. Then Nathaniel Oliver said, 'My love, I think I may not, after all, come with you to Marianne's wedding. Weddings do not, as you know, interest me a great deal. Would you mind if I left the party when we reach the Bath Road, and take the stage instead to London? You have the two grooms to protect you.'

'Do not do anything rash, Nathaniel.'

'I would just like to see for myself if Lady Walcot is

ill. If not...perhaps we could test Mr Jonas Damned Guthrie's feelings. Do you think you could let someone in Combe St James know of our change of plan?'

'Let me see.... I could arrange for one of the men here to fetch something for me...something I had forgotten. I could write a note to Mrs Desmond. Now, what could it be...?'

Lady Walcot expressed surprised delight at seeing her niece so soon after her last visit, and her husband came in several times to interrupt Eleanor's conversation with her aunt just to say how pleased he was that she was back in London again.

'I've laid on a horse and groom for you, Eleanor, my dear. Don't let your aunt dissuade you from your early morning rides. Best time of the day.'

But, in the privacy of Lady Walcot's bedroom that night, the Walcots gave voice to their shock at the change in their niece's appearance. 'Anthea didn't say what was wrong. She merely asked me to take care of Eleanor until she was herself again. What can it be, Charles?'

'Has she been ill?'

'I don't think so.'

'Perhaps she's been crossed in love? That's often the case with females when there isn't any other explanation.'

'That's it, Charles! That is it! It's that man Guthrie! Oh, I know everyone hints now that he has been misjudged—though how that can be I don't know—but I *knew* no good would come of Eleanor's association with him. How could Anthea have sold Stanyards to him? It was simply asking for trouble.'

'Er. . .better not say anything to Eleanor, Hetty. If it isn't Guthrie, you'll have wasted your breath, and if it is. . .'

'Do you take me for a fool? We must distract her mind from it all until she forgets him. Once I am certain she is strong enough, I intend to show her a great deal more of London than she had time for in the spring. When are you free in the next few days, Charles?'

So after a day or two's rest Eleanor was taken on what was to prove a relentless round of pleasure. She welcomed the fact that she never stopped meeting people, visiting exhibitions, seeing the sights, that she never, ever seemed to have time to think—during the day.

It was different at night. Then, however exhausted she was, sleep eluded her till the early hours of the morning, and her mind turned and turned on a tread-mill of despair. She despised Jonas Guthrie for the creature he was, but, worse, she despised herself for falling victim to his lies. She had thought him honest. He was a liar and a cheat. She had thought him an idealist. He was a shabby trickster, filling her mind with his visions for the future, while all the time he had merely been making use of her. How could she live with the thought of her idiocy? She, who had taken such pride in the quickness of her wits, had congratulated herself on the independence of her opinions!

But, gradually, her aunt's care and her uncle's obvious pride in his niece had their effect. Her bruised spirit slowly began to heal, and Eleanor at last started to recover her self-respect.

She had been in London for two weeks, and was reluctantly beginning to think of returning to Somerset. If she had had only herself to think of, she would have stayed in London much longer, although, she thought bitterly, Guthrie had been right—she was a country girl at heart. After a while, life in the capital seemed too confined; there were too many streets and not enough greenery, too much smoke and not enough air. Her reluctance to go back was not so much a desire to stay in London, but more a dislike of returning to Stanyards.

But her mother was on her conscience. She really should not be left alone for too long. Perhaps she might persuade her to think of moving elsewhere? There was nothing to keep them at Stanyards now, and, as far as Eleanor was concerned, every reason why they should leave. There must be other places in Somerset which were as attractive—or nearly. She must talk to her mother when she got back.

Of course the Walcots were disappointed that she was planning to leave them so soon. They had made plans for the next month at least, and were already talking of Christmas for everyone on their estate in Kent. But Eleanor was adamant—for the moment she must return.

'Well, if you must, you must, Eleanor. And I have to say that you are looking a great deal more the thing than when you arrived. London has done you good.' Lady Walcot hesitated, then added, 'I have not enquired what was wrong, though I have my own ideas on the subject. But I should like to congratulate you, Eleanor, on the way you have refused to give in to your unhappiness. I have been full of admiration for the breeding and discipline you have shown—it has almost caused me to change my mind about this independence of yours.'

Eleanor was so touched at her aunt's tribute that she almost ruined the occasion by bursting into tears! But not quite. The hard days and even harder nights had taught her a great deal. She might have experienced uncontrollable passion, and, for a short while, paid for it with uncontrollable pain. But feelings of any kind were now firmly in her control again, and that was how they would stay.

Lady Walcot went on, 'I think you should choose what you wish to do before going back. Is there something that we still have not shown you?'

'You have shown me so much, I don't think there can be. . .unless. . .'

'Yes?'

'I should dearly love to see Vauxhall Gardens, Aunt Hetty. I've heard they are very pretty.'

'My dear, I think they have closed till next year—or are they open till the end of September? Let us hope so.'

It was soon established that the gardens were still open, and Lady Walcot set about arranging a party there with enthusiasm. In the end, a group of twelve people of varying ages set off a few nights later across the Thames to the famous pleasure gardens. The river was busy, and it was not surprising that the party failed to notice one of the other boats which was taking passengers to Vauxhall. It might have given rise to comment if they had, for one of the three men in it looked strangely out of keeping with the other two. The first was undoubtedly a gentleman. His two companions were quite as obviously not. . .

# CHAPTER THIRTEEN

LORD WALCOT had taken two of the best boxes for the evening, and Eleanor was so delighted with the lights and the music which wafted through the night air that she forgot for a little the stony feeling in her heart. There was a certain coolness in the air—it was, after all, September—and the ladies kept their wraps on. In company with the younger members of the party Eleanor wandered along the colonnades lit by hundreds of lamps, stood before the orchestra and watched the musicians, and took some refreshment in the rotunda. But when her companions went in search of other, more lively amusements she decided to return to her seat in the box to watch the world parade by.

By this time she was feeling a little tired and, truth to tell, weary in spirit as well as in body. When the rest of the party went in search of supper Eleanor was relieved to hear that Lord Walcot was staying where he was and she elected to stay with him.

'Does it live up to your expectations?' he asked when they were alone.

'Oh, yes, Uncle Charles!' she replied, rousing herself. 'It's like a fairyland! The lights, the music. . .'

'You don't have to pretend with me, you know. You have been splendid during your stay with us, but you don't have to keep it up before me. Has your aunt told you how proud we both are of you?'

'Don't!' she whispered. 'Please! I. . .'

'Yes, well, that's enough of that. I've told you and we can now forget it. Are you sure you don't want supper—a glass of wine, even? It would be warmer there, and I would take you if you wished.'

Eleanor looked at the noisy crowds streaming in and out of the rotunda. 'If you don't mind, Uncle Charles, I would rather stay here. The supper-rooms are a little hot and. . .airless. Would you object if we just sat quietly for a while? I have a touch of the headache—and the megrims. To tell truth, I am not looking forward to going back to Somerset.'

'Then stay in London,' he said promptly.

'You mustn't tempt me,' Eleanor replied with a smile. 'I must face it like a man! Besides, Mama looks to see me before too long. Perhaps we shall come to Kent, both of us together.'

'That would be delightful.' They sat in companionable silence for a while, and Eleanor felt some of her stretched nerves easing. The crowds were thinning now—the night air was cool enough to tempt them inside. Even Eleanor started to feel the cold. She gave a little shiver.

'Right, that's it, Eleanor! It's time we went. I wonder where your aunt can have got to? If you'll wait here for a moment—you'll be perfectly safe if you stay well back in the box—I'll fetch her. Don't leave the box, mind!'

His tall figure disappeared in the direction of the rotunda and Eleanor closed her eyes. . .

'Please!' The voice broke in on her thoughts and she sat up and leaned forward to see who or what it was. A young woman was standing in front of the box. 'Are you Miss Southeran?'

When Eleanor said she was, the girl, for she wasn't much more than that, went on, 'It's your aunt, Miss Southeran. She's hurt her foot on the way back from supper. She can't walk. Is Lord Walcot with you?'

'No,' said Eleanor, standing up, alarmed. 'He thought she was still having supper, and has gone to fetch her. Where is my aunt?'

The girl pointed towards the avenue of trees leading away from the central walk. 'She's sitting under that tree—can you see her?'

Peering, Eleanor could just make out a muffled figure on the grass under the first of the trees. 'Lord Walcot is probably in the rotunda—could you please let him know? I'll see if I can help her.'

Quite forgetting her uncle's admonition, Eleanor left the box and ran over to the tree, only to stop with a cry when a ruffianly-looking man stepped out from behind it, and advanced towards her. She looked down—a second man lay there laughing at her. She turned and made to run back, but they caught her with ease.

'Here's a little beauty! I didn't know we were going to catch such a queen, did you, Jack? Look at this!' Between them the two men had dragged her further down the path to a more secluded spot, and had now paused in their endeavours.

'It's a real shame to spoil this,' said the one called Jack, examining Eleanor while the first man held her, his huge hand over her mouth.

Eleanor had been paralysed by fright and the unexpected attack, but she now suddenly recovered. She bit the hand over her mouth, and as the man swore and pulled it away she screamed as loudly as she could. The scream was broken off abruptly as Jack clamped his hand roughly over her mouth, and snatched her into a rough embrace. 'You should've watched out for that, Bart—she's a girl of spirit, this one. I like her!' He grinned evilly down into her face, his breath stale and reeking of brandy. 'I think we could have a bit of sport with her, don't you? There's no hurry, is there?'

'Yes, there is—they'll be lookin' for her soon,' said Bart sullenly, sucking his hand. 'Come on, let's finish it, then we can get our money and be off.'

Suddenly the man holding her was torn away and hurled to the ground. Eleanor stood in shock as she heard Mr Guthrie's voice say, 'Miss Southeran! Are you all right? Here, lean against this tree.'

She held on to the tree for dear life while her rescuer turned on the second man, who was rushing up to attack. Mr Guthrie met him head-on and Eleanor watched, horrified, as the man doubled up in pain, then was jerked up and lifted bodily by a blow to his jaw. He fell heavily some feet away and lay motionless. The first man started to get up, but fell back as Mr Guthrie turned to stand over him, his fists clenched and an expression of raw fury on his dark face. Eleanor had never before seen anyone look so dangerous.

'Have you. . .have you killed him?' she whispered, looking at the unconscious form of her attacker.

He turned, his face still grim. 'Not even half,' he assured her. 'He'll wake up with a headache, that's all. What do you wish me to do with them?'

Eleanor thought, half hysterically, that he might be offering to murder them if that was what she wanted! 'I. . . What did they want with me?'

Mr Guthrie gave the man on the ground at his feet a none too gentle nudge, and hauled him up by the collar. 'Tell her!'

'We was. . .we was hired.'

'To do what?'

'Not to kill 'er, I swear! Just frighten her for a bit. He said you'd come.'

There was a sudden significant silence. Then Mr Guthrie rapped out, 'Who?'

'He didn't say who he was—no, don't hit me, I swear that's true! Bart would tell you the same. . .if he was conscious. He said we 'ad to frighten her, mebbe knock her about a bit. Aaggh! You're choking me!'

'You scum!'

'No, we didn't like the idea a bit, guv'nor! But he paid us a good bit on account, and said there was more. . . And he said you'd come before any real damage was done to her. If you didn't, we was to leave 'er here.' He added resentfully, 'But he didn't say you was a prize fighter!'

Guthrie turned to Eleanor. 'I think I know what happened and why.'

'Then tell me!'

'I will, but not here and now. Do you want me to give these two some more of their own medicine?'

Eleanor shuddered again. 'No! Leave them where they are. I'd rather forget them.'

'They ought to be handed over. . .'

'No! I don't want the fuss! I want to go. . .to go. . . back. Leave them!'

'Very well.' He poked the first man with his foot. 'Have you had enough? Or would you like another round?' His teeth gleamed in a ferocious smile, and the man cringed back, shaking his head. 'Then make yourself scarce—and take the other piece of vermin with you.'

The man on the ground nodded vigorously, and Mr Guthrie turned away to Eleanor. 'Come, let me help you, Miss Southeran.'

'No,' said Eleanor, nervously backing away.

He gazed at her in astonishment. 'But you are very shaken, I can see you are! You must allow me to help you!'

'You will help me best by leaving me alone!' said Eleanor, her voice rising slightly. 'I am obliged to you—very obliged to you—for rescuing me from those men, but I do not wish for anything more.'

'This is absurd! Eleanor——'

'And I would be obliged if you would not make free with my name, sir.'

'God damn it. . .' At a snort of derision from the man behind him, Mr Guthrie swung round dangerously.

'Just going, guv'nor,' Jack said hastily, and hurried off.

But Eleanor had seized her chance and was now some distance away, running to meet the Walcots. The incident which had seemed to last an eternity to her had, in fact, lasted the same length of time it had taken her uncle to find his wife and return with her.

They were horrified when she began to tell them what had happened, and their first reaction was to put it down to the general lack of supervision in the

Gardens which accompanied the end of the season, and the consequent increase in crime. But when Mr Guthric arrived, incidentally much to their surprise, he put the affair in a different light, and it began to acquire more sinister overtones. Lord Walcot was seriously concerned.

'We cannot let this pass, and I should like to discuss it further with you, Guthrie. But this is clearly neither the place nor the time. May I suggest that you come round to South Audley Street tomorrow—at ten?'

Eleanor went to bed exhausted, but found sleep once again impossible. Shivering in her bed, she relived her terrifying experience over and over, and whenever she dozed off she would wake up with a start, and it would all begin again. That there was some kind of unpleasant mystery behind it she did not doubt. Those men had known who she was, had enticed her deliberately into the avenue.

And how had Mr Guthrie turned up so fortuitously? She would rather have been rescued by almost any other man in London. She was haunted, too, by the violence of his attack on the two men, and the expression on his face as he'd looked at them afterwards. The memory of that dark, violent face kept her awake, and when she did sleep she was back with her nightmare.

Eleanor was not present during most of Lord Walcot's discussion with Mr Guthrie, but was invited to join them towards the end. She had spent the time alternately fuming at not being included in a matter which concerned her so closely, and feeling relieved at not having to be in the same room as Mr Guthrie for longer than was necessary. This was not because she might be distressed or feel regret for what was lost, but rather because she felt such distaste for his company. Even the night before, in her vulnerable state after being attacked, her only desire afterwards had been to escape from him.

So when she entered her uncle's study she was composed, but in no mood to suffer any attempt to treat her as if she were a defenceless woman needing male support.

'Eleanor, come in and sit down.' She went over to the chair her uncle indicated, giving a cool nod to Mr Guthrie on the way, but without actually meeting his eye. 'What Mr Guthrie has been telling me has astonished me beyond belief. May I ask you a few questions, my dear? Or would you rather not talk about last night?'

'Of course I will, Uncle Charles. What do you wish to know?'

'Your uncle wishes to know how the men enticed you to come over to them, Miss Southeran. Can you recall the woman's exact words?'

Eleanor thought for a moment, then, looking at Lord Walcot, she said, 'I cannot remember the order exactly, but she told me that Aunt Hetty had hurt herself, and was lying under the tree. She asked if you were there, Uncle Charles.'

'How did she describe your uncle?'

Eleanor looked at Mr Guthrie and said dismissively, 'I don't know what you mean. She didn't describe him at all.'

'I think Mr Guthrie meant, did she mention my name? Or simply call me "your uncle"?'

'She called you Lord Walcot.'

'And you?' her uncle went on. 'Did she call you by name, too?'

'Yes. She called me Miss Southeran.'

Mr Guthrie, who had been sitting forward in his chair, now sat back with the air of a man who had just proved a point.

Lord Walcot looked very grave. 'You were right, Guthrie. The plot was specifically against Eleanor. It is a pity you did not wait till the men could be apprehended and questioned.'

'I've told you, Lord Walcot. I know who the real villain is. And it isn't either of those two men.' He turned to Eleanor. 'Before I came, did they say anything about waiting for me, or expecting me?'

She turned to her uncle. 'Do you wish to know that, Uncle Charles?'

'Good God, Eleanor, we're not going to get very far if you persist in treating me as if I don't exist!'

'I know you exist, sir.' Her tone implied that she found this regrettable. 'And I have no desire to get anywhere as far as you are concerned.'

Lord Walcot had listened to this exchange with some amusement, but he now said, 'Mr Guthrie is right, Eleanor, my dear. The affair is too serious to play with. Did the men mention Mr Guthrie—or anyone else?'

Eleanor thought again. 'I think so. They. . .one of them said that he would. . .would like to h-have some sport.' In spite of herself her voice trembled, and Mr

Guthrie got up and went over to the window, swearing under his breath. He came back.

'I should have killed them,' he said baldly.

'Sit down, Guthrie!' said Lord Walcot. 'I agree with the sentiment, but it would not have solved anything, only complicated things even more. Go on,' he said gently to Eleanor.

'Can't you see she's on the edge? At least give her some time to recover herself!' Mr Guthrie exclaimed.

'I am perfectly ready to continue now. The other one said, "they'll be looking for her soon"—I thought that meant you, Uncle Charles. He wanted to get his money and go.'

'Where?'

Eleanor looked blankly at Mr Guthrie. 'Where they were to go? I don't know.'

'The money, the money. Where were they going to collect the money?'

When Eleanor repeated that she didn't know, Mr Guthrie gave a snort of impatience. This roused Eleanor to say coldly, 'Do forgive me—I suppose I should have asked, but I forgot. I had other things on my mind.'

Lord Walcot shook his head with a smile, but then grew very serious. 'I apologise, Guthrie, for not believing you. I think you are right. Eleanor is under threat while she stays in London.'

'She is under threat wherever she is, until Oliver is caught. As yet, there isn't any real proof, and he appears to have gone underground. He is now certain which is his quarry, of course. I'm afraid I revealed my hand by following him to London to protect Eleanor.'

'What are you talking about?' asked Eleanor. 'Threats, proof, protection—what is it all about?'

'Mr Guthrie is certain that a man called Oliver intends to hurt him by hurting you, Eleanor. It seems incredible, but, I must say, the evidence of last night seems to confirm that. Mr Guthrie advises that we send you back to Somerset in his care, where he feels he can give you better protection. London is too full of villains for hire of all kinds. You'd be safer in the country, where strangers would stand out.'

Eleanor rose with dignity. 'I am not,' she said clearly, 'going anywhere with Mr Guthrie. Not now. Not ever.'

'Eleanor——'

'I have asked you not to be so free with my name, Mr Guthrie.'

Lord Walcot intervened. 'I think,' he said carefully, 'that I am going to leave you two alone for a few minutes. It seems to me,' he continued, overriding his niece's cry of protest, 'that, before we can get very far with this question of protection, other matters must be resolved first. No, Eleanor, I insist that you stay. I should like you both to remember that nothing— nothing at all—should be allowed to endanger Eleanor's life.'

He went out, leaving Mr Guthrie standing by the window and Eleanor glaring at the door.

'Eleanor, why are you so very angry with me?'

She turned to find him gazing at her with that same quizzical gleam in his eye which had disarmed her so often before. 'I am not angry with you, Mr Guthrie, although I wish you would do me the courtesy of listening when I ask you not to call me by my given name.'

'I thought I had been given that privilege?'

'It is withdrawn. If I appear angry, it is because I deeply resent my uncle's insistence that I stay in this room with you.'

Mr Guthrie came towards her. 'He loves you and wishes you to be protected.'

'The only protection I need at the moment is from you!'

'Isn't that what I said? I can protect you far better than anyone else.'

'That is not what I meant, and you know it! But why? Why are you doing this? What have you told my uncle to persuade him that you should be responsible for my safety? I find that intolerable.'

'I told him I loved you.'

There was a sudden silence. Then Eleanor said harshly, 'And he believed you? I must tell you that I do not.' He started to say something, but she went on, 'And if you try to say any more on that topic I will risk my uncle's displeasure and leave this room immediately.'

'But I do, God damn it— No! Don't go! I won't mention it again if you'll only stay. It's important that you listen to the rest. Please, El—Miss Southeran, come away from the door!'

Eleanor took her hand away from the door-handle and turned round slowly.

'Would you. . .would you sit down? This may take some time.' He had the sense to walk right away from her, after offering her a small upright chair not far from the door.

'I am waiting, Mr Guthrie.'

'I know, I know. It's just. . .'

Eleanor realised with surprise that he was nervous, and she wondered why. What lies was he preparing now?

Finally Mr Guthrie began, 'Rumour has it that I seduced Evadne Anstey. That is not true. When she came to me after Henry Anstey died and told me that she was having a child, she told me then that Oliver was the father. She said that he was prepared to marry her if she could find some money—a dowry, so to speak. I knew Oliver, and I advised Evadne to have nothing more to do with him. I offered to help her to go away until the child was born and could be adopted. She could then come back afterwards to resume her life in Boston. I wish now I had insisted.'

He walked about the room. 'Instead I gave her the dowry Oliver demanded.' He came to a halt in front of Eleanor. 'I had the money, and it was what she wanted,' he said, as if to explain.

Eleanor remained silent, though the words she had overheard in the library were echoing in her mind. Evadne Anstey had *blackmailed* Mr Guthrie into giving her the money. It hadn't been the voluntary, charitable gift he was claiming. What had been Evadne's hold over him, if not the fact that he had seduced her? And what about the settlement on the child once it had been born?

Mr Guthrie gave up waiting for a response and went on, 'Oliver was—is—a strange man. Evadne found that he already had a young man, Christopher Digby, living with him, of whom he was. . .very fond. In fact, he was devoted to him. Christopher is that curious

phenomenon, a person without any moral sense whatsoever—not immoral so much as amoral. When Oliver
learned that Amelia Anstey, his wife's mother, stood
to inherit my estate if I should die before marrying, he
decided to have me killed off. Christopher was his
intended instrument—fortunately an incompetent one.
You yourself witnessed one attempt in Hyde Park.
There were others, including the last, disastrous
attempt which might have cost you your life.'

Eleanor made a sudden movement. 'The man on
the hill,' she said. 'It was Christopher?'

'Yes. I had hoped that they would give up when I
moved to Somerset. I kept my destination a secret
from all but a few people in London. But then Amelia
came to Combe St James and my efforts were wasted.
I had to act—so I decided to deprive Oliver of his
tool. I abducted Christopher Digby, and sent him
willy-nilly to Madras. I have friends there, and they
will keep an eye on him.' He added with a slight grin,
'One way or another.'

Mr Guthrie had so far been talking almost dispassionately, as if the events he had been recounting did
not concern him closely. But now the atmosphere
changed, and he said very gravely, 'Oliver has taken
the loss of Christopher very hard. He won't risk
attacking me himself—but the accident on the bridge
has given him the idea of making me suffer through
you. He has sworn to damage, maim, even to kill any
woman I love, anyone I intend to marry.'

Eleanor rose from her chair. She was paler than
ever. 'And that was the reason for the attack on me
last night? The man is a madman!'

'He is all the more dangerous if he is. It is fast becoming an obsession with him.'

'But you must tell him that you do not love me!' she cried.

'He will not believe me—especially as I raced to London the minute I heard you and he were both here. I see now that that was what he intended. It gave the confirmation he was seeking. I must take you back to Somerset, Eleanor—Miss Southeran.'

'Tell him that I do not love you!'

He was pale. 'Is that true?'

'Yes, it is! How can you ask? I would not, could not, think of loving you ever again.'

'Why? Because I was unkind to you in the stable yard? Don't you think you are being excessively sensitive about that? I've told you the reason—it was to put Oliver off the scent.'

Eleanor was in a dilemma. She could not bring herself to tell him that she had overheard his conversation with Evadne when he had denied that he loved Eleanor Southeran. Yet the pain she had suffered because of it lay at the heart of her refusal to consider that he might now be sincere. How could she ever trust him unreservedly again? He had been totally convincing in his denials of any interest in her, his claim to have been dallying.

'Tell him!' she said again.

'It would make no difference,' he said grimly. 'As long as he believes you are important to me, you are at risk.' He turned away. 'Is it not ironic? I have as little chance of convincing him that you are not important to me as I apparently have of convincing you that you are—that I love you, and want more than anything in the world to marry you.'

'What about your title?' said Eleanor bitterly. 'I wouldn't be much of a great lady!'

'What do you mean?' His eyes narrowed. 'When did you hear of my title?'

'Never mind. I am not travelling to Somerset in your company, Mr Guthrie!'

'And if your uncle insists?'

'He knows me well enough not to insist.'

'Eleanor—— Oh, God damn it, Miss Southeran! This is not a game! Lord Walcot would be risking your life if he does not see that you have adequate protection. I tell you, Oliver is dangerous!'

'I do not think the risk is nearly as great as you fear. But in any case I would take it—and more—rather than suffer your company for two days.'

On this Eleanor would not be moved, not by Mr Guthrie, nor later by her uncle.

'May I suggest, Lord Walcot, that your niece at least has an escort to Hounslow? That might be far enough from London—especially as Oliver can have no suspicion that she is leaving tomorrow instead of later in the week.'

Lord Walcot was not at first at all happy with this compromise, but finally gave in. Eleanor would leave the next day in the Walcot coach, and would change over to a post-chaise at Hounslow. Lord Walcot's coachman would see to the post-boys and horses himself, before he returned.

Eleanor left London the next morning. In contrast to her departure earlier in the year there was little ceremony, for the aim this time was to make it as unobtrusive as possible.

She had said her farewells the night before, and had been touched and relieved when her uncle had returned unusually early from his club to spend some time with her. Lord Walcot had clearly been impressed with Mr Guthrie, and she had been afraid that her obstinate refusal to have anything to do with the man might have offended him. But he had been as affectionate as ever, merely anxious for her safety. He had told her that, though the Walcot coach and driver would return from Hounslow, John, the groom, would stay with her all the way to Somerset.

'I can be sure then that you will travel in comfort and safety, my dear. Please don't refuse this precaution as you did the others!'

'Thank you, Uncle Charles. I confess I shall be relieved to have someone I can trust with me.'

'You could have had Mr Guthrie.'

'I trust John.'

No more was said on that score, and the following morning Eleanor climbed into her uncle's well-sprung coach and set off on the first stage of her journey.

They made good time through Kensington village, Hammersmith and Brentford and arrived in Hounslow about nine o'clock. Here they stopped, and Eleanor went into the inn to have a light breakfast while John arranged for a post-chaise and horses. There were always plenty to choose from. Hounslow was said to stable over two thousand horses, and was one of the busiest posting centres in England—all the Western Mails stopped here. Travellers could be reasonably certain of finding a comfortable chaise and some good, reliable horses.

She finished her breakfast, was shown one of the bedrooms where she could tidy herself up, and then decided to go in search of John. He would be in the stable yard behind the inn. At the bottom of the stairs she hesitated, uncertain of the way.

'It's to your right, ma,am,' said one of the maids who was flitting past. Eleanor took the doorway on her right and walked up the passage. The morning sun streaming in through the opening at the end dazzled her, and she could hardly see where to put her feet. Suddenly someone grabbed her from behind, put a gloved hand over her mouth and dragged her into a dark store-room to the side of the passage. She struggled and kicked, and once almost escaped, but in the end it was to no avail. Whoever it was had a grip of iron.

'Put the sack on her. You'll have to tie it on— there's no time to waste,' said a hoarse voice. A rough sack was put over Eleanor's head, and tied round her middle. The hand had been removed and she screamed, but the sound was lost in the folds of the sack.

'Scream away, darlin'. They won't hear you through there in the taproom, and there ain't anyone else,' said a second voice.

Eleanor felt completely helpless. The rope which held the sack in place also bound her arms to her sides, making resistance impossible. She tried to kick, but her feet were caught and tied together. Then she was slung up over a man's shoulder like a bundle of rags.

'Where do you want 'er, guv'nor?' said the second voice. There was no reply that Eleanor could hear, but she was carried along the passage and out into the fresh air. 'Hold the door and mind 'er 'ead. We don't want to damage 'er, do we?' said the same man, with a spine-chilling laugh.

Eleanor was deposited on a narrow strip of floor, the door was slammed shut and the coach—for that was what she surmised it was—set off. She strained her ears for any sound, any clue as to what was happening, but she could hear nothing out of the way, only the ordinary noises of the inns and houses lining their route.

She seemed to be alone inside the coach. It travelled sedately till it was on the high road, then it picked up speed. Eleanor was unable to prevent herself from rolling backwards and forwards as they went over the potholes and bumps in the road. She was very uncomfortable, but, more than that, she was very frightened. What were they going to do with her?

If they were travelling over Hounslow Heath, which she rather thought they were, then anything could happen, for it was a long stretch of deserted road, with plenty of bushes and scrub in which to hide a body. Was that what they were going to do—kill her? Or were they going to abandon her, as they would have done the other night, but this time on the Heath, a known haunt of highwaymen and thieves? The sack suddenly semed unbearably constricting, and she felt choked, panic rising within her.

She must think about something else quickly. What about John? What had happened to him? Perhaps he was now lying injured, or worse, in some dark corner in Hounslow. Oh, how could she have been so pig-headed? Her uncle had been right to be anxious, and she should have paid more attention to him, especially after the attack at Vauxhall. Why had she allowed her dislike of Guthrie to override her common sense? She was about to pay dearly for her stupidity.

Eleanor's spirits were rapidly reaching a low ebb when the coach suddenly turned off the road and stopped. She held her breath and braced herself. The door was opened, two people climbed in, and she was hauled up and placed on the seat. They sat down, one each side of her. Oh, God, what were they going to do? There was a knot of fear in her stomach, and she felt sick.

But then the coach started off again! One of her captors grasped her arms and held her, while the other started to release her bonds. What on earth were these people up to? Unless she was very much mistaken, the person holding her was a woman! Suddenly the sack was removed and she was gazing into the face of the maidservant from the inn!

'You are a formidable woman, Miss Southeran. You fought so fiercely that we had to truss you up like a chicken before we could persuade you to come with us. I'm sorry if you have been uncomfortable.'

Eleanor whirled round. Mr Guthrie sat looking at her with a sardonic smile on his face.

# CHAPTER FOURTEEN

ELEANOR was overcome with a mixture of relief and scorching fury. 'You. . .you villain!' she shouted. 'You heartless, scheming villain!' She swung her hand to hit him, but he laughed and held her wrists. She snatched her hands away and beat her fists against his chest, out of her mind with anger. Then she burst into tears. Mr Guthrie put his arm around her, but she leapt up, only to lose her balance in the lurching of the coach and fall on to the seat opposite. He leant forward, and she backed away into the corner.

'Don't touch me!'

'I wasn't going to touch you, only to try to speak to you. Pull youself together, Eleanor.'

'My name is Miss Southeran,' she shouted.

'I shall call you Miss Southeran when you start behaving less like a child and more like a lady.'

Eleanor stopped short. She looked down at her dirty dress, at the inelegant way she had pulled her legs up on to the seat to avoid contact with him, and was shocked. She straightened herself and tried to smooth her hair with hands that still trembled.

'May I help you, Miss Southeran?' It was the maidservant.

'Not until I know who you are, and what you are doing here.'

Mr Guthrie replied for her. 'Her name is Maggie

Carver. When she heard of the danger you were in she agreed to help me. She is an old friend.'

'I'm sure she is,' agreed Eleanor sweetly.

'Er, excuse me, Miss Southeran, but what Mr Guthrie should have said is that my husband, Sam, and I are old friends of his. Both of us,' said Maggie calmly. 'I'm not sure Sam would like your tone, begging your pardon.'

'You can hardly blame me for thinking the worst. Abduction is hardly the work of honest people,' said Eleanor, not giving ground.

'Sam is driving the coach now. I should prefer not to stop again, but if you wish to meet him I will ask him to draw up for a second,' said Mr Guthrie.

'I would prefer not to have met any of you. I can do without meeting Mr Carver—his wife was enough.'

'Eleanor, stop this. Maggie and Sam have done you a favour, possibly even saved your life. Now let Maggie help you to get yourself in order. Your hair needs urgent attention, and your bonnet must be here somewhere. We threw it in after you.' He picked up a sad confection from the floor. 'Er. . .I think you must have rolled on it.'

'Of course I did,' said Eleanor, her temper rising again. 'I rolled on everything! I couldn't stop myself. I must have bruises everywhere.'

He grew serious. 'We didn't intend to hurt you. That was the last thing I wanted. But you were fighting like a wildcat. Where *did* you pick up some of those tricks? We had seen Oliver arriving in Hounslow, so we had to hide you and get away with speed. That's why you were on the floor of the coach.'

'Oliver?'

'Yes, he's a determined man. God knows how he picked up your trail. Did you make a great fuss when you left? I advised your uncle against it.'

'My uncle—that reminds me! What have you done with John?'

'He has gone back to London to report that all is well.'

'Gone back! To report! You mean that my uncle knew about this?'

'We planned it together last night, after you had been so stupidly determined to let your prejudice against me override all caution. I'm glad we did. You might otherwise be facing Oliver here on the Heath, instead of me.'

'Are you trying to tell me that all this rough treatment of me was with my uncle's consent? I don't believe you!'

'You must, of course, believe what you choose. I don't think he realised quite what an Amazon you are. I certainly never expected to have to fight you, or to tie you up so comprehensively. Nor to have to deposit you on the floor. We released you as soon as we could, but we had to get well clear of Hounslow before stopping. Now, if you stop complaining, and concentrate instead on repairing the damage, Maggie will soon put you to rights. I'll look the other way.'

Maggie opened a small dressing-case which was on the seat beside Eleanor. She took out various toilet articles, and a clean tucker, and set to work.

'Thank you, Mrs Carver,' said Eleanor reluctantly. 'I'm sorry if I insulted you before. I was angry. In fact, I still am.' She glared at Mr Guthrie, who was studying the drear landscape outside.

'It's very natural, miss. You must have suffered a terrible shock. And I didn't like lying to you back there at the inn, but Mr Guthrie said it was vital that we got you away. We all know Mr Oliver.'

'You do? How?'

'We were in Mr Guthrie's service while he was in Boston. Mr Oliver is a wicked man.'

'Well, now, Miss Southeran,' said a voice from the other corner of the carriage. 'May I look round?'

'I am in your power, sir. How can I stop you?' said Eleanor coldly.

'You know that's not true. If you were, I should do a lot more than look round, believe me. Ah! You've worked miracles, Maggie. What about Miss Southeran's bonnet?'

'I'm afraid the bonnet is beyond repair, sir. I'll get another one out of her valise when we arrive at Salisbury.'

'We are staying the night at Salisbury, Miss Southeran,' said Mr Guthrie, turning to Eleanor. 'We should make it easily. Maggie here will look after you at the inn, though it won't be the most comfortable in the town. We shall stay somewhere less conspicuous, somewhere from which we can observe Oliver without being observed ourselves. Then when he sets off tomorrow we can see which road he chooses— Shaftesbury or Blandford—and we shall take the other. It will make for a more relaxed journey.'

'Mr Guthrie, I have been frightened half to death, tossed about like a sack of potatoes, am forced to endure your company to Somerset when you know the thought is anathema to me—how can you say that this journey could in any way be relaxed?' Eleanor's voice rose on these last words. It was obvious that she was not at all reconciled to her circumstances.

Mr Guthrie pulled a face and said to Maggie grimly, 'Would you object to joining Sam on the box for a while, Maggie? I think some matters are best sorted out in private.'

Maggie smiled sympathetically at him and said she would like a breath of fresh air. It would do her good.

When the change had been effected Mr Guthrie turned to Eleanor and said, 'Now you may give free vent to your spleen, Miss Southeran. Let us have it out in the open. Why *do* you dislike me to this extent, when I have given you no real reason?'

'No real reason? What of your treatment of me in Hounslow?'

'That isn't the issue, and you know it. Don't fence with me, Eleanor. It isn't worthy of you! This question is far too important to both of us.'

Eleanor was silent.

'Eleanor?'

'Don't call m——'

'God damn it, girl, stop playing! You know I have a right to call you Eleanor! Or have you forgotten that you once lay in my arms, begging me to kiss you again, lost to all sense of time or place, caught up in a passion over which you had no control? I am not too much of a gentleman to remind you that it wasn't you who called a halt before we reached the point of no return, Eleanor Southeran!'

Eleanor had listened to this impassioned speech with growing horror. She had tried to stop him, but he swept on, disregarding her frantic pleas.

'You love me, Eleanor Southeran, every bit as much

as I love you. Don't try to deny it, or claim that you have forgotten any part of the episode by the combe!'

Eleanor, who had taken pride in the way she had suppressed her feelings, who had refused to let them surface for the past two weeks, was now almost beside herself with pain. The stoic restraint, the iron control she had exercised, at least in public, were shattered, and the storm of tears over Jonas Guthrie's perfidy, which she had never before allowed herself, now broke.

'Stop it, stop it!' she cried. 'Of course I remember! I can't stop remembering! I would to God I could forget! You are not worthy of all this pain. You do not love me—you are a liar and a cheat, and I despise myself for having been deceived into thinking you were ever anything else!'

She huddled into the corner and cried as if her heart was breaking—hard, dry sobs which were not any easy relief from shattered nerves, but deep, bitter grief.

Mr Guthrie looked at her incredulously. 'Eleanor! Don't! Don't, my love, I can't bear it. What is all this for? What have I done? Oh, my God, tell me. . .' He looked helplessly at her, not daring to approach her, for once in his life at a complete loss.

Finally, when the storm of grief was calming down, he said quietly, 'You must talk to me again. I didn't realise. . . I thought you were simply being difficult. . . But this. . .' He stopped abruptly. Eleanor took her hands from her face and looked up. He was gazing at her uncertainly, with such baffled misery in his eyes that a tiny seed of doubt was planted in her mind.

He went on, 'I honestly don't understand why you think so badly of me. I love you, Eleanor, more than my life. Why can't you believe that? You had such amazing, such incredibly illogical trust in me before — against all reason, all reputation. Why has that gone?'

'You never said that you loved me,' she whispered. 'You only ever offered me friendship. But I thought you did. . .love me. You. . .we behaved as if you did. You talked of the future.' The tears came now, rolling down her cheeks unchecked as she went on. 'And then you. . .then you said that you didn't, that you never had loved me. You were very convincing.' She turned her head away from him. 'I don't know what to think. But I can't quite believe anything you say any more.'

He was frowning. 'When did I say this, Eleanor? That I didn't love you?'

Eleanor was feeling wearier than she had ever felt in her life before. The experiences of the morning, on top of the many sleepless nights preceding them, had overwhelmed her. She was incapable of fencing with him. She yawned and made an effort to respond. 'I. . . can't remember. . .'

Her voice trailed away. She heard Jonas get up and sit beside her. He took her into his arms and when she somewhat half-heartedly protested he said soothingly, 'Have a rest, my love. Things will be better when you wake. We can sort all this out another time. Sleep now.' That was the last Eleanor knew.

Jonas sat with Eleanor asleep in his arms for the rest of the way to Salisbury. Occasionally he rested his cheek on her hair, or kissed the top of her head. But for the most part he simply sat there, deep in thought. It was clear now that Eleanor had been told something of his conversation with Evadne Oliver. But who had done this? There had been no witnesses. Had Evadne herself spoken to Eleanor? It was unlikely, but not impossible. Though Eleanor had disappeared to London quite soon after the scene in the library, she hadn't left straight away.

His mind turned to that visit to London. To help Lady Walcot while she was ill, it had been said. This wasn't so, of course—Mrs Southeran had told him her daughter had fled to London 'unhappier than she had ever been in her life', and she had taken him to task for it.

Evadne must have seen Eleanor! And if Eleanor had been told what he had said to Evadne in the library, and had believed it, then he was not surprised at her distress when she had fled to London. His mouth tightened as he thought of what she must have suffered.

It was dark when they reached Salisbury. They found an inn slightly off the beaten track but not too far from the centre. After a short meal Eleanor, still exhausted, went upstairs accompanied by Maggie, who was to sleep on a truckle bed in her room. Sam went out as soon as he had eaten on a tour of the inns and taverns in the town. He came back after an hour or so and gave Mr Guthrie a nod. Oliver had been spotted.

'I hope you don't mind, guv'nor—I've given a couple of lads some of the ready to keep an eye on the gent. He won't go without us knowin' about it.'

Jonas and Sam spent a convivial half-hour in the taproom, and if there were some who looked askance at the oddly assorted pair neither of them minded.

They had known each other a long time, and been through a good many fights together.

The next morning the party, having been informed that Mr Oliver was taking the more popular route by way of Blandford and Dorchester, prepared to leave for Shaftesbury and Sherborne.

Eleanor woke up much refreshed after an uninterrupted night's sleep—the first for some weeks. Maggie was standing by her bed, holding a cup of chocolate. 'I wasn't sure whether you would want this, Miss Southeran,' she said. 'But Mr Guthrie insisted I should bring it up. He was concerned that you had so little to eat last night. Very thoughtful, is Mr Guthrie, ma'am.'

Eleanor lay back on her pillows and smiled at Maggie.

'I can see you're his friend, Maggie—and your husband,' she added, with a twinkle.

'That we are. But *I* can see you're feeling better, ma'am. Wonderful what a night's sleep will do. Would you like me to help you dress? I've ironed your clothes, and laid them out. I think Mr Guthrie would like to leave in half an hour.'

Eleanor finished her chocolate, then leapt out of bed and, with Maggie's help, was downstairs in a surprisingly short time, ready to go.

'My goodness, you look better!' was Mr Guthrie's greeting. He looked admiringly at Eleanor's yellow muslin dress, and grey pelisse. 'And I like this bonnet better than the last!'

Indeed, it was very pretty—a grey silk, lined with white sarsnet, with a small yellow ostrich plume at the side, and it framed the face beneath it delightfully. Eleanor looked at him sideways, uncertain how to respond. She was feeling better than she had done for weeks, but her emotions, now having surfaced, so to speak, were still raw, still easily disturbed—especially by this man.

'Shall we set off?' said Mr Guthrie, not sounding unduly perturbed by her lack of response.

They went out to the yard where Mr Guthrie's coach was already waiting in the morning sunshine, the boxes tied on the back. Here Eleanor met Sam—a fearsome-looking character with a voice she had heard the day before. He looked as if he would be more at home in a dockside fight than driving a coach. But when she greeted him he shifted nervously and said, 'Maggie told me off yesterday, ma'am. She said I'd been too rough. I'm sorry, and I hope as how you will forgive me.'

He thereupon smiled, and Eleanor, who had been wondering how a decent-looking, respectable body like Maggie had brought herself to marry him, could suddenly see why. Sam's smile was like sunshine breaking through storm clouds.

'I am perfectly sound in wind and limb now, Mr Carver. It was good of you to feel you ought to help me. And if there *is* any blame, I know where to apportion it!' She glanced darkly at Mr Guthrie, who laughed, but merely ordered them to stop wasting time.

'I would like to reach Stanyards before dark,' he said.

Maggie climbed up beside Sam, and Mr Guthrie held the door open for Eleanor. She hesitated, then got inside. As soon as Mr Guthrie joined her, Sam wasted no more time, but set the coach in motion. She could see now that, though it had a plain exterior, it was luxuriously appointed inside, with velvet squabs and handsome woodwork.

'I see that you believe in comfort when you travel, Mr Guthrie,' she said nervously.

'It depends on my company. Sometimes I prefer a high-perch phaeton, Miss Southeran,' was his solemn response.

She shot him a glance. He was smiling at her with that familiar quizzical smile in his eyes. 'Don't. Please don't,' she faltered.

'What was I doing?'

'You were smiling at me. . .in a particular way. I. . . I don't want you to.' She paused, then they both started to speak together. 'Mr Guthrie, I——'

'Miss Southeran——'

They stopped, then Mr Guthrie said, 'You first, Eleanor.'

'I only wanted to say that I am sorry.'

'*You* are sorry?'

'For the exhibition I exposed you to yesterday. You were very patient.'

'I'm glad you think so. I didn't know what to do, I confess. Are you feeling better this morning? You look it.'

'Thank you, yes. And I am obliged to you for all the trouble you took to save me from my own foolhardiness. If I seemed ungrateful at the time, you must forgive me.'

She looked at him to see how he would take this. He was smiling as he said, 'Now that really isn't fair. You ask me not to look at you in a particular way, then you immediately offer me provocation!' He hesitated, then added, 'There are a number of things I wish to tell you, Eleanor. The most important, and one that I hope you will not immediately reject, is that I do love you. No, don't say anything. I can see that you are still too vulnerable at the moment, and the last thing I want is to upset you again. All I wish is that you should know it. We shall talk about it when we are back at Stanyards.'

'Thank you. If I have misjudged you yet again, then I am sorry for that, too.'

'Your feeling of betrayal was perfectly justified if Evadne Oliver reported verbatim what I said to her.'

'How did you know it was that. . .?' asked Eleanor, astonished.

'Something you quoted. It must have been the conversation with her—I haven't talked to anyone else in those terms, and never wish to again. I lied, but not to you, Eleanor. Never to you. I had guessed that Evadne would report everything I said to Oliver, and was fighting to prevent him from knowing the truth. I wasn't very successful, as it turns out. All I did was to cause you unnecessary distress, and now I may have lost you because of it. Damn Evadne and her malice!' He stared moodily at the passing landscape.

There was silence in the coach for a while. Eleanor thought she ought to say something, but what could she say? She didn't know herself what she felt. Mr Guthrie's sudden transformation from complete hero to complete villain and back again was too much for her overburdened emotions. She wanted time to think, to get rid of old scars, before entering into a new relationship with him. But one thing she must clear up.

'Jonas,' she began, using his name deliberately.

He was very still for a moment, then he turned towards her.

'Yes, Eleanor?'

'I ought to tell you. It wasn't Evadne Oliver. She didn't report what you said. I heard your conversation with her for myself.'

She could see him thinking. 'You weren't in the room with us, I'm certain of that. You weren't outside the door, either—in any case, the door is too thick. A concealed passage? A priest hole? Stanyards is old enough to have one. But why have I never been told?'

'You would have been eventually. The Southeran archives are hidden in it. I was consulting them for the catalogue when you and Evadne came into the library that day. I couldn't escape, but because I'd left the door to it slightly open I. . .I heard everything.'

'Oh, God! You were listening while I was working to convince Evadne. . . I can't remember everything I said—I was watching her all the time to see how she was taking it, and inventing as I went along. I must have sounded completely heartless.' Eleanor nodded. 'But why didn't you come out and face me with it afterwards?'

'I never wanted to see you or Stanyards again.'

'And you fled to London. I see. I wish to heaven you had let us know you were there, Eleanor.'

'I couldn't! Not without betraying the secret of the room—to Evadne as well as to you. And then I was too. . .too disturbed.'

He took a deep breath. 'So what is to happen now? I'll look after you while there's any danger, there's no doubt about that. But Oliver must give up some time—he hasn't the funds to stay long in England. What happens then, Eleanor? Will you never wish to see me again after that?'

'No! I mean, I would like to see you, but. . .we've had such a stormy acquaintance, Jonas. I need time. I don't know what I want, except time to think—and peace. . .no demands.'

He smiled down at her. 'Undemanding friendship, Eleanor? Is that what you want of me for the time being? You shall have it. It won't be easy, but I'll try—for a short while.'

'That's it, then,' she said contentedly. But if she had seen the expression on his face as she sat back and closed her eyes, she would have wondered how long the friendship would remain undemanding!

The rest of the journey passed without incident, and they arrived at the Dower House in the evening just before dark. Mrs Southeran was not expecting them, of course, and there was a flurry of activity while Daniel and Betty worked to make the rooms ready. It had been decided that Maggie and Sam would stay for a little while in Somerset, and Jonas wanted them near the Dower House, to act as a kind of extra bodyguard for Eleanor. Mrs Southeran was easily persuaded to offer them rooms in the newly refurbished stable block. Daniel eyed Sam somewhat doubtfully at first, but after a few careful exchanges he decided to accept the stranger's presence gracefully. Betty and Maggie were instant friends.

Jonas had a meal with the Southerans and over it Mrs Southeran brought them up to date on the news.

It was much the usual, familiar gossip, but there were two items of particular interest.

'Evadne Oliver is alone in Church Cottage. Her mother has decided to stay in Oxfordshire to be near Marianne—I hear she has been offered a small house on the Morrissey estate. The redoubtable Phoebe is staying with her at present. It must be quite sensational to have two such beauties as Phoebe and her sister living so near to each other, wouldn't you say? And quite difficult for the elder sister to have to give precedence to the younger! But I doubt it will be long before Phoebe has a coronet of her own.'

'Have you heard anything of Mr Oliver, Mama?' asked Eleanor. She and Jonas had decided not to frighten Mrs Southeran more than they had to. They would not tell her of the attack in Vauxhall, nor of their journey.

'Nothing! He did not return with Evadne from the wedding. But he must come back soon, if only to help her remove. The cottage will be let to someone else before long.'

Just as Jonas was leaving he said, 'You said there were two items. What was the other?'

Mrs Southeran glanced at Eleanor. 'Threlfall has gone from the farm, but they say he's out of his mind with fury at losing it. I'm afraid he is seldom sober now, and is issuing dire threats against you, Jonas. You'll watch out for him, won't you?'

'I'm not afraid of Threlfall, ma'am. He's a poor thing. It's natural he should rage against me—how could he possibly acknowledge the truth, that he only has himself to blame? But I'll watch. I don't want

matters made worse. Goodnight, Mrs Southeran,
Eleanor.' But Eleanor followed him to the door.

'You will be careful, Jonas?'

He smiled at her. 'I like it when you are so concerned. But you needn't be. Get some rest—you're
looking tired again. I'll see you tomorrow. If you can
bear it, I should like you to show me where this
famous room of yours is. I don't like the thought that
it is there without my knowing where precisely.'

'We should have told you before now. I'll show you
tomorrow. Goodnight, Jonas. And. . .and thank you.'

He bent and kissed her swiftly, then walked away
towards the path to Stanyards.

Mr Oliver had arrived home the same evening, but
not to the same enthusiastic welcome. Evadne was
distinctly jaded over their meal, and though she gave
him the gossip of the neighbourhood she was
impatient with him even in front of the servant.

After the covers had been removed and the girl had
gone to bed, she asked him how he had fared in
London. What he had to say displeased her, and when
he would have excused himself, when he talked of
waiting for the right moment, she said, 'Nathaniel, you
have had several opportunities to get rid of Jonas and
now he has changed his will and it is too late! I went
to considerable trouble to establish who it was that
Jonas really preferred, and what have you done to
dispose of Eleanor Southeran? Nothing!'

'Did I not tell you about Vauxhall?'

'Vauxhall!' she said contemptuously. 'It was all
there for you and you couldn't bring youself to tell
those men to get rid of her. You are a procrastinator

and a coward, Nathaniel, no better than poor Threlfall, who raves about what he will do, but does nothing.'

'Perhaps you're sorry you married me,' he sneered.

She looked at him dispassionately. 'Well, yes,' she said. 'I rather think I am.'

He went pale. 'Evadne! You cannot mean it. You love me!'

'Did you think for one moment,' she said cruelly, 'that I would have married you if I had thought Jonas Guthrie would look twice at me? You were mistaken if you did.'

'So I was a poor substitute? When you swore you loved me, when you had my child, it was Guthrie you really wanted?'

'There was never any question of Guthrie wanting me. And you were there, making sheep's eyes at me.'

'I never thought I would marry, Evadne. You know that. But you were so young, so alive... You made me laugh. And when I knew you were having my child I loved you enough to marry you...in spite of Christopher.'

'With suitable recompense, Nathaniel. Guthrie gave me a very good dowry.'

'Gave you! That's rich. The blackmail idea may have been yours, but it was I who had the evidence about your father, don't forget.'

'And what have you done with it? You've allowed Guthrie to destroy it! We can't even get anything more from that! You're a fool as well as all the rest.'

'Evadne...why are you like this? I would have had you without any dowry, you know that. Don't say you regret our marriage—now that Christopher has gone I...I depend on you.'

'I can get more money from Guthrie if you will forget this stupid affair and come back to Boston with me.'

'No! Not yet. I have a score to settle—now more than ever.'

'Then settle it! But I won't wait much longer. And now I am going to bed. I have had my mother's room prepared for you. Goodnight, Nathaniel.'

Evadne swept out, leaving her husband a prey to his fears and fantasies. He sat at the table, drinking, until the candles were guttering and the bottle empty.

So Evadne had wanted Guthrie all along. Damn him! Everywhere he looked Guthrie was in the way, first taking Christopher and now Evadne. Evadne was right—he must brace himself to act.

But how? He was not brave like Christopher; he was afraid. Why was Christopher not here, when he needed him? There was no one else to depend on, no one else who loved him as Christopher had. . .

Mr Oliver put his head down on the table and wept. Damn Guthrie! Damn him!

But after a few minutes he lifted his head. There was someone he might be able to use. . . A germ of an idea formed in his mind. God, he was tired—he couldn't think any more tonight and this would need careful planning if he was to remain unsuspected. Tomorrow he would consider it more carefully to see if it could be done. It had a number of merits. If it worked, he could rid himself of his enemy and a lot more besides, with little risk to himself. He would show Evadne!

# CHAPTER FIFTEEN

As IF to compensate for the rain and dull weather in August and early September, Somerset was having an Indian summer over Michaelmas. The sun shone day after day, and, though it was chilly at night and in the early morning, during the day it was hot and dry. It was the season of the Goose Fairs, and the excitement among the farmers and countryfolk ran high as the pedlars and chapmen, gypsies and jugglers started to gather in the small country towns.

For the people who worked hard in the fields for most of the year this was the great holiday. During the three days of the fair they could meet exotic travellers from afar and buy goods and trinkets with their hard-earned pennies before returning home to prepare for the winter. The people of Stanyards were no exception. It was a tradition that the estate and its gentry were left to fend for themselves for one day while everyone else attended the local Goose Fair, farmers, servants, stable hands alike.

Jonas was worried. Though he said nothing to anyone else, it seemed to him an ideal occasion for Nathaniel Oliver to strike. Time was running out for the man, and he must do something soon or go back to Boston defeated. Well, let him try! At least it would clear the situation once and for all. It infuriated Jonas that, though he knew all about Oliver's crimes and criminal intentions, there was no evidence, nothing with which to charge him before a magistrate. Perhaps, after the Goose Fair, there might be.

If he were to be trapped, however, Oliver must not be put off from making an attempt, so Jonas decided that any precautions he took must not be obvious. He had a word with Sam, but he kept his own counsel otherwise and let the rest carry on with their plans. Daniel and Betty had filled Maggie's head with tales about the fair, and she could hardly wait to see it for herself. Even staid Mrs Cartwright was accompanying Annie and Dora and the other staff from Stanyards and the Dower House—though she managed to convey the impression that she was not going for her own enjoyment but rather to keep an eye on the maids!

Jonas had managed to get himself invited to the Dower House for the day, which suited his plans very well. He would be able to keep a close eye on Eleanor, while Sam watched from his vantage point over the stable for any unwelcome visitors.

The expedition to the fair set off early in the morning with much merriment and noise. Maggie had been somewhat annoyed with her Sam for his refusal to go to the fair, but even she cheered up when he bade her a most affectionate farewell and gave her money to buy herself a trinket or two.

'I'm not the sort to enjoy all that bustle,' he said to her. 'I'll have a nice easy day here and wait for you to come back and tell me all about it.'

Stanyards seemed very quiet as Jonas walked along the path to the Dower House. The park and fields around it were empty, the house deserted. Jonas was not a fanciful man, but it seemed to him almost as if the place was waiting for something to happen—it was like the silence in a theatre just before the play began.

Mrs Southeran was unaffectedly glad to see him. Her manner to him had always been as direct as his own, and the slight coolness which had appeared when Eleanor had gone to London in such distress had quite gone. It was now clear to anyone who chose to look that Jonas was deeply in love with her daughter—and that Eleanor's spirits visibly improved every time he appeared. She was now certain that the hope she had cherished almost from the moment Jonas had bought Stanyards was about to be realised.

Eleanor herself was very subdued, still struggling to cope with the after-effects of the flood of emotion which had almost swamped her. Until Jonas Guthrie had come into her life she had remained a child, emotionally speaking. Of course she had felt normal family affection, and she had always been devoted to her mother. But, until Jonas Guthrie had appeared, her deeply passionate nature had remained largely dormant, its only outlet her love and care for Stanyards. Jonas had aroused a tumult of feeling such as she had never before experienced, and she had been exhilarated, astounded, and frightened that any other person could have this profound effect on her.

Then, still in this highly vulnerable state, she had been forced to listen to his conversation with Evadne in the library, had heard his careless dismissal of their relationship, his declaration that he did not, in fact, love her, that he had been making use of her. During the days that followed this she had almost succumbed to despair. It had taken all the courage of which she was capable to pull herself together, to paper over the feelings of betrayal and self-contempt and face the world.

Now she could hardly take in the fact that it had all been unnecessary, that Jonas had loved her all the time. Whatever he had told her afterwards, however much her head told her it was reasonable, her deeper feelings were still numb with shock. But she was slowly coming to look more and more for Jonas's arrival, to hear his deep voice, to see his tall figure coming up the path, to feel that the world was right when Jonas was there.

The three of them—Jonas, Eleanor and Mrs Southeran—had a pleasant meal, which had been carefully prepared early that morning before Betty and the others had departed. They were still sitting at the table when the sound of a horse coming up to the Dower House put Jonas instantly on the alert. He got up and walked calmly to the door. As he had thought, it was Nathaniel Oliver.

'Don't bother getting off your horse, Oliver. You're not coming in here,' Jonas said grimly.

Oliver stayed where he was, but called out, 'I've come to make peace, Guthrie. Evadne tells me that she won't wait any longer before she goes back to Boston, and I've decided to give it up. Miss Southeran is safe. I was. . .overwrought and made threats which I now withdraw. May I come in to discuss it?'

Jonas made no move to welcome him, but stood like a rock in front of the door. He said coldly 'And London?'

'That was a mistake. I've had a talk with Evadne since. She tells me you have offered her money to return. I. . . We should like to take you up on the offer. May I come in?'

'Of course you may, Mr Oliver,' said a voice behind Jonas. It was Mrs Southeran. 'Is anyone else with you?'

'No, I am alone.'

'In that case——'

'No, ma'am! Pray do not invite him into your house! You do not know him as I do. He is dangerous and untrustworthy,' said Jonas with urgency.

'Nonsense! He will surely not attack all three of us at once. Take off your coat, Mr Oliver, and come inside.'

'My coat?'

'I will give it back to you once Jonas has made sure you are not armed.' As Mr Oliver dismounted and busied himself with the coat, Mrs Southeran murmured, 'Sam Carver is not far away, I take it, Jonas?'

He smiled unwillingly. 'You are a witch, ma'am! But I still cannot like exposing Eleanor to this man.'

'I sent Eleanor upstairs.' She turned as Oliver came up the steps. 'Come in, Mr Oliver.' Jonas waited at the door with Mr Oliver's coat until the gentleman had passed into the hall. Then, having checked that Sam Carver was now in the yard and coming towards the house, he closed the door to, without actually shutting it. He was taking no risks.

'Would you like your coat back, Mr Oliver? Now, what can we do for you?' said Mrs Southeran, once they were in the sitting-room.

Mr Oliver put on his coat and settled back in the chair she had indicated. Jonas stood with his back to the window, looking watchful.

'If you could persuade Guthrie that I am sincere in
my wish to forget the whole matter and return to
Boston, I should be obliged to you, Mrs Southeran. I
have lost one very dear friend and I do not wish to
risk losing my wife as well—as I shall if I don't give
up this. . .vendetta. She has set her heart on leaving
England within the week, and I have told her we shall
do so. Unfortunately. . .'

'You're short of money,' said Jonas sardonically.

'Well, yes.'

'But even supposing Mr Guthrie were generous
enough to give you some money, what will you do
when you get to America, Mr Oliver? The firm of
Anstey and Oliver is finished, is it not?'

Oliver sighed. 'I shall have to look for something
else to do. It will not be easy. I was hoping that
Guthrie here. . .?'

'What? Give you enough to live on for the rest of
your misbegotten existence? Or did you think I would
give you an introduction to my unsuspecting business
acquaintances? Not on your life, Oliver!'

'Let us not be too hasty, Jonas,' murmured Mrs
Southeran. 'Mr Oliver must be left with some prospect
of a future.' She turned to Oliver. 'I have a letter here
from a Mr Bitteridge of Tremont Street in Boston. I
believe you know him?'

'He was a friend of my father's,' said Oliver sullenly.

'What are you up to, ma'am?' asked Jonas sus-
piciously. 'And how is it that you have suddenly had a
communication form Bitteridge? He's an important
man in Boston—one of the town's most worthy
citizens.'

'Then why are you surprised that I have correspondence with him? He was a friend of my husband, a fellow bibliophile.'

'Ah, yes! I had forgotten his hobby. I only came across him by way of our trading connections.'

'But I actually wrote to him to ask about the Ansteys and you. I found what he has to say extremely interesting.' She turned to Oliver. 'He seems to think that the part you and your wife played in the Anstey story was, to say the least, dubious, Mr Oliver.'

He started to protest, but Mrs Southeran overrode him. 'However, his friendship with your father inclines him to take a more tolerant view of your conduct than others might. He mentions that he has plans to expand his trading interests westwards. I think you might well profit from a visit to your father's old friend when you get back to Boston, don't you?'

Mr Oliver got up. Almost without appearing to move, Jonas was at Mrs Southeran's side, between her and her guest.

'Really, Guthrie!' Mr Oliver exclaimed. 'What do you suppose I am about to do? I object to your excessive suspicion of me! I find it offensive.'

'Object away,' said Jonas curtly. 'I am not concerned with your feelings. What are you about to do?'

'I would like to thank Mrs Southeran for her interest in my future.'

'It is my daughter's continuing future with which I am concerned, Mr Oliver. I would like you to go back to America and not return. I am willing to intercede for you with Mr Bitteridge, if you think it would help.'

'I think it would, ma'am, indeed I do. Meanwhile. . .'

'Meanwhile you need some money,' said Jonas. 'I

am prepared to make good my promise to Evadne, in spite of your activities since.'

'Too good, too kind,' said Mr Oliver with mock-humility. 'Though a more sensitive soul might find this haste to have me gone a touch hurtful. Still. . .shall I return here later this evening? I should like to leave as soon as possible. Letters of credit would do.'

'I don't have the necessary papers here—nor do I wish you near this house again. I will give you what you need at Stanyards. Shall we say five o'clock?'

'In the library?'

'Right! And now go!'

'So unpolished,' murmured Mr Oliver. 'I shall take leave of my hostess first. And Miss Southeran?'

'I shall give her your good wishes myself, Oliver. She is not available.'

'Goodbye, Mr Oliver. Do not disappoint Mr Bitteridge.'

After Oliver had gone, Mrs Southeran looked anxiously at Jonas. 'Do you think it will work? Will he leave?'

'I don't know, but I won't take any chances. I'll be with Eleanor for the rest of the day until I go to Stanyards to meet Oliver, and Sam will be on guard while I am up there.'

'He seemed to be interested in Mr Bitteridge's offer, but. . .'

'I know. He didn't mention consulting Evadne, and leaving Boston would be a major step—he'd never take it without first talking it over with her. On the other hand, she is apparently eager to go back without further action. Perhaps he thinks she would approve.

They must be finished as far as the Boston people are concerned. All the same. . .'

'Take care when you're up at Stanyards, Jonas.'

'It isn't my skin he is after, Mrs Southeran. He wants me to suffer, and he knows it would hurt me far more if Eleanor were hurt. I'm safe as long as Eleanor isn't with me. I haven't told her about Sam, by the way. I didn't want her to know how worried I was.'

Mrs Southeran understood and agreed with him on this. Eleanor's equilibrium was still in a fragile state.

The rest of the afternoon passed pleasantly, and no one would have guessed, as Jonas chatted with Mrs Southeran and played a game of croquet with Eleanor, how heartily he was wishing that the time to leave for Stanyards would come. Eventually he set off at four o'clock, having first extracted from Eleanor a promise that she would stay with her mother, without actually telling her why. On his way to the house he called in at the stables and warned Sam to have extra care.

He had given himself the extra time to write out the necessary instructions to his bank, and prepare for Oliver's visit. He was fairly certain that the house would be safe as yet, for Sam had kept a look-out along the drive and had seen no one. As Jonas walked up the path to the house he was considering what Oliver might do. It could be that the man had concluded that enough was enough, had decided to take the money and go. But Jonas somehow didn't think that this was the case. There had been something about that conversation this morning. . .

Still, it was worth a risk just to see whether matters could be settled by negotiation. There had been no reports of strangers in the district, so Oliver was on his own. Jonas decided that the danger was not great, once he had removed any weapons Oliver might bring with him—he must remember to search him for a knife...

Once inside the house he checked the library carefully and then locked the door. He wrote out his intructions to the bank and laid them out ready for Oliver to see. Then he went into the secret room, which he had taken to using for valuables since being shown where it was, and counted out some money. This he put into a small bag, came back into the library and set it beside the envelope on the desk. It was nearly five o'clock. He unlocked the library door and waited by it. Someone was coming up the stairs...

Nathaniel Oliver came into the room, and Jonas seized him from behind, searched him, and removed a pistol from the side-pocket of his coat. There were no other weapons. Only then did he release his guest and invite him to sit down to read the letters.

'Well, I will, though I have a damn good mind to call off the truce, Guthrie. Is this the way you treat your other business associates?'

'It's the only way to treat you, Oliver. And you are no associate of mine, not in any sense . Read the letters and go!'

'I see you are making it a condition that I leave Combe St James by eight o'clock tomorrow morning?'

'You will need to leave immediately if you are to catch the October packet to New York. My carriage will take you both as far as Axminster. You can pick up the London mail from there. You will also observe that the payments are in instalments, and are conditional on the fact that you collect them in person on certain dates and in certain places.'

'An unnecessary complication, surely?'

'It's the only way I can be sure that you actually do travel back in the way you say you will.'

'Such a suspicious nature,' mocked Oliver, but he seemed to be satisfied.

'What about Evadne?' asked Jonas abruptly.

'Oh, she'll be pleased,' said Oliver with a smile. 'She'll be impressed.' Jonas frowned at his tone and Oliver explained smoothly, 'It's a handsome sum of money altogether.'

'Right, I'll just have your signature...' Oliver signed, and the documents were sealed and packed up. Jonas handed Oliver the bag of guineas, and stood up. 'You're getting away with more than you deserve. But it's worth it, just to be free of you. Don't come back to England in a hurry, Oliver.'

'I shan't, Guthrie, I shan't! I'll bid you farewell, then. No, I don't expect you to shake my hand. I'm really quite a reasonable man...' They were walking out of the door, and Oliver started down the stairs, looking up and giving Jonas a mock-salute as he went. Jonas watched him go. At the last minute he sensed danger, but it was too late. Something came at him from behind. He turned to defend himself, but felt a crashing blow on the head, was dimly aware of a loud voice shouting curses and then fell to the ground unconscious...

'Good,' said Oliver, coming back up the stairs. 'Now help me to drag him back into the library. That's it. Over here, I think, by the window. It'll look as if he was trying to get out. I don't suppose he could, if he did come to before it was too late?'

'Have a look out of that window, Mr Oliver,' said Threlfall. Oliver shuddered as he gazed down. Stanyards was surrounded on this side by a deep moat, now filled with iron spikes. 'Excellent! Now, Threlfall, we want kindling and tinder. Did you get it?'

'I hid it in the barn yesterday. Shall I fetch it?'

'Do so. Did—er—did anyone see you with it?'

'Only Tom Briggs, and he won't think twice about it.'

'Right! Fetch the stuff and we'll build a little bonfire for our dear friend here. I'll just see if there's anything worth keeping. . .'

'I'm not a thief, Mr Oliver. You do what you please, but I don't want anything but the money you promised me.'

'You are right, Threlfall. Now hurry!'

Threlfall went away while Oliver stood in the centre of the library, deciding how best to arrange the straw and tinder for maximum effect. But once his accomplice had gone he hurried to the desk and searched the drawers. Nothing but the pistol Guthrie had taken from him a few moments before, which he pocketed. Damn Guthrie and his careful ways!

Then he smiled. He had his passage and the letters. He and Evadne could leave tonight for London and go back satisfied to America, while poor old Threlfall took the blame for the fire. A piece of luck that this Tom, whoever he was, had seen the kindling in Threlfall's possession. . .

As if on cue Threlfall came in carrying a huge bundle of straw and other combustible material.

'I'll fetch some more,' he said. 'You could start laying a trail, if you would, Mr Oliver.' With his experience of burning off the stubble in the fields, he showed Oliver how to set the fire, then went to fetch more straw. 'It's going to be a right good blaze. That'll finish Mr Bloody Know-all Guthrie!' he said as he went.

Meanwhile Eleanor sat in the sitting-room at the Dower House in the fever of suspense. She had listened to the conversation between Oliver and Jonas, though she had remained unseen. She, too, had heard undertones in Oliver's voice. Jonas was in danger, she was sure, and she could suddenly no longer bear to sit there doing nothing.

'Mama, I think I shall just go out for a little air,' she said.

'You promised to stay with me, Nell.'

'But——'

'You will stay, Eleanor.'

Jonas, too, had known there was danger, and had obviously asked her mother to make sure that Eleanor remained in the Dower House. Mrs Southeran very seldom used such a tone, but when she did there was no disobeying it. Or, at least, not overtly.

Eleanor eyed her mother, who was working on a poem at her desk. A little guile was necessary, a little patience. She must go to Jonas, she must. . . But she would have to wait a while.

Eleanor got up.

'Where are you going, Nell?'

'To open the doors on to the terrace, Mama. Since I

cannot go out, I'll sit by them, just round the corner
from you, and read.'

The book was fetched, and the two women sat in
silence, Eleanor apparently absorbed in her book and
Mrs Southeran concentrating on her poem. In a few
minutes, as Eleanor knew she would be, Mrs
Southeran was lost to the world. She would not notice
what was happening for a minute or two. It would be
enough.

Eleanor laid her book down and silently crept along
the terrace, ducking under the window by her mother's
desk as she went. She avoided the steps at the end of
the terrace which led down into the yard, instead
crossing the lawn and scrambling through the hedge
on to the path to Stanyards. Here she took to her
heels and ran swiftly along it, driven by a single aim—
to get to Jonas. The scent of danger was getting
stronger all the time.

She met Threlfall at the foot of the stairs up to the
library, and her heart gave a thump when she saw the
consternation on his face as he caught sight of her. He
was covered in pieces of straw.

'Where is he?' she cried. 'What have you done with
him?'

'Miss Nell! Don't go up there, Miss Nell!'

But Eleanor was already halfway up the steps. She
burst into the library, and was horrified to see Jonas's
body lying under the window at the far end of the
room.

'Jonas,' she screamed. 'Jonas!' She did not see
Oliver, pouring oil from the lamp over a bundle of
wood and straw, as she ran forward and knelt down
beside the figure on the floor. A trickle of blood had

dried on Jonas's face. It came from an ugly wound on the side of his head, and as she gently touched it he groaned. He was alive! She got to her feet and looked for Threlfall, but was stunned when she saw Oliver standing by the door, smiling at her. In his hand was a lighted brand.

'Miss Southeran,' he said. 'An unexpected but wholly delightful pleasure to see you here. But I am afraid you will never now marry—either of you!'

Eleanor screamed again as Oliver threw the flaming piece of wood on to the nearest bundle of straw, then slammed the library door shut and locked it. The straw caught immediately, blazing up in a great fan of flame. . .

Outside the library door Threlfall and Oliver were struggling for possession of the key. Threlfall was beside himself, shouting, 'Let me have it! Give it to me, you bastard! Oh, God, not Miss Nell; you're not going to kill Miss Nell! Give it to me, I say!'

He caught the hand which held the key, but Oliver was holding a pistol in the other, and he pulled the trigger. Threlfall staggered back, then with a roar he attacked Oliver like a maddened bull. Oliver did not stand a chance. He went crashing down the stairs, the key slipping from his fingers as he fell. It tinkled down the steps behind him, finally coming to rest next to his body at the foot of the stairs.

Gasping and groaning, Threlfall lurched down the steps, his eyes only on the key. Oliver was lying with his head at an unnatural angle, his neck clearly broken, but Threlfall didn't wait to look. He climbed the stairs again, slowly, agonisingly slowly, his brow covered in sweat. He gave forth little grunts as he went, as if he had no breath for more than that.

When he reached the door he fumbled with the key for several moments, unable to see the lock, only feeling for it with fingers that were growing numb. Finally the door swung open and he fell into the room. A sheet of flame engulfed him, but he was already dead. His last words, heard by no one, had been a desperate cry to Eleanor.

At the far end of the room Eleanor was huddled over Jonas, her eyes wide with terror at the noise and power of the blaze in front of them. She rose to look out of the window. If only she could open it. . .

'Don't do that, Eleanor! It'll be the end if you do!'

Jonas was sitting up, holding his head. For a mad moment she thought she was back in the park, so many months ago. . .

'Eleanor! For God's sake, pull yourself together!' he whispered hoarsely. 'If we are to stay alive you've got to help me. We must get into that room—it's stone and our only chance!'

'The room? Of course!' Quickly she pressed the knob and the wall beside the window slowly opened, revealing the stone passage. 'I'll help you, Jonas,' she said as he got painfully to his feet. He was sheet-white, and it was clear that he was exerting every ounce of his strength to control his limbs. He was frowning with concentration.

'Quickly!' said Eleanor, trying not to sound as panic-stricken as she felt. 'You go first; I'll close the door behind us. Don't argue—save your strength.' Her voice wobbled and she cleared her throat. 'We'll be fine in there.'

They made their way into the passage.

'Make certain the door is shut tight!'

'I have, I have! Now hurry!'

A breath of cool air met them as they made their way into the little room, and sank gratefully to the floor. Eleanor snatched the cushion she had left there in her precipitate flight almost a month before and put it under Jonas's head. He was lying with his eyes shut, still frowning. Eleanor sat by him, holding his hand and listening to the roar in the library. A sudden crash made her jump.

'The beams in the ceiling? Or the floor?' said Jonas.

'Don't talk. Try to stay perfectly still.'

'It's difficult to do anything else! There isn't room for it,' he said, with a hint of his smile. Eleanor tried to smile back, and for a while there was silence again, during which Jonas gradually relaxed and his face regained a little of its colour.

'I thought you were dead, Jonas,' said Eleanor, her voice trembling. 'For a moment I thought you were dead. And all I could think was that I had never told you. . .'

'Told me what?' he asked, his eyes still shut. He was hardly daring to breathe.

'That I love you,' she said, quite simply. 'I never realised how much.'

He let out his breath in a long sigh, then said slowly, but with a hint of his old, quizzical tone, 'It takes a lot to persuade you to be kind to me, Eleanor Southeran! It needs an ambassador to get you to dance with me, a fire before you'll come looking for me, and you have to think I am dead before you realise that you love me after all! I can see an eventful life ahead. What do you demand before you will marry me? Carlton House? A visit to the moon? Immortal life?'

'An assurance of your love,' she said. 'That's all I have ever wanted.'

'Oh, my love, my very dearest, most precious love, you have that and to spare,' he said, rolling over and taking her into his arms.

'Jonas, be careful. . .' Eleanor's protest died away as he kissed her gently, but at great length. . .

The sound of another crash brought them to their senses, and they realised that the stones on the library side of the little room were growing warm. Jonas got up and went into the passage. When he came back he said tersely, 'I expect that was the floor in the library giving way. Don't look like that, Eleanor, we'll be all right. The stones here are part of the tower and very thick; they're not going to crack unless the fire burns for longer than I think it will. Oliver had put down straw and wood, you say?'

When Eleanor described to him what little she had seen, he said thoughtfully, 'He set out to create a sudden, overwhelming blaze—which he obviously did. The bookcases, ceiling and floor are all of wood— they'll go. The roof might, too. But the walls will hold. They are all of stone. Thank God for your ancestors' distrust of their neighbours, Eleanor! This house was built with the strength of a fortress.'

'I suppose the books will all have been destroyed,' she said sadly. 'My father's treasures.'

'I'm afraid so. But the best are still with Wilkes. That's one consolation.' He saw that tears were rolling down her cheeks. 'Don't cry, my love. We'll build it all up again—Stanyards, the collection, the lot! Together.'

'Yes, Jonas,' she said, trying to smile. 'Yes, I know.'

'We'll assess the damage and start on the repairs right away. You'll see. Stanyards will soon be itself again.'

'I'm not sure that is what I want any more. Perhaps we should plan something new, for a new age?'

'I'd like that! But we could build the new alongside the old—why shouldn't they mix?'

He saw that this subject intrigued her and encouraged her to talk of her ideas. But suddenly she said, 'We are going to get out, aren't we?'

'Oh, yes! The fire will burn itself out soon enough. Meanwhile, we shall have to stay here—we might get warm, but we won't burn.'

'How long, Jonas?'

'I should think it might be all right by morning.'

'Morning!'

'The fire will die down pretty soon now, I should think, but the wood and stone and rubble will be hot for some hours. We're stuck here till tomorrow. Are you afraid that you're ruined, spending the night with me? There's no danger to your virtue. I regret to say that I'm not capable of attacking you—I'm as weak as a kitten. And anyway, I'll make an honest woman of you just as soon as you'll allow me—I'll marry you.'

Eleanor smiled at this sally, but shook her head. 'It's my mother,' she said. 'She'll be frantic.'

He grew grave immediately. 'I'm sorry. I hadn't thought of that aspect; I was just relieved to find that we were not about to be roasted alive. What about

Threlfall? Won't he...? No, I suppose not. It would be tantamount to admitting his own guilt. Oliver certainly won't tell anyone. If I know him, he and Evadne will have left the area by nightfall. He has all the necessary funds, and he'll be anxious to exchange the letters I gave him for cash. Sam and your mother will see the smoke, of course...' Jonas put his arm round Eleanor. 'We'll have to sit it out, and so will they, my darling.'

# CHAPTER SIXTEEN

THEY made themselves as comfortable as they could. The floor was hard, the atmosphere stifling, and they were hungry and, above all, thirsty. Jonas was obviously still in some pain, but he insisted on giving Eleanor the cushion to rest on. In turn, she made him sit next to the window slit. At least the air coming in was cool and fresh.

The noises in the library were dying down. Before long they heard calls and shouts. Mrs Southeran and Sam were frantically circling the building, shouting and calling. Eleanor leapt up and leaned over Jonas till she could get her hand out of the slit. She waved, but there was no response. The old builders had done their job too well. The window was completely invisible from the ground.

'Here,' said Jonas. She was astonished to see him rip off his shirt and tear it into one long strip. 'Wave that,' he said.

Eleanor waved again and eventually heard an excited exclamation under the window. 'Mrs Southeran, Mrs Southeran! Ma'am! Look at this!' It was Sam.

They heard Mrs Southeran call tremulously, 'Eleanor? Are you there? In the room?'

'Yes,' shouted Jonas. 'We're both here. We're safe enough, but I doubt we'll be able to get out for some time. Don't worry. Have you seen Oliver?'

'Oh, thank God, thank God! Eleanor, say something—I shan't believe you're safe till I hear you.'

Eleanor put her face to the slit and shouted as best she could. 'Mama? I'm sorry. But I had to find Jonas.'

'Have you seen Oliver?' shouted Jonas.

'Yes. Was it you?' shouted Sam. His voice echoed round the little room.

'What do you mean?'

'He's dead. Neck broken,' bellowed Sam. 'We'll tell you about it later. I'll have a look at the stairs again. See if we can get you out.' He was gone.

'Is there nothing we can do?' asked Mrs Southeran.

'I don't think so. We're trapped till it's cooled off a bit. What is that about Oliver?'

'He was at the bottom of the stairs. Jonas, I cannot shout much more; my voice is going. Here's Sam again. Eleanor, take care!'

'She'll be all right, ma'am,' they heard Sam say. 'She's with Mr Guthrie.'

Jonas smiled. 'I wish I had his confidence!'

'Well, I have. Listen!'

A sound of singing and laughter came thinly on the air. The merrymakers were returning. But as they aproached their songs died down and exclamations of horror took their place. Soon Stanyards was surrounded by a throng of worried people. Sam took charge, ordering some to fetch water to make an attempt to put out the last remnants of flame, some to take Mrs Southeran back to the Dower House, and others to start getting rooms ready for those who had lost their sleeping quarters. The best men he kept with him to make an attempt to reach the window slit.

Eleanor and Jonas were going to need water and perhaps some food soon.

With the aid of some ingenious devices and skilled climbing, Sam got water and some biscuits through the slit. That would have to do till the morning. During the attempts, the two in the room heard that the library was completely gutted, and its floor had collapsed—there was no safe way out through it at the moment. Fortunately the fire had spread in the other direction away from the corner where the secret room lay. But some parts of Stanyards' roof had given in; others were still burning. 'It'll burn itself out very soon, Mr Guthrie. Don't you worry!'

'Is it bad, Sam?'

There was a silence, then Sam said, 'It's not good, sir. You'll see in the morning.'

With that he was gone. By this time it was dark, and it was with difficulty that Eleanor and Jonas ate their rations. Then they settled down for another rest. Eleanor's fingers came into contact with Jonas's bare chest. She let them roam. . .

'Don't,' said Jonas in a strangled voice.

'But you're cold,' said Eleanor. 'The floor, no shirt. . .'

'I am not,' said Jonas, 'cold. Not at all.'

'Oh. I just thought. . .'

'Well, don't!'

'I quite understand,' said Eleanor mournfully. 'And you did say that you were feeling not quite the thing. Weak as a kitten, you said.'

He pulled her into his arms. 'I suddenly find, my scheming, conniving, tormenting darling, that I am not as weak as I thought. Come here. . .'

'But Jonas.' Eleanor's voice was muffled againt his chest. 'You said my virtue was in no dang——'

'I lied! Now be quiet and let me seduce you like the villain I am!'

The next morning Eleanor and Jonas were rescued from their prison. Eleanor was swept off to the Dower House, and Jonas was carried away, protesting that he didn't need a damned doctor. When they met later that day in the Dower House, Jonas went straight over to Eleanor and took her into his arms, holding her close, as if he could not bear to be away from her, while Mrs Southeran watched them with a satisfied smile. Then the three of them talked of the events of the previous day, and Jonas added what he had learnt from Sam and the others.

Threlfall's badly burned body had been discovered in the ruins below the library, but it was still possible to see the bullet wound in his chest. Oliver's body was now lying in one of Stanyards' surviving rooms till the coroner should see it. A gun had been found near him.

Eleanor shuddered and hid her face in Jonas's coat. 'Please let us not talk of it any more. I can't bear to think of it. Poor Threlfall!'

'Poor Threlfall indeed! He was trying to murder me, Eleanor!'

'Well, if you hadn't been so hard on him——'

Mrs Southeran intervened. 'Now, now! It would be quite wrong of you to quarrel about Threlfall yet again. Or do you intend to continue after you are married?'

'Mama! You've spoiled my surprise—how do you

know? I haven't mentioned it. Have you?' said Eleanor, turning to Jonas.

Mrs Southeran said severely, 'No one has told me a thing, Eleanor. But I should certainly hope you are getting married—after last night.' Then she watched in amusement as Eleanor's face grew scarlet. 'I thought as much,' she said.

Jonas laughed out loud. 'I shall marry Eleanor as soon as she has something suitable to wear, ma'am.'

'And the licence?'

'That has been in my pocket since before I left London. But we shan't have anywhere to live for some time. May we lodge with you?'

'Well, I too have a surprise for you. I might be going to visit Boston for two months in the spring. And before that I shall be in London.'

Eleanor stared at her mother. 'What do you mean, Mama?'

'Mr Bitteridge is coming over to Europe very soon, and I shall stay in London with your aunt Hetty and show him the sights. He has invited me to go back with him to Boston, and I think I might.'

Eleanor sat down rather suddenly. 'Is he...is he married?'

'Goodness me, what a question! As it happens he's widowed—like me. But pray do not start adding two and two together and making five, Eleanor. I shall return next summer—if I go at all.'

They were interrupted by Betty. Her eyes were round as she said, 'It's Mrs Oliver, ma'am. Shall I... shall I say you're not at home?'

'No, of course not. Come in, Mrs Oliver.'

Evadne Oliver walked in, as composed as ever. She

was dressed in black, and, curiously enough, the clothes suited her. After an awkward few minutes during which everyone except Evadne tried to find something to say, she announced, 'I know what they are saying, and I think it probably true. Nathaniel tried to kill you, and was killed in the process. I knew nothing of his plan, Jonas. I merely wanted to get away as quickly as possible from England. Do you believe me?'

'Let us say for the sake of argument that I do, Evadne. You may have the money and the rest that I gave your husband. Sam will bring them down to you. Is that what you want? I take it that you still hope to take the boat to New York?'

'New York? Certainly not! I shall go to Madras.'

'Madras?' exclaimed Eleanor.

Evadne Oliver smiled. 'Madras,' she said. She went to the door, then turned. 'The late Mr Oliver was not the only member of our. . .somewhat peculiar household to like both men and women. And Christopher was much nearer to me in age. I shall go to Madras. Goodbye.' She went out, leaving the three people in the room speechless.

Mrs Southeran followed her extraordinary guest out, and Eleanor and Jonas were left alone.

'What about Stanyards, Jonas?'

'It's badly damaged. Parts of it are no longer safe. I should like to build a new house, Eleanor, perhaps incorporating some of the old. Would you live with me there?'

'A mansion, for a great lord with a title?'

'No, a family house—a large family house for our

large family! I shall never be a great lord, but the house will have a great lady for its mistress.'

'No, no, no,' said Eleanor, putting her arms around him and holding him close. 'A pretty little country girl—one who will help her husband to while away the odd hour—all of them, for the rest of his villainous life!'

# MISS WESTON'S MASQUERADE

by

Francesca Shaw

## Dear Reader

*Miss Weston's Masquerade* grew from a wish to send our heroine on an adventure with excitement, exotic places and a touch of danger. The European Grand Tour offered all of these – but no well-bred young lady would be allowed to undertake such a trip, and certainly not with the hero!

We decided to disguise Cassie, escaping a distasteful marriage, as the hero's valet. For Nicholas, it seemed simple enough to deliver her to her godmama in Paris. By the time they arrived in Paris to discover Godmama had moved on we were enjoying ourselves almost as much as Cassie was. It would take Nicholas many miles, a number of embarrassing encounters and some hair-raising adventures to realise the troublesome child he had carelessly taken on his travels was in fact an attractive, intelligent and spirited young lady.

For Cassie and Nicholas, their safe arrival at her Godmama's in Vienna meant they had to discover each other all over again. Of course, the path of true love proved anything but smooth until Cassie, driven to desperate flight once again, discovered that Nicholas truly loved her. We revisited some of our favourite European cities and saw them through Cassie's eyes. We hope if you know Paris, Venice and the other towns on their tour you will enjoy visiting them again; if not, perhaps Miss Weston's adventures will encourage you to discover them. We wish you as much fun reading our romp through Europe as we had in writing it.

*Francesca Shaw*

**Francesca Shaw** is not one, but two authors, working together under the same name. Both are librarians by profession, working in Hertfordshire, but living within distance of each other in Bedfordshire. They first began writing ten years ago under a tree in a Burgundian vineyard, but although they have published other romances, they have only recently come to historical novels. Their shared interests include travel, good food, reading and, of course, writing.

**Other titles by the same author:**

Master of Winterbourne
The Unconventional Miss Dane
The Admiral's Daughter
A Compromised Lady

# CHAPTER ONE

THE Audley Street Chapel clock struck nine, echoed by others more distant, their chimes carrying clearly on the still morning air. Cassandra Weston emerged with caution from the shelter of a dusty laurel bush and stood brushing down her cloak as she surveyed the Square.

There were people abroad, but only servants and tradesmen hurrying about their masters' business: mercifully none of the Quality who might pose a danger to her. At home in Hertfordshire she and Papa would have already breakfasted; the workers at Home Farm would have finished the milking and the streets of Ware would be bustling with market-goers by now.

A small cart rumbled past over the cobbles, causing her to draw back into shelter. Now it was full light, Cassandra felt even more conscious of the awkwardness of her situation, but nothing would be gained by hesitating. She ran her hands through her disarrayed chestnut hair, swallowed hard and picked her way across the cobbles to the steps of number 6, Grosvenor Square.

The knocker was heavy and cold in her hands but still she hesitated before letting it fall. It was five years since she had last seen her Godmama: what if she had miscalculated, presumed too much on the lasting affection of her mother's best friend? Perhaps Lady Lydford would take one look at her and pack her straight back to Hertfordshire and Papa. And if she did that, what recourse would be left to her? She thought of the oily, sliding waters of the Thames and shuddered, letting the knocker fall from her fingers with a resounding thud.

The door swung open with startling suddenness to reveal not the expected footman, but the stately figure of the family butler whose eyebrows rose at the sight on the doorstep.

'The tradesman's entrance is at the rear.'

The door was already closing before Cassandra found her voice. 'Wait, please, Peacock. It is Peacock, isn't it?'

The butler hesitated and looked more closely at the small dishevelled figure. 'And what if it is?' he asked cautiously, obviously puzzled by the contrast between the sight before him and an educated voice.

'I must see Lady Lydford.'

'The Dowager Countess is not at home.'

'Then I will wait,' Cassandra said more firmly.

'I did not mean that her ladyship is not At Home, I mean that her ladyship is not at home. She is, in fact, not even in the country: a fact that any of her ladyship's acquaintances well know.' Peacock began to close the door again.

'Out of the country?' In her desperation she had never considered the possibility that her godmother would not be in London. Shock, compounded by hunger and fatigue sent her head reeling. Her knees gave way and she sank onto the cold stone steps, whispering 'Godmama not here. . .?'

The butler, who had stooped to seize her arm roughly, froze, his eyes suddenly alert, scanning her face. 'You cannot remain here on the steps. Come inside.' He cast a rapid glance across the Square, but the only people in sight were a milkmaid emerging from Brook Street, pails suspended from the yoke across her shoulders, a street sweeper and a hurrying page boy.

Breathless, Cassandra found herself standing in the hall, an expanse of black and white marble. The light from the central lantern gleamed richly on the balustrade of the curving staircase and the few pieces of elegantly arranged furniture.

A footman slipped silently from an anteroom to disappear through a door under the stairs. Peacock sighed almost imperceptibly, his eyes on the man's back. 'I think it best you should see his lordship and not wait where the other servants can see you.'

'The Earl is at home?' For some reason she had assumed that with her Godmama away, all members of the family would be absent.

'For the present. He leaves for the Continent today.' Perhaps regretting his impulse to admit her, Peacock gestured abruptly to her to follow. A slight figure in the dusty cloak, Cassandra followed the butler's disapproving bulk, trying not to let her ill-fitting shoes clatter on the polished stair treads.

With a glance behind him to ensure the unwelcome and embarrassing visitor was still there, Mr Peacock halted on the second floor landing and scratched lightly on the door in front of him.

As it opened, Cassandra craned her neck, but could glimpse only a portion of the room past Peacock's square shoulders and nothing at all of the man inside who was speaking.

'. . .how the Devil would I know how many neck-cloths I will need before we reach Paris? Does it matter? Do they not manufacture such articles on the Continent?'

Nicholas Anthony St John Cheney, Seventh Earl of Lydford, was evidently out of humour. Cassandra fought down an urge to turn and run down the staircase, across the chequerboard hall, out into the morning-quiet street beyond, and stood her ground.

'None of the quality we would accept my lord.' The valet coughed softly. 'Mr Peacock is at the door, my lord.'

'I am aware of that, Franklin. Well, Peacock? Have you come to announce some further disaster to overset my plans?'

'I could not say, my lord. There is a young. . .person to see you.'

'What makes you think I would wish to interview a young person—or, indeed, anyone else—at this hour in the morning?' A flash of vivid crimson brocade was intermittently visible: the Earl was obviously pacing impatiently.

'I believe you will wish to see *this* one.' The butler spoke with a curious emphasis, stepping aside as he did so to reveal the shrinking figure behind him to the irritable gaze of a tall gentleman wearing a dressing gown shrugged carelessly over shirtsleeves and breeches.

'Have you been at the port, Peacock? Why should I wish to see this scrubby boy?'

'The young person was asking for the Dowager Countess, my lord.' Peacock was very much on his dignity. 'In view of her ladyship's absence, I thought it best to escort the young...'

'Will you stop referring to this boy as a Young Person! Here—you boy, come in, stop skulking in the shadows. Have you performed some service for my mother which requires recompense?' He turned impatiently to the butler. 'I do feel, Peacock, that you could have dealt with this.'

'Perhaps, my lord, if you were to enquire the young person's name... Meanwhile, there is a matter which requires Franklin's urgent attention in the laundry room.'

The valet grimaced as he slipped out onto the landing. 'Got out of bed the wrong side and three hours too early,' he muttered *sotto voce* as he passed them.

Peacock propelled the cloaked figure into the bed-chamber and shut the door. Cassandra's heart sank at the disappearance of her only ally, however reluctant.

Lord Nicholas stood regarding her unfavourably, arms folded across his chest. The bright sunshine streaming in through the long casements caused him to narrow his green eyes assessingly. To Cassandra, quaking in her borrowed clothes, he resembled, with his aquiline features and high cheekbones, nothing more than a sparrowhawk who had sighted an insignificant but tasty mouse.

'Should I know you?' A hint of puzzlement touched the assured voice.

Pushing aside the folds of cloak, she stepped forward into the sunlight, which shone on the boards behind her. 'Yes, although it must be nearly ten years since we last met.' Cassandra was aware she was blushing. She had not expected to find herself in a gentleman's bedchamber, least of all that of the man who had been her hero since she was eight years old. 'I. . . I was hoping to see Godmama.'

'Your Godmama! My mother, you mean? Then you must be. . .' He looked her up and down, frankly incredulous.

'Cassandra Weston.' She let the heavy wool fall to the floor revealing the jerkin, breeches, coarse woollen stockings and the ill-fitting shoes she had borrowed from the stableboy in yesterday's urgent flight.

'Little Cassie? Good G. . .' He checked the oath and walked slowly round her, his expression half-way between amusement and exasperation. 'What prank are you engaged on? You shouldn't be jauntering around London in those clothes: where is your maid?'

'I don't have one.'

'No, I suppose not, at your age.' He came to a halt in front of her, hands on hips, amusement winning out over irritation. 'How old are you? Twelve?'

'Certainly not!' She was about to tell him she was all of eighteen, then some instinct made her hold her tongue. Let him believe she was still a child, at least until they were in more proper surroundings with a maid as chaperone.

'Well, fifteen, then, you cannot be much more! You look the most complete urchin—what have you done to your hair?' The Earl leaned forward and lifted a strand between fastidious fingers. 'It appears to have been cut with shears and it's full of cobwebs.'

'Embroidery scissors; they were all I could find,' Cassandra replied bleakly. The loss of her mass of chestnut curls had seemed a small sacrifice at the time;

now, seeing herself through his critical eyes, she regretted it. 'And I had to hide in the gardens of the Square. The stage arrived at ten last night and it took me so long to find the house, I thought it too late to knock.'

'If we retire before two in this household we consider it a dull night, but I suppose in the wilds of Hertfordshire all activity ceases as the sun goes down.' He was watching her face as he teased her. She saw his eyes narrow. 'You're as white as a shirt under that dirt, child. When did you last eat?'

'At noon yesterday.' And she could not tell him that after her father's ultimatum she had run from the dining-room and been violently sick.

The Earl tugged the silken bellpull beside the hearth and gestured her into a chair with its back to the door. When a footman brought chocolate, ham, bread and sweet rolls, he watched her eat hungrily for a few moments before pouring himself a cup of chocolate.

'Would you care for some ham?' Cassandra suddenly remembered her manners.

'Not at this unearthly hour of the morning!' he gave a snort of amusement at her expression.

'But it is almost ten o'clock! Surely you would not still be abed?' Her father was always railing against the laxity and dissipation of London life: perhaps he was right.

'Indeed I would if I were not taking the Dover road this afternoon. But never mind that: what mischief are you about? Your father is not going to be pleased to receive you home looking like that.'

Cassandra jumped to her feet, heedlessly overturning the plate of rolls in her agitation. 'I am not going back! He mustn't know I am here!'

'You've run away?' All the amusement was gone from his face. 'This is not some prank hatched in the schoolroom, then? Have you no concern for your reputation?' He read the answer in her desolate face. After a moment, he got to his feet and began to pace in thought, hands thrust deep into the pockets of his dressing gown. 'You really could not have chosen a more inconvenient time to quarrel with your father. . .'

'It is more than a quarrel,' Cassandra cried.

She realised the Earl was not taking any notice of her, his brow furrowed in thought. Eventually he announced: 'If you stay here with Mrs Mitchell, the housekeeper, and write to your father, then no harm will be done. With the family away, no-one of consequence will visit us here. You must stay in your room, of course, until your father comes to take you home. . .'

'I will not go home.' Cassandra grasped one brocade sleeve with frantic hands. 'If you try and make me, I will throw myself in the Thames.'

There was a short silence while he freed her fingers from his sleeve and smoothed out the rich fabric. 'What melodrama are you playing out?' His voice— and face—were cold. 'You ridiculous child, you are not between the pages of a novel.'

'Papa does not permit me to read novels,' Cassandra said stiffly. 'I am not a child, pray do not treat me as one. Oh, if only Godmama were here—I cannot expect you to understand, you are a man!'

'That I cannot deny,' he said drily, recovering some of his humour. 'Sit down and tell me the story from the beginning.' The clock on the mantel chimed ten. 'But without embroidery. I am in no mood for a melodrama: time is pressing, we must resolve this before I leave London.'

'I doubt you can help me,' Cassandra stated despairingly. 'Only Godmama could do that. . .'

She broke off as the valet slipped into the room with an apologetic murmur. 'The luggage my lord?'

'Take the dressing case, the rest can wait—for a few minutes.'

The Earl's obvious impatience to be gone spurred Cassandra to blurt out the truth as soon as they were once more alone. 'My father insists I marry Lord Offley.'

'*Lord Offley*?' He was every bit as outraged as she could have hoped. 'That disgusting rake? Why, he must be thrice your age! He's no fit husband for any decent woman, let alone a young girl of your sheltered upbringing. Are you sure you have the name right? I cannot believe your father would have anything in common with such a man.'

'Nor has he. Father has not left home this last decade since Mama died, except for a few visits to the London booksellers. In Hatchards last year, he chanced to meet this widow, Lord Offley's sister, and now he is besotted with her. . .'

'Bella Mainwaring?' The Earl grimaced. 'Bella Mainwaring and your father! She has been on the catch for a complaisant husband these last six years, but I cannot imagine a man of your father's. . .habits being attracted to such as she.'

'Please do not attempt to be polite about Papa's

character,' Cassandra interjected bitterly. 'He is a mean, reclusive, tyrannical, selfish. . .'

'Quite. Although I doubt a dutiful daughter should say so.'

'Since my mother died I have been his companion, I have kept house for him on a pittance. I have been loyal and dutiful and obedient.' And very, very lonely, she thought to herself, but could not voice it aloud. 'And now he wants to marry this woman. He is infatuated with her. But she will not countenance it while I am still in the house. She knows I see her for what she is: a fortune seeking female, who will see my father in his grave as swiftly as she saw her first two husbands into theirs.'

'You are well-born and no doubt well dowered.' Nicholas leaned back in his chair regarding her critically. 'You are young, but not impossibly so. And presumably, when correctly dressed, passably presentable. Why does he not permit you to have a Season next year and find an eligible husband you can accept?'

Cassandra chose to ignore his unflattering description of her looks and prospects. 'The Season costs money and requires planning. He will spend neither time nor money on me, although I am his only child.' She knew she was sounding bitter, but was beyond caring. 'Yesterday at luncheon, he told me if I did not agree to marry Lord Offley, I would be shut in my room until I acquiesced, however long that took.' She shuddered. 'Have you met Lord Offley? He has a wet mouth, and he keeps wanting to touch. . .'

She had all the Earl's attention; his mobile mouth was drawn into a thin line of distaste. 'I know him only too well, although he is not of my circle. Your instincts about him are quite correct: there are tales I could not possibly tell an innocent girl.' He got to his feet and walked to the window, pulling back one of the drapes to stare out over the Square.

Cassandra could not read his mood, but she felt reassured by his anger on her behalf. When she was eight years old he had come to visit with his mother. He had rescued her kitten from a tree and she had thought him the most wonderful youth in the world. Now, regarding his broad shoulders, she felt the same security she had experienced when he had swung down from the tall oak clutching the terrified cat.

'My lord,' she began as the silence stretched on.

'Nicholas, call me Nicholas,' he said absently. 'We are almost cousins. I must think what to do for the best. . .' He was interrupted by a loud crash and the sounds of splintering wood.

'What the Devil!' Nicholas wrenched open the chamber door, Cassandra at his heels. Leaning over the landing balustrade, they had a birdseye view of the hall below. Franklin, the valet, was flat on his back on the marble floor, one leg twisted beneath him. Mr Peacock was directing two footmen to lift a valise from his body. Shirts cascaded from the split leather and neckcloths fluttered on the splintered ends of the banisters.

'Is he all right?' Nicholas called down.

The butler raised his face to his employer. 'I think not my lord. He is unconscious and I fear his right leg is broken.'

'Send for the surgeon.'

'At once, my lord. We will carry him through to the anteroom sofa.'

The Earl thrust Cassandra back into his room. 'Wait there.'

As she wandered round the chamber, a fresh cup of chocolate in her hand, Cassandra felt her spirits lighten despite her concern for the unfortunate Franklin. She had no idea what was to become of her, unchaperoned in this great house with a nobleman who was about to leave the country, but she had an irrational confidence that Nicholas would take her side, would not allow this marriage to take place.

Behind a small screen she found a ewer and basin. One glance in the glass hanging on the wall sent her flying to pour water and wash her hands and face, but even dragging a comb through her hair did nothing to tame it. Experimentally, she dipped the comb in the water and wetted her hair, smoothing it closer to her head and back off her face.

Critically she examined the result: really, she thought, she made a very passable boy. Her lashes were rather long over her blue eyes, but she had dark, definite brows, high cheekbones and a firm mouth. Cassandra was accustomed to being told she was a passably handsome girl, a description she had taken to mean she would never be pretty. Now that seemed an advantage.

By the time Nicholas returned, a furrow of worry between his brows, she had brushed down her clothes and straightened her necktie. 'Has the surgeon been?'

'He has,' replied Nicholas shortly. 'Franklin will be going nowhere for at least a month; his leg is badly broken. There is no hope now of finding a valet willing to travel in time. Well, there's the end of it, I shall have to postpone my departure, I cannot possibly travel without my manservant.'

'You do not seem very concerned about Franklin.' Cassandra was slightly shocked, and disappointed her hero seemed so unsympathetic.

Nicholas's brows rose haughtily. 'He is being attended by an excellent surgeon, he has a comfortable bed and has nothing to do but lie in idleness at my expense until his leg knits.'

'You make it sound as if the man has done it on purpose in order to inconvenience you!'

'You have to admit, Cassie, I have had my full share of inconveniences today,' he said wryly. 'Now what are we going to do with you?'

The question went unanswered. Distantly, from the stairs, Peacock's voice could be heard raised in what even Cassandra realised was untypical agitation. '. . .his lordship is not yet out of his chamber, my lady. He is not receiving visitors yet. . .'

'Nonsense, Peacock, my nephew will see me.' A forceful female voice overrode his protests.

'Oh, my God!' Nicholas sprang out of his chair, dragging Cassandra to her feet and thrust her behind the screen. 'Aunt Augusta!'

Outside the chamber door, Peacock was making a despairing last effort. 'I believe his lordship is not yet dressed. . .'

'Well, he should be, idle young hound.' The door swung open as Peacock gave up the struggle. 'Lady Augusta Armitage, my lord.'

'So you are up, after all, Lydford.' Through the crack in the screen, Cassandra could see a formidable matron wearing a crimson mantle and an alarming turban. At the look on the Earl's face, Cassandra was hard pressed to suppress a giggle.

'Good morning, Aunt. To what do I owe the pleasure?'

'Why are you not properly dressed? I do not hold with the habit you young men have of lolling about until all hours. Wait until you are married, all this will stop!'

'I am sure it will, Aunt. Won't you take a seat? Let me ring for fresh chocolate.' While his aunt arranged her gown, Nicholas whipped Cassandra's cup and saucer off the tray and hid them behind his back. His aunt had eyes like a hawk and a nose for scandal second to none. If she knew he had a girl in the house, let alone his room, they'd be married by lunchtime. He shuddered at the thought.

'That would be very refreshing, Lydford, thank you. And now, to the purpose of my visit. Sit down, stop fidgeting, why don't you.'

Cassandra had to stuff her sleeve in her mouth to stifle her laughter as Nicholas sat down cautiously, manoeuvring the cup under the chair.

'Of course, I am always delighted to see you Aunt, but you say you have a particular purpose for your visit today. . .?'

'I certainly have—to bring you to some sense of your duty, since your poor mama seems unable to. I know you are about to set off on some wild escapade round the Continent. . .'

'A series of cultural visits only, I assure you, Aunt. Now we are at peace with France again, the opportunity presents itself. . .'

'It is to be hoped the Corsican Monster is safely caged this time.' Lady Augusta paused long enough to allow him to pour her chocolate. 'I shudder every time I think of that upstart Napoleon. However, I did not come here to speak of politics. It is time you were married, Lydford. I met my dear friend Lady Hare at a reception yesterday evening. Her niece was with her, a charming girl, eminently suitable. I have asked them both to stay next week at Woodham Park and I want you to postpone your departure and join us there.'

Cassandra realised from the hunted look on Nicholas's face that this was a familiar theme. 'Aunt, grateful as I am for your invitation, what you suggest is impossible. I have a boat to catch tomorrow morning.'

'Not without your valet, you won't,' his aunt retorted triumphantly. 'I have heard of this morning's accident. Do not try and gull me! You, of all men, will not leave without someone to look after your linen.'

The look on Nicholas's face was so comic, Cassandra stepped back quickly before laughter got the better of her. Unfortunately she backed into a small table, sending an ornament tumbling.

'Nicholas! What is that? Is there someone in the room?'

Desperately Cassandra seized a pile of freshly pressed shirts and scurried head down from behind the screen towards the door.

As she pulled it closed behind her, she heard the formidable voice demanding 'Who was that?' Controlling her breathing with an effort, Cassandra pressed her ear to the panels.

'Why, my new valet, of course, Aunt.'

'That scrubby boy? Are you out of your senses?'

'It's Franklin's nephew. He will do until I reach Paris. Beggars can't be choosers.' Even through the oak, Cassandra could hear the enjoyment in Nicholas's voice. She suspected he rarely had the advantage over this formidable lady and was relishing it now. Abandoning her post, she tiptoed down the landing and let herself into the next room.

She realised she was in Nicholas's bedchamber: through the linking door to the dressing room she could hear Nicholas's voice and the more strident tones of his aunt. Goodness knew how long Lady Augusta would stay, she may as well make herself comfortable.

The bed looked inviting, freshly made. Cassandra put the shirts carefully on a dresser, kicked off her shoes and sat on the edge of the bed. It was wide and soft with a mountain of white pillows. Surely it would do no harm to settle down here for a few minutes?

'So that's where you've got to.' Cassandra struggled back to consciousness to find Nicholas standing at the end of the bed regarding her. 'You can come out now—she's gone.'

'Are you going to Woodham Park to stay as she asks?' Cassandra sat up, rubbing the sleep from her eyes.

'And abandon my trip for a week of hideous embarrassment while she throws the simpering niece of Lady Hare at my head? I think not.'

Cassandra saw a wicked gleam in his eyes. 'Your aunt will be very displeased.'

'All the more reason for not being here.' Nicholas

riposted. 'Hurry, get up. I have had an idea. We have a lot to do—finding you clothes that fit for a beginning.'

'Why, you are running away from her! I do believe you are frightened of her!'

Nicholas's mouth twisted humorously. 'There is not a man in Christendom who isn't! Her late husband was terrified of her. But we will not be here to experience her wrath.'

Cassandra pricked up her ears at the 'we'. It sounded as though, whatever the plan, he did not intend leaving her with the housekeeper after all.

'You have a scheme for me?' She looked into his face eagerly, but he was not attending to her. His expression was preoccupied.

'I must do something about trimming your hair,' he began. 'And I think I can find you some clothes to fit.'

'But Nicholas,' Cassandra shook his arm to gain his attention. 'What are you going to do with me if you're going to France? And how can you go to France without a valet?'

He looked down at her, a slow, mischievous smile curling his lips. 'But I have a valet. I'm looking at him—or rather, at her.'

# CHAPTER TWO

'YOUR *valet*?' Cassandra said incredulously, as Nicholas's words sank in. 'You want me to pretend to be your valet?'

'I don't *want* you to pretend to be anything. I want you to be twenty-five miles away in Hertfordshire under your father's eye. But you're not, are you? You're here in my bedroom.' He crossed his arms across his chest and leant against the bedpost, ignoring her blushes. 'And if Aunt Augusta walked in now and found you, I'd be marrying you, not Emily Hare.' He grinned at her. 'I don't think either of us would thank her for that! Well? Do you have any better ideas?'

'I...why cannot I stay here with your housekeeper until Godmama returns?' Under the coarse neckcloth, Cassandra could feel the rising heat of embarrassment. Marry Nicholas! He had been her idol for so long, a wonderful 'big brother', she could never think of him in *that* way. He was jesting, of course, believing her to be so young. And, of course, he was making it quite evident how unthinkable the idea was.

She pulled herself together, realising he was still talking. '...there is no saying when my mother will return. After all, she is her own mistress with no-one to please but herself. My aunt, on the other hand, will not give up organising my life so easily: she must not find you here.'

'But surely she'll think the house is empty...'

312

'All the more reason for frequent visits to supervise the servants. You cannot hope to remain here undetected and, I can assure you, my aunt is of the old school: if your father says you must marry Lord Offley, then marry him you will. She would have no truck with disobedience.'

Cassandra could well imagine Lady Augusta's reaction if she discovered an unmarried girl who had run away from home and taken refuge in a gentleman's chambers! She would have to marry Lord Offley or Nicholas or be ruined in the eyes of Society.

She was conscious of Nicholas's silence: he had made a suggestion, now it was up to her to decide. Go with him and take the risk of public exposure and ruin, or go back and face a marriage she abhorred. She shivered, remembering Lord Offley's lascivious gaze. She may have led a sheltered life, but she knew exactly what was in his mind when he looked at her like that.

She raised her eyes to meet those of the very different man who was offering her the chance of escape.

'Cassandra,' Nicholas prompted gently. 'I realise I have given you an impossible choice: you are between the Devil and the deep sea, but we have no time to waste. You must decide now.'

An impossible choice! What seemed impossible was to hide her elation from him, make him think she was the frightened, vulnerable child he believed her to be, not the determined eighteen year old she was. Cassandra could think of nothing she would rather do in the entire world. To journey abroad—to Paris! And with Nicholas, whom she had idolised since she was eight years old! Hastily she cast her eyes down before he could see the welling excitement there.

'Yes, Nicholas.' She managed to sound demurely obedient and trustful. 'If you think it would work. . .'

'All we have to do is to get you to Paris. Mama will know what to do with you. No doubt she will announce that she invited you to stay and invent a suitable chaperone for the journey. And, this way, at least I catch tomorrow's boat.'

And escape Aunt Augusta's schemes, Cassandra thought wryly, although she did not voice it aloud. Life with Papa had taught her that men needed their dignity preserving, however ridiculous they could be.

'Do you trust me to look after your linen?' she enquired with mock seriousness, eyeing the careless elegance of his attire. The dressing gown had gone, to be replaced by a dark blue double breasted coat, a snowy cravat and shining Hessians over buff breeches.

'Looking at the way you are turned out, I have the deepest misgivings.' He eyed her dubiously. 'Where did you get those garments? The stableboy?'

'Yes, as it happens. They are his Sunday best.'

'But hardly suitable for the valet of an Earl. I'll see what I can do with your hair, meanwhile. . .' He tugged the bellpull. 'Come back into the dressing room.'

Cassandra hopped off the bed with alacrity, glad to escape from the bedchamber. Not that she felt threatened in any way: naturally she had no experience of how a man *should* react to finding a girl in his bed, but it seemed to her that Nicholas was unflatteringly unmoved.

In the dressing room, she submitted meekly to being swathed in a towel while he dragged a comb ruthlessly through what remained of her curls. 'This will have to be a severe crop if you're not to look as though the moth's been at it.' He snipped quickly and deftly, the fine hair falling on to her face and making her sneeze. Nicholas brushed it off her cheeks with surprising gentleness.

Peacock entered the room silently, a suit of dark clothing over his arm, disapproval etched on every feature. 'The underfootman's church clothes, my lord,' he announced frostily. 'An undersized youth. They should fit Miss Weston.' He departed stiff-backed.

'He knows who I am?'

'He has been with the family twenty years, he certainly knows who my mother's godchild is.' Nicholas tossed aside the towel impatiently. 'Hurry up and get dressed, it will soon be noon. We will eat on the road at the first change of horses.' He paused with one hand on the doorknob. 'If you need anything, ring for Peacock. Don't be seen outside these rooms—and hurry,' he urged as the clock chimed once more.

The underfootman's Sunday best was a good fit. Cassandra tucked the ends of the neckcloth into the black cloth waistcoat and straightened a wrinkle in one of her stockings before examining herself in the long glass. The waistcoat was rather tight, but that was a good thing, she reflected. It served to flatten her small breasts; when she shrugged on the coat, the effect was complete. No-one would guess she was not a boy, she assured herself.

Ten minutes later, Nicholas's keen scrutiny confirmed what she had seen in the glass. 'Passable, in fact, more than passable. It's a good thing you're not pretty. Just remember to stride when you walk, stand up straight, and don't say anything unless you have to.' He seemed oblivious to the hurt look Cassandra gave him. She knew she wasn't pretty, but he might at least have said she made a good looking boy! 'That's good: scowl like that,' he added, blithely piling insult on injury.

Cassandra followed him down the curving staircase to the hall where Peacock handed him into his caped driving cloak. 'Is the luggage stowed, Peacock?'

'It is, my lord, and the heavy baggage should have reached Dover this morning. Your gloves and hat, my lord.'

Ignorning the butler's disapproving glance, Cassandra ran blithely down the steps to where the curricle waited, a diminutive Tiger holding the heads of four matched bays. 'I shan't be needing you, Jem.' The Earl swung up onto the box, gathering the reins in his gloved hand and steadying the team.

'What, m'lud? Not taking me? Who'll sort the 'orses out?'

'I think I'm capable of giving simple instructions to ostlers, Jem. You can follow tomorrow and bring the team back from the *Shoulder of Mutton* at Dartford. Get up, er. . . Cass.'

Cassandra scrambled up to sit beside him.

'Cross your arms and sit up straight,' Nicholas hissed out of the corner of his mouth. 'Let them go, Jem!'

The team was fresh and enough of a handful to occupy his lordship's attention for the first ten minutes as he negotiated the thronged streets leading to Piccadilly and Green Park. Sitting up straight as she'd been bid, Cassandra hardly knew where to look first. The quiet streets had been transformed into bustling life, so crowded she wondered that the traffic was moving at all.

Carriages of all kinds wove their way around tradesmen with barrows, a man driving pigs, a broken down hackney carriage with the wheel off while two coachmen quarrelled over who had caused the accident. . .

'Look at that beautiful lady, Nicholas.' She uncrossed her arms to tug at his sleeve. 'Oh, I wish I had a dress like that!'

Nicholas glanced in the direction she was pointing and snapped, 'Sit still and cross your arms! And don't gawp. . .'

'But I've never seen a dress like that, so daring. How does she make it cling so?'

'Never you mind,' Nicholas said grimly, swearing under his breath as a coalman shot a load of coal noisily down a cellar chute making the wheelers shy. He was beginning to think that a fresh team and Miss Cassandra Weston were more than any man should have to deal with at once. 'No woman walking the streets unaccompanied is any better than she should be!'

'Oh, Nicholas, is that the Banqueting Hall?' Cassandra was quite uncrushed by his irritation. 'Slow down, please, I want to look at it.' She was swept up by the exhilaration of being driven through London, seeing before her eyes all the sights she had read about.

'Perhaps you would like me to stop and buy you a guidebook?' he enquired politely.

'I wish you would.' His sarcasm was lost on her; she had almost forgotten why they were there, who she was with. 'Papa has Mr Pennant's *London*. If I had thought, I would have brought it with me, for Papa swears by it as a guide.'

'Cassandra, I have no intention of sightseeing, gawping at streetwalkers, visiting bonnet shops, calling on the Prince Regent or any of the other diversions you seem to have in mind! Now, you tiresome child, you will sit still and be quiet, or I will set you down on Westminster Bridge and you may throw yourself in the Thames or walk home to Ware as you wish.'

They both subsided into smouldering silence. Cassandra waited until Nicholas had turned the team onto the bridge, then asked in a small voice, 'Do you regret bringing me?'

'I must have been mad.' He spoke grimly. Cassandra realised he was looking at her and sniffed defiantly: she would not let him see she wanted to cry. It wasn't her fault it was all so new and exciting.

'Don't sniff, child. I don't allow Jem to sniff—and besides, your nose is getting pink.' The Earl smiled at her, his irritation suddenly gone, as they passed the new obelisk in St George's Circus. 'If you want to sightsee, how about that magnificent building on our left?'

'What is it?' Cassandra enquired eagerly, craning to look.

'The King's Bench Prison.'

Cassandra shuddered and averted her gaze from the grim walls, her appetite for sights disappearing. Soon the wide streets of Southwark were behind them; Greenwich and Blackheath with their palace and parkland passed and the horses were breasting the long pull of Shooters Hill at a steady trot.

'Are there highwaymen?' she asked apprehensively,

gazing at the thick wood which grew right down to the road edge and inching closer to Nicholas.

'Probably. There are horse pistols in the holster beside you. If we're attacked, it's the groom's job to fire them.' He glanced at her pale face. 'Don't worry, I'm teasing you, we're safe enough in daylight and there are other travellers on the road. Besides, the Mail is a far more tempting target. If you look out at the crossroads, you might see a corpse on the gibbet,' he added slyly.

Mercifully Cassandra was spared the sight. It was nearly two o'clock before they arrived at the *Shoulder of Mutton* in Dartford. Cassandra's stomach grumbled as she climbed down from the high seat and stood quietly to one side like a good servant, while Nicholas gave orders to the ostlers for the return of his team and looked over the horses which were to replace them for the next stage to Chatham.

This was another side to him she had not seen before: the cool assumption of authority, the way the inn staff jumped to his every order. No wonder he was so confident, he was used to receiving compliance everywhere he turned. Not for the first time Cassandra realised how much easier life would have been if she'd been born a boy. Meanwhile, she was going to enjoy pretending—all the way to Paris.

'There's time for some bread and cheese and ale.' Nicholas shouldered his way into the inn and found them a corner table. 'I should get a private parlour with you here, but this will be good practice for you. Just remember to act like a boy—and drink your ale, don't sip it.'

Cassandra copied the way he lifted his tankard and

drank deeply, shuddering as the bitter liquid ran down her throat. 'It's disgusting! How can men drink this for pleasure?' But Nicholas not was listening. He had turned, one long arm across the back of the settle, and was watching the arrival of the Dover coach which had just clattered into the yard and was disgorging its noisy cargo. 'What's the matter?' His watchfulness made her suddenly uneasy.

'Nothing, I hope, so long as no-one who knows me is on board and stops to talk. Drink up, we'd better get on our way.'

They pushed their way back through the group, an ill-assorted collection of all social classes from young blades to plain-dressed artisans, all stretching to relieve the stiffness caused by the coach's rattling progress.

Cassandra let her breath out in a sigh of relief as they regained the road without anyone hailing Nicholas. So caught up was she in her own predicament, she was only now beginning to realise what an embarrassment she might be to him. He seemed unruffled, but his broad shoulders relaxed as he drove the new team well up to their bits down the old Roman road to Rochester.

The green countryside with its rows of neatly kept hops marching up the slopes and the groups of oast-houses was pleasant enough to distract her thoughts until Rochester. She hoped they would change horses there: perhaps find time to look at the castle and the ships lying at anchor on the wide Medway, but Nicholas pushed the tired team on to Chatham for the next change.

They made good time, but still it was well past five

before they entered Canterbury and even Cassandra's enthusiasm for sightseeing was blunted by tiredness. She passed the cathedral with scarcely more than a glance at the twin towers soaring over the narrow streets. They changed horses for the last time at Bridge.

The good weather that had favoured them all day mellowed into a still, warm June evening and their shadows were lengthening on the road before them as they drove, at last, down the long hill into Dover.

The castle crouched on the clifftop, dominating the port straggling down the valley to the sea's edge. Cassandra sat up, straightening her weary shoulders and crossing her arms like the perfect servant. She ached in every limb from the joltings of the road, yet all she had done was sit alongside Nicholas.

He had driven the strange horses for mile after mile, negotiated potholes and tollgates, avoided village urchins and stray dogs, and yet he looked as fresh as when they had set out from Grosvenor Square. Only the crinkles of tiredness at the corners of his eyes betrayed any sign of fatigue. Cassandra watched his hands, sure and strong on the reins, the long flexible fingers sending almost imperceptible signals to the leaders.

The curricle was bowling down to a wide esplanade and, suddenly, there was the sea sparkling grey in the evening light, the salt tang filling the air—and filling Cassandra with a strange exaltation.

'Stop bouncing,' Nicholas chided, but he was grinning. 'You really are the most irrepressible child! Have you never seen the sea before?'

'No! I've imagined it, of course...but it's so big, so...'

'Wet?' Nicholas supplied wryly. 'Now behave yourself, we're nearly at the *Ship Inn*.'

'Oh.' Cassandra said flatly, noticing for the first time the abundance of inns and lodging houses that lined the street, all of them disreputable and dirty.

'Don't worry, it's not one of these. You'll find the *Ship* comfortable enough. And the bedlinen is at least clean.' As he spoke, he wheeled the team into a cobbled yard under a gaudily painted sign of a galleon in full sail, which swung so low that Cassandra ducked instinctively.

The yard was bustling with other sporting carriages, like their own, and a number of chaises with piles of luggage strapped high behind. 'Now you see why I was so eager to leave on time: we would have lost the accommodation otherwise.'

Cassandra climbed down stiffly, pleased to see the yard was freshly strewn with clean straw and that neatly dressed grooms hurried forward to take the horses.

She stared in awe at one of the passengers alighting from a closed carriage on the arm of a foppishly dressed gentleman. The lady was wearing a Spanish pelisse in a dove grey sarsenet trimmed with Chinese binding. Her delicate hands and feet were both gloved in dainty lemon kid: Cassandra watched openmouthed as this vision stepped down onto the cobbles without a thought for her exquisite footwear.

She was jolted out of her study by Nicholas stepping forward and raising his hat. 'Lady Broome. What a pleasure to see you here: are you making the crossing?'

'My dear Earl!' The lady fluttered forward, extending her gloved hand. 'You know my brother George?' The gentlemen exchanged nods. 'Nothing would prevail upon me to brave the Channel, not even for a glimpse of Paris fashions before they reach Town. I am here to meet my sister-in-law. And you?' She raised a coquettish brow, laying one hand on the Earl's sleeve and turning towards the inn door.

'Alas, the perils of the ocean for me—and without your presence to stiffen my resolution. . . Cass! Don't stand there with your mouth open, boy, bring my dressing case!'

Resentfully Cassandra tugged at the leather straps securing the bags. Mouth open, indeed! The heavy case fell off the top of the pile wrenching her arms.

'Need a hand with those, lad?' One of the grooms was beside her. 'Amazing what these nobs put into their cases, feels like a load of bricks, don't it?' The man swung the remaining pieces down and took them into the *Ship*, Cassandra following behind, trying to manage the heavy case and stride manfully at the same time.

The Earl was leaning easily against the mantelpiece in the coffee room. Seeing Cassandra, he hailed a passing waiter. 'Show my man to my chamber with the luggage. Cass, check the heavy luggage has arrived and unpack my evening dress: I shall dine with Lady Broome and Sir George this evening.'

Cassandra opened her mouth indignantly, then closed it again with a snap. After all, what else did she expect? She'd freely entered the charade, she couldn't complain when she was asked to act the part. But Nicholas didn't have to act his with such relish!

The room was a good one with a bow window overlooking the main street and affording a glimpse of the sea beyond. A maidservant was mending the fire and the heavy luggage was piled high in one corner. With a nod at the girl, Cassandra began unpacking the dressing case, laying out the silver backed brushes and shaving gear.

Poking into the various valises, she found what seemed appropriate evening wear and clean linen. She was laying a nightshirt on the bed when a thought struck her: where was she to sleep? Where did servants sleep in establishments like this? And more immediately, where was she to eat?

What time was it—and when would Nicholas require warm water? How little she knew! It was all very well to have to act like a boy. That was easy, compared with learning to act like a valet!

'Oh, hang the man!' Cassandra stamped her foot, angry that Nicholas had abandoned her in this strange place and, suddenly, not a little frightened.

'Language, infant!' Nicholas was leaning against the door jamb. He seemed lazily amused, his eyes narrowed as he watched her.

'I am not an infant! How could you leave me without giving me some idea what to do with all this!' She gestured wildly at the pile of cases, irrationally more angry now he was there than she had been before.

'What did you expect me to do?' he enquired, strolling into the room. 'Invite you to take tea with Lady Broome?' He shrugged off his coat and handed it to her. 'Brush this will you, it's dusty from the journey.'

'Brush it yourself!' Her chin came up and she threw the coat onto the bed. 'You just go off with that *woman* and leave me. . .'

'Calm down, Cassandra—and don't treat my coats like that! I'm sorry I left you, brat. To tell you the truth, I keep forgetting you're not a boy, you're so good at it.'

He straightened and strolled across to look down at her, his eyes warm with amusement. One long finger tilted her chin up, forcing her gaze to meet his. 'Stop sulking, Cassie. I couldn't just leave Lady Broome, it would have looked most odd. Besides,' he smiled reminiscently, 'what better way to kill an hour than in the company of a beautiful woman? Moreover, you seem to have managed well enough. Have you ordered hot water?'

Cassandra bit her lip, acknowledging to herself that her real complaint was Nicholas's preference for Lady Broome's company over her own. 'No. I didn't know what time you wanted it. I'll get it now.' She paused, her hand on the door knob, 'Nicholas. . .where am I to sleep tonight?'

He paused, arrested, his cravat half undone. 'Lord, I hadn't thought of that. Go for the water, I'll think of something.'

Cassandra returned with a steaming ewer to find Nicholas pulling a battered screen across one corner of the room. 'What are you doing?' She set the jug down on the dressing table and came to peer round the edge. 'Where did you get that from?' A low truckle bed was set behind the screen.

'It was under the bed. I'll take this, you have the bed.'

'I can't do that, Nicholas,' she protested, scandalised. 'I cannot sleep in the same room as you! It's. . .'

'. . .the only thing we can do,' he finished for her. 'What would you prefer? To share with the male inn servants?' He looked at her pink face and added ruefully, 'You're as compromised as you're ever going to be, Cassie. By running away with me dressed as a boy, you burned your boats, child: a night in my company can make it no worse.'

Cassandra knew her blush was deepening; her tongue felt too clumsy to get round the words. 'But we. . . I never thought. . .'

'I don't believe you thought from the moment you left home! But then, neither did I—at least, not about this.' He hesitated, 'Look, Cassie, I'll pull the screen across. It'll be almost as if we're in two separate chambers.'

Cassandra cast round for other reasons not to share the room. It wasn't as though she didn't trust Nicholas . . .it was just that the big bed was strangely disturbing. Her eyes fell on the shortness of the pallet. 'Your feet will stick out of the end. You won't be able to walk tomorrow. I'm much shorter, I'll sleep in it.'

'You are in my care, Cassandra, and you will do as I tell you.' The Earl's tone brooked no argument. 'You're my mother's godchild and I must see you safely delivered to her. It's bad enough that you're jauntering around in boy's clothing, unchaperoned, without sleeping in a servant's bed in an inn!'

Cassandra knew when she was beaten. 'Thank you,

Nicholas.' She gestured to the jug. 'Your water will be cooling.'

Her capitulation appeared to surprise him. With a slight shrug, he moved the screen round the dressing table and disappeared behind it. Cassandra dithered in the centre of the room. She had begun to feel more comfortable in the valet-master role, now Nicholas had turned it on its head by treating her as a girl, if not a lady.

However, it seemed now the question of the bed was settled, he had no further qualms. A shirt came sailing over the top of the screen followed by a crumpled neckcloth. 'Pass me a clean shirt, please.'

Cassandra handed one round the screen and busied herself with brushing down the corbeau blue coat and cream kerseymere breeches. 'Which waistcoat do you want? The sage green or the white?'

'Green. Can you pass me my, er. . .' For once Nicholas seemed at a loss.

Silently Cassandra handed the unmentionable nether garments round the screen. It was a good thing he couldn't see the smile on her face. Really! Did he think she was *such* an innocent? Who did he think sewed on her father's buttons?

By the time the Earl emerged, smoothing down his cuffs, Cassandra had her face under control. She had polished his quizzing glass and found a fine cambric handkerchief. 'Cologne, my lord?'

'Naturally.' He wasn't rising to the bait, although Cassandra saw his mouth twitch briefly, as if in amusement. 'Now, for your supper, go down to the kitchen and bring something back up here. I don't want you eating in the Inn—it would be hazardous as well as unseemly.'

'Yes, my lord,' said Cassandra demurely.

'Cassandra. . .'

'Yes, my lord?'

He paused at the door, a tall, lean figure in the severe evening dress, the candlelight honing his features into an unfamiliar austerity. 'Go to bed early like a good girl, we've a long journey tomorrow. And stop calling me "my lord", you are beginning to sound like Peacock.'

The door shut behind him with a distinct click. As sounding like the butler had been Cassandra's aim, she was rather pleased with the rebuke. Nicholas was inclined to treat her like a child and while that had its advantages it was beginning, for some reason, to gall her. Teasing him—very gently—was the only way she could assert her character without alarming him with her femininity.

She began to tidy the room, gathering up discarded clothing and straightening the dressing table, her mind on this man who had unexpectedly taken control of her life.

Revealing her true age would not matter once they were on the other side of the Channel; Nicholas would hardly abandon her on the road to Paris. And yet. . . Cassandra paused, her arms full of the opulent folds of his dressing gown. Something told her that he would not be pleased when he discovered how she had deceived him, fooled him into thinking she was a child.

But that was still days away, now she was starving. She would see what the kitchen had to offer.

\* \* \*

The cook had been too busy in her steamy kitchen to pay much heed to one undersized valet and Cassandra had secured a plate of mutton stew and bread and a mug of ale without drawing attention to herself. But in trying to find the back stair in the gloom of the labyrinthine corridors of the *Ship* she took a wrong turning. Light streamed through a door which stood ajar in front of her; through the gap came the chink of glass, the scrape of cutlery and the sound of voices.

Her curiosity got the better of her: by dint of flattening herself against the wall, Cassandra could see a wedge of the dining-room. It was warm, full of light and bustle and infinitely more enticing than the prospect of her own room. Besides, the plate of stew was cooling fast. Quietly she moved a stool closer to the door, perched on it and began to eat.

The room was crowded with diners of the Quality. Cassandra chewed absently, her eyes and mind full of the shifting colours of the women's gowns, the richness of the men's attire. She wanted to be there, part of it. Her father had denied her the chance to join even the provincial social life that Ware had to offer. If dinner in a Dover inn was this glamorous, how much more wonderful was Paris going to be!

She was almost lost in a reverie of elegant gowns and charming men when the party sitting nearest her door rose to reveal Nicholas and Lady Broome sitting alone at a table. Of Sir George, there was no sign.

Cassandra gasped as her eyes took in Lady Broome's gown cut so low it scarcely contained the full swell of her breasts. What fabric was showing was silver gauze over deep rose silk. Her dark hair was cropped dashingly short in the latest mode, its only adornment a silver filet threaded through with its loose ends fluttering at her cheek.

It was only then that Cassandra noticed her companion: Nicholas was lifting his glass to toast her, a lazy smile curving his lips as their eyes met and held. Lady Broome leaned towards him to touch her glass to his. The two dark heads almost touched before Nicholas leaned back, still holding the look.

Cassandra drew in her breath with a sharp hiss. This was a very different Nicholas to the safe elder brother who had teased and bullied her all day. Not, of course, that she wanted him to look at her like that. . .

Absently, she took a sip of ale. Lady Broome was speaking now, her rippling laugh cutting across the hubbub of the room to reach Cassandra in her dark corner. She had obviously put a question to the Earl, who was shaking his head, a look of regret evident on his face. His fingers caressed the delicate filigree of silver on her cheek as his lips moved with soft words.

'Silly goose!' Cassandra exclaimed crossly, unsure which of them she was referrring to. Couldn't he see how blatantly she was flirting, playing with him? Of course he could—and he was enjoying every moment of it. . .

When Cassandra regained the bedchamber, she still felt nettled and vaguely disappointed in Nicholas for being so easily beguiled. She unbuttoned her waistcoat, taking a deep breath: boy's clothing gave considerable freedom, but it pinched in unexpected places. She sat on the bed and peeled off her stockings, then realised she had no nightgown to put on. She held Nicholas's up against herself, but it was far too long. Casting about to find something to put on she padded barefoot across the boards to a valise and tugged out a shirt. Pulled over her head it brushed the top of her knees: not quite seemly, but then she had little alternative.

The bed was high and deep with an old fashioned feather mattress which closed round her as she climbed in. Cassandra looked guiltily at the truckle bed, then hardened her heart. Nicholas had ordered her to take this bed, and after all he had enjoyed *his* evening! *He* hadn't had to sit in the dark eating greasy stew while other people dined and flirted.

She snuggled down into the pillows, stretched her aching legs and waited for sleep to overtake her. But, despite all that had happened over the past twenty four hours and her lack of rest the night before, her eyes refused to close.

She supposed she ought to be worrying about what her father would be doing. Somehow she doubted he would have gone to the expense of hiring a Bow Street Runner to pursue her. Now she was out of the house, Bella Mainwaring would agree to marry him, and provided Cassandra's flight caused no local scandal, he wouldn't care if he never saw her again. Cassandra knew she was undutiful in thinking like this, but their relationship had never been characterised by affection and she had long since given up hope of his changing.

No, what was keeping her awake was the enigma of Nicholas. Enough lingered of her old hero worship to make her trust him implicitly, but she could not deceive herself that he had taken her with him for any other reason than his own convenience, and his desire to avoid delay. But the Earl of Lydford was used to getting his own way under all circumstances:

Cassandra had a sinking feeling that with her in tow, and no valet to smooth their path, things were not going to go with the ease which he had come to expect. This was hardly likely to improve his uncertain temper.

Not that he was out of temper this evening, far from it. Cassandra replayed the scene in the diningroom, Lady Broome's curls bent close to the Earl as she fluttered both fan and eyelashes. She remembered Nicholas's gaze lingering on the vivacious face and creamy throat before him.

Cassandra let her mind drift into fantasies of how she would look in evening gowns of silk and gauze; of feathers and jewels; of kid gloves with innumerable pearl buttons and fragile slippers. In clothes like that, no gentleman would call her 'brat' or 'infant' or think her a child.

She had just reached this gratifying conclusion when the door opened cautiously and Nicholas slipped in, his hand cupped round the flame of his candle. 'Asleep, infant?' he whispered, flattening Cassandra's fantasy most effectively.

'No,' she said baldly.

'Why not? Did you get some supper?' He was keeping his distance from the big bed. In the flickering candlelight his face was underlit, expressionless, the face of a stranger.

'Mutton stew.'

'That's all right, then.' He turned towards the screen.

'Is it? I would rather have had guinea fowl and Dover sole and claret.'

'You must have hung around the kitchen a long

time. Wasn't that rather tempting fate?' He shrugged off his coat.

'It wasn't in the kitchen,' Cassandra began, then realised she was getting onto dangerous ground.

'Where then?' Nicholas turned and faced her. 'Have you been prowling around the inn?'

'I saw you in the dining-room with that woman,' she burst out.

He sauntered over to the bed and looked down at her. In the semi-darkness his shirt was very white, his face inscrutable. He seemed to loom above her.

Cassandra scrambled up against the pillows, clutching the quilt to her throat. The silence stretched on, then he said slowly, 'There are moments, brat, when you seem a lot older than your tender years. Goodnight.'

Cassandra held her breath until he was safely behind the screen. There was a clatter as he tossed his shoes into a corner and rustlings as he shed his clothes, then the truckle bed creaked and the light was blown out.

She found it impossible to give herself up to sleep. She had never shared a bedroom with anyone, let alone a man! There were several minutes of creaking and tossing while Nicholas adjusted his long frame to the narrow bed, then the only sound in the room was his breathing, regular and slow.

Her last thought as she finally drifted off was that innocent though this night was, she was now, in the eyes of Society, ruined beyond redemption. The surprising thing was, somehow she didn't care.

# CHAPTER THREE

'NICHOLAS.' Cassandra tugged his sleeve as he stood in the stern surveying the port of Dover as it receded slowly into the early morning mist. 'That sailor says that with this breeze we're only going to be four hours reaching France.'

'Thank heaven for that,' his lordship remarked absently, then focused sharply on his charge's eager face. 'And what the devil are you about, talking to common sailors?'

Cassandra blinked at his vehemence. 'He's a very nice man, and his wife lives in Dover with their three small sons and they all want to be sailors, too... I know why you're so mumpish!' She broke off and studied his frosty profile. 'You're feeling seasick.'

'And you, I suppose, are not?' He could not doubt it, looking at her shining eyes and wind blown hair. She was licking the salt from her lips with relish and the sea breeze had whipped colour into her cheeks.

'Not in the slightest, I wish we could sail all day.' She looked closely at Nicholas's set face. 'If you are feeling unwell, you must not go below. It is too close and full of others being sick. The smell is disgusting.'

'Thank you for your advice,' Nicholas said stiffly. 'There is nothing amiss with me save the effects of trying to sleep in a bed several sizes smaller than I.' He buttoned his greatcoat firmly to the neck and set off to stride up and down in the small deck space not occupied by roped piles of barrels and boxes destined for the Continent.

Cassandra grinned to herself and settled on a barrel in a sheltered corner to watch the sailors coiling the maze of ropes cast off when the ship left port. Well, she had offered to sleep in the truckle bed. . .

One of the deckhands passed her, saying with a wink, 'You're faring better than your master, lad! Having trouble with his breakfast, is he?'

'I think he's feeling sick—not that he'll admit it.' Cassandra felt a prick of guilt at discussing Nicholas with this sailor. She had never seen Nicholas other than in complete command of himself: it seemd her idol had, if not feet, then one toe of clay. 'Is there a cure?'

'Well. . .' The seaman scratched his grizzled head under the knitted cap. 'I doubt he'll relish it, but what you need is a nice piece of fat bacon. Tie it on a long thread, swallow it down and jiggle the thread up and down. . .'

'Yes, thank you very much!' Cassandra interjected hastily, her stomach rising in sympathy with Nicholas's. The sailor grinned amiably and moved on down the deck with the rapid rolling gait they all shared.

Her nest among the barrels was snug and yet afforded her an uninterrupted vista of the grey Channel waters widening behind them as England slowly receded. She had expected the sea to be a great lonely expanse, but it was not. In the brightening morning light, coastal scows paralleled the shore; the fishing fleet was returning to harbour accompanied by a wheeling cloud of gulls clamouring raucously for scraps. And in elegant contrast, a sleek private yacht, its sails snowy, glided past headed for Newhaven.

She was so absorbed it was some time before she realised the Earl was standing at her shoulder. 'Enjoying yourself, brat?' he asked softly.

'You startled me!' Cassandra's heart thumped unaccountably in her chest, then she glared at him indignantly as he ruffled her hair with a careless hand.

He was smiling, the colour once more back in his cheeks. 'Aren't you afraid of all this deep, cold water? I presume you cannot swim? What will you do if you fall in?'

'You'd save me,' Cassandra said confidently. Her hero seemed himself once more. 'Are you feeling better? One of the sailors told me a certain remedy. . .'

Nicholas held up his hand hastily. 'If it's the one with the piece of fat bacon, I don't need it repeating.'

All too quickly for Cassandra the coast of France filled the horizon, the cliffs dipping down to long sandy beaches. The hundled roofs of the small port of Calais grew steadily closer, then unaccountably the boat hove to and dropped anchor. Nicholas hailed a passing crewman.

'You there! What's going on? Why are we not entering harbour?'

'Can't, sir. It's low water. Look, boats are coming out already to take you and your baggage off. Cost you a guinea, sir.'

'A guinea!' exclaimed Cassandra, her housewifely instincts revolted. 'But we've already paid to cross, why must we pay again?'

'Quiet, Cass, don't draw attention to yourself,' Nicholas commanded. 'Those rogues have the upper hand. If we want to land on French soil, we must pay French prices!'

They hung over the rail together, watching as the swarm of flat-bottomed rowing boats hove up. They were crewed by men and boys wearing rags no better than beggars, their feet in wooden sabots.

There was a chaotic period while negotiations took place to secure a boat for each party, then they and their luggage were roughly loaded. Cassandra was dangled dizzily over the edge of the packet boat by her wrists before being seized by the men in the craft below and dropped among the bags. She noticed a momentary look of concern on Nicholas's face as she was manhandled, then relief as the crew seemed to sense nothing amiss.

On the quayside their luggage was seized and carried away by a gang of brawny females, their skirts kilted up to show bare, muscular calves.

Jostled by the crowd, Cassandra struggled to keep an eye on their things. 'Nich. . . My lord! Where are they taking the baggage?'

'The Custom House. Follow me and keep your mouth shut.'

Nicholas strode off in pursuit of their porters, Cassandra scuttling to keep up through the press of touts all shouting the names of various inns.

In the Custom Hall officials searched their bags with an insolence that shocked Cassandra. 'Why do you not protest?' she whispered, scandalised as dirty hands rummaged through the fine linen.

'Quiet, or they will deny us a passport.'

'But you have one.'

'An English passport will not serve here, we need a French one for the onward journey.'

Cassandra jumped in alarm as a hand was thrust into her pocket. The searcher tossed her pocket handkerchief onto the bench, then turned with obvious attention of searching the rest of her clothing.

She felt the man's fingers touch the breast of her coat, then Nicholas's hand whipped out and clamped onto the official's wrist.

'*Un moment, mon ami*! I think this is what you are looking for.' There was a glint of gold coin and the man turned away, waving them through the throng to the row of desks where clerks were writing passports.

Cassandra stood swaying, hardly conscious of what was going on around her until the Earl's firm hand under her elbow guided her out into the fresh air.

'Cassie? Are you unwell?' His face was close as he bent over her. Cassandra blinked, forcing herself to concentrate on him; for the first time she noticed brown flecks in his green eyes and the way one brow slanted up fractionally more than the other.

'Cassandra!' Nicholas's voice was preremptory. 'You can't faint here, pull yourself together. We're going to an inn now, you need food.'

Obediently she stumbled over the cobbles beside him, following the handcart loaded with their luggage. She was hungry, yes, but it wasn't that that had made her feel faint. It was the thought of those dirty rough hands pawing her body, the reek of garlic and sweat in the Hall and the land seeming to move under her feet.

By the time their porter delivered the bags to the doors of the *Hotel d'Angleterre*, Cassandra was feeling more herself and able to look around at the scurrying servants and throng of well-dressed guests. The air was full of noisy English voices raised in demands for food and wine, and the shouts of ostlers backing horses between the shafts of travelling carriages.

Eyeing the hubbub, Nicholas remarked, 'It's as well I reserved a private parlour. This place has regained all its popularity with the Grand Tourists after the war: they say the owners have made a fortune here.'

They dined alone in their private parlour, ignoring the waiter's raised eyebrows at the Earl's latitude in permitting his valet to share his table.

'Won't they think it odd?' Cassandra asked as the door closed behind the man.

'It's of no matter, they think the English are mad, anyway,' Nicholas shrugged. 'Pass the buttered crab, I believe it is the speciality of the house.'

Drowsy with food and sea air, Cassandra fell asleep as soon as her head touched the pillow in the tiny chamber Nicholas secured for her.

Next morning she tumbled downstairs rubbing the sleep from her eyes to find him already up and dressed, impatiently tapping his foot on the cobbles as he watched the first carriages leaving the inn yard.

'Hurry up, Cass, if you want any breakfast,' he ordered. 'And, for heaven's sake, do something about that neckcloth, you look more like a scarecrow than a valet.'

She was becoming accustomed to his uncertain temper first thing in the morning. By the time they settled themselves in the carriage hired from the inn, the Earl's mood was positively cheerful. Cassandra gathered he approved of the horses they had obtained and that even the French postillion passed muster.

After the dismal streets of Calais the wide open countryside with its fields of green corn and red poppies came as a surprise and a pleasure. There were no hills or deep valleys to slow the horses, only a rolling greenness which pleased the eye until interrupted by small, squalid villages, or collections of tumbledown farm buildings.

'Bored?' enquired the Earl, sometime later, as she settled herself back against the cushions with a deep sigh.

'I expected it to be so different: but it could be Hertfordshire.'

'What did you expect?' Nicholas grinned at her, his teeth flashing white with amusement. 'Dragons or strange costumes? This is France, not Cathay.'

'But after the sea crossing, everything seems so ordinary,' Cassandra lamented.

'Can you play cards?' Nicholas produced a pack and started to shuffle them. 'No? I'll teach you to play picquet.'

By the time they passed through the gate of Amiens that evening, Cassandra had won several sixpences. 'Are all card games this simple?' she enquired disingenuously, as Nicholas put away the pack.

'I am learning a little about you, Cassie. Under that country girl exterior beats the heart of a gamester.' He regarded her wryly. 'My mother will not be pleased with me, teaching you to gamble.'

Despite the warmth of the cheerfully lit inn, Cassandra felt strangely chilled as she carried the dressing case inside. For a time she had forgotten how close the end of their journey was. Her adventure was almost at its close. Nicholas would leave her in Paris—with relief, that much was evident—and she must learn to be a young lady again.

The Earl sensed her mood. Poor child, she had borne up far better than he could have expected. Most delicately raised young women of his acquaintance would have had the vapours inside five minutes: but then, he was forgetting just what a child she was. He patted her arm. 'Bear up, Cassandra, we're nearly there. By this time tomorrow you'll be safe with Mama.'

'And you?' She raised her eyes to his face, hoping to see some hint of regret that she would not be with him.

'Ah, well. . .' He paused in the act of tying a clean neckcloth, a slight smile curving his lips. 'I intend enjoying Paris to the full. I think I deserve a little diversion after playing the governess.'

Stung, Cassandra bit out, 'Have I been such a burden then? After all, it was your idea to bring me!'

'You ungrateful brat!' He swung round, fists on hips, to regard her coldly. 'I would have left you on the doorstep if you hadn't threatened to throw yourself in the Thames.'

'It wasn't that at all,' she flared. 'After your valet broke his leg, it simply suited your convenience to bring me with you. But, of course,' she added sarcastically, 'I should have realised, you're regretting not going to stay with Aunt Augusta and meeting the eligible Miss Hare!'

'If nothing else, Miss Hare would be more amenable!'

'And such a suitable match!'

'You provoking brat...' he seized her by the shoulders and gave her a little shake. 'You ungrateful, ungracious...'

'You needed a valet.' Cassandra struggled, but only succeeded in making him tighten the hold. 'If I hadn't come with you, you wouldn't be here now! So don't try to pretend you did it out of the goodness of your heart—it suited your purposes, that's all!'

His eyes narrowed as he studied the flushed, angry face raised to his. 'How old did you say you were, Cassandra?'

Hastily she struggled to remember what she'd told him. 'Fifteen,' she stammered.

'So I thought.' He dropped his hands and stepped back. 'I suggest you curb your temper in future dealings with gentlemen. Some might take it as a provocation.'

'And you wouldn't?' Some devil tempted Cassandra to persist.

'All you provoke me to, brat, is an urge to paddle your britches! Come on, I need my dinner.'

The next day's journey from Amiens to Paris was accomplished in an atmosphere of cool politeness. Both Cassandra and the Earl suspected they had gone too far, but neither was prepared to admit it and apologise.

If they had thought the formalities at Calais irksome, they were much worse at the gates of Paris, where officials of the *Bureau du Roi* examined the carriage and its contents at tiresome length.

'Why don't you bribe them?' Cassandra enquired

irritably, tired of being jostled by the importuning crowd of touts and trinket sellers who had descended on the travellers.

'I am more inclined to hire a new valet from amongst those offering their services,' the Earl remarked, gesticulating at the crowd of smartly dressed young men who noisily proferred references from previous employers.

'They're wearing earrings,' Cassandra observed censoriously.

'But no doubt they can tie a cravat.'

Her smouldering silence lasted just as long as her first glimpse of the Seine and the sight of the fashionable quarters where the great houses of the nobility still existed despite the Revolution. At first, Cassandra was enthralled, but she soon turned to Nicholas, her nose wrinkled with disgust.

'It's filthy! The mud! And there are no pavements— look at that lady there.' She pointed to an elegantly dressed woman hopping from one stepping stone to another, her gown gathered up. 'And it's so noisy and crowded.'

'I believe it to be the most populous city in Europe,' Nicholas remarked. 'But there are compensations. When my mother begins to take you about, you will enjoy the gardens and the shops, no doubt.' He spoke absently. Cassandra was convinced he had all but forgotten her now they were almost at his uncle's house and he could be rid of her.

'And what will you do?'

'Meet with friends, play cards, go to the opera. . .' he replied airily, twisting in his seat to admire a handsome young woman promenading slowly along the edge of the Tuileries gardens.

Cassandra ran her hand through her tumbled curls and twitched her neckcloth into some sort of order, ready to meet her godmama. What a pity it was, she thought, that a nice boy who rescued kittens from trees should grow up to be frivolous, bad tempered, arrogant. . .

'Why are you glaring, Cassie? And try at least to stop sulking. We're here. If you look like that my mother will pack you straight back to your father.'

The postillion wheeled his horses to swing through the elaborate ironwork gates of the *porte cochere* of a great *hôtel*. Immediately servants ran into the wide cobbled courtyard to fling open the carriage doors and let down the steps.

Cassandra climbed down and stood looking around her, mouth half open at the magnificence of the classical pilasters and the regular ranks of many-paned windows. 'Does your uncle own this?' she whispered, awed.

'No, he hires, like everyone else who visits. He is never here long enough to warrant a permanent establishment.' He broke off to acknowledge the bow of the Steward who stood at the head of the steps to greet him. '*Bonjour*, Gaston. Is my uncle at home?'

'I fear not, milord. Sir Marcus has been recalled to Vienna. *Helas*! He will be *desolé* at missing your lordship—but, *c'est la vie*, these are the inconveniences of the life of the diplomat.'

Cassandra felt a wave of relief. She had not relished the thought of being introduced to Sir Marcus Camberley, who could not help but disapprove of her actions. Now she would have Godmama to herself and could explain it all. Feminine company and sympathy; a woman to talk to who would understand her dilemma. . .

Gaston was ushering the Earl across the wide marble entrance hall, bowing him into the salon when his eye fell on Cassandra following behind. With a snap of his fingers he summoned a footman, 'Take his lordship's valet to his suite.'

'No, Gaston, I want him with me.' Ignoring the Steward's raised eyebrows, he enquired, 'Is the Countess at home?'

'*Pardon*, milord, I have not made myself clear, *Madame la Comtesse* has accompanied *Monsieur* her brother to Vienna. She acts as his hostess this Season, you understand.'

If Cassandra had not been so distressed herself, the look on Nicholas's face would have been almost comical. 'Not here?' He pushed his hands through his hair, then sat down in the nearest chair, his long legs thrust out in front of him. For a long moment he looked from Cassandra to the Steward and back again. The silence stretched on, then he came to a decision.

'The brandy, Gaston. Bring it yourself and close the door. I need to consult with you.'

'*Certainment*, milord.'

Cassandra sat numbly on the edge of a brocade covered sofa. She hadn't thought beyond Paris, beyond the sanctuary Godmama would provide. Now her mind seemed blank, all she could do was wait, watching while Nicholas warmed the brandy glass between his palms, apparently lost in thought. The

Steward waited patiently, his intelligent dark eyes flicking from the Earl to the young lad.

'This person, Gaston, is not my valet. It is Mademoiselle Weston, the god-daughter of my mother.'

'Indeed, milord.'

'Indeed. She has had to leave the shelter of her home for reasons I do not propose to enter into, and finding my mother away from home has accompanied me here. For purposes of discretion and propriety she has been dressed as you see her. Now I find *Madame la Comtesse* is not here to take charge of her. You see my predicament, Gaston?'

'Indeed, milord,' the Steward repeated. 'A situation of some delicacy.'

'You have had experience of many delicate matters in your years with my uncle. Does any solution present itself to you now?'

The Steward hesitated only briefly. 'If I may suggest, milord: the housekeeper, Madame Robert, is a woman of intelligence and refinement. She would be an excellent chaperone for the young lady until *Madame la Comtesse* returns. I presume there is no question of Mademoiselle Weston going out into Society until then?'

'Certainly not! That will do admirably.' Nicholas finished the brandy and began to get up. He'd known Gaston would come up with a solution to his problem. A respectable housekeeper was just the person to take charge of the child. His duty as her godmother's son was quit.

'Do I have no say in the matter?' Cassandra enquired frostily. The play of emotions on Nicholas's face was all too plain; he'd rid himself of an inconvenience, now he could get on with enjoying himself.

Nicholas eyed her sharply. 'No.'

'So I am to be a prisoner in this house, bored to tears, with no diversion. . .'

'There is no alternative, unless you want me to pack you straight home again, you ungrateful br. . .' He stopped suddenly, aware of the Steward's presence. 'I shall do my best to make sure you are not bored. If I arrange a small allowance for you, you may engage a dressmaker. Tomorrow I will find you a dancing master, a French master and a drawing master. That way your days will be filled, and by the time my mother returns, you may be fit to go about with her, perhaps even attend young people's parties.'

Cassandra felt a rush of contrition. She was acting like the child he thought her. Nicholas was trying to do his best for her under the most difficult of circumstances. The suspicion that he would have done almost anything to get rid of her was unworthy.

'Thank you, Nicholas, that is very kind of you,' she said meekly.

'That is settled, then.' He shot her a suspicious glance, as if he had expected some resistance. 'Go with Gaston, then, he will take you to Madame Robert. And behave yourself, child.'

He kept calling her 'child'. It galled, but it served her purpose.

The sharp-eyed Frenchwoman to whom Gaston handed her with an explanation in rapid French was not so easily fooled.

'I thought Monsieur Gaston said you were fifteen,'

she commented an hour later, handing Cassandra a towel as she climbed out of the bath.

'I. . .' Cassandra was within an inch of confirming the lie when she looked up and met the other woman's beady regard. The dark eyes were not unkind, but they were shrewd. 'I am eighteen,' she confessed. 'But the Earl believes me to be younger.'

'And you thought it wise not to set him right,' the housekeeper said drily. 'I see.'

'You do, *madame*?' Cassandra was surprised.

'But, yes. You have to leave home—an *affaire* of the heart, no doubt?—the Earl is your only friend. Why embarrass him with the truth?'

Cassandra smiled to herself, but said only, 'You speak excellent English, *madame*.'

'My late husband was a wine merchant. For many years we lived in Bristol. When he died I returned to France: the English climate does not suit me.'

She bustled around gathering up the discarded boy's clothes. 'When you are dressed *à la jeune femme*, we will engage for you a lady's maid. Until then, we must be discreet, I will look after you.' She held up a peignoir borrowed from the Countess's wardrobe. 'Put this on and I will fetch you a little supper. Tomorrow we will find you a few simple dresses. While the Earl is here, it is best you remain fifteen.' Her lips quirked in amusement.

Cassandra relaxed, curled up in an armchair before the fire. The warmth of the day had turned to evening cool in the high-ceilinged mansion. Despite everything, she felt happy. She was in Paris, her father would never find her here, and Madame Robert was a wonderful ally. She was going to enjoy herself, and when Nicholas returned from his Grand Tour, he was going to find a young lady of quality and accomplishment staying with his mother. He would never call her brat again.

'*Bonjour, ma petite.*' Madame Robert swept the curtains open with a rustle of taffeta. The sunlight streamed in across the parquet floor, striking colour from the rich Turkey rug.

'*Bonjour, madame.* What time is it?' Cassandra sat up in the big bed, hugging her knees and gazed round. She'd been too exhausted the night before to take in all the details, the magnificence of the room. Now she looked wide-eyed at the crystal chandelier, the Chinese wall-paper and the ormulu furniture.

'Almost noon. I have ordered you a light *repas.*' As she spoke, there was a tap on the door. *Madame* took a tray from the servant and put it across Cassandra's knees. The inviting smell of sweet rolls and hot chocolate filled the room and Cassandra ate hungrily while the housekeeper bustled around the room.

'Where is Lord Nicholas?'

Madame Robert arranged the silver-backed brushes on the dressing table to her satisfaction, then came to stand at the foot of the bed. 'He has gone out. Many people have left cards in anticipation of his arrival; he is a gentleman who moves in the very best circles.' It was evident that this was a source of pride to the staff.

'But what about me?' Cassandra asked indignantly. 'I thought he was going to find me a dancing master.'

'And so he will,' *madame* soothed. 'He asked me to tell you he will take supper with you. No doubt he will tell you all the arrangements he has made then.

Meanwhile, the dressmaker will arrive at two; I have
sent orders already for a few simple gowns. I trust she
will have something suitable to hand so that you can
leave this room. Until then you must remain in this
chamber, as his lordship ordered.'

Cassandra could not dispute the wisdom of this: it
would be indiscreet to be seen in the valet's clothes
and she could hardly leave the chamber dressed in
Godmama's peignoir. Her breakfast finished, she
made her toilette, amusing herself for almost an hour
trying to coax her ruthlessly cropped curls into something resembling a coiffure and failing dismally.

At two o'clock promptly, Madame Robert appeared
with the dressmaker, who had brought half a dozen
ready made gowns and her sewing basket with her.
She fussed around Cassandra, pinching and tweaking
fabric, pinning and tucking until three of the gowns, a
sprigged muslin, a twilled sarsenet and a printed pop-
lin, could be made to fit Cassie's slight figure. While
the dressmaker whipped seams and let down hems,
Madame Robert sorted through muslin fichus and
collars to ensure the shoulders and necklines of the
new dresses were suitably modest.

'Ah, *charmante*,' the dressmaker murmured, as
Cassandra tried on the sprigged muslin again. 'It is a
pity English girls have no figure and are so tall, but
*mademoiselle* has a certain something in her *deporte-
ment* that is most attractive.'

'These dresses will do very well indeed,' Madame
Robert was saying, while Cassandra viewed herself in
the pier glass. 'Now *mademoiselle* will need at least
two walking costumes. . .'

The two women lapsed into rapid French which

Cassandra made no attempt to follow. She looked critically at herself in the mirror: she may not have much of a figure, but what she had was certainly improved by the clever cut of the simple gown with its high waist and neatly draped skirts. She twisted and turned to get a view of the back, pleased to see how slender and feminine she looked after several days in boy's clothes. Would Nicholas still call her 'brat' dressed like this?

The novelty of her new dresses and her restricted surroundings soon wore off as the afternoon dragged on. The few dreary tomes by French philosophers which the bookcase held were of no interest to her. Outside there was sunlight and movement and voices carrying over the high wall from the city streets beyond.

Somewhere out there was Nicholas, visiting friends, enjoying himself, flirting, no doubt, with an army of desirable, elegantly dressed women. She crossed to the glass again, uncertain now that the dress was as grown-up and flattering as she'd first thought. When she compared its modest, pale lemon fabric with the heavy luxury of the silk peignoir, she felt positively dowdy.

By supper time there was still no sign of Nicholas. Eventually she ate alone in her room, bored almost to tears with her own company after being used to Nicholas's for the past few days. She wanted to show him her new gown, hear about his day, gossip of Paris, this wonderful city she'd only glimpsed. And she wanted to hear when her lessons could start and how soon she could go about with Madame Robert. . .

It was almost midnight and Cassandra was in bed when she heard the noise of carriage wheels on the cobbled courtyard beneath her window. She leapt out of bed and ran barefoot to the long casement. Below her, Nicholas was getting out of the carriage, but he was not alone. Another carriage pulled up behind and men and women in evening attire alighted from both.

Cassandra could not see them properly from above, but she could hear their laughter as they passed between the flickering *torchérès* into the house. The beast! Cassandra stamped her foot with fury. He'd promised to meet her at supper and instead he'd been out carousing with these people...he'd probably forgotten she existed. She'd spent all day by herself waiting for him to come home...

Angrily she wrenched open the door, careless of the fact she was wearing only the silk peignoir. Gaston was ushering the party into one of the drawing-rooms as she peered over the banister. They must have come on from the theatre, the three women in the group were bejewelled, gems flashing on the milky expanses of *décolletages*.

'Make yourselves at home, *mes amis*,' Nicholas called over his shoulder. 'I will be with you in a moment.' He began to run up the staircase, his opera cloak flung over one shoulder. Hastily Cassandra retreated to her room, her heart beating hard.

Well, at least he was coming up to apologise for missing supper with her! She sat on the edge of the bed and fluffed her hair up. Several minutes passed, but no knock came at the door.

He'd gone to his room without a thought for her! Furious, Cassandra swept her skirts around her and marched out of her room and down the corridor.

Nicholas's door was ajar: she stood silently outside watching him.

In the candlelight, the black and white of his evening clothes were in stark relief. He had tossed aside the cloak and was adjusting his cravat before the glass. Cassandra moved slightly and the change in light must have caught his eye for he turned and saw her.

For a long moment Nicholas did not recognise the figure in the doorway. The brighter light from the landing cast a halo round tumbled dark curls and gleamed on the rich emerald silk which pooled around the pale bare feet which peeped provocatively from the folds. One white shoulder showed where the fabric had slipped with the woman's agitated breathing.

Instinctively he stepped forward, drawn by the sensuality of the still, silent figure. Then he saw who it was.

'Cassandra!' He stopped, scandalised as much by his own arousal as her appearance. With an effort he got his reactions under control. 'What are you doing out of your room—and dressed like that?'

'How else should I be dressed?' she demanded. 'It *is* bedtime, after all!' Her chin came up defiantly. Strangely, seeing him made her even angrier, although she could not have said why. 'You promised you'd be home for supper. . .' She could hear the childish whine in her voice even as she said it—and so did Nicholas. His expression changed from one she could not read to one of annoyance.

'You stupid child! Get back to bed this instant. If anyone were to see you. . .'

Her eyes sparked and she shrugged dismissively, sending the gown slithering down the other white shoulder. 'They'd only wonder who that child was—who should have been in bed hours ago.'

'Not dressed like that, they won't.' Before she could move, he had taken one rapid step forward, seized her by the shoulders and brought his mouth hard down on hers.

Nicholas held her crushed hard against him as he deepened the kiss with an erotic expertise that made her dizzy. Fireworks exploded behind her closed lids, her bare skin where the gown had slipped from her shoulders seemed to burn against the fabric of his shirt and his hands on her back moulded her body to his insistently.

Cassandra was beyond rational thought, surprise or any idea of resistance. Of their own volition, her fingers sought the crisp curls at his nape, twining and inciting with a quite instinctive knowledge.

A little moan of wanting began in her throat and he freed her as sharply as he had taken her. Bewildered, she staggered, her eyes on his face, trying to understand this new Nicholas, trying to fathom why he had broken the embrace so brutally.

'Nicholas?' The timid whisper appeared to goad him to fury.

'Let that be a lesson to you.' His voice was as harsh as his face. 'You must learn that if you provoke gentlemen, they will respond to what you have offered.'

'I was not provoking. . .' Her eyes were huge in her white face, the hurt in them shaming him even more than he felt already.

'What do you call that?' His fingers pulled up the silken ruffles to cover her bare shoulders. 'If you come into a man's room dressed like a whore, you must expect to be treated like one. I taught you a lesson for your own good. Now go to bed.'

He strode past her and out of the room. From the foot of the stairs his voice drifted back to her, light and careless. 'Have you drinks, *mes amis*? Dice or cards?'

# CHAPTER FOUR

CASSANDRA threw herself across her bed and pummelled the pillows until her clenched fists ached and the memory of Nicholas's contemptuous face faded.

'Pig! Pig!' she sobbed into the coverlet. How could he treat her like that! Gradually her fury subsided, leaving her feeling sick with humiliation at the way Nicholas had used her—the way she had responded to him. She hadn't intended to provoke him, she told herself, then felt her cheeks burn at the way she'd responded to that kiss and the strength of his arms as he'd crushed her body to his.

Cassandra had had no experience of men, but she knew now that this was exactly what she'd been wanting him to do ever since she'd walked into his bedchamber in Grosvenor Square. She lifted her hot face from the pillow, scrubbed the tears off her cheeks and sat up. Well, however attracted she felt to Nicholas, his cold dismissal proved he felt nothing for her. As far as he was concerned, she was an embarrassing child and tonight's incident would only make him more determined to leave her safely chaperoned in Paris while he continued his Grand Tour unencumbered.

The sound of laughter from the salon below sent her to the open casement. Light streamed from the long windows across the paved courtyard painting the shadows of the miniature orange trees against the walls of the *hôtel*.

'It's not fair!' Cassandra fumed to her reflection in the panes. All along Nicholas had misunderstood her, had treated her like a boy even when she didn't have to act the part, then when all she'd wanted was to be noticed, he'd treated her like a... She remembered what he'd called her and couldn't say it.

She was just another possession as far as he was concerned, like his servants and his house and his carriages—something he didn't notice until it discommoded him. Well, it was about time the Earl of Lydford did notice her!

Cassandra looked at herself again, but this time with more calculation. The shock had left her pinched and white about the face, her hair damp and flattened on her head. The soft femininity of the afternoon had gone: the boy Cass stared back at her with reddened eyes.

Ten minutes later Cass peered silently through the balusters as a footman deposited a tray of glasses on a side table in the hall. Before he could return, she sped swiftly down the stairs and picked up the salver. Her heart was thudding against her ribs, but no-one looked up as she slipped through the door into the salon.

Four men were lounging around a card table throwing dice. Beside them, flushed with excitement and wine, four women were egging them on with sharp little cries of encouragement. The light from the mass of candles glinted off jewels and bullion lace, cut crystal and silverware.

Cass's hands shook, setting the wine glasses tinkling and she put the tray down hastily just as the footman brought in the decanters. His eyes widened at the sight of her, but she took them from him, shutting the door in his startled face.

The gamesters still paid her no attention. The women were laughing, teasing one of the men whose luck seemed to be out.

'Throw a double six, my dear Comte, and I will give you the rose from my bosom,' the redhead said throatily, leaning towards him to show off the prize nestling between her scarcely covered breasts.

The Count, a dark, sardonic man with a beak of a nose smiled lazily at her. 'I shall want more than the rose if I score high, my dear Juliette.'

His voice, as warm as honey, did nothing to disguise his meaning, even from Cassandra. Her small gasp of outrage was audible. Several heads turned towards the dark suited figure but Nicholas, without looking up, ordered, 'Pour the wine and go. We will serve ourselves.'

Cassandra lifted the heavy decanter with both hands and began to pour the red wine gingerly, one eye on Nicholas's dark head. This wasn't what she'd planned when she'd scrambled into the valet's clothes. She'd wanted to give him the shock of his life by appearing as a boy, pay him back by forcing him to play act in front of his sophisticated friends.

She'd only meant to appear for a minute, give him a fright. Now she was trapped—and he hadn't even looked up from the dice, or noticed it was her.

The woman perching like a bird of paradise on the arm of the Earl's chair was running her fingernails absently through the crisp curls at his nape. Cassandra met the woman's eyes and registered with shock that she must be a good ten years older than Nicholas, although her beautifully painted complexion belied it.

'Nicholas, my darling,' she drawled, 'where did you find such a delicious boy? I declare, he is positively edible—and so young! Why, look, we shock him!' The fingers were still on Nicholas's neck, all her attention was fixed in that gaze.

Cass could feel the scalding blush flood up from her neckcloth as the woman sauntered over and touched one cheek with a long finger. '*Regardez, mesdames*, his cheek is smooth like a peach.'

Nicholas turned, his expression of mild irritation freezing into a mask of disbelief at the sight of Cassandra dressed in the dark suit he'd given her in London.

Juliette, the redhead, laughed. 'Oh, Mariette! Even for you, he's a little young. And so innocent. . .how could you think of bespoiling it?'

The tip of Mariette's tongue touched her upper lip fleetingly. 'Just watch me. . .'

'Leave the lad alone!' Nicholas spoke quietly but with an underlying edge of menace. 'It is his first time out of England and I don't want his head turning, or he'll never be any use to me.'

Mariette turned from Cassandra with a flounce of bad temper. 'You are so high minded, milord! All this concern over a lackey.' She snapped her fingers, 'Wine, boy!'

Cassandra moved round the table proferring the salver, her head giddy with relief at her close escape. It had never occurred to her that anyone would take her seriously as a boy—in *that* way!

She kept her eyes averted as Nicholas leaned over

to take his glass: she sensed he was too angry to risk a meeting of eyes. She came to the Count last. He lounged back in his chair, a malicious smile playing on his lips at Mariette's discomfiture. As Cassandra served him, he gave her a conspiratorial wink. Grateful, she smiled warmly at him and failed to see his eyes narrow with sudden speculation.

'That will be all, Cass,' Nicholas ordered. 'Get to your bed.'

Thankfully, Cassandra put down the tray, bowed and left as quickly as she could. The cool of the deserted marble hall was delicious after the overheated atmosphere of the salon. She sank wearily onto the bottom stair, pushed her sticky hair off her temples and drew a long, shuddering breath.

Of all the stupid, foolhardy things to do—to risk exposure in that way and at the hands of a rapacious female like Mariette! Cassandra shuddered and dropped her hot forehead into her hands. Goodness knew what Nicholas would do in the morning! Throw her out onto the streets of Paris probably—and who could blame him?

'Oh, no. . .this is the *end*,' Cassandra moaned. How could she have provoked Nicholas like that?

'Come, come, *ma petite*, things cannot be so bad.'

Cassandra started to her feet at the sound of the warm, sympathetic voice, then realised, as she found herself staring into the deep brown eyes of the Count, that he had addressed her in the feminine form.

'What. . . Sir. . .?' she stammered. 'I think you must be mistaken. I am. . .'

'A young woman and a very pretty one at that.' His gaze travelled slowly from the top of her cropped head to her small feet in the buckled shoes. His eyes were knowing, yet somehow compassionate. 'We have a little *mystère* here, I think. I love a mystery; life is too predictable.'

Cassandra's eyes flew to the door, expecting at any moment someone to come in search of him.

'Do not fear.' He seemed to understand her apprehension. 'They know I dislike the dice—they are not easy to manipulate, unlike cards and women.' The laughter lines creased at the corners of his eyes and Cassandra found herself smiling back: the Count seemed to be something of a rogue, but a likeable one for all that. 'They will think I have gone into the library. We can talk there.'

'But I don't want to. . .' Cassandra found herself being propelled firmly into the booklined room and the doors were closed behind her.

'And I think you need to talk to someone, *ma petite*.'

Cassandra's mind raced. She did need someone to talk to: could she trust this man, about whom she knew nothing, not even his name? No, she dare not tell him anything. Nicholas would never forgive her if she compromised him so.

Warm hands cupped her chin and gently tipped it up, forcing her to meet his eyes. 'We will have a glass of Madeira, my little one, you are shivering. Then you will tell me what is troubling you, and why a well-bred young lady is involved in some masquerade that necessitates these garments.'

Cassandra found herself sitting meekly, watching his long, beringed fingers flicking dismissively at her fustian jacket. 'But I know nothing of you, not even your name.' Despite herself, she felt her guard slipping in the face of his charm.

'That is easily remedied. I am Guy de Montpensier, Comte de Courcelles, at your service, *mademoiselle*.' He swept her an elaborate bow before subsiding elegantly into the chair opposite. He raised an interrogative brow then sipped his wine, apparently entirely happy to wait until she was ready to confide in him.

Cassandra knew she should not be in this position, alone in a room at night with a strange man—a Frenchman to boot! She watched him from beneath her lashes as he lounged in the wing chair. He was not as tall as Nicholas, nor as muscled. No, the Count was altogether more languid and almost a dandy in his dress.

The big nose dominated his face. He should have been ugly, but for the charm of his wry smile and the warmth in his brown eyes. All of a sudden the urge to tell someone everything was overwhelming.

'It began when my father announced he was marrying again,' she blurted and soon the whole sorry tale was tumbling out. The Count sat sipping his wine, nodding occasionally when she faltered.

'. . .and he said I looked like a. . .like a. . .' Words failed her at last.

'And so you decided to pay him back? Very understandable. And that is how we find ourselves having this talk, *n'est pas*?'

Cassandra took a gulp of Madeira, feeling it warming its way down her throat. She shouldn't have told him, but she was glad she had.

The silence stretched on. The Count had finished

his wine and sat, apparently deep in thought, his fingers steepled.

'Monsieur le Comte. . .'

'Guy.'

'Guy. . .what am I to do?'

'*Malheureusement*, little one, I can offer no better solution than the one you have already before you. Wait here until your *marraine* returns from Vienna.'

'But Nicholas will be so angry, he will throw me onto the streets!' Cassandra wailed.

Guy leaned forward and took both her hands in a warm clasp. 'Nonsense, he is too much the English gentleman! He will be very angry, *sans doubte*,' he shrugged. 'But you will feel braver in the morning.'

'But. . .'

'Should that happen. . .' he was saying as the door opened.

'Cass, what are you doing in here?' Nicholas sounded more mildly irritated than the anger she expected.

Cassandra shot out of the chair, knowing her face must be a picture of guilt. 'Nicholas, I was just going to my room. . .'

'Indeed, you are,' he said levelly. His eyes, resting on the Count, were cold. 'Really, Guy, one never knows where you will turn up next.'

The Frenchman swept him an ironic bow, but his expression was wary. 'Miss Weston and I were merely discussing her impressions of France.'

'Miss Weston? So, Cassandra, you have been confiding in my friend here? A pity, he is known as one of the worst gossips in Paris.'

'You do me an injustice, *mon brave*—surely you

mean the best!' His insouciance did not quite disguise the edge of tension in the room.

'A warning, *monsieur*. Miss Weston's predicament is not a subject for one of your witty stories.'

'But Nicholas, *mon ami*, it is so *piquant*. . .so irresistible!' Guy spread his hands, 'With the names changed, of course. . .'

'Indeed. And how irresistible will you find it if I send my seconds to wait on you?' Nicholas enquired amiably.

There was a long silence. Cassandra looked from man to man, unable to read how serious Nicholas was.

'Nicholas,' she said imploringly. 'Please stop talking about duels, you're frightening me!'

'*Cherie*,' the Count remarked with a grimace, 'you are not alone! He frightens me, too.'

Suddenly she realised the two men were grinning at each other and that her alarm was quite misplaced. The realisation made her angry. 'Men!' She stamped her small foot and flounced out of the room, carefully not slamming the door behind her.

Through the crack she heard the clink of glasses and Nicholas's short laugh. 'I do declare, Guy, the child is more trouble than a barrel-load of monkeys. Thank heaven, I do not have a daughter.'

'Not one you know of, at any rate, *mon brave*.'

Cassandra stamped upstairs, their laughter ringing in her ear. Men! They were all as bad as each other.

The Earl was no less infuriating the next day, nor more inclined to forgive her.

Madame Robert was just attempting to arrange

Cassandra's cropped locks into a more feminine style when Nicholas swept into the chamber.

'Milord!' The housekeeper cast a scandalised eye over his shirtsleeves and crimson dressing gown.

'You may leave us, *madame*. I wish to speak to my ward alone.'

Madame Robert dropped a curtsey and left stiff-backed.

'I am not your ward.' For some reason, she preferred to be called 'cousin'.

'I wish to blazes you were not my anything!' He had obviously had very little sleep. It had done nothing for his temper but, Cassandra thought wistfully, it had not marred his looks. 'Unfortunately you have made yourself my responsibility and after last night. . .'

Cassandra blushed deeply, remembering the heat of his body crushed against hers. 'How could you be so unkind as to talk about that?'

'After you confided the truth to one of the worst rakes in Paris, we need to talk!' They were obviously at cross-purposes: her indiscretion with the Count was obviously more important than the encounter in his bedroom. 'Guy will never be able to resist the joke, it will be all over the City.'

'Is he a rake?' Cassandra enquired, momentarily distracted. 'I've always been warned about them, of course, but I never thought I'd ever meet one.'

'Cassandra, of course, he's a rake and a gamester to boot! Not that he'd have believed a word of your story, of course. He assumes you're my mistress, I've no doubt.'

Cassandra gasped in horror. 'Nicholas! Why would he assume that? Didn't you tell him how old I was?'

'I doubt if it would have made any difference what I told him after you'd sat there batting your eyelashes at him and holding his hands. He's quite well aware you are only fifteen. You are so naive, Cassandra! You make me feel forty.' He ran his hands through his hair and broke off to pace around the room.

Cassandra sat nervously fingering the muslin of her gown, wondering what was going on in his head as he paced about like a caged panther. With a sinking heart, she recognised how foolish she'd been. Nicholas's whole plan had depended on her staying quietly in the house so no whiff of scandal leaked out. Now she had compromised both of them, and possibly her beloved Godmama, too. She could hardly be expected to give countenance to a girl widely believed to be her son's mistress.

'Nicholas?'

'What?' He came to a halt before her, green eyes serious on her face and she realised how much she was going to miss him.

'I must go home, mustn't I?'

'Impossible. I refuse to send you home to Offley's tender mercies. No, there is only one solution. You must go to Vienna.'

'Vienna? To Godmama?' Cassandra leapt from the chair with excitement. She took two steps towards him, ready to throw her arms round him, then thought better of it. 'Oh, Nicholas, thank you, it's more than I deserve, I know.'

'Indeed, it is,' he observed tartly. 'Now sit down and stop prattling, I must think.'

'I wasn't. . .' Cassandra began, then subsided into silence, her eyes on his thoughtful face. Vienna!

Godmama would bring her out and there'd be balls and receptions and beautiful gowns—and Nicholas would have to admit she was no child.

'Mama's travelling carriage is in the stables, which is fortunate. Gaston will know of a reliable courier to take charge of the journey and Madame Robert will be able to recommend a firm duenna to look after you.' He was jotting notes on a set of tablets. 'Four fully armed outriders, I think, better to be safe than sorry. . .'

'But Nicholas—aren't you coming, too?'

'Why should I?'

'But I thought you were going to Vienna next.'

'No of course not, that was never my plan.' His eyebrows shot up. 'I never intended to follow the direct route which you will now take. Once I leave here—sooner than I'd intended, thanks to your foolishness—I am meeting an old acquaintance in Marseilles. And then I have my papers to travel into Italy. . .' He broke off at the sight of her disappointed face. 'Cassandra! You did not believe I was about to change my plans in order to escort you personally to Vienna? Heaven help me, child—haven't you caused me enough trouble already?'

'But Godmama would expect. . .'

'Mama would have expected me to have boxed your ears back in London and packed you off to your father! Never have I done anything I regret more than bringing you here.'

'That I doubt,' Cassandra responded waspishly.

'Meaning?'

Cassandra recognised his rising temper, but was too angry to heed it. 'What's done is done, and you are responsible for me, you said so yourself. I don't want to go by myself with some hatchet-faced female. And it will be dangerous: you shouldn't abandon me.'

'I am flattered you should think I could protect you where four armed outriders could not. What you are really afraid of is being forced to behave yourself for a change.'

They were glaring at each other now. Nicholas slipped the tablets into his pockets and stood up. 'You will do as you are told while you are under my protection. I have a cultural itinerary planned and I intend to follow it.'

He had turned towards the door, dismissing her. 'Cultural activities like last night, I suppose?' she jibed. 'Intellectual conversation with half-naked women? A philosophical study of games of chance? I can imagine what an exhausting time you will have. No wonder you won't come to Vienna with me—it might stop you enriching yourself culturally.'

'You are your father's daughter, Cassandra Weston.' Nicholas swivelled slowly to face her, anger etched in his features. 'You are a shrew, sharp-tongued, devoid of feminine graces and intolerant to boot. Well, I capitulate. You have your victory.'

Cassandra swallowed her resentment at his insults. 'You will accompany me, then?'

'On the contrary, Miss. You will accompany *me*. You can see what pleasure there is to be had in travelling on rough roads, sleeping in flea-infested inns and eating disgusting food. And, of course, I shall rely on you to draw my attention to all the cultural sights along the way.'

He was exaggerating the difficulties to frighten her,

of course. Cassandra turned sparkling eyes on his face. 'Oh, thank you, Nicholas. I knew you wouldn't have been so unkind as to have left me! Marseilles and the Mediterranean and Italy! Will we cross the Alps?'

'I sincerely hope not. I despair of you, Cassandra: this is not a treat, this is a punishment. Now, get ready and pack your bags. We will leave after luncheon, before the Count has spread the news of your presence round every gossip in Paris.'

'Shall I travel as your daughter or your niece?' Cassandra smoothed her muslin gown. 'We had better decide for the passports.'

'Daughter?' Nicholas grinned wickedly, showing a gleam of white teeth. 'Oh, no, Cassandra. I have no intention of dragging a lady's maid across Europe to lend you countenance. I brought you here as my valet, and my valet you will remain.'

'I will say this for you, Cassie, you don't sulk.' Nicholas leaned back against the brocade squabs of his uncle's travelling carriage and eyed her with more favour than he had for several days.

They had been handed back their documents duly stamped at the *Porte d'Italie* and Cassandra was folding them carefully back into the leather satchel on the seat beside her.

'There's never been much point in sulking,' she observed, with a last regretful look out of the window as Paris receded behind them. 'When you spend all your time alone, nobody notices.'

'Poor brat. What a very dull life you must have led. No wonder you wanted an adventure.' Nicholas closed his eyes and settled his shoulders more comfortably. 'Wake me up if anything interesting happens.'

Cassandra sighed and gazed out of the window. It was as if the three days in Paris hadn't happened: perhaps she'd dreamt it. Her fingers came up involuntarily to brush her lips. No, that embrace had been no dream. She shivered with mixed pleasure and apprehension. It was foolish to dwell so on her first kiss. It hadn't meant a thing to Nicholas, that was plain. And now she must settle back into the master-servant relationship when they were among people. When they were alone she must be careful: if she continued to provoke and tease him, he would soon realise she wasn't the child she pretended.

Or did he realise, anyway? The Earl of Lydford was no fool. Perhaps he was pretending to believe her for her own sake. If the truth came out into the open, he would have no choice but to send her off to his mother and hope she wasn't ruined irretrievably.

On the other hand, his taste in women seemed to run to the older, elegant, experienced and, no doubt, married ladies like Lady Broome. He wouldn't notice well-scrubbed, innocent country girls. The carriage lurched on the rutted surface of the dry road and Cassandra grabbed a hanging strap to steady herself, wishing she'd brought a book with her. An Italian one would have served to polish up the reading she'd already done in her father's library.

Nicholas dozed on, seemingly unaffected by the jolting. Cassandra sighed. This was about as exciting as driving to Ware market on a Wednesday: perhaps foreign travel wasn't as stimulating as all the books said.

# CHAPTER FIVE

AFTER four long, dusty, uncomfortable days on the road, Cassandra was rueing ever challenging Nicholas to take her with him. The roads East would have been no better, it was true, but at least she would have been treated as a young lady, with all the status of travelling as the ward of the Earl of Lydford.

Instead, at the end of the interminable roads, mercifully shaded with the poplars Napoleon had had planted to shelter his marching troops, all she could look forward to was a hard truckle bed behind a screen in the corner of Nicholas's chamber.

The inn at Briare had been acceptable, but the food at Nevers had been every bit as bad as Nicholas had threatened; swimming with grease and heavy with garlic.

As the coach swung out of Macon, bouncing over the cobbles behind a fresh team, Nicholas caught her eye and asked, 'Comfortable?'

'Perfectly, thank you.' Cassandra had vowed not to complain, to give him no excuse to say 'I told you so'. Instead, she smiled back, tried hard not to scratch the additional flea bites she had acquired the night before in the inn, and distracted herself with catching glimpses of the river traffic on the Saône.

'Not much more of this,' Nicholas remarked, studying the post road map he had bought in Paris. 'We should reach Lyons this afternoon.'

'I'm quite all right. At least your uncle's carriage is well-sprung and clean, unlike those filthy hired coaches. Or the diligences,' she added, as they swung out to overtake one of the public coaches with its creaking wicker sides and piles of luggage, lumbering along at four miles an hour.

'Well, you might be all right, but I'm as stiff as a post.' Nicholas stretched his long legs as far as he could, then put his hands behind his neck to rub the sore muscles. 'I need some exercise and a change of scene from these squalid hovels and dusty verges.'

'I have to admit the scenery has been disappointing, although the river's interesting.' Cassandra knelt up on the seat to look out over the wide river, glittering grey in the sunlight. 'Everyone seems so poor,' she added, her eyes following a group of ragged children waiting to beseige the diligence with outstretched palms.

'The women are handsome, though.' Nicholas was admiring a slender young woman, her skirts kirtled up to show strong tanned calves. Catching his eye as the coach slowed to negotiate the herd of pigs she was driving, the woman smiled, exposing a few blackened teeth. 'Perhaps not,' he added quickly, withdrawing back into the coach.

'None of them seem to have many teeth left,' Cassandra observed. 'The guidebook says it's caused by the frequent fogs, but I can't see how, can you?'

'No, but it is a powerful aid to virtue. Come, let's play cards.' He pulled out a pack from one of the numerous pockets lining the doors of the coach and began to deal. 'Your picquet is becoming passable.'

Cassandra even managed to win a hand, feeling

decidedly in charity with her companion for a change. He was so nice, she thought wistfully, while he was like this, just like an older brother, not the arrogant Earl of Lydford. Those older women weren't good for him, she decided censoriously, they encouraged him to be hard and frivolous.

'A penny for your thoughts or can't you decide what to do with that hand?'

Hastily Cassandra discarded a red three and answered honestly. 'I was thinking how nice you were being.'

'You make me sound like an ogre. Of course I'm being nice, you're behaving yourself.' He grinned, 'And that was a very foolish discard. My point.'

Cassandra swung one buckled shoe back and forth, fighting the urge to kick him on the ankle. Aggravating man! At least he was still treating her like a child which, all things considered, was safest.

The Saône and Rhône met at Lyons, cutting their way through a ridge of hills down which the city tumbled to the quaysides. After the succession of squalid villages and provincial towns through which they'd passed, Lyons seemed almost as splendid as Paris.

The postillions turned the carriage in to the yard of the *Dauphin*, one of the best inns in the city. The tired horses stood steaming in the traces as Cassandra climbed down and began giving instructions in rapid French to the porters, while Nicholas was greated by the *patron*, effusive in his greetings to the English milord.

'We are in luck tonight,' Nicholas commented, as the innkeeper bowed them through the front door. 'I have secured two bedchambers and a private dining-room.'

'Yes, I overheard.'

Nicholas arched a laconic eyebrow. 'You are turning into an passable valet, Cass. The state of my linen is improving—although I cannot say the same for my boots—and your French is excellent.'

'Your lordship is too kind,' Cassandra murmured, sketching a bow as she stood aside for him to enter the room.

'Impertinent brat,' Nicholas murmured in return. 'Wine and biscuits, my good man. And send hot water and two baths. I dislike dirty servants,' he added, catching the innkeeper's surprised look at such consideration for a valet.

The luxury of soaking in hot water, after days of surreptitious dabbing with a rag and cold water, was blissful. Cassandra emerged pink and glowing to rummage in the medicine chest for the salve to dab on her flea bites. The jar was almost empty, obviously Nicholas was similarly afflicted. She put on her one remaining clean shirt, buttoned her waistcoat firmly over her breasts, checked with a sideways glance in the mirror for betraying curves and, satisfied, tapped on Nicholas's door.

He was sitting, feet up, in the window seat, languidly paring his nails and watching the street below.

'We need to go shopping,' Cassandra remarked. 'I need a shirt and you need neckcloths and we both need flea salve. I don't believe oil of lavender does *anything* to keep them away.'

'And you need another haircut.' Nicholas was looking at her critically. 'Those wispy little curls are really quite fetching. . .' His green eyes were suddenly warm on her face and Cassandra felt the blood rush to her cheeks. '. . .but not on a valet. Come here, I'll do it now while I have the scissors out.'

Reluctantly, Cassandra came and perched on the edge of the window seat. 'Look down so I can do the back.' His fingers seemed to burn on the skin at the nape of her neck as he lifted and snipped each curl. 'Stop wriggling,' he ordered, dropping one hand to her shoulder to hold her steady as he trimmed around her ear.

Cassandra could feel the heat of his body, warm from the bath as hers was, his breath feathering her ear, the coldness of the metal as he rested the scissors on her cheekbone for a second. Her breath came short, and under the constricting waistcoat she felt her nipples harden against the fine linen shirt. Instinctively she turned her face to his, her lips slightly parted and found him watching her, the scissors still in his fingers.

There was a long silence, heavy in the hot room. The only movement was the motes of dust dancing in the sunlight. Nicholas bent towards her, his eyes fixed on her parted lips. The scissors dropped from his heedless fingers and skidded across the polished boards with a clatter; it was enough to jerk both of them back to reality.

Cassandra leapt to her feet. 'Where's the clothes brush? I've got hair all over my waistcoat.' She was almost gabbling, avoiding his eyes as she rummaged in the dressing case for the brush.

A tap on the door and a waiter bringing in a tray of wine and almond biscuits was a merciful distraction. Nicholas seemed quite relaxed as he sipped the wine, but Cassandra still could not bring herself to meet his eyes.

Nicholas had once more made himself comfortable in the window seat, thumbing through the guidebook for references to Lyons. 'At least the shops here are recommended, both for clothes and for luxuries. It's getting cooler, shall we go now and eat when we return?'

'Er. . .yes.' Cassandra shrugged her coat on. He seemed quite calm, she must have imagined he had been about to kiss her again. It was extremely immodest of her to feel like this, to *want* him to kiss her, she told herself severely, trying to look as masculine as possible by matching his long stride as they crossed the yard.

The streets were bustling, the crowds jostling in the *traboules*, the narrow alleys which threaded their way between the medieval houses to the river quays. The *Lyonnais* were noisier, more lively than the northern French. They were darker, more voluble and their French was alarmingly fast to Cassandra, trying to catch phrases as she walked.

When they reached the shopping quarter, Cassandra found an apothecary's shop, its window full of jars of vipers in oil and even a stuffed crocodile. She purchased a large jar of unguent, guaranteed to repel even the most virile flea, more oil of lavender and a good supply of olive oil soap in angular brown lumps.

There was no shortage of linen drapers and, acting the good servant, Cassandra was soon loaded with parcels of shirts, neckcloths and body linen. Nicholas was striding on ahead when she caught a glimpse of sunlight on vivid colours and he found her, nose pressed against the glass, gazing longingly at a display of the most exquisite painted silk fans. There were flower patterns, roses, Chinese scenes, lovers in arbors. Small fans and large fans and fans with feathers and beads.

'Cass, come on, I want my dinner.' Cassandra turned to find him laughing at her. 'Valets do not stand lusting after fans! You are being stared at.'

'I don't care, Nicholas,' she breathed. 'They are beautiful. Look at that one at the back with the classical scene. It's Arcadia, I think, see the nymphs and fauns.'

'Wait there.' He left her standing on the pavement and went inside, shaking his head ruefully. When he emerged, he had a flat package tucked under his arm, silk ribbons streaming.

'What's that?' Cassandra demanded, tripping over her feet as she tried to keep up with him, while looking over her shoulder at the shop window.

'Never you mind. You gave me an idea. It's a present for a lady I know.'

Cassandra glared at the blue broadcloth stretched taut across his shoulders. So that was it, a trinket for one of his married mistresses when he got home to England.

However, it seemed the lady was nearer at hand. As the waiter brought food into their private dining-room, Nicholas strode in, fastening his cloak over his evening attire.

'You're not going out?' she demanded.

'I certainly am. I've ordered you an excellent dinner, you'll be quite comfortable here with no need to go out. And don't wait up,' he added as the door closed behind him.

Cassandra tore a roll apart and spread butter on it with a lavish hand. He obviously wasn't going out for dinner—he could have had a perfectly good dinner here with her, even if that was a fricassee of frogs' legs she could see at the end of the table. And she very much doubted if an evening of cultural activity was what the Earl had in mind, although she suspected the theatre would feature in his plans. Cassandra had heard about opera dancers, who apparently provided much of the entertainment for gentlemen bored with the play.

Cassandra was still wide awake as the clocks were chiming two and the door to the adjoining chamber creaked open. About time! He was so inconsiderate—there was she, lying imagining him with his throat cut by pickpockets in some darkened alley. . .

No, it wasn't that keeping slumber at bay, she admitted to herself. It was the thought of Nicholas in the arms of the lady for whom the fan was intended, of her gratitude for the pretty gift.

Candlelight showed under her door and footsteps crossed the floor. To her surprise, her door opened slowly, and Nicholas tiptoed in. Cassandra froze, her fingers grasping the coverlet. What was he doing in her room? Even when she'd had to sleep behind a screen in his chamber, he had never once entered that private space.

She half closed her eyes, trying to feign sleep, certain he would hear the sound of her racing pulse in the silent room. Under her lashes she watched him move towards her bed and bend down. Cassandra closed her eyes and almost stopped breathing: she knew he shouldn't be there, knew she should cry out, but she could not—she didn't want to. She felt him gently place something on the foot of the bed, then he tiptoed out again.

Gradually she relaxed her fingers as the door closed behind him and sounds made it obvious Nicholas was preparing for bed. The candle next door was snuffed. Cautiously Cassandra sat up and peered down at the foot of the bed. In the moonlight she was able to discern the shape of an oblong package with a tangle of ribbon. He had given her the fan.

When she woke in the morning the package was clutched in her arms like a child's doll, the ribbons crushed. Eagerly she pulled off the paper to examine the prize in the daylight. Gold leaf gleamed around the edge, the ivory sticks were smooth as butter under her fingers. Slowly she opened it up, tracing the delicate painted figures with a fingertip.

The door of Nicholas's chamber banged, startling her out of her reverie. What time was it? Judging by the bustle in the street below and the strength of the light flooding through the windows, she had overslept. Nicholas must have gone out without her.

Cassandra balanced on one foot, tugging on her other shoe, worrying about oversleeping. Usually she was up well before Nicholas and had his hot water, clean linen and breakfast all organised before he shouted for the first cup of coffee.

In his room, yesterday's shirt was tossed on the floor and in their private parlour, the remains of rolls and an almost empty coffee pot showed he had eaten before leaving. Cassandra rang for chocolate and rolls for herself and began tidying the bedchamber.

Should she pack their valises or not? Nicholas had not said how long he intended to stay, nor what their route from here would be.

When the chocolate came, she curled up in the window seat, the opened fan propped up at her feet, sipping the hot drink. Beneath her the street was thronged with tradesmen making deliveries both to the inn and to the private houses on either side. There were few carriages abroad at this hour and few gentry on the street: Nicholas ought to be easy to sight when he returned.

Warm in the sunlight bathing the window seat, Cassandra wriggled comfortably against the cushions and realised to her surprise that she was happier than she had ever been in her life. Despite the fleabites, the boy's clothes, the bumpy roads and Nicholas's uncertain temper she felt alive, vital—free. For nearly eighteen years she'd been her father's silent companion. Showing emotion was frowned upon, as were high spirits, or any display of temperament.

At best, her father had treated her as a rather unintelligent housekeeper. Now she was discovering that she could live off her wits. Rubbing shoulders with all classes, speaking French, pretending to be a boy, were all new experiences. A few weeks ago she would never have believed this could happen. When she'd run away from home she was only seeking sanctuary, not this new world of experiences.

But the most unexpected boon was this companionship she and Nicholas had achieved. If that was what it was. . . Cassandra looked at the fan again, biting her lip with indecision. If only she knew what he felt about her, what his reasons were for giving her the fan.

She'd missed Nicholas in the street below: the door behind her opened and he strolled in whistling, hands in pockets.

'You sound very cheerful,' Cassandra remarked, wondering who was responsible for putting the twinkle in his eye and the spring in his step.

'The sun is shining and not every young woman in Lyons is toothless.' He tossed his cane and gloves to one side. 'So, you decided to get up at last. Are we packed?'

'No! You didn't tell me we were going.' Cassandra scrambled off the seat, then remembered the fan. 'Thank you for the er. . .' She could feel herself blushing and blundered on. 'The fan. . .it's very beautiful.' She gazed at the buckles on her shoes, wondering why it was so difficult to thank him.

'Oh, it's nothing. You've been a good child, and I couldn't resist the look on your face, like an infant in a toyshop.' He flicked open the top of the chocolate pot to see if any remained, then threw himself down in a winged chair. 'You can put it somewhere safe until you're grown up.'

A good child! Cassandra burned with indignation, within an ace of telling him just how old she was, then bit back the words. What would he do if he realised she was eighteen? Pack her off to Vienna with a respectable widow—or give in to the instincts that had brought them so close to a kiss yesterday?

Cassandra couldn't decide which would be worse: all she wanted was to stay with Nicholas on this long route to Vienna, to build on the friendship that was growing between them. Anything else was too complicated.

'Cassandra?' Nicholas had obviously been speaking to her for a few moments. 'Do wake up! The cases need to be packed: see to it while I talk to the postillions. We've got a boat to catch.'

A boat? Cassandra was still asking questions when they arrived on the quayside. The postillions unhitched the horses, were paid off by Nicholas and clattered away, leaving the carriage stranded on the cobbles.

'But where's the boat? And we can't leave the carriage here. . .'

'Stop tugging at my coat tails and watch.'

A group of men swung a crude wooden crane over the carriage and heaved until it dangled precariously in the air. The wheels were removed and handed over the quayside into a large, flat-bottomed boat where they were laid in the bottom, half submerged by dirty bilge water. To Cassandra's horror, the body of the carriage was swung over and down until it rested upon them.

'We can't go in that,' she protested looking at the crude boat rocking on the swift flowing River Rhône. 'It's nothing but a giant punt!'

'That giant punt is costing me seven guineas. Would you rather jolt over miles more road? Or perhaps crowd onto the public boat? We can stop at night, there are inns all along the banks.'

Cassandra looked dubiously at the vicious swirl of the current and felt her stomach contract. 'I can't swim, Nicholas. . .'

'Nonsense, nobody's going to fall in. And look how much you enjoyed crossing the Channel.'

She wouldn't let him see how afraid she was. Cassandra watched the four boatmen making ready their long poles and sorting ropes. A rather more practical problem asserted itself.

'Nicholas.'

'Um?' He was watching them make the carriage secure with a lashing of cords.

'Will we be on the boat all day? I mean. . .they're all men and I. . .'

Nicholas grinned at her discomfiture. 'Don't worry, infant. The very latest in travelling commodes is in the carriage which, as you know, is equipped with curtains.'

'Oh, thank you! I didn't think it would occur to you.'

'It didn't, but it's suggested in the guidebook. Now climb down and let's be off.'

Once the moorings were let go, the boat was pulled swiftly into the current. Two of the boatmen pulled on the primitive rudder, a long oar protruding through a hole cut in the stern; the others fended off with poles on either side.

'Cass, what are you doing? Get in.' Nicholas was already in the carriage, but Cassandra perched on one of the thwarts keeping her feet out of the bilge water with difficulty.

'I'm staying here,' she stated flatly. 'If this thing goes down, I'm not going to be stuck in the carriage.'

The wind was stronger on the water. Cropped as Cassandra's hair was, it was whipped into her eyes making them weep. Gradually the novelty of being on the river overcame her nervousness and she started to enjoy herself.

The tall houses and warehouses began to diminish as they left the city behind them, but the river was surprisingly busy with traffic crossing from bank to bank, or boats like their own laden with every cargo from sheep to bales.

The men had to work hard to keep a straight line down the Rhône, using their poles as brakes and steering oars. Other boatmen waved or shouted comments, some of them obscene enough to bring a blush to Cassandra's cheeks. Unsteadily she stood up and spoke to Nicholas. 'They all seem very rough. Are they reliable?'

'This was the most respectable crew I could find.' Nicholas seemed relaxed, but Cassandra noticed the coach pistols were out of their holsters and very much to hand. 'This is hardly a pleasure trip on the River Thames. When the boat reaches Arles, it will be broken up for firewood and the men will have to make their own way back upstream. They need to be tough.'

The banks seemed to fly past: Nicholas speculated they must be travelling at six miles an hour. The bridges were the most perilous to negotiate and at most of them, Nicholas and Cassandra disembarked and walked round to wait for the men to pole the boat between the piers.

'You are looking rather pale, Cass. Are you feeling sick?' Nicholas climbed down from the carriage, carefully picking his way to keep his feet dry.

'Not sick—hungry. It seems ages since we had breakfast.'

'They will pull into the bank at that village at the next bend.' Nicholas pointed and Cassandra could see a straggle of houses with one rather more respectable building on the water side with its own jetty into the river.

The crew had a struggle to pull the boat out of the mainstream current into the quieter water that lapped the grassy banks. A man came down from the inn to catch the mooring rope and a scrubby boy was dispatched to warn the *patron* that guests were on their way. Cassandra's legs felt as wobbly as when she'd crossed the Channel, and the quiet inn with its dabbling ducks at the waterside was very welcome.

The inn was surprisingly clean and the food wholesome, although all that was provided was the simple *ordinaire*: cheese, olives and crusty bread with rough red wine to wash it down.

Cassandra made excuses to avoid reboarding the boat until Nicholas got quite short with her, pointing out that they would not reach Vienne for their night's lodgings if she tarried any longer.

'What *is* the matter with you?' he demanded, exasperated.

Cassandra shrugged and climbed reluctantly aboard. The fact that one of the men was baling out did nothing to soothe her fears, but they made a safe landfall at Vienne as the sun was setting and the air was cooling.

By the third day, as they re-embarked after a night in Montelimar, Cassandra was beginning to feel quite confident; able to make her way from one end of the boat to the other without mishap, and even exchanging badinage with the crew. Nicholas was in despair at the development of her vocabulary, but Cassandra pointed out that a few choice curses all helped her masculine disguise.

By mid-morning the weather had changed: the sky turned grey, a cold wind began to cut at their backs and the water, already turbulent, was whipped up into choppy wavelets.

Nicholas spoke to the boatmen, who shrugged their shoulders and muttered about the cruel winds of the Rhône. They were aiming to leave the boat at Arles, but the men seemed doubtful they would reach it that day, especially as the weather would make the difficult bridge at Pont St Esprit even more dangerous than usual to negotiate.

The crew seemed edgy and joked and sang less as they swept downstream. Nicholas showed Cassandra the map: Pont St Esprit was just below the junction of the Rhône with the Ardeche. The smaller river came tumbling down from the mountains swollen with snow-water.

'*Messieurs*!' The chief of the crew hailed them. 'We will put into the bank soon to let you off. You will have to walk to the other side of the bridge. It is not safe for you to remain on board.'

The boat was already tossing uncomfortably, the murky water sucking at the sides as the men struggled against the vicious current to turn into the bank. Cassandra could see an inn at the waterside and a group of people on the jetty watching the men's exertions. She felt nervous, but after almost three days afloat, she had trust in the skills and strength of the men.

They were within hailing distance of the shore when there was a loud crack. One of the side oars had snapped under the strain and, with a despairing wail, the crewman toppled into the water. The other men were powerless to assist him. Nicholas threw a rope from the stern, but the man had already disappeared below the choppy water.

In the confusion, and with only three oars, the boat had already spun back into the main current.

'Hold tight, *messieurs*!' the steersman shouted. 'We must all shoot the bridge together!'

The stone arches with their sharp prows slicing the current loomed large ahead of them. As they hurtled towards the piers, the bridge seemed to grow larger and larger, while the gap through which they had to pass appeared to Cassandra's terrified gaze to narrow.

Nicholas scrambled to her side, crushing her to the side of the coach and holding on for grim life as they sped inexorably towards the smooth slide of water under the central arch.

For a moment it seemed they would slip safely through, then an eddy caught the prow and sent it crashing against the stonework. Cassandra was aware of a great rending of wood, then the world turned upside down. She was wrenched from Nicholas's arms and thrown into the chilly, dirty water of the Rhône.

There was no light, only a thick green darkness which filled her eyes, ears and nostrils. She was going down and someone seemed to be beating her all over with sticks.

Desperately she kicked off her shoes, and felt a sudden relief as her coat was dragged off by the force of water. Surely any moment she must come up, but a great hand seemed to be holding her down, pushing her towards the muddy depths.

Her mind called 'Nicholas!', but her mouth was full of water, spilling down her throat. She was going to

die. She had time to realise that, to wonder if Nicholas
had made it to the shore, to start to say a prayer. Then
everything went black.

Treading water in a patch of still water mercifully
clear of the current, Nicholas scanned the surface
feverishly for any sign of Cassandra. The water was
opaque, too thick to see. It was pointless to dive, he
could only pray the undertow would throw her clear.

The onlookers had launched boats: he could see two
of the boatmen pulled out safely. If he did not see
Cassandra soon, he too would have to swim for shore.
His legs felt like lead with the weight of the water and
the insistent pull of the current. He had almost given
up when a sudden flash of white that could have been
a fish broke the surface downstream. It was a hand.

Nicholas struck out strongly towards it, promising in
his mind anything in the world if it was Cassandra, if
he could reach her before she sank again. The white-
ness was only a glimmer under the surface when he
reached it, his fingers clamping around the wrist.

As soon as he touched the narrow bones, he knew
it was Cassandra. Desperately he pulled her up,
encircling her ribcage with his arm and striking out
backwards for the shore. There was a warning shout
behind him, the back of his head grazed painfully on
the wood of a rowing boat and arms dragged them
both into the sanctuary of the craft.

Nicholas hung over the side of the boat retching,
suddenly too sick to help either of them until his lungs
cleared. The next thing he knew, they were on the
river bank, the grass feeling wonderful under his
grasping fingers.

'The boy is dead, *monsieur*.' Someone was touching

his shoulder in clumsy consolation. Nicholas shrugged the man off and staggered to where Cassandra was lying, her mud-streaked face colourless, her lips pinched and blue.

He lifted her shoulders, but there was no sign of life, no answering flutter of the eyelids as he shouted her name.

# CHAPTER SIX

'CASSANDRA!' Nicholas couldn't, wouldn't, believe she was dead. He lifted her shoulders, but there was no sign of life, no answering flutter of the eyelids as he shouted her name again.

She hadn't wanted to come on the boat, had been afraid, however well she'd hidden it, and he'd ignored her fears. Because it had suited him, he had treated her like the boy she was not. . .and now she was lying lifeless in his arms.

'*Monsieur*, leave him, you can do nothing. The priest is coming down. . .' One of the boatmen was tugging at his shoulder.

'Damn you, no!' Nicholas snarled, too angry to respond in French. He would not accept it, not admit she was dead. His rage at himself cleared his mind: he remembered a man being dragged from the village pond when he was a child and the blacksmith turning him over and beating the water out of him until he came back to coughing life again.

Ruthlessly he tipped Cassandra's limp body over his knee and with his clenched fist struck her hard between her shoulder blades repeatedly. Under his fingers there was a fluttering pulse, then a sudden cough, a retch and she was violently sick.

Cassandra struggled feebly against the rough hands that were beating her. It was bad enough to be dead without being struck. Perhaps she was already in Hell, which seemed unfair, so she said so.

'Not fair...' it was only a croak, but the hands stopped pummelling her and turned her over gently. Someone was cradling her, stroking away whatever was clogging her eyes and nostrils; it felt as though lips were grazing her cheek, her temples, her closed eyes.

The world beyond her eyelids was no longer green and she could feel the sun on her face. Someone was saying repeatedly, 'Thank God!' Perhaps it wasn't Hell, after all, but Heaven. A voice she knew said 'Cassandra, Cassie, open your eyes...please, look at me.' It sounded like Nicholas, but the imploring tone was one she had never heard on his lips before.

Clean, cool water was splashing over her face and she managed to open her eyes. Above her, Nicholas's face, white and out of focus, swam close.

'I told you I couldn't swim,' she managed to croak.

'And I told you I'd save you, you ungrateful brat,' he replied, but his voice broke on the last word.

Cassandra's body convulsed in a violent shudder and her eyes closed despite herself. There were voices on the fringes of her consciousness. 'A blanket, monsieur...wrap the boy warmly...the *Veuve* Aubrac sends to say there are beds ready. Hurry, *monsieur*, before an ague sets in...'

Strong arms lifted her from the muddy bank and Cassandra knew she was being carried. With an effort of will, she forced her eyes open and saw Nicholas's face, set with effort, as he picked his way over the rough ground.

'Lie still, brat, don't wriggle,' he ordered, his breath

coming short. 'There's a good inn here and you will shortly be safe in bed.'

There was a babble of voices with one, a well-modulated woman's voice, commanding and organising. Cassandra was aware of the change from sunlight to gloom as they entered the inn, of jolting as Nicholas carried her up a short flight of stairs and then there was a wonderfully soft, warm, safe feeling as she was lain on a bed.

Fingers unwrapped the swathing blanket; then there was silence. Nothing happened. After a moment, the woman's voice said, '*Monsieur?*'

Cassandra opened her eyes to find a tall, middle-aged woman looking down at her with raised eyebrows. Painfully, she turned her head and saw the expression of astonished horror on Nicholas's face as he, too, looked at her. Suddenly she was aware of just how little she was wearing. Slender bare feet protruded from the torn remnants of her stockings, her wet breeches were moulded to her hips and with her jacket and waistcoat gone the sodden, white linen shirt was as transparent as gauze across her breasts.

Without the constricting upper garments, every curve of her eighteen year old body was revealed. With a gasp, Cassandra grabbed the edges of the blanket round herself as the woman said, 'A word with you, *monsieur*.'

If she hadn't felt so ill and been so embarrassed, she could have found humour in the situation. Nicholas appeared to have been poleaxed, and the obviously highly respectable Widow Aubrac was completely in control of the situation.

Snatches of low-voiced discussion reached Cassandra's

ears from the two who had withdrawn into the window embrasure.

'You expect me to believe you were unaware. . .'

'That she was a girl. . .not that she was a woman. . .'

'You prefer to travel with a *child* in disguise! *Monsieur*, this is a respectable house!'

'*Madame*. . . I assure you. . .' Nicholas was the picture of guilt, digging himself into a deeper hole with every word he uttered.

He obviously needed rescuing before *Madame* decided he was a total roué and threw him out. Painfully Cassandra levered herself up on one elbow and croaked. '*Madame*. . .'

Instantly the woman hurried to her side. 'Do not worry, *ma petite*. You are safe here. I have heard of these decadent English milords.' She shot Nicholas a cold look. 'Under my protection he will not touch you! I will write to your family and *Monsieur le Curé* will give you sanctuary under his roof until they come for you.'

'But it is not his fault—it is I who have been dishonest,' Cassandra protested. 'The Earl is the son of my godmother: I deceived him into thinking I was much younger than I am. Listen, I will tell you everything. . .'

'When you are warm, fed and rested, *ma petite*,' Slightly mollified, the woman turned to Nicholas. '*Monsieur*, you and I must talk later, but for now I must ask you to leave.' There was a knock at the door and servants staggered in with a hip bath and flagons of hot water. 'Your chamber is at the other end of the landing, you will wish to bathe and rest, *sans doubte*.'

Much later, warm, dry and lulled, Cassandra drifted

off to sleep, aware only of the comforting crackle of logs in the grate and subdued noises from the outside world penetrating the closed shutters.

She woke to find the room full of sunlight, the shutters thrown open and the smell of chicken broth in her nostrils. *Madame* was setting down a tray, but when she saw Cassandra was awake, she bustled over to plump up the pillows and help her sit up.

Every muscle in Cassandra's body seemed to protest. Under the starched sheet her legs were stiff and sore, and when she picked up the spoon, her wrists were purpled with bruises.

'Nicholas?' she asked anxiously, suddenly fully awake, the memories of yesterday flooding her mind. '*Madame*, is he all right?'

*Madame* smiled slightly. 'Stiff and bruised as yourself, *m'selle*, but quite well. Somewhat chastened in spirit, I believe: I have remonstrated with him on his foolishness in indulging in such a charade.'

Looking at the aristocratic face, Cassandra could well believe it! What such a woman was doing running a country inn was a mystery, but in post-Revolutionary France, many people were forced to make shift as best they could.

*Madame* continued to talk as she straightened the bedclothes. 'I will never understand Englishmen! How could he have been so blind? You would not have deceived a Frenchman for one moment!'

'How long have I been asleep?' Cassandra swallowed the soup hungrily, it seemed days since she had eaten.

'You have slept the clock round. Now eat, and sleep again. Tomorrow, perhaps, you can get up.'

'But I need to talk to Nicholas.' All Cassandra could think of was the expression on his face as he realised just how she had deceived him. What would he do? Such impropriety would not be countenanced by polite society. Even the reputation of the Earl of Lydford would be damaged by such a scandal: no mother of a marriageable daughter would have him in the house again. Godmama would never forgive her if she prevented Nicholas from making a suitable marriage, as surely he soon must.

'Not in your room! It would be most improper for the Earl to visit you here. Besides, he, too, is resting. He came close to losing his own life in rescuing you.'

So it *had* been Nicholas who had dragged her from the water, and brought her back from the edge of death. Unconsciously she rubbed her wrist where his strong fingers had marked her. 'And the others? Our boatmen?'

'They are all safe, thank God.' *Madame* crossed herself piously. 'Even the one whose fall caused the accident will live, although he has a broken leg. Now rest again, that is enough talk for now.'

Cassandra was too weak to argue, even if *madame*'s autocratic manner had permitted it. 'Yes, *madame*,' she capitulated, her eyes closing even as she spoke.

When Nicholas found her the next day, Cassandra was sitting quietly on a settle by the fire in the back parlour. In the high-necked grey gown *madame* had found for her and with her cropped hair, she looked like a novice nun. Her face was porcelain pale except for a livid bruise running from cheekbone to jawline on one side and she was flexing stiff fingers painfully in her lap.

'Cassie,' he said quietly.

Cassandra jumped, then bit her lip with pain at the sudden movement. Nicholas took one step towards her as if to comfort her then stopped, sitting abruptly in the wing chair on the other side of the fire.

'We have to talk.' He looked not at her but down at his clasped hands, and Cassandra wondered if he was too angry at her deception to face her.

'I know, Nicholas... I'm sorry. I was headstrong and foolish and I should never have allowed you to go on believing I was so young. But I knew you would not have brought me with you if you knew the truth.' For a moment the thought of Lord Offley's wet lips on hers, the prospect of marriage with such a man came flooding back and she shuddered. 'I would rather have died than remain!'

'You almost did,' he said sardonically.

'*Madame* told me it was you who saved me.' Still he did not look at her. 'Thank you for saving my life, risking your own for me. I am truly sorry.'

'*You* are sorry!' The words burst from him. 'I should never have taken you on that boat. You were frightened and I ignored it.' His anger was palpable. 'This has been a sorry escapade.' He got to his feet and thumped the mantelpiece with his clenched fist. 'I must have been mad that day in London!'

'But you weren't to know my true age,' Cassandra protested. 'It was I who let you go on believing I was fifteen.'

'Just how old are you, Cassandra?' he demanded,

his voice hard. He was standing over her and she had to look up to meet his scrutiny.

'Eighteen,' she confessed quietly.

'Oh, Cassie!' He took her chin between long fingers, turning her face from side to side. 'Of all the stupid things to do!' There was a heavy silence, then he sighed and released her. 'What a damn fool I've been—I think I must have known all the time, I just didn't choose to see it. For heaven's sake, I nearly kissed you in Lyons!'

'You *did* kiss me in Paris.' Cassandra could have bitten her tongue as soon as she said it: the expression in Nicholas's suddenly hooded eyes warned her she was still on dangerous ground.

'Precisely! Cassandra, you are a woman, however little experience you may have of Society and the world...'

'Are you telling me I cannot trust you?' she whispered.

'Yes!... No!' He spun away, pacing the room in his inability to explain to her. 'That night in Paris I had been drinking, you had made me angry—and then to see you looking like that... I didn't stop to think.' He struggled to find the words to explain to this sheltered girl-woman just how provocative her behaviour had been. 'Our Society keeps unmarried girls and men apart for a reason: sometimes our natures overrule both sense and honour.'

Cassandra swallowed hard. The delicacy of Nicholas's carefully chosen words could not disguise the truth of what he was saying. If it had happened in Paris, it could happen again if they were thrown together in such intimacy. 'You are saying that you must send me back,' she stated bleakly. 'That you have no alternative.'

'I only wish I could send you back! Don't think I haven't considered it.' His smile was rueful. 'But I could not consign you to Offley's tender mercies! Nor can I send you directly to my mother: from here you would have to travel back to Lyons, then across the Alps into Switzerland and on to Vienna, and that is too perilous a journey even with a reliable escort.

'No, I have weighed all this since yesterday: you must continue to travel with me, but as my ward, under my protection. It is no further to Vienna through Italy than to retrace our steps.

'*Madame* will find you a wardrobe of discreet clothes such as you are wearing now and we must hope you can pass as a schoolgirl. I will engage a maid.' He broke off and looked at her. 'It will seem unconventional, but we are on the Continent: foreigners think all the English are mad, anyway. We must just avoid the company of our own countrymen.'

'But Nicholas, you will be sacrificing so much, missing so much of the Grand Tour if we have to avoid everywhere where English tourists will be.'

He shrugged. 'So be it. I doubt I'll have a decent night's sleep until I can deliver you safe to my mother, never mind an appetite for art galleries and antiquities!'

Cassandra knew she should feel guilty, perhaps she did. But overriding all other emotions was the thought that she would still be with Nicholas, for days, weeks to come. He was arrogant and dangerously disturbing, but he also laughed with her, shared with her and looked after her. For the first time in her life, she had a friend, a companion.

Her life before she'd run away had been desperately lonely. No doubt when she reached Vienna, Godmama would introduce her to girls of her own age who would become friends, but for the moment there was only Nicholas to fill that gap.

'Thank you, Nicholas,' she said fervently. 'I promise I'll behave with discretion—I made a good boy, but I'll make an even better schoolgirl!'

She fixed him with an imploring gaze, which he met with narrowed eyes and a slight, dubious, shake of the head. 'You'll be bored to tears back in skirts and with a chaperone. When the novelty wears thin. . .'

Whatever he was about to say was drowned by the rumble of carriage wheels on cobbles, followed seconds later by the raised voice of an Englishman. Nicholas jumped up and opened the door a crack. 'Hell and damnation! Upstairs quickly!'

'But Nicholas. . .'

'Don't argue.' He propelled her to the door, one hand painfully between her bruised shoulder blades. 'There's a party of about a dozen English. . .three carriages. Of all the cursed bad luck!'

In her room, Cassandra set the shutters open a crack so she could safely observe the new arrivals. There seemed to be two families with their servants. The older men appeared to be brothers, both florid and overdressed. They were accompanied by their wives—one stout and perspiring in the afternoon sun, the other thin and languid—and their sons.

Cassandra saw at a glance they were not of the *ton*. Rich merchants from their dress and manner, she guessed. The yard soon emptied, the noise transferring to the interior of the inn as they and their luggage were distributed among the available rooms.

Did this mean she would have to be confined to this chamber until these people—or she and Nicholas—moved on? Cassandra sighed heavily, already beginning to chafe at the restrictions of her new rôle. At least as a boy she could have slipped down the back stairs and into the stableyard and no-one would have spared her a second glance.

There was a light tap at the door and *madame* came in, accompanied by a pretty blonde woman in her early twenties, whom she introduced to Cassandra as Madame Vernet, the apothecary's wife. '*Monsieur* entrusted me to engage a companion for you, *m'selle*, and he has requested me to ask you to come down to dinner this evening with Madame Vernet.'

'But the other visitors. . .'

'They are not of the best society, *m'selle*.' The widow spoke with hauteur, as if her inn were used to better. '*Monsieur le Comte* thinks it would be useful for you to practise your new rôle among people who do not know him.'

'Oh, good!' A chance of escape, a change of company. 'What am I to wear?'

'*Monsieur* and I consider what you are wearing entirely suitable for a young lady not yet out.'

Cassandra smoothed down the light grey stuff of her skirt and sighed. Her new resolution to behave was being sorely tested sooner than she would have expected.

The rest of the party was assembled in the dining-room by the time Cassandra and her new chaperone entered. Colette Vernet had proved to be a friendly companion and an excellent dresser of hair. Despite her drab dress, Cassandra was pleased with the shining curls Colette had teased from her crop, and the Frenchwoman had brought her own rice powder to cover the bruise on Cassandra's cheek.

Daringly, Cassandra had crushed geranium petals to colour her lips and touched rose water behind her ears. All eyes turned to the two women as they entered, Nicholas's with relief at her modest demeanour, the touring party with frank curiosity that turned to indifference at the sight of two uninteresting females.

'My ward, Miss Jones. Ca... Catherine, Mr Bulstrode and Mr George Bulstrode and their families.'

Cassandra bobbed a neat curtsey, then took the seat next to the Earl, Colette at her side.

'You are most indulgent to bring your ward with you, my lord,' the elder Mrs Bulstrode observed archly. 'My two sweet daughters, Phoebe and Ariadne, pleaded with their dear Papa to permit them to accompany us, but Mr Bulstrode would not countenance it. Would you, Mr Bulstrode?'

'Certainly not,' her spouse replied robustly. 'I don't spend good guineas for them to attend Miss Simpkin's Academy in Bath so they can fritter their time on continental travel. No way to catch a good husband that, is it, my lord?'

Faced with a direct question, Nicholas was forced to participate in a conversation he clearly found distasteful. 'I am afraid I have no opinion on the matter, Mr Bulstrode. I am delivering my ward to the care of her great aunt in Nice: that is the sum total of my experience of the rearing of young girls.'

Cassandra could hardly contain her laughter. How Nicholas managed to convey such total boredom and a complete distaste for the subject without being openly offensive fascinated her. She could well believe all the stories she had heard of the arrogant Earl of Lydford.

The Bulstrodes appeared oblivious to the snub. They ignored Cassandra and her companion completely, except to request them to pass the buttered crayfish or the mustard, and addressed all their remarks to poor Nicholas.

Cassandra knew she had to avoid his eye or they would both set off laughing. But all desire to giggle left her when, to her utter astonishment, she heard her own name mentioned.

'Of course, Earl, you have been out of the country and will not be aware of the latest *on-dit* in Society. Poor Lord Offley has set off such a hue and cry after his young bride-to-be, who has quite vanished from her home. Why, he believes Miss Weston to be abducted, so sudden was her disappearance!' The younger Mrs Bulstrode was positively quivering in her inappropriately overtrimmed gown with the excitement of the tale.

'And he must be right,' her sister-in-law chimed in, 'for what young girl would fly from such a distinguished connexion!'

Cassandra felt the colour rise up her throat and her heart began to thud painfully. Not for a moment had she expected anyone to make her flight public, let alone Lord Offley. But, of course, when she thought about it she could understand why. Her father might live cut off from Society, but he hoarded every penny and was known to be a warm man. Lord Offley, as profligate with his money as with his morals, would want Cassandra—and her dowry—back.

'Why, we have shocked dear Miss Jones,' Mrs Bulstrode senior said patronisingly, misunderstanding her flushed cheeks. 'I am sorry, my dear, but such sad stories should be told: they hold a moral for young girls.'

'In what way, since you hold her to have been abducted? If that were the case, it could not be her fault and the story holds no moral,' Cassandra remarked coldly. 'Or do you suggest she had connived in her own abduction? If that were so, I am sure it is not fit for my ears!'

Nicholas tapped her warningly on the ankle with the toe of his shoe, but Cassandra was enjoying the look of outrage on Mrs Bulstrode's florid features. The older woman was not to be so easily snubbed, however. Ignoring Cassandra, she turned to the Earl. 'I believe Miss Weston is a connexion of yours, is she not, my lord? This sad news must be a terrible shock for you.'

'One of my mother's numerous godchildren, I believe,' he said in tones of utter boredom. 'A scrubby child given to masquerades when I last saw her. The Dowager has always been more generous than wise in her patronage. Catherine, my child, if you have finished that Rhenish cream, I suggest you retire.' He turned to Mrs Bulstrode. 'She is not yet out, you know,' he remarked, by way of explanation for such an early dismissal.

Cassandra was glad to escape the overheated atmosphere and the ugly curiosity of the Bulstrodes. In her room she thanked Colette, who promised to attend her in the morning, but once the Frenchwoman had gone, she felt too agitated to undress and get into bed.

Instead she curled up in the window seat and rested her hot face against the cool green glass. In the moonlight, the dark Rhône slid silently past, its smooth surface giving no hint of the murderous currents beneath.

Those odious women! The thought of vulgar persons like that gossiping, bandying her name about! It had never occurred to her for one moment that news of her flight would reach more than her immediate and restricted circle. She had believed no-one would care, no-one would find her of any interest.

Now what was she going to do? What would Godmama say when she heard? The humiliation made her go hot and cold all over. The thought of waiting until the morning to talk to Nicholas was insupportable: she must see him now, find out if he would still take her with him in the face of this scandal.

When she reached his room, it was empty. Too agitated to sit, she perched uneasily on the end of the bed until she heard his feet treading lightly on the polished boards of the passage.

Almost as soon as he closed the door behind him, she had flung herself into his arms, sobbing against his chest. The candle he was holding guttered and snuffed with the draught she created, leaving them clinging together in the darkness.

'Cassandra. . .for goodness' sake,' he began, trying to free the arms that encircled him, but then the extent of her unhappiness and humiliation must have reached him and he said no more, but held her close until the sobs turned to hiccoughs.

His arms around her felt strong and sure, his body was a rock to which she clung. Gently he stroked her hair from her crown to the nape as if he was gentling a kitten and instinctively Cassandra snuggled closer.

'You shouldn't be here, you know,' he remonstrated gently.

'Those horrible people, Nicholas! Talking about me! Everyone knows. . . I'll die of shame. What am I going to do?'

'Pay them no heed—they'll find another scandal next week,' he said matter-of-factly.

Cassandra tipped her head back to look at him. In the moonlight his face was a white mask, but it seemed to her his breathing was not as regular as it had been.

'Cassie. . .you must go.'

'Not yet, we must talk about what to do, Nicholas,' Cassandra insisted, no less vehement for having to whisper.

'Not now, not here!' Nicholas freed himself from her embrace and gave her a little shake. 'Cassie, this isn't proper and it isn't wise!'

'Oh, I know what you said, but I trust you, Nicholas. . .'

He looked down into the pale oval of her face, at her parted lips and her dark, shadowed eyes. 'Stop it, Cassie, I'm not made of stone! Be a good girl and go to your room.'

'Stop treating me like a child when you know I am not,' she said vehemently. 'You've seen I'm not a child. Why won't you discuss this with me? You just keep saying "Cassie, do this, Cassie, do that, don't worry, it'll be all right". But it won't be all right, will it?'

'If you don't get out now and go to your room it will never be all right,' he said between clenched teeth. 'What if someone finds you here? Do you *want* to be ruined?'

'But I *am* ruined in the eyes of Society, anyway. I've been travelling with you day and night for more than two weeks. What has changed? I need to talk to you, Nicholas. . .' She reached out her hands to him again, but he caught her wrists, holding her away from him.

'I tried to warn you in Paris you were playing with fire. There is a lot of difference between being ruined in name and in fact. You are not such a child; you understand what I am saying to you. Get out of this room *now*.'

He freed her wrists and turned from her, one hand clenched on the carved bedpost. In the sudden stillness of the room his breathing was ragged.

Cassandra could not pretend she did not understand him, not after his plain speaking earlier. He had obviously been attracted to her in Paris, and in Lyons, but had fought against it because be believed her so young. Now he had seen with his own eyes that she was a woman. Cassandra burned with the memory of his eyes on her body, but mixed with the embarrassment was a tingling pleasure.

And Nicholas was a passionate, experienced man, used to the company of women as experienced and willing as Lady Broome. Innocent young ladies were a bore—until such time as he would have to enter the Marriage Mart in search of a suitable wife.

With her trustfulness and in their enforced intimacy, she was putting an intolerable strain on him. And suddenly, staring at his wide shoulders, the crisp curl of dark hair at his nape, the strong hand gripping the bedpost, she realised she didn't care, she *wanted* him to feel like that about her.

Five minutes ago she had been in his arms, held close to him and she yearned to be there again. With a shiver, she remembered the heat of his mouth on hers in Paris, the strength of his arms as he held her on the river bank. 'Nicholas,' she began, then broke off, uncertain of what she meant to say.

'Damn it, Cassandra,' he ground out without turning. 'Will you get out of here!'

'But. . .' she stammered.

'Go!' He gestured abruptly with his hand and she turned and fled, banging the door behind her.

# CHAPTER SEVEN

'THEN I can go back to being a boy?' Cassandra started to sit down on the low stone parapet of the bridge, remembered her skirts and checked the movement.

Nicholas gazed past her to the edge of the river where an old woman was collecting driftwood. 'I think it would be as well.' His tone was studiedly neutral, as it had been since the rather stilted breakfast they had shared that morning.

A little devil prompted her to ask, 'Why?' The question was rewarded by a sharp glance from Nicholas's green eyes.

'If people such as the Bulstrodes know of your disappearance, those in Society certainly will. The Bulstrodes are in no position to know whether I have a ward or not, but the *ton* most certainly do. The coincidence of my mother's missing goddaughter and a mysterious young woman travelling with me would be too marked to overlook.'

'Yes, Nicholas,' Cassandra averred demurely. 'That is a very good reason.'

And it was. But she knew the real reason as well as he did. Nicholas did not want the constant reminder of her femininity. Dressed as a boy and with the formality of the master-servant relationship restored, it would be easier to pretend she was simply young Cassie again.

In the cold light of day, she realised what a narrow escape they had had last night from something they would have both bitterly regretted. She had only Nicholas's self-control to thank for that. . .

'Will we be moving on today?' she asked, gathering up her skirts to cross the cobbled bridge. 'I haven't any boy's clothes.'

'The apothecary's wife is buying some. I asked her this morning while I was making arrangements for the carriage.'

'And the rest of the luggage?' Cassandra rested her palms on the bridge parapet and watched the treacherous sucking water below that had so nearly taken her life.

'We can buy everything we need in Orange, according to Madame. Stop looking at the river, Cassie, dwelling on the accident will not help you recover from it.'

She shivered and decided he was right. Her restless sleep the night before had been full of swirling green water overlying the image of Nicholas's face and the remembered sensation of someone touching her skin with cold lips.

Raising her eyes from the surface to the water's edge, she watched a group of urchins chasing minnows in a muddy pool, shrieking with laughter. 'The river is not all bad,' she remarked with a smile, which froze on her lips at the sudden appearance of the Bulstrode family party strolling along the far bank.

The Mesdames Bulstrode were a startling vision, the elder in lilac, the younger in an argumentative shade of puce. Both were having trouble controlling overlarge poke bonnets in the strong morning breeze.

'Oh, yes, Cousin Nicholas,' Cassandra remarked in a high, clear tone. 'You are so right in observing that the state of the deserving poor in this country is much worse than that of our own. Good morning, Mrs Bulstrode.' She dropped a neat curtsey. 'The Earl and I were discoursing on the condition of the lower orders in these parts. The absence of a benevolent landowning class must be much to blame.'

'Well, they are all Papists,' the older woman announced sweepingly, before turning her attention to the Earl.

Nicholas, however, was too experienced in the ways of social climbers to be trapped by the Bulstrodes into a lengthy exchange.

'You are so right, Madam,' he agreed, straight faced. 'I wonder why that did not occur to us. Come Cas. . . Catherine, the wind is getting quite keen.' He raised his hat to the Bulstrodes and shepherded a demure Cassandra back towards the inn.

'You baggage!' he accused, as soon as they were out of earshot. '"Benevolent landowning class", indeed! Where did you learn to spout such nonsense?'

'The vicar's wife talks like that all the time. I did it rather well, I think,' she congratulated herself.

'You do like to sail close to the wind, don't you, Cassie?' he remarked drily. 'Now stay upstairs until the carriage is ready. I doubt my constitution will stand any more encounters between you and the Bulstrodes.'

How and when Cassandra would transform herself from demure young lady to valet exercised them both. It would not do to risk encountering the sharp eyes of the elder Mrs Bulstrode with Cassandra in boy's guise and Nicholas cravenly refused point-blank to risk the icy disapproval of Madame Aubrac by enlisting her aid. Nor could Cassandra change in an inn along the way or the postillions would gossip.

Eventually she hurried out to the carriage while the horses were being hitched up, drew the blinds and scrambled out of the dress and into her shirt and breeches. She was just tying her second garter when Nicholas joined her.

She was perfectly decently clad but, for some reason, she felt exposed in her shirt sleeves and stockinged feet. Hastily she pulled on the jerkin and fastened the buttons tight, jammed on her shoes and began to fiddle with her neckcloth. She knew she was mangling it, but Nicholas made no move to help her as he would have done two days before: he seemed as conscious as she of the changed condition between them.

But by the second day, as they neared Aix en Provence, it seemed the illusion of the clothes had worked, the truth about her age was forgotten and they were at ease with each other again.

Aix lived up to Cassandra's expectations of what a 'proper' foreign city should be. There were wide, clean avenues of limes, fountains on every corner and gracious squares where the inhabitants took the air in the evening.

To Cassandra's delight, it was warm enough to sit out after dusk. In the larger squares, enterprising restaurant owners had set tables out under the plane trees for couples to watch the promenaders while sipping wine and nibbling almond biscuits.

Cassandra had acquired a very decent suit of super-fine, and with her best linen and polished shoes, black looked respectable enough to sit with Nicholas pretending to be his *courier*.

'You are causing much interest amongst the young ladies,' she teased slyly. As the respectable family groups strolled past, several of the pretty daughters on their fathers' arms were sliding interested looks under demure lashes to where they were sitting.

Nicholas snorted. 'It's not me,' he teased back. 'I think the little redhead has taken a fancy to you. Take care, Cass, I don't want outraged fathers banging at our door.'

Far from being chastened, Cassandra burst into laughter, choking on her wine until Nicholas threatened to slap her on the back. 'It's good,' she finally managed to say. 'If I can deceive those girls, I can deceive anyone.' Greatly daring, she added, 'I do believe you're jealous of my success, Nicholas.'

'Impudent whelp!' Nicholas aimed a cuff at her ear. 'I would have you know that respectable bourgeoises hold no fascination for me.'

No, she thought, taken unaware by a sudden stab of jealousy. It wasn't inexperienced, unsophisticated chaperoned girls he wanted, it was the older, knowing, society women who attracted Nicholas. Preferably those safely married to complaisant husbands.

Cassandra gave herself a little shake and picked up the *Gentleman's Guide*. 'It says here that Aix will please us more than any city we have seen in France.'

'If you're going to start quoting the guidebook, it's time you were in bed. Come on, brat, you've broken enough hearts for one evening.'

\* \* \*

From Aix, they turned due East and took the winding road through St Maximin and Brignoles. High ground rose sharply on either side covered with a fragrant scrub of lavender and wild thyme, baking under the hot sun.

Even glimpses of snow on the distant Alps could not make the journey seem any cooler. Nicholas tossed aside his jacket and loosened his cravat and Cassandra followed suit, too hot to worry about her shirt sleeves and exposed throat.

The road was rough and the low scrub of the *maquis* crowded close. The postillions were nervous. In every inn along the way, people were telling vivid tales of banditry, and now they were convinced every clump of trees contained brigands waiting to attack the carriage.

As the shadows lengthened, Nicholas cleaned and checked the pistols in the carriage holsters. When he reached for the balls to reload, Cassandra could contain herself no longer. 'Please show me how to shoot them, I've always wanted to try.' She leaned forward, eyes shining and reached for one of the long-barrelled weapons.

'Don't touch!' Nicholas looked quite shocked at her bloodthirsty interest. 'They aren't toys, Cass.'

'Yes, but what if we're attacked?' They, too, had heard the tales of brigands at every inn along this coastal route to Nice.

'The postillions have horse pistols,' he began, then broke off, looking thoughtful. 'Perhaps there is something in what you say. Look, it loads like this. Leave the hammer down and don't point it at anyone. When you need to fire, you cock it like this.'

Cassandra watched as his strong thumb lifted the hammer, then eased it back down slowly.

'Here.' He handed her the unloaded gun. 'Try with this one.'

The hammer was stiff and she had to use both hands to cock it, the metal cold and unfriendly against her hot hands. Suddenly she didn't want anything to do with guns, but he took her hand in his, aiming it and the weapon out of the window.

'Like this. Hold it steady and squeeze the trigger. Aim for the body, it's the biggest target, you are more likely to hit something than if you aim for the head.'

Cassandra swallowed hard and handed the gun back. 'Thank you.' There was nothing exciting in the prospect of killing or maiming a man, however villainous.

Frejus, however, was reached without incident. They put up for the night in a passable inn where the patron boasted of the parties of English tourists who had passed that way the week before. 'They all took the sea passage, of course, milord. To avoid the brigands, you understand.' He rolled his eyes to emphasise the dangers. 'Desperate men, milord! They would slit your throat for the clothes on your back. Much safer to take my brother-in-law's boat.'

Nicholas turned from the landlord's cheerful relish of the dangers ahead to see Cassandra turn as pale as a ghost.

'Nicholas...no...please, not a boat! You didn't say anything about another boat!'

'All right, Cass,' he spoke calmly. 'We'll say no more of it today: tomorrow we can look at the sea.

Perhaps you'll feel better when you see how calm it is.'

Next day the sea was indeed calm, but Cass was not reassured. Panic tightened her chest and her feet seemed rooted to the shingle beach. In vain, the landlord's brother-in-law demonstrated the fine lines of his boat, the strong arms of the boatmen and the wisdom of the captain. Cass shook her head mulishly and refused to move.

'The lad was almost drowned on our way down the Rhône,' Nicholas explained to the landlord, who was obviously of the opinion that a firm master would simply toss the young valet on board and be done with it.

'*Les anglais*,' he muttered, shaking his head in disbelief at such indulgence.

'Thank you, Nicholas,' Cassandra whispered fervently, some of the colour restored to her face. 'I know I shouldn't be such a coward.'

Nicholas cast a swift glance round and finding them alone gave her a swift, hard hug. 'No, you're not a coward. You very nearly lost your life: I should never have suggested it.'

Cassandra shivered, despite the hot sun on her back. The casual embrace was meant to reassure, she knew that, but she could still feel the pressure of his fingers on her skin beneath the fine lawn shirt. He was already striding ahead, shouting at the postillions to harness the horses. The gesture had obviously been as fleeting as the moment to him, she thought, with a tinge of regret.

The road left the coast to cut inland through the thick forest of pine and chestnut hugging the slopes of

Mont Vinaigre. The rutted dusty track climbed steeply in hairpin bends up the flank of the mountain to a height of almost a thousand feet.

Jolted by the deep ruts, Cassandra watched Nicholas as he sat with one hand resting on the holster set in the coach door, his eyes alert, despite the heat that seemed to bake through the very fabric of the coach. Eventually the heat and the motion lulled her into an uneasy doze from which she woke stiff-necked and dry lipped as the coach descended into the little fishing village of Cannes.

'Are we there?' she asked, not too certain where 'there' was.

'Almost.' Nicholas relaxed against the cushions with a long sigh. Cassandra realised just how alert he had been for the last twenty miles, despite his reassuring words to her earlier.

Cannes was no more impressive than Frejus had been and the inn considerably worse. They were relieved to be leaving the next morning after a breakfast of coarse bread and evil coffee and now with the threatening mountain road and its danger of brigands behind them, they were both in almost holiday mood.

The route from Cannes to Nice lay along the coast: a winding, often alarming road hanging on the very cliff edge. The sea sparkled blue below them, sometimes hidden by clumps of pines, and white farmhouses set in the hillside made the land seem peopled, even though they saw scarcely anyone except a goatherd and his dog.

After the insignificant village of Antibes, the road dropped almost to sea level offering a continuous view over the dazzling Mediterranean with fishing boats bobbing at anchor. Cassandra stuck her head out of the carriage window and breathed in the smell of hot pine resin, the crisp tang of the sea and the scent of herbs in the dusty air.

Nicholas seized the hem of her waistcoat and hauled her back into the carriage. 'Get back in, brat—or you'll be out of the window at the next bump in the road!'

'Why are you laughing at me?' Cassandra demanded, seeing the grin on his face.

'You look like a retriever pup who has just had her first scent of game!' But as he looked down into her indignant face, flushed with heat and excitement, her hair awry, her eyes sparkling, he thought he had never had the urge to kiss one of his gun dogs.

The carriage suddenly slowed and one of the postillions shouted out. Nicholas put his head out of the window. 'What is it? Why are we stopping?'

From the other window Cassandra had already spied the problem: a broken-down farm cart was slewed across the road, its meagre contents spilling out and the ancient driver tugging at the reins of an equally ancient mule.

'Get down one of you, and help him or we'll never get to Nice,' Nicholas ordered. The man did as he was bid, walking awkwardly in his heavy boots. He vanished round the cart: seconds later there was a sudden cry, then silence.

'What the Devil!' Nicholas jumped down, leaving the door swinging. 'Stay there, Cassie, while I see what is happening.'

As he strode towards the cart, the driver took to his heels. Then there was a thump swiftly followed by a cry: from her vantage point Cassandra watched in horror as the second postillion slumped to the ground, a knife-hilt protruding between his shoulder blades.

For a moment she was frozen, then she scrambled across the carriage to the open door. 'Nicholas! Behind you!' she shouted, seeing two ruffians emerge from behind the cart, each with a cudgel and a curving knife in his hands.

Everything happened so fast it was blurred. Nicholas stooped, picked up a rock and threw it with unerring accuracy to catch the nearest brigand in the centre of the forehead. The man fell as if poleaxed. The second man cursed and began to back away, holding the murderous knife in front of him.

Nicholas had already snatched up the fallen man's knife and was advancing when a shadow seemed to slip from behind the horses, arm raised.

'Behind you!' Cassandra shrieked again, but too late. The man had brought the cudgel down in a crashing blow on Nicholas's shoulder, sending him sprawling to the ground.

Cassandra saw red. Unknowingly her fingers curled round one of the pistols, slipping it from its holster. The smooth wood of the butt felt right in her hand and this time the hammer pulled back smoothly under her thumb.

Without conscious thought, she brought the muzzle up, aimed at the broad, leather-jerkined back and fired. The recoil shot her backwards painfully onto her tailbone. Eyes streaming, shoulder numb, she scrambled down from the coach, brandishing the other pistol.

'Get away from him! Get away or I'll kill you!' she

yelled in English. The message was clear enough: the brigand grabbed his injured colleague and stumbled off into the pines. Of the man Nicholas had hit there was no sign.

Cassandra ran, stumbling in her haste and fell on her knees beside Nicholas. He was stirring, his eyes black in a deadly white face. 'Nicholas!'

'Stop pointing that pistol at me,' he managed to say, then broke off, retching painfully.

'Sit up.' Cassandra half dragged him into the shade of the cart and propped him against the wheel. 'I'll fetch some water.'

After several deep draughts, he reopened his eyes and looked at her, a ghost of a smile on his lips. 'Bloodthirsty brat! Where are all the bodies?'

'One of the postillions is all right, he only had a tap on the head. He's looking after the other one in the carriage. The brigands have gone.'

'I'm not surprised!'

'I only shot one of them,' Cassandra protested. 'I think the others were taken by surprise; they didn't know there was anyone else in the carriage.'

Nicholas shifted his position and grimaced. 'I think they've broken my collarbone.'

Cassandra probed gingerly, wincing as he did. 'I don't think you have—but it is bound to be very badly bruised. Can you get up? We need to get all of you to a doctor—and besides, what will we do if they come back?'

Unsteadily, leaning on her shoulder, Nicholas made his way back to the coach. The stabbed postillion was slumped silently in one corner, the other stood holding his head and moaning.

'There's money in it for you if you can drive us on to Nice,' she said firmly to the man with the headache. 'You have done well, the Earl will not fail to reward you.'

It was almost dusk by the time they entered Nice at a decorous trot. Cassandra was too preoccupied with her patients to heed the famous groves of oranges and lemons or admire the white *bastides*, their doors and windows smothered in brilliant blooms.

To her relief, Nice was every bit as civilized and fashionable as the other coastal towns were not. The hotelier summoned a doctor with dispatch and made them comfortable in his best suite, while the postillion was carried off to the servants quarters to have his wound dressed by the barber surgeon.

'*Monsieur le docteur* will be here soon,' the hotelier announced. 'It would be best if you get your master undressed and into bed while you wait. I will send up wine and hot water.'

'Undress. . .er, I. . .'

'You are his valet, are you not?' The man shrugged his shoulders at the stupidity of the English. 'You have not had a blow to the head? You understand what I am saying?'

'Perfectly,' Cassandra replied haughtily. 'I will look after *Monsieur le Comte*. You may leave.'

Nicholas was slumped back against the pillows, his face faintly green in the subdued light. Cassandra bit her lip, undecided how best to get him undressed. She told herself that she was being unnecessarily modest, and that in an emergency such as this, propriety could not count. Even Godmama would tell her not to be such a little ninny.

She pulled off his shoes and stockings then his neckcloth. He did not stir. Emboldened, she unbuttoned his shirt, pulled it loose from the waistband of his breeches and tried to ease it off his shoulders. After a few minutes struggling to no avail, she sat on the edge of the bed and pulled him forward to rest against her breast while she slid the shirt free.

She should have let him back down onto the pillows, but instead, Cassandra found herself holding him, his naked back warm and smooth under her fingers, his heart beating rhythmically against her chest. She had never realised that a man's skin could be this smooth, that the play of strong muscles would be so alluring to the fingertips.

Her hesitant, gentle touch seemed to rouse him and he stirred, murmuring incoherently. His lips moved against her throat and Cassandra stiffened with shock at the intimacy and pleasure of the sensation. How long they would have stayed like that had not the doctor's knock at the door intervened, she did not know.

Doctor le Blanc greeted Cassandra in excellent English, clucked with disapproval to find Nicholas still half-dressed and had him out of his breeches, into a nightshirt and between the sheets in a trice.

She was relieved to see how competent and efficient the doctor seemed. He kept up a constant flow of inconsequential but reassuring chatter while he probed and checked Nicholas from top to toe.

'Very good, my lord, very good,' he said as Nicholas stirred and opened his eyes. 'No breaks, I am happy to say, although that is a most serious contusion on your shoulder. It will be painful for some time as it is so near the bone, but nothing a fit young man like yourself cannot endure!

'. . .and you have found a most excellent hotel which is fortunate when you consider the number of your countrymen resident already in our lovely town.'

'Does that account for your excellent English, *monsieur*?' Nicholas asked between clenched teeth as the doctor pulled his nightshirt back over his shoulder.

'But *certainement*, milord. Many of my patients are of the English nobility, here for the excellence of the climate and the efficacy of our seabathing. I would recommend a course of immersions for your wound.'

Cassandra had retreated to the window when the doctor arrived, glad of the opportunity to regain her equilibrium. She rubbed her fingertips together, still feeling Nicholas's body so warm and strong and yet, for once, so vulnerable.

It had seemed such a good idea to reassume her former rôle, but however much she might play the boy, she could no longer deceive herself that her feelings for Nicholas were anything but those of a woman for a man.

'Cass. . .that is your name, is it not?' The doctor was at her elbow and had obviously been talking to her for some time. 'I have sent a message to the apothecary to prepare a salve. It must be applied three times a day and rubbed in well. The day after tomorrow, milord must go down to *la plage* and immerse himself in the sea for ten minutes: it does not matter if he cannot swim.'

'He swims very well,' Cassandra replied absently.

'So much the better. *Au'voir*, milord, send for me if you have the slightest discomfort.' He bowed himself out of the chamber as Nicholas shifted uncomfortably against the piled bolsters.

'Slightest discomfort! French understatement, no doubt.' He looked across at Cassandra's pinched face and held out a hand to her. 'Cassie! Come over here. You saved my life, you know...'

Cassandra walked to him as though he pulled a string and took his warm, strong hand in hers. His fingers closed over hers and stroked the knuckles.

'And how are you? It must have been a terrible shock.'

His sympathy was enough to precipitate tears. Two large drops gathered and rolled down her cheeks and she hung her head to hide them.

'I thought you were going to be killed...and the knife in the postillion's back and the blood...and those terrible men...' She took a deep breath and asked, 'Do you think I killed him?'

Nicholas didn't answer. Instead he pulled her onto the bed beside him, gathered her against his good shoulder and held her until the tears dried. Gradually in the safety of his arms, Cassandra's tense body relaxed, her eyes felt heavy. Without conscious thought, she snuggled closer and let herself drift. Under her cheek, Nicholas's breathing slowed and they both slept.

They were roused by a soft knock on the door. For a long moment, Cassandra could not remember where she was. She blinked and looked up to find her eyelashes almost grazing Nicholas's unshaven chin. 'Cassie! What on earth..?' he began.

The knock was repeated and she scrambled off the

bed, scarlet with confusion, avoiding Nicholas's eyes as she pulled down her jerkin.

'*Entrez*!' he called when she was a safe distance from the bed, but his voice carried less than its usual authority and Cassandra guessed he was as shaken as she at the position they had woken up in.

The door opened to reveal a little party assembled outside: the apothecary's assistant with a package sealed with wax, a chambermaid with a tray full of food, a waiter equipped with cutlery and a cloth, and the *patron* to supervise all.

Cassandra was relieved at the diversion: a glance at the clock on the mantel showed her that she had slept in Nicholas's arms for over an hour and she had no notion of what she should say to him.

By the time she had laid a tray on Nicholas's knees, poured him a glass of wine and settled herself with chicken casserole, she had decided that the only thing to do was to play Cass the valet to the hilt. She must drive from his consciousness all awareness of Cassandra, the woman who had slept beside him in his embrace. She was honest enough to recognise that if he took her in his arms again, she would do nothing to stop whatever might follow—and she wanted him to hold her so much. . .

'You look much better,' she said briskly, whipping away the tray and bringing him warm water and cloth. 'I think you ought to go back to sleep again. I'll leave you in peace and go and find out about the seabathing.'

'Cassie?' He seemed bemused by the transformation from vulnerable femininity to brisk efficiency. 'Is anything wrong?'

'Wrong? Of course not.' She shook out the starched tray cloth with a snap, not meeting his eyes. All she wanted to do was throw herself back into his arms and tell him... What? That it was the only place she felt content?

To her intense relief, Nicholas was up and about when she tapped on his door the next morning.

'What about the salve?' she asked, gathering up discarded clothing to avoid looking at him.

'It's all right, I put it on myself. Smells disgusting, so it must be doing some good.'

Cassandra could feel herself blushing with relief. Her sleep had been troubled by half dreams, half fantasies of rubbing the salve into Nicholas's naked shoulder. She had woken angry with herself for such immodest thoughts. The thought of what Nicholas might assume if he realised how her thoughts dwelt on him was mortifying. Why, he might imagine her to have a *tendre* for him!

All it was, she told herself firmly, was the natural attraction of finding herself in the constant company of one of London's most eligible men, a man who had offered her sanctuary and a means of escape when her world had been turned upside down. Why, as soon as she reached Vienna, this attraction, the dreams she had of him, would fade as other companions filled her life.

'Should you be up?' she enquired, folding a shirt.

'Of course. I can't lie in bed on a beautiful day like this. It would take more than a blow from a ruffian's cudgel to keep me on my back. Now, here's some money: go and do some shopping, buy what you like—

some lace or some sweetmeats. I'll see you here for dinner, I'm going to try the good doctor's seabathing.'

'Shouldn't I come?' Cassandra asked thoughtlessly.

Nicholas caught her eye and pointed to the window. 'Lean out and to your left and you can just see the men's bathing beach. I assume you didn't go and look last night!'

'No.' Cassandra did as she was bid, then gasped with shock at the glimpse of bare flesh. 'Nicholas! They have no clothes on!'

'Then I suggest you stay well away from the shoreline, Cassie! In fact, take care where you wander if you go out.' The door banged shut, leaving Cassandra gaping after him.

Despite the money burning a hole in her pocket, Cassandra didn't feel like mingling with the crowds. She headed away from the centre, climbing through the narrow streets past the close-packed stone houses to the ramparts crowning the town. Below her lay a vista of the sea to one side and, in the distance, white capped mountains. In between the land was full of fruit trees, already heavy with oranges, lemons and pomegranates; the hot air hummed with the song of cicadas.

Even the simplest house among the groves was neat and white painted, hung about with bougainvillea, roses and climbing vines. Cassandra wandered down into an olive grove touching the ancient twisting trunks in wonderment; they seemed a thousand years old.

She found a shady patch under an olive and sat watching the spear shaped leaves trace patterns as they filtered the sunlight. Below her a goatherd was leaning on his staff and flirting with a dark-eyed girl who had brought him a dinner basket.

Cassandra leaned back against the gnarled trunk and closed her eyes. This was all she had ever wanted: to get away from home, to travel, to experience foreign ways and see strange sights. This place was idyllic, almost paradise, yet, like Eden, it had its serpent.

Every time she closed her eyes, she could feel the touch of Nicholas's body under her palms, feel his lips on hers, hear the warm strength of his voice caressing her. It was no use pretending to herself any longer: she was falling in love with him.

And he would never love her, however much it seemed on occasion he was physically attracted to her. The Earl of Lydford had no time for gauche girls fresh out of the schoolroom.

She could imagine his embarrassment, how kind he would be if he discovered her *tendre*. She could live without his love—somehow—but she couldn't bear his pity.

# CHAPTER EIGHT

'CASSANDRA! Wait a moment!'

She hesitated on the threshold of the bedchamber, her arms full of Nicholas's freshly pressed shirts, then reluctantly came back into the room.

'Yes?'

'I need to talk to you, sit down.' Nicholas gestured to the chair opposite him in front of the cold fireplace. 'I've scarcely seen you the last two days, you haven't even eaten your meals with me.'

Cassandra sat down awkwardly, still hugging the shirts to her chest. 'The doctor said you had to be quiet,' she said defensively. 'And you did say I could explore the town.'

'I have no complaint if you wish to go about enjoying yourself.' He hesitated, obviously at a loss to know how to deal with her in this uncommunicative mood. 'I was worried about you.'

Still she wouldn't look at him, risk meeting his troubled eyes. Instead she sat scuffing the parquet with the toe of her shoe.

'I know what it is that's troubling you,' he began, then broke off in surprise at the tide of scarlet confusion that swept up to the roots of her hair.

Cassandra felt sick with humiliation. How could he have guessed how she felt for him? Oh, the mortification of it! He was going to be kind about it, she could tell. Tolerant of this puppy love. . .he wouldn't take her seriously, or worse, he would pity her. . .

'I can see I was right,' he began. 'It pains me to embarrass you, but I think we should talk of it.'

'How did you guess?' Cassandra whispered, raising haunted eyes to meet his concerned look.

'It was natural you should be upset to find you had fallen asleep in my bed the other evening. After all, you are a gently brought up young girl: but we shouldn't reproach ourselves for what was entirely innocent.' He leant forward and patted her hand gently. 'We had both suffered a terrible shock, it was natural we should fall asleep like that. Try not to feel so conscious of it, Cassie, nothing happened, after all.'

Cassandra could only gape at him, she was so taken aback at his words. And she had very nearly blurted out her love for him!

Nicholas misinterpreted her shocked expression. 'Don't look at me like that, Cassie!' He stood up and ranged around the room while he searched for the right words for what he had to say. 'I admit there have been moments when my. . .instincts have led me to regard you in a way I now regret. . .'

'Like that evening in Paris?' Cassandra's voice was sharp with reaction.

'Yes, like Paris.' Nicholas turned to face her. 'But I promise that won't happen again, Cassandra.' He managed a laugh, although it sounded hollow in the high-ceilinged room. 'Do you realise how good you are for me? Why, I declare, by the time we arrive in Vienna, my mama will not recognise the dissolute rake she left behind, so responsible and sober will I have become.'

\* \* \*

He was as good as his word. Two weeks later as their carriage neared Venice, Cassandra reflected that she could hardly have had a more sober, correct, *boring* companion if her Godmama had appointed a strict chaperone for her.

Nicholas had dutifully pointed out the beauties of the Plain of Lombardy, encouraged her to read improving passages from the guidebooks he acquired along the way and ensured she went to bed early after a good dinner.

Even the excitements of passing from one independent kingdom or duchy to another were kept from her, for Nicholas insisted she stay in the carriage while he ruthlessly bribed officials and negotiated passports and health certificates at the endless customs posts.

By the time they reached Padua, Cassandra had decided she had been quite mistaken: far from being in love with the man, she actively disliked him.

With bad grace she clumped on board the *burchio* waiting to take them down the Brenta Canal from Padua to Venice and glowered out at the unlovely town crowding the banks.

'Stop sulking, Cassie,' Nicholas said sharply, then seemed to relent. In a softer tone, he added, 'I'm sorry, I should have realised: are you frightened to go on a boat again?'

'No.' She scowled down into the greenish depths of the still water. It was true, she wasn't afraid, she was quite simply bored. 'I'm bored: I'm tired of dirty inns and bumpy roads and greasy food—and no diversions *at all.*'

That was only part of it. Nicholas had withdrawn into the half avuncular, half patronising manner of their first meeting in London. If he had ever found her tempting or alluring, it was quite plain he no longer did. Sulking was not going to improve matters, but she was too hot, tired, dusty and cross to care.

'If you don't take that mulish look off your face, I'll tell the officials in Venice that you haven't got a bill of health and they'll shut you up in the Lazarrette for forty days with all the pestilential seamen!'

Cassandra glowered at him: he was only half-joking. 'Well, it would have to be more entertaining than the last fourteen days!'

Nicholas's eyes narrowed, and not against the slanting evening sun. 'You are asking to be put across my knee and have your britches paddled, my lad,' he began between clenched teeth.

'I would like to see you chance it!' Cassandra knew she was going too far, but she couldn't stop herself. She had tried being good and obedient and meek, and he treated her like a troublesome scrub of a boy. The knowledge that she must look like one only rubbed salt in her wounded vanity. Her hair was full of dust no brushing would remove, the fleas last night had been worse than usual and she had had no clean linen for three days.

'When we get to the *palazzo*...' Nicholas began, real displeasure in his voice.

'Oh, be quiet!' Cassandra was on the verge of tears and didn't care who knew it. Abroad was dangerous and squalid, travel was boring and uncomfortable and Nicholas was a beast. Or perhaps he was just a man and they were all like that.

She sniffed loudly and cast him a darkling look, half expecting him to carry out his threat and put her across his knee. She was saved from whatever retaliation Nicholas was contemplating by the arrival of another party of travellers with a pile of baggage.

Wordlessly he handed her a large pocket handkerchief and then ignored her: they embarked for the fairytale city of Venice in a mood of sullen antagonism.

The *burchio* was a long, flat-bottomed craft with an awning of canvas over metal hoops; the passengers were a mixed bag who would have entertained Cassandra under different circumstances. Opposite her a soberly dressed lawyer, with his equally sober young family, divided their disapproving glances equally between the two loud-voiced gallants perched precariously in the stern and a gaudily dressed and painted woman who winked at all the menfolk unwise enough to catch her eye. A party of peasants complete with malodorous goat added to the general discomfort.

By mid-afternoon on the second day, Nicholas, glancing sideways at Cassandra's set face, began to worry that she was not sulking but sickening. 'Cass,' he began in a low voice, then saw her face light up for the first time in many days.

'Oh, look!' She pointed out under the half-moon of the awning to where the banks of the canal opened out into a vast lagoon. Across the shimmering water the towers and palaces of Venice hung like a mirage. Cloud shadows chasing across the water and mud made the whole scene unreal and dreamlike. 'Nicholas, it's beautiful,' she whispered, hardly able to speak.

'It is rather fine,' he remarked casually, then grinned at her fierce expression, 'Oh, yes, you're right, it *is* wonderful—a dream city.'

Their passage across the lagoons of Chioggia and

Malamocco gave them different vistas every few minutes as the boatmen wove between mud banks and islets. At last they entered the Canale della Giudecca, a waterway as wide as the Thames at London and as crowded, with craft of all sizes, from sea-going galleys with banks of oars, to the narrow black gondolas Cassandra had read so much about.

Reading of Venice in the seclusion of her father's study bore no resemblance to the reality of the scene before her amazed eyes. The noise of bargemen shouting, the bustle of constant activity between the shore and the boats, the vivid colours under the brilliant sun and the exotic shapes and colours of the buildings were so overwhelming, Cassandra forgot her miseries and discomforts.

'Ouch! Cass! Let go of my arm.' She hadn't even realised she had hold of him. Hastily she let go and smoothed down the creased cloth of his sleeve with a penitent hand. 'Never mind that.' He was pointing ahead. 'There's St Mark's and the Campanile.'

Cassandra was trying to find the correct page in the guidebook without taking her eyes off the gorgeously exotic facade of the Doge's Palace, its delicate pink and white walls seeming to float on the water, its walls crowned with Arabic ornaments and spikes.

No sooner had the barge drawn up alongside the crowded pavement than Cassandra had scrambled ashore and was hopping from one foot to the other with impatience, while Nicholas retrieved their luggage. 'Come on,' she urged, 'we go up here to get to the Piazza. . .'

Nicholas had to seize her by the collar to restrain

her. 'Not now, Cass! Wait here and guard the luggage while I hire a gondola to take us to the *palazzo*.'

'A *palace*! We're staying in a palace?' All thoughts of exploration fled.

'If you hadn't been sulking for the last sennight, I would have told you. It's been hired by my friend Beckwith, but he's been summoned to Rome by his uncle at the Embassy, so we'll have the place to ourselves.'

Cassandra felt immense relief at the thought of such privacy and comfort. In a private lodging she would have only the servants to deceive, no sharp-eyed noblemen to avoid, no sharp-tongued harridans to gull.

Travelling in the gondola after the heavy barge was like riding a horse after being in a carriage. The gondolier, dextrously propelling the swift craft with strokes of his oar, dodged between the shoals of boats ferrying people of all classes about their business.

They made their way up the Grand Canal, under the Rialto Bridge, then turned sharply into a little side canal no more than twelve feet wide and flanked by twisting alleys and landing stages.

Their gondolier finally drew into the side of a minute square with marble steps leading down to the water. The paving was decorated with coloured inlays and in the centre a little fountain bubbled.

Close to, Cassandra saw how the fine frontages were stained with water marks and the stucco was peeling to expose the stonework. Greenish water lapped at the walls and Cassandra's nose wrinkled at the smell. Nicholas noticed her expression and laughed. 'The tide will not flush these little waterways as it does the main canals. Is the palace not as grand as you expected?'

'It's wonderful,' Cassandra protested. 'So old and mysterious.' She would have said more but for the appearance at the door of a black-coated major domo flanked by footmen. With a gesture, he dispatched them to unload the rowing boat loaded with luggage which had followed the gondola and advanced on Nicholas.

'My lord!' He bowed low. 'Welcome to the Palazzo Lucca. Signore Beckwith is devastated that he cannot be here to greet you, but all is prepared. Pray enter!'

Nicholas rolled his eyes at Cassandra and followed the self-important little figure as it swept up the steps to the main door. Cassandra would have followed, too, but she paused, her eye caught by a flash of colour at a window in the facade to her right.

A woman, dressed in a robe of emerald green taffeta, was leaning on the sill watching their arrival, idly brushing out the mass of coppery-gold curls which cascaded over one bare shoulder. Cassandra knew she was staring, but she had never seen such a gorgeous creature before. As she watched, a man's bare arm appeared, caressing the naked shoulder and the woman turned and disappeared into the shadowy room.

'I thought you said there was no one else staying here,' she hissed to Nicholas when she caught him up in the monumental entrance hall.

'There isn't.' He turned in surprise as she tugged at his sleeve.

'But I thought I saw someone in the window over there.' She pointed to the wing of the *palazzo*.

'That's another house,' he explained. 'Every building is crowded in against its neighbour, land is so scarce.' He turned away and mounted the staircase in the wake of the major domo.

Cassandra raised her eyebrows behind his back and mused to herself that she was certainly learning a great deal about the world. She could hazard a guess at the woman's profession, but somehow the broad daylight made her state of undress seem even more scandalous.

They were shown into a suite of rooms overlooking the canal at the front and the courtyard at the side. Nicholas's bedchamber faced directly across from the courtesan's balcony and Cassandra hurriedly closed the carved wooden shutters. 'The sunlight's bad for the draperies,' she explained, as Nicholas blinked in the sudden gloom.

'The perfect housewife,' he remarked drily, but made no move to re-open them. 'Baths and hot water for myself and for my valet,' he commanded the major domo, but the man was already ushering footmen in with hip baths and brass water jugs.

Cassandra retreated to her own room, which adjoined Nicholas's with a shared balcony between them. As she closed the shutters, she peeped across at the opposite window, but it, too, was shuttered.

The magnificence of her chamber stunned her with its cool, high ceiling adorned with cherubs and gods disporting on swirling clouds. The walls were lined with painted and gilded panelling interspersed with vast, cloudy mirrors. The bed was piled high with silk-covered pillows and hung with billowing draperies.

Cassandra caught a glimpse of herself in the glass and shuddered. Her hair was dark with dust and perspiration; her skin was dirty, too, but under the grime she suspected that she was not only tanned, but freckled also. She tore off the restricting jerkin with a sigh of relief and threw off the rest of the clothing. The wide boards were cool under the soles of her feet and she wandered naked across the room to peer more closely at her reflection.

Her shoulders and breasts were milk white in contrast to the golden tan of her face and hands. The poor food and the strains of the journey had honed her already slender body and the unaccustomed freedom of striding around in breeches had sculpted her leg muscles, chasing away all traces of girlish plumpness.

Suddenly self-conscious, Cassandra crossed to the door onto the landing and turned the key. The major domo would not be inclined to knock before entering the room of a mere valet. Doubtfully, she contemplated the tall double doors connecting her chamber with Nicholas's. There was no key in this escutcheon.

Need she worry? Nicholas had always been scrupulous in respecting her privacy, even when they were sharing a room. But yet, she felt uneasy. Perhaps it was the opulent femininity of the room, the air of decadence hanging over the whole city. She carried the painted and gilded chair from the dressing table and wedged it as best she could under the door handles.

The bath was deep and hot and when she had washed all over once, she unlocked the door, retreated behind a screen and rang for yet more water. Luxuriating in the scented warmth, she let herself drift, running through memories of the journey in her mind. It was remarkable how quickly being clean lifted her spirits and improved her temper. Why, she felt quite in charity with Nicholas again.

Unbidden, the memory came back of lying against his long body, safe in the shelter of his arms, and more disturbing, the recollection of that kiss in Paris, the response it had kindled in her...

Idly, she squeezed out the sponge and saw how wrinkled her fingertips had become. Time to get out before she resembled a prune! A pile of large linen towels were heaped on a chest and Cassandra draped one around herself under her armpits, tucking it in at the front. She found a smaller one and began to rub her wet hair, so much easier to dry now in its boyish crop.

Glancing up, she gazed at the ceiling once more, the painted scene suddenly making sense. Why, it was no innocent pastoral scene as she had thought: instead, gods and satyrs chased—and caught—naked nymphs through wooded glades And when they caught them... Her mouth dropped open at the explicitness of what was depicted there. Did men and women *truly* do that? And, if they did, was it as pleasurable as it was depicted here?

Fascinated, Cassandra walked slowly backwards, her head tipped right back as she followed the unfolding scene.

'Cassandra?' Nicholas's voice called, but she was scarcely aware of it. The next second there was a crash, a curse and Nicholas was lying on top of her, inexplicably entangled in a chair.

'What the devil!' he gasped. 'Why was that chair there? Are you hurt?'

Cassandra pushed the wet towel from her mouth

and the hair from her eyes. He had knocked the wind out of her as they had fallen together and for a moment she couldn't speak.

'Cassandra?' His green eyes, full of concern, were very close and her damp limbs were entwined with his.

'I'm all right,' she managed to say. 'You knocked the breath out of me. Why didn't you knock?'

'I did—but there was no reply. I was worried about you, thinking you might have fallen asleep in the bath and drowned yourself!'

It seemed to Cassandra that indeed he was concerned for her: he was pale, his breath uncertain and he held her to him strongly. He was stroking her bare shoulder lightly and his gaze was on her mouth. . .

'Nicholas. . .' she began hesitantly.

'Yes?' His voice was husky, his face so close his breath fanned her cheek.

'I wanted to ask you something, but I think you will be shocked.'

He brushed the wet hair away from her temples and smiled down at her. 'You can ask me anything, Cassandra.'

'Well. . .this ceiling.' She freed an arm and pointed upwards. 'I. . . I mean. . .does that sort of thing really go on between men and women? I thought I knew. . . you know. . .what happens. But nothing like *that*!' She pointed to a particularly rapacious and inventive satyr.

Nicholas seemed stunned, then he broke into helpless laughter, rolling over and releasing her as he did so. He sat up, hands on knees and regarded her as she gathered up the folds of towelling.

'Cassie, my mother would thoroughly approve of your influence on me!' He ignored her puzzled frown and got to his feet, ruefully rubbing a bruised knee. 'Hurry up and get dressed, dinner will be ready. And,' he paused in the doorway, 'what the blazes was that chair doing there?'

'I. . .er. . . I couldn't find the key.'

'For future reference, Cassie, that trick only works when the door opens towards you. Although, if you wish to cripple your would-be ravisher, this method is quite effective.'

'But Nicholas—what about the ceiling?'

'Ask my mother. It is a godmother's duty to explain such matters to a young girl. I am certainly unequal to the task!'

The servants had left clean linen set out on the chair and Cassie dressed swiftly. Nicholas's sudden eruption into her room had driven everything from her head, even the impropriety of finding herself scarcely clad in his arms. Now everything she had felt while she sat under the olive tree in Nice and thought of Nicholas came back to her. She felt again the touch of his caressing fingers on her bare skin and a shiver ran through her, bringing with it, inexplicably, a vision of the woman in the green robe. Nicholas might anger and irritate her, make fun of her, but she was still in love with him and she still yearned for his touch.

And it was so improper to feel like this, she scolded herself, as she tied her neckcloth. A well-bred young lady should admire and respect a man she believed she loved, but the warmth of affection was all that should animate her. Surely this desire to be in his arms, to taste his skin again with her lips, to feel his strong body against hers was shameful and sinful?

She was feeling somewhat shaken when she

knocked on the door of his chamber, but outwardly she was composed as Nicholas opened the door to her.

The marble-floored dining salon was even more ornate than the bedchambers. The long table had been laid with two places at one end and candles cast pale shadows on the polished wood. The shutters were still half-closed against the early evening light and the air was warm and heavy.

'Nicholas,' she whispered, as servants began to carry in dishes. 'Is it the Venetian custom for master and valet to dine together like this? And why has the major domo given me such a magnificent bed-chamber?'

He waited until the servants had withdrawn to their station against the wall before replying, and even then seemed strangely reluctant to look her in the eye.

'I...um, suspect that Antonio, the major domo, has penetrated your disguise.'

'Oh.' Cassandra was surprised at the man's perception, but even more puzzled by Nicholas's diffidence. He was fiddling with the long stem of his wine glass, uncharacteristically ill at ease. 'Then he knows I'm a ...girl? Doesn't he think that's odd?'

'I believe he has jumped to the obvious conclusion. Have some turbot.'

'The obvious conclusion?' Her brow furrowed in puzzlement, then the serving forks fell with a clang onto the silver serving platter. 'You mean he believes we're...that I'm your... But that's absurd! You must tell him, Nicholas—at once—that I'm no such thing!'

'And how do I explain you to him if you are not my mistress?' he asked drily, finally looking her in the eye. 'An Englishman with a mistress in Venice is so commonplace as to be beyond remark. . .'

'Dressed as a boy?' Cassandra interjected in amazement.

'Dressed as *anything*.' Nicholas sipped his wine thoughtfully. 'But a runaway, especially a well-bred female runaway, will be a cause for gossip and rumour. Remember where we are: this is Venice, the home of intrigue. There are many English residents and tourists in the city.'

'But what about my reputation?' she wailed, then realised how ridiculous she was being. She had abandoned that the moment she had donned breeches and escaped from her home. Too late now to quibble over the precise cause of her disgrace.

The same reasoning had obviously occurred to Nicholas. He said nothing, but gave her a hard stare and continued to eat his fish fastidiously.

Finally, after the servants had served a platter of quail, he remarked, 'And I'm not certain what the penalty for abduction is in Venice: breaking on the wheel, probably.'

Put like that, masquerading as his mistress seemed the lesser of two evils. They finished the meal in virtual silence, both lost in their own thoughts. When at last Nicholas pushed back his chair and stood up, Cassandra demanded, 'What are we going to do now? It's a lovely evening, can we go to St Mark's Square?'

'You are going to bed and I am going out,' he announced firmly.

'Where to?'

'Really, Cassandra, you are beginning to sound like a nagging wife. You need a good night's sleep.' He sounded out of patience with her. 'I need a game of cards, some good company and perhaps some dancing.'

'Dancing? Ha!' she ejaculated scornfully. 'Painted women, more like!'

'What a good idea,' he said smoothly. 'Why didn't I think of that? Some grown up company for a change.'

He was gone before she could think of a suitable retort. Back in her room, she kicked angrily at the flounced drapes around the bed, then threw herself down among the cushions. She complained bitterly out loud about being left behind, suppressing the small voice inside that told her she was being very unfair and that after two weeks of playing the duenna, he deserved some entertainment.

Her eyes focused on the painted ceiling again. Did gods and goddesses really do that sort of thing? Did anybody do that sort of thing? Was that what the courtesan across the square spent her time doing? Did Nicholas like. . .? Her hectic thoughts were interrupted by a soft tap at the door.

'Come in!' She sat up hurriedly.

'Good evening, *ma donna*. Do you have any commands for the household?' The major domo seemed quite unperturbed to be addressing a young lady in valet's clothing as if she were mistress of the household.

'Yes.' Cassandra sat up straight, suddenly full of enthusiasm. 'I want some new clothes—some nice clothes.'

'Men's attire or women's?' Antonio enquired calmly.

'Men's, I suppose,' she said gloomily. 'But some fine fabrics, please, Antonio. Silk and linen. . .'

'It will be as you wish, by noon tomorrow. Does *ma donna* require wine and biscuits now?'

'No, thank you. I don't want anything to eat, I want to go out.'

'But, of course, I will bring you a cloak, and perhaps a mask would be wise.'

So, it seemed that guarding her formed no part of Antonio's duties! Cassandra threw open both shutters and windows and walked out onto the balcony. Below her the previously quiet canal was now busy with gondolas, each bearing a cargo of richly attired men and women out for the night's entertainment.

'Shall I order you a gondola?' Antonio had reappeared with a cloak of dull black silk, a half-mask dangling by its strings from his fingers.

'No, I will walk—I have a map in this guide-book.'

As she swung the cloak around her shoulders, Antonio pointed from the window. 'Follow this *calle* here and eventually it will take you to St Mark's Square.' He looked at the map she had opened out. 'You will be quite safe if you avoid these *sestieri*—in those areas, the low types inhabit. Stay with the crowds and carry only a few coins secreted in your clothing.'

Cassandra put on the *domino* and mask, which covered the upper part of her face. Behind it she felt anonymous and irresponsible: no longer Miss Cassandra Weston of Ware, but a citizen of Venice going out to enjoy the evening like any other.

The narrow *calle* flanking the canal twisted and turned, sometimes widening into the forecourts of *palazzi*, sometimes into little squares where several paths met. Several times she had to flatten herself against the brickwork or stand in a doorway to let a group pass noisily on their way to the Opera or to one of the many public balls whose music floated across the water.

Finally, more by good luck than by careful attention to her map, Cassandra reached St Mark's. The entire square was a confusion of people and a babble of languages. Cassandra spied an elderly gentleman rising from a table outside a coffee house and darted quickly to seize the seat.

'*Uno caffè*,' she ordered, pleased with her few words of Italian gleaned from her father's books.

Languages she could only guess at filled her ears: as she sipped her coffee, she began to differentiate one from the other.

A group of naval officers, swarthy and dark-haired were Greek—she recognised a few words close to the classical form. Two tall men, deep in a business discussion must be Jews by their long ringlets and fur-trimmed hats, and to her delight a group of turbanned and berobed Turks strolled across looking arrogantly about them.

There was a multitude of fortune-tellers, minstrels and conjurors—even a man with a dancing bear—all soliciting for money in loud voices and with extravagant gestures. Cassandra pushed the pocket containing her money more securely into her inner garments: pickpockets were the same the world over from Ware market to Venice, and as she watched she saw an embroidered handkerchief vanish into a voluminous sleeve without the owner being any the wiser.

As the night became darker, the flares and lamps lighting the piazza shone more brilliantly. Cassandra ordered more coffee, then nearly dropped the cup in shock as a courtesan swept into sight, a small black page at her heels. There was no mistaking her trade: her hair fell loose, dyed an improbable array of colours, plumes topping a silk turban. Heavy earrings brushed her shoulders, but the most shocking thing was her gown, cut so low in the bodice that her breasts were totally exposed, the nipples painted gold.

Respectable people passed her with scarcely a glance, then Cassandra saw others like her, drawn like moths from the darkness into the illumination of the piazza.

With a start, she found someone bending over her, whispering in her ear. Her Italian could not cope with the rapid words, but the tone of invitation was unmistakable in any language. His garlic-laden breath was hot on her face and lacking words she pushed him roughly away. He fell against another table and wandered off laughing, quite unperturbed by her rejection. In alarm, Cassandra doubted her disguise: even behind the concealing mask had he realised she was a woman?

At that moment a youth strolled past with an older man, the latter openly fondling his shoulder. With a deep sense of shock, she realised that being a boy was no protection here. The next rake who wandered in her direction was met with a scowl so ferocious, he veered away at once, and Cassandra relaxed slightly.

The crowd fell back and a group of men wearing strange silken togas strolled across the square. Her reading of the guidebook told her that these were some of the senators who governed *La Serenissima* under the Doge.

The clock in the tower struck twelve and Cassandra knew she should retrace her steps and be safely home before Nicholas returned. But her feet were aching now and the darkened lanes beyond the Square were subtly threatening. She would hire a gondola and glide home in style.

She was hesitating on the water-steps, unsure of how to hail one of the many gondoliers when a man and a woman passed her so close the silk of the woman's gown swished against her cloak. Cassandra stepped back, a word of apology on her lips, then froze as she realised the man was Nicholas.

He handed his companion down into the narrow craft and waited until she was settled on the heaped cushions before joining her. Cassandra had ample time to take in the woman's appearance. She was undoubtedly a courtesan but young and beautiful, her fresh skin subtly tinted, her hair loose on her shoulders, confined only by a twist of silk scarf. Her gown was as outrageous as the others and Cassandra realised she must be wearing tight stays to thrust forward her small, naked breasts. Her nipples had been rouged a deep ruby and a single red stone quivered on a gold chain between them.

As soon as Nicholas joined her she insinuated herself into his arms, long ruby-red fingernails scoring lightly down his thigh. Cassandra watched, mesmerised, until he bent to nuzzle the courtesan's white throat, then turned with a small, choking sob and stumbled away into the shadows.

She was hardly conscious of the journey back, but

some instinct must have guided her footsteps for, at last, she found herself standing under the awning of a wine seller's booth at the head of the *calle* leading to their *palazzo*.

'*Signore*?' The man was proffering a horn beaker brimming with red wine. Unheeding, Cassie took it and drained it in three gulps, unprotesting as he filled it again. This time she sipped it slowly, her mind full of dark thoughts of how she would like to deposit that courtesan in the deepest, dirtiest canal in Venice— then pitch Nicholas in after her!

So much for his fine talk of reform and responsible behaviour! Why, he had just abandoned her so eager had he been to go out—she groped for a word and came up with the ugliest she could remember—*whoring*! Images of the painted ceiling flashed through her mind, but it was Nicholas's face on the satyr's body, the painted breasts of the courtesan on the nymphs.

She tossed the wine seller a few coins and stumbled miserably towards home. The door was open and a watchman blinked sleepily at her from his chair in the hallway as she dragged herself up the stairs. She pushed open the door into Nicholas's chamber, driven by an obscure need to touch something belonging to him.

On the bed lay his brocade dressing gown and she picked it up, smelling the ambergris he used. 'Oh, Nicholas,' she whispered miserably. What did she expect? He was a man of the world, used to indulging himself. He had not asked to chaperone a sulky, inexperienced girl across Europe. . .

'*Where the hell have you been*!' Nicholas roared at

her, standing framed in the connecting doorway to her room.

Cassandra was so startled she jumped, dropping the robe to clutch the bedpost in shock. Her heart thudded in her throat. 'I. . . I thought you were out.'

'That is all too obvious!' He strode into the room and took her roughly by the shoulders. 'Where have you been sneaking off to? I managed to get Antonio to admit he'd allowed you to go out—but that's all I'd expect from a Venetian rogue of a servant!'

'Let go, you're hurting me!' Cassandra tried to free her arm from his iron grasp, but he only pulled her closer, a look of revulsion crossing his face as he smelled the wine heavy on her breath.

'You're drunk!' he snarled. 'Who have you been drinking with?'

'No one,' she protested, twisting in his grasp.

'Don't lie to me,' his eyes glittered: Cassandra had never seen him so angry. 'And what else have you been doing tonight?'

The implication was clear, even through the fog of wine that was muddling her thoughts. 'You think I've been. . .that I would. . . How dare you!'

'What am I to think, with you wandering the streets like a. . .'

'Like a courtesan?' she finished for him. 'I know what a courtesan looks like.' Her chin came up and she looked him straight in the eye. 'She has long, unbound hair twisted with a vermilion silk scarf; she paints her face, but lightly if she is young. Her breasts are bare and her gown is sequinned and she paints her nails to match other parts of her body which should remain concealed. She laughs a lot and when she does, the ruby round her neck...'

Nicholas jerked her against his chest, glaring down into her defiant face. 'You little witch! You followed me!'

'I did not—but if you flaunt your whore across St Mark's Square you should not wonder if you are seen!' She wrenched herself free and ran acrosss to the balcony, desperate for air. She felt sick with the heat and wine and the sordid argument.

He followed her swiftly and before she knew what he intended, he had upended her across his knee and brought his hand down hard across the seat of her breeches. With the strength of pure outrage, Cassandra twisted free, bringing up her hand to fetch him a vicious crack across the cheekbone.

The force of the blow snapped his head back and brought tears to her eyes. Nicholas stood frozen, one hand to his face, then turned on his heel and slammed the window shut with a clap that bounced off the walls of the little square.

Cassandra clutched the balcony rail as a wave of sickness swept her from head to foot. When she recovered herself, she raised her head slowly and found herself meeting the quizzical gaze of the woman in the room opposite. She was lit by a branch of candles at one side and Cassandra saw a fleeting smile touch her lips. The woman raised her hand in a small salute, then slowly turned and vanished into the room.

# CHAPTER NINE

A THIN dawn light penetrated the little courtyard, touching warm fingers on the damp stonework behind Cassandra's head. She blinked and shook her head, wincing at the pain behind her eyes. So this was what an excess of wine felt like. . .

Cassandra struggled to her feet, grimacing at the stiffness in her cold limbs. She must have dozed off eventually, after a miserable hour or two. Instantly the memory of the terrible quarrel with Nicholas hit her: the shocking words she had used to him, the humiliation of being put over his knee like a recalcitrant schoolboy—and worst of all, to have raised her hand to him. How could she, how *could* she, have struck Nicholas!

No gently brought up young lady would use violence under any circumstances, save to protect her virtue or her life. And however hypocritical he was being, she sensed Nicholas's anger was prompted by his wish to protect her.

Cassandra heard the creak of oars and leant out over the rail to watch a vegetable boat emerge from the miasma of mist rising from the canal. The city was beginning to wake and go about its business: a servant from the *palazzo* ran down the steps and hailed the vendor. After much haggling and jesting, conducted in whispers, the servant returned, his wicker basket laden with saladings and fruit.

451

Silence fell again, broken only by the slap of the boat's wake against the greenish stonework of the landing steps. Cassandra turned unhappily towards her chamber window, then paused as a man's voice, low and sensual, broke the peace in the courtyard.

Standing back in the concealing shadows of the architrave, Cassandra watched as a cloaked figure stopped on his way from the house opposite to the steps. He was looking up to the window where the Titian-haired woman in the green wrapper leaned out, calling softly down to him.

As the church clocks began striking five, the gentleman swept an elaborate bow, gesturing to a sleek black gondola which had drawn up in readiness. Intrigued by the pantomime of parting, Cassandra forgot her woes, watching the lovers. The woman beckoned, and as the man approached again, tossed down a round object. The gallant caught it one-handed, laughing up at his lady as he broke open the fruit.

A pomegranate. Cassandra had never tasted one, but she recognised the faceted red flesh and smooth exterior of the fruit. Somehow, it added to the fairytale mood of the scene with the mist rising off the canal and the sleeping city slowly rousing all around them.

The magic held Cassandra until the carved stern of the gondola slipped from sight, then with a sigh she turned to slip into her room. As she moved, she found herself caught in the steady gaze of the courtesan. The woman smiled as she had before, then beckoned with one long-nailed finger.

'Me?' Cassandra mouthed foolishly, looking round, but there was no one else in sight. The woman nodded and gestured again. Cassandra hesitated, intrigued by the summons, yet unwilling to run the gauntlet of the servants, who would all be about their business by now.

Suddenly emboldened, she swung a leg over the balustrade, gripped the heavily carved stonework, and in a moment had reached the safety of the courtyard, with only a scraped knuckle and a burst seam to show for her foolhardiness.

The door opened silently as she approached and closed just as quickly when she entered. A maid-servant holding a candle ushered her upstairs in silence, then abandoned her at a chamber door with a bobbed curtsey.

Cassandra scratched tentatively on the carved panels and a soft voice called, 'Come in, little one.' It was English, exotic and musically accented, but English none the less.

The chamber was heavy with brocade hangings, dominated by a huge canopied bed and lit by many candles, each multiplied over and over in the silvery mirrors which hung on every wall. The air was redolent of attar of roses and a hint of cinnabar, and Cassandra's feet sank into the deep pile of a Turkey carpet as she hesitated inside the door.

'Come in, little sister,' the woman said gently, sinking gracefully onto a sofa with a gesture for Cassandra to come and sit by her.

Startled, Cassandra blurted out, 'You know I'm not a boy?' Mesmerised, she sat as she was bid, next to the courtesan, unashamedly staring.

'But, of course. You may call me Lucia. And you are?'

'Cassandra.'

'Cassandra.' Lucia rolled the name round her tongue as if tasting it and nodded in approval. 'You will take your *colazione* with me.' It was an assumption, not a request and Cassandra abandoned all thought of her English Society manners. This was no afternoon tea party at the Vicarage.

The maid was already laying the breakfast table with hot rolls, fruit and chocolate. The mixture of warm fragrances was so appetising that Cassandra could hardly contain her hunger.

To her surprise, her hostess showed as hearty an appetite as she, and for several minutes neither spoke. At last, Cassandra sat back with a contented sigh, warm, full and clear headed.

Lucia shifted slightly to regard her guest. 'So! Now you feel like a human being again. It is always a mistake not to eat, my child. How old are you?'

'Just eighteen,' Cassandra confessed. Being lectured on the importance of eating properly was not what she had envisaged when she had entered this house.

'Ah.' Cassandra shifted uneasily under the courtesan's appraising gaze. 'Just eighteen, just arrived in Venice and you have had a *disputa*, a, what do you call it. . .?'

'Quarrel?'

'*Si*. A quarrel, with your lover.'

'He is not my lover!' Cassandra protested hotly. 'He is the son of my godmother and I am travelling under his protection.'

'Dressed as his valet? And it is part of the masquerade that he beats you? You English!' She cast her eyes heavenwards.

'He doesn't beat me! Well, that was the only time and I had been very provoking. . .' Her voice trailed away as the resentments of last night resurfaced. 'But he deserved what I said about his whore.' Then she realised in whose company she found herself and went scarlet with embarrassment.

'There is no need to avoid the word in my company, although courtesan is more accurate, both for myself and for the lady who the Earl of Lydford was escorting.'

'You know who he is?' Cassandra looked at Lucia with new respect, noting for the first time the shrewd intelligence in her eyes.

'It is my business to know.' She shrugged, a lazily sensuous movement, even in the presence of another woman. 'My sisters and I are well-informed. We are professionals, after all.'

'Your sisters?' Cassandra was confused.

'Venice is a city of women. Men rule it—and we rule the men. Men work against each other for their own power. Our strength lies in our combined power: even the wives of the men who come to us are our sisters. We trust each other. It is accepted.'

The idea of women selling themselves, yet still retaining their independence and their dignity, astonished Cassandra, yet, looking at Lucia, the only comparison she could draw was with her godmother, an independent great lady.

'But why did you ask me here?' she blurted out.

'Because you need my help.' Lucia snuggled back into the cushions and tucked her long, bare feet up. 'You say he is not your lover, this Earl of Lydford. . .'

'Nicholas.'

'*Niccolo.*' Lucia tried out the name. 'But you do love him?' Her plucked eyebrows rose interrogatively.

'Yes,' Cassandra whispered. Having said it out loud, she knew it was true. This was no hero-worship, no *tendre* of a young woman for an experienced man. It was certainly not gratitude. She wanted him in every possible way, and forever. 'But it's impossible.'

'Perhaps. Do you want his heart or his body?'

'Both,' Cassandra confessed. 'I want him to love me and marry me.'

'Ah,' Lucia looked thoughtful. 'This is more difficult. He wants you, that is self-evident.'

'It is?' Cassandra's eyebrows shot up. 'There have been occasions. . .' She blushed. 'We have been thrown together by circumstance and he is a man of the world. . .'

'So he starts to make love to you and then he feels guilty and stops. Oh, the English and their sense of guilt!' Lucia frowned at her. 'Silly little virgin, do you think he would be so angry with you if he did not want you?'

'Perhaps not. But I am a great nuisance to him, I have ruined his Tour, perhaps even his reputation, if we are found out.'

'You keep making excuses for him, yet you are angry and hurt,' Lucia remarked shrewdly. 'Why?'

Cassandra got to her feet and began to fidget around the room. The question was disturbing, forcing her to confront her real feelings. 'I'm jealous,' she said eventually. 'I want him to see *me*, not an irritating child he's been saddled with or a distracting body he must try and ignore. If he thinks of me at all, it's either as the little girl I was when he last met me, or as a package he must deliver intact to his mother, because his duty demands it.'

'So you want him to recognise you are a woman. A woman who can say "yes" or "no" to him. . .'

'I suppose so.' Cassandra bit her lip, forcing herself to be honest. 'But I want him! I know it's wrong, but I want him to love me. . .to make love to me. He has always had everything he wants. . .'

'And now there is something you desire?' Lucia laughed. 'And you need to learn how to use a woman's power to make him see you and only you.'

'But how?' Cassandra sank down on the sofa, suddenly aghast at what she was saying.

'You go home and go to bed, little one. Sleep. Eat your dinner in your room. Let your Niccolo believe you are not well, and when he goes out to the Turkish Ambassador's ball this evening, come back here to me.'

'How do you know where he is going this evening?' Cassandra asked, although nothing about this amazing woman would surprise her now.

'All Society goes to the Ambassador's masque. And so do the courtesans. And for one evening you will be one of us, for your Niccolo only. And then you may love him or not, as you decide. Now go—and take care no one sees you leave.'

Remaining in her room was simpler than Cassandra had feared. The encounter with Lucia seemed some sort of mad dream. How could she even contemplate anything so outrageous as to seduce Nicholas? She sent a message by Antonio that she was feeling unwell and would take her meals alone and received by return a curt note from Nicholas.

It is not to be wondered at that you feel unwell after your behaviour last night, he wrote. For myself I have no wish to set eyes on you until you have had time to reflect on your conduct and make amends. The servants have been informed that you will remain in your room until they receive my orders to the contrary.

It was signed curtly, Lydford.

Cassandra read this missive through twice, unable to believe her eyes. So, he wanted her to confess her faults, while he offered no word of contrition for his conduct in putting her over his knee like a child! All doubts about Lucia's wanton plan vanished: she would show him she was a woman!

Cassandra screwed up the paper and hurled it at the wall. It missed, sailed out of the open casement and into the canal where it sank gently beneath the greenish waters.

It was nine in the evening when she watched Nicholas emerge from the front door and make his way down the steps to his waiting boat. He was obviously dining out before the ball. Despite her anger with him, Cassandra felt her heartbeat quicken at the sight of him, magnificent in full evening attire. A heavy opera cloak lined with scarlet silk was thrown back over an evening suit of corbeau blue cloth. His neckcloth was immaculate in its complex folds, a single fob glinted against the dull sheen of soft silver threads in his waistcoat.

The major domo hovered, in his hand Nicholas's mask dangled by its strings. Against the Venetian servants, Nicholas's rangy height was even more apparent.

More than anything else, Cassandra wanted to be

with him, on his arm. To be helped into the boat by him with the solicitude he had shown his companion of the night before... But after tonight, perhaps...

With the Earl's departure, the public rooms of the *palazzo* rapidly emptied of servants, making it easy for Cassandra to slip out and across the courtyard. The door opened before she even knocked and once again she was conducted silently into Lucia's presence.

The courtesan was already dressed in evening finery, although without paint. A large bathtub, lined with white linen stood in one corner, a manservant filling it with flagons of warm water. Lucia sent him away and paused to consider a collection of glass phials.

'Sandalwood, I think,' she mused. 'Heady, but not clinging. You will be able to wash it off later, and that may be important, for you may yet change your mind, little sister! Now, take off your clothes, and into the bath with you.'

An hour later Cassandra was being laced into a corset which produced a figure which she had no idea she possessed. She looked down, startled, at a surprising amount of cleavage, but oiled, warm and faintly lightheaded from a glass of sweet wine, she felt no inclination to protest.

The maid helped her into a gown the colour of crushed raspberries and began to fasten it. 'But what about my hair?' The boyish crop, even though it was beginning to grow into soft curls, was ludicrously at odds with the soft folds and low cut bodice of the silk gown with its gauze overdress.

'But a wig, of course!' Lucia sat Cassandra to the dressing table, pulled back her hair with a ribbon and arranged a blonde mass of ringlets on her head. 'There!'

Cassandra gazed into the glass and a creature who was not Cassandra gazed back. Only her dark, direct eyes, shadowed by uncertainty, were familiar.

'Now, to paint your face. We will do it together.'

Cassie sat obedient as a child as Lucia went to work with her brushes and myriad little pots. She brushed kohl around her eyes until they were huge and dark, then thickened the lashes with a black powder. She brushed Cassandra's skin with rice powder, clucking over the fading sun-freckles. And then she painted her mouth with a red gloss the exact colour of the gown.

The sensuous touch of the brush following the curve of her lip made Cassandra pout. 'Perfect,' Lucia murmured. 'Now, remember, do not bite your lips and be careful when you drink.'

Lucia, satisfied at last, led her to a full-length glass. 'There!'

Cassandra gasped. A total stranger stood there, sophisticated, beautiful, intriguing. Yet despite the paint and the tumbling blonde curls, there was no hint of coarseness or wantoness. The neckline teased, but did not reveal, the lines of the gown flattered rather than flaunted.

'Now: slippers, a fan, a mask and you are ready. Not even your father would recognise you!'

Cassandra smiled ironically. What her father would say if he could see his only child now beggared description. 'Lucia, this is beautiful,' she stroked the gown, 'but I'm still not certain I can go through with this.'

Lucia steadied the kohl brush as she shaded her own eyes. 'We are going to the Turkish Ambassador's ball and you will dazzle your Niccolo. What comes after is in your hands.'

'I can't do it, Lucia!' When he found out, his anger would be unimaginable! Cassandra looked round wildly for the maid to unlace her gown.

'Silly child!' Lucia swept over and pressed her into a chair. 'I do not recognise you and I created you myself. You do not have to decide anything. . .yet. Follow your instincts. Here, drink this slowly and try on your mask.'

Cassandra slipped the heady wine then tied the strings of her mask. It covered her eyebrows, cheekbones and subtly altered the shape of her nose. Lucia was right; she could not recognise herself. And besides, she thought philosophically, there would be such a throng that perhaps Nicholas would never see her.

'But my voice? What if he should speak to me?'

'Oh, he will speak to you, that is certain.' Lucia smiled her slow, mysterious smile. 'You speak French? Good, then lower your voice, use a French accent and say only a little, with many French words. That will intrigue even more.'

Cassandra shrugged, still sceptical that Nicholas would even notice her among the throng of beautiful women but the heavy scents of the room, Lucia's confidence, the sweet potency of the wine, all came together, and suddenly she was careless of what the night might bring.

'Wait,' said Lucia suddenly, as the maid settled their cloaks around their shoulders. 'One jewel is all you need.' She clicked her fingers and the maid brought a casket, waiting while her mistress stirred the contents with one long finger. 'Ah, yes, the very thing. This is a little gift for you, my child.'

She held up a flexible gold necklace, fashioned in the shape of a serpent. In its delicate jaws it held a rose quartz egg on a gold chain. Lucia fastened it around Cassandra's neck where it hung, the jewel trembling on the swell of her breasts.

'Thank you,' Cassandra breathed, touching the ornament as she followed her companion from the room.

The journey was short, but their gondola had to wait, jostling for position with the dozens of others at the watergate to the Ambassador's imposing *palazzo*. Despite Lucia's assurances, Cassandra was amazed to see groups of courtesans arriving, rubbing shoulders quite openly with nobility of all nationalities. English voices carried on the night air, mingling with the growl of Russian, German gutterals and mellifluous Mediterranean accents.

The entrance court was as bright as noon with turbanned servants lining the walls, each with a flambeau to light the guests threading slowly up the marble stairs to where the Ambassador greeted the company.

Lucia ignored the main throng and insinuated herself through a side door, up a flight of stairs and emerged, Cassandra in her wake, virtually at the Ambassador's elbow.

He recognised her at once, bowing low over her hand with an intimate murmur of greeting. Cassandra realised all at once why Lucia had been so confident of her plan: the Turk was obviously a favoured client. The Ambassador's dark eyes gleamed appreciatively as he bowed to Cassandra and she found herself smiling back at the hawkish, moustachioed face.

He snapped his fingers and an elegant young man, dressed like the Ambassador in national dress, hurried to his side. Cassandra heard Nicholas's title murmured and the aide nodded and gestured politely for the ladies to precede him into the crowded salon.

It took some minutes to locate the Earl. He was standing listening to a middle-aged man whose evening dress was bedecked with orders and medal ribbons. Cassandra recognised Nicholas's rising boredom and stifled a giggle before sudden panic gripped her.

'I must be *mad*,' she whispered, pulling back against Lucia's light grip on her elbow.

'Do not worry, little one,' Lucia whispered in return. 'Go and fascinate your Niccolo: he will never know it is you—unless you choose to tell him! I will not be far away.'

The aide waited politely until the senior diplomat noticed him and broke off an exposition of the Russian situation.

'His Excellency, my master, has commanded me to introduce these ladies to your eminences. . .' The aide allowed his words to tail off discreetly as he melted backwards into the crowd.

The diplomat's obvious irritation at the interruption vanished abruptly as his gaze fell on Lucia. She looked magnificent in her favourite emerald green, her white bosom scarcely contained in a jewelled net bodice, her Titian hair tumbled in artful disarray.

'Hurrumph!' He stared for a moment through his quizzing glass, then it fell from his fingers as he surged forward to bend over Lucia's proferred hand.

'*Madame*! Your most obedient!' He had no eyes for anyone, let alone Cassandra in her more modest attire and the Russian situation had obviously been instantly forgotten.

'Sir Humphrey,' Lucia purred. 'I have met you at last! I have heard so much about you: tell me, is it true that only your subtle intervention saved the talks at. . .' She had already borne him off towards a curtained alcove and Cassandra never did discover Sir Humphrey's great contribution to European statesmanship.

She was looking after them with bemused admiration for Lucia's tactics, when Nicholas's voice in her ear remarked, 'Very prettily done—it is always a pleasure to see an expert at work.'

Cassandra started, realising with horror that she was all alone with Nicholas. He was looking at her with blatant admiration in his eyes, a warm smile playing round his lips. For the first time, she was experiencing all his charm, uncomplicated by their difficult, ambiguous relationship.

This was the man whom prudent London mamas warned their susceptible daughters against: not because he was a seducer of innocents, but because he would steal their hearts without for a moment taking them seriously. Many lures had been cast before the eligible Earl of Lydford, but none had hooked him.

Cassandra took a long, unsteady breath and the rose quartz jewel quivered between her breasts, drawing Nicholas's eyes to the soft swell.

'Monsieur?' Cassandra hastily remembered the rôle she was playing and held out her hand to him. Nicholas took it and turned it so that his warm lips met the inside of her wrist in a lingering caress. Her heart leapt so she thought he must feel it in her pulse, but he drew her hand through his arm and began to stroll towards the terrace.

She forced herself to relax and move sinuously against him as he bowed and nodded to various acquaintances as they progressed through the crowd. A black page paused before them with a tray of wine glasses and Nicholas took two, offering one to Cassandra.

She took a cautious sip and realised it was champagne. The bubbles tickled her nose, but the taste was unthreatening and she drank more deeply.

Nicholas was intent on reaching the less crowded terrace and skilfully evaded all attempts to detain him with conversation. Outside it was much quieter, although couples and small groups strolled and chatted along the wide, balustraded space overhanging the Grand Canal. He found her a bench, its cold marble smothered in heaped cushions, and leaned against the wall at her side.

Cassandra could hear the slap of tiny waves as gondolas disturbed the water below, then quite forgot her surroundings as Nicholas spoke to her.

'Will you tell me your name, *ma belle*?' he asked. 'I am Nicholas...'

'Earl of Lydford,' she finished for him, rolling her r's.

'You know? I am flattered.' He dropped onto the bench beside her, stretching out his long legs, quite at ease.

'I make it my business to know,' she said, remembering Lucia's words. 'You may call me Antoinette.'

There was a small silence as they sipped their wine,

their eyes meeting above the rim of the glasses. A vague uneasiness stirred somewhere in Nicholas's mind, an evocation rather than a memory. A frown creased his brow and his companion noticed it at once.

'Something is wrong, Nicholas?' Her voice was husky, low; the dark gaze behind the mask questioning.

He tried to express what he was feeling. 'I thought you reminded me of someone. . .but no, it is a passing fancy. I cannot even recall who it might be.'

'I, Antoinette, have never met you, Nicholas.' Cassandra let her hand rest lightly on his sleeve. 'I would have remembered *you*.' Panic gripped her: there must be something about the way she moved, the way she held herself, that could not be disguised, and she was still not ready to commit herself to this masquerade.

Very well, then, she would use Lucia's arts to divert his thoughts. He had known her in many rôles in their weeks together: tomboy, nurse, demure young lady— but never seductress. This was frightening, but excitement was racing in her veins.

She let her hand drift down his arm until her fingertips brushed his knuckles, then flexed her fingers, grazing the smooth flesh with her nails. She felt his instant reaction, and suddenly she was aware of her own power over him. This was what Lucia had meant when she spoke of the power her sisters wielded over men.

His free hand came over hers, trapping it. Again, he turned it, but this time, instead of carrying it to his lips, he rubbed one fingertip over the sensitive palm, the swell at the base of her thumb. A wave of tingling heat passed over Cassandra's body, absurdly out of porportion to the lightness of his touch.

She met his eyes, unaware that her painted lips were parted invitingly, that the snake on her breast rose and fell with her tremulous breathing. Nicholas was intrigued by this courtesan who responded like an innocent girl. It had to be artifice, she was obviously a professional, but the fantasy of inexperience was powerfully erotic.

'You are refreshingly different, *ma belle*,' he murmured against her hair. Cassandra felt herself swaying instinctively against him, driven by her love, her need, for him. His warm lips grazed tantalisingly down the curve of her jaw to the soft hollow of her throat.

She had to touch him. She was beyond thinking how a courtesan should behave, beyond teasing and flirting. Cassandra put up her hand, caressing the nape of his neck and instantly her memory supplied the recollection of his bare back under her palms in Nice.

Spreading her fingers in his hair, her thumb rubbing the strong tendon of his neck, Cassandra was hardly aware of the balustrade behind her shoulders, the yielding cushions beneath her.

Nicholas could feel the pulse jumping beneath his lips, the warm, supple body yielding in his arms and knew he had to stop this now, whilst he still could.

Footsteps rang on the marble and with a mixture of relief and regret, Nicholas sat up, running one hand through his hair and tugging at his cravat.

Cassandra, her heart in her throat, came back to reality with a start. The terrace was now virtually empty, but Lucia was approaching them with Sir Humphrey in her wake. All that had happened, Cassandra told herself, was that he had taken her in his arms, yet she felt stripped naked before everyone.

Behind the mask, Lucia's eyes were quizzical. 'We came to tell you that supper is being served and dancing will follow. Will you not join us? It would give us great pleasure, would it not, Sir Humphrey?'

The diplomat was totally under her spell. 'Of course. . .of course. Damned good supper, by the look of it.'

Nicholas responded readily, taking Cassandra by her hand to escort her once more into the salon.

'One moment,' Lucia put out her hand. 'Look, my dear, your lace is torn. Gentlemen, allow us a moment while I pin it up. Please, go ahead, we will meet you inside.'

As soon as they were alone, she pushed Cassandra back on the seat and stood before her. 'What are you about, little one! You must tease, tantalise, flirt with him. Inflame him, yes—but not yield to him! At least,' she added thoughtfully, 'not yet.'

'I couldn't help it,' Cassandra wailed. 'I love him, I do want him. . . How could I realise it would be like this? What am I to do, Lucia? I have no experience. . .'

'You have two choices: flee now while you can; or take him back to my *palazzo* and there give yourself to him.' She shrugged her shoulders. 'You want him to know you as a woman. But I wonder if you understand truly what that means. . . I cannot dictate to you whether you follow your heart or your head, you must decide. Come now, they will be becoming impatient.'

Nicholas had heaped a plate of dainties from the buffet for her and Cassandra ate with an appetite, telling herself it would mop up the wine, clear her head.

To her own amazement, she kept up her part in the lighthearted badinage which passed between their party, remembering to keep her voice low and accented. Yet, all the while, she was aware of Nicholas at her side, the touch of his sleeve against her bare arm, the caress of his fingers as he handed her peeled sections of fruit. .

His regard was warm on her; she sensed his impatience to touch her was reined in only by the demands of good manners. Even as she chatted and flirted, her mind whirled on a treadwheel of indecision. What should she do?

The safest thing would be to disappear now. But meeting his eyes as he smiled down at her, she knew she wanted more than anything to be in his arms, for him to kiss her again as he had in Paris, for her to show him her love.

She wanted to be his wife, to be with him always. By giving herself to him tonight, he might come to love her as she loved him. But it was a terrible risk. He might reject her and an illicit love affair would be a betrayal of everything she felt for him, of her upbringing and sense of what was right.

'You are very thoughtful, *ma belle*,' he said lightly, tipping up her chin.

The touch sent the blood burning through her veins and she smiled at him, moving closer, wanting to be held. 'Let us dance, Nicholas. Listen—the waltz.'

She had never performed this daring, intimate dance with a man as her partner. The Vicar's four daughters, with whom she was friendly, had wheedled their dancing master into teaching them the waltz and Cassandra had learned it from them.

But dancing and giggling with Verity Lamb while sister Charity played the spinnet was quite a different matter than standing close to Nicholas, his hand resting lightly at her waist, the other clasping hers. She gathered up her skirt gracefully in her free hand and tried to concentrate on the steps of the dance, not the touch of his palm against hers.

At home to have danced more than twice with the same man would have been shockingly forward, but in Venice, such conventions held no sway. Dance after dance passed, and Nicholas took no other partner, had eyes for no-one else.

As the clock struck three, he pulled her closer than the dance demanded and whispered huskily, 'I can bear it no longer, I must be alone with you. Come to my *palazzo*.'

'No.' Cassandra was startled into bluntness, then remembered Lucia's whispered instructions earlier in the evening. 'I never go to a gentleman's house. . .'

The look of disappointment on his face gave her a feeling of power, of strength, she had never before experienced. This assured, experienced man was in her thrall, hanging on her decision. She wanted him—and he was hers.

'You would leave me?' His eyes were dark and glittering, although he kept his voice light.

'No, my lord. I did not say that. Come, instead, to my *palazzo*. Come home with me.'

# CHAPTER TEN

THE blaze of torchlight on the Grand Canal seemed almost to ignite the water, so bright were the reflections on its dark surface. To Cassandra's relief, she had to give no orders to the boatman: Lucia's gondolier followed his mistress's instructions to return speedily to her *palazzo*, but by a route his passengers would not recognise. He steered south, not north, turning off to avoid the main waterways.

Cassandra was lost within seconds, but their route was of small importance beside the effect of being alone with Nicholas in the intimacy of the gondola. Now, in the velvety darkness, with the discreet silhouette of the gondolier above them, she felt panic, and a sudden doubt. Despite her overwhelming love for this man, was she doing the right thing? Would he understand that she was driven to break all the codes by which she had been raised only because she loved him?

Through the thin silk of her gown, Nicholas's thigh was warm and hard against hers. He put his arm around her shoulders, drawing her close against his chest, his lips moving in her hair.

Cassandra stiffened, then made herself relax as one hand slipped under the lace at her shoulder and he began to caress her skin. Any maidenly shrinking would betray her instantly—but how was she to restrain his mounting passion until they reached the *palazzo*?

'Nicholas,' she whispered. 'Do you intend to stay long in Venice?'

'Umm?' He was disinclined for conversation, his response merely a mumble as he nibbled delicately at her ear.

'How long do you stay in Venice?' she persisted, unable to prevent her treacherous body moving more closely into his embrace.

Reluctantly he freed his mouth. 'That depends on what there is to stay for.' He bent his head and trailed kisses across the swell of her breasts, his lips fretting at the confining lace.

Cassandra swallowed hard, filled with a strange mixture of panic and desire. 'Oh, there is much to stay for Nicholas,' she managed to gasp out.

'As I am discovering,' he responded huskily. An unwelcome thought seemed to strike him, and he straightened up, still holding her close. 'I am not entirely my own master in this matter,' he said with heavy irony, his eyes on the dark water.

In the light from a lighted courtyard, Cassandra saw his face harden with remembered anger. 'Why not, my lord?'

'I am encumbered,' he said shortly. 'Encumbered by a troublesome child for whom I have responsibility. I must take her to my mother in Vienna. If I do not strangle her first,' he added bitterly.

Some devil prompted Cassandra to probe further. 'You jest, of course, Nicholas! You have your little daughter with you? Do you not like *les enfants*?'

'She is no relative of mine, thank the Lord! And she

is not truly a child, although she is as unruly and ungovernable as one.'

There was real feeling in his voice and Cassandra realised she was still unforgiven, both for her words and for the blow. 'Surely, if you are giving her your protection, she should be meek and grateful in return? Why,' she fought to keep the anger from her own voice, 'I am sure you must have been like an indulgent elder brother to her, *mon cher.*'

It was too dark to read his face, but Nicholas shifted uncomfortably on the cushions beside her and Cassandra felt a small stab of triumph. So, she had pricked his conscience had she?

But not so much, it seemed, to make him forget his grievances! 'The wretched chit had the impertinence to lecture me—*me*—on my behaviour and morals. When I consider that I saved her from the most dissolute, the most diseased rake in London...' Nicholas had forgotten the woman beside him in his bitterness.

Cassandra was frightened by his vehemence, then remembered Lucia's suggestion that his anger was fuelled by his desire for her. It seemed difficult to believe, looking at his set profile and stiff back. His hands no longer caressed her, but rested tensely on his thighs.

To her relief, the gondola bumped up against a landing stage and the gondolier jumped ashore to secure it. Cassandra realised they had reached the back of Lucia's *palazzo* and set herself to distract Nicholas in case he should recognise their surroundings.

'You are very quiet, my lord,' she purred, as he

handed her out of the gently rocking boat. She kept her fingers linked with his as she drew him towards the door already standing ajar. 'Forget your troublesome ward—you are with me *ce soir*. . .' She let the phrase trail off provocatively, and it had the desired effect.

Nicholas gave himself an almost imperceptible shake and smiled down at her as they passed into the darkened hallway. 'No man could forget he was with you, *ma belle*,' he murmured.

His ardour led him to catch her in his arms as they mounted the stairs, spanning her slender waist with his hands and turning her towards him as he stood on the step below.

This position brought them mouth to mouth. He kissed the corner of her lips, then ran the tip of his tongue around their curve, the strength of his hands pulling her tight against his hard body.

'Nicholas,' she protested gently, against his lips. 'Upstairs. . .we will be more comfortable upstairs in my chamber.'

'Then let us make haste, or I swear I will have you here where we stand!'

Cassandra felt the scalding blush sweep from her toes to the roots of her hair. She had never dreamt that the depth of a man's passion and urgent desire could lead to lovemaking on the stairs! She was just reflecting that it was fortunate that the darkness masked her dismay, when he stopped and swept her up in his arms.

'This door?' He hardly waited for her nod of acquiescence before shouldering it open.

Cassandra expected him to set her on her feet as

soon as he had kicked the door closed behind them. Instead he tightened his embrace, crushing her breasts against the soft linen of his shirt front as he bent his head to claim her lips.

This was what she had been waiting for, yearning for, since she had realised her love for him. She tightened her arms around his neck, unconscious that she was inciting, compelling with her fingertips.

His mouth was hot, sweet and demanding, invading hers with an intimacy that shocked yet thrilled. Cassandra felt certain that if she did not draw breath in the next few seconds she would surely faint, yet rather than withdraw, he deepened the pressure with erotic expertise, teasing her tongue tip with his own. Her senses spinning, she forgot all her doubts, all her fears, in the tide of her love and longing.

She was aware of him moving towards the bed, although he never freed her lips. He stooped, laying her gently amongst the yielding cushions, and sat beside her.

Cassandra lay fighting to control her tumultuous breathing, watching him through the slits in her mask. A small branch of candles afforded enough light to gild the sheen of perspiration on his taut face, and his eyes glittered greener with desire.

Nicholas watched her for a long moment, deliberately it seemed to her, prolonging the tension in the room. When at last he did move, it was to reach out with one long finger and free the jewel that trembled beneath the lace, caught in the cleft of her breasts.

The merest brush of his fingertip left her quivering with desire; he took the rose quartz between thumb and forefinger rubbing its cool smoothness gently, insistently, his eyes never leaving her face. While he fondled the jewel, his little finger stroked the satin sheen of fine skin, gently at first, then with increasing pressure.

A tiny gasp of shock and surrender escaped Cassandra's parted lips: if he kissed her now, she would be lost, would give herself to him utterly without heed to anything... But it would be worth it, worth anything, if there was a chance he could come to love her, too.

'Damn these masks,' he growled, fumbling in her hair for the strings. 'Intriguing they may be, but they're damnably inconvenient...'

In a moment they would be face to face, not Nicholas and Antoinette, but Nicholas and Cassandra. Suddenly she knew she, Cassandra, could never do the things that 'Antoinette' would do. To make love to him in disguise would be pointless, empty, wanton. To make love to him as herself, she realised, was impossible.

It would betray her own honour and, in doing so, tarnish everything she felt for Nicholas. The realisation doused her passion more effectively than a douche of cold water. With a sinuous twist, she slipped from beneath his hand and off the bed.

'When I return, Nicholas,' she whispered huskily, 'then you may take everything...starting with the mask. But I must fetch wine and fruit for later and make certain we are not disturbed.'

'I'll wait then, *ma belle*—but impatiently.' He swung his long legs up onto the bed and leaned back against the cushions. The smile he sent her was melting with desire as she escaped, pulling the heavy door closed behind her.

She leaned her shoulders against the panels, achingly aware of Nicholas on the other side, fighting to control the urge to run back into his arms, whatever her conscience told her.

Lucia's sharp hiss brought her to her senses. 'Why have you left him?' She was standing at the foot of the stairs as Cassandra ran down. 'What is wrong? Why are you not in your Niccolo's arms?' Her sharp eyes missed nothing in the flushed face turned to hers.

'I cannot do it, it would be wrong! Oh, but Lucia, I love him so.' Her voice broke on a sob.

'Make haste then!' Lucia drew her into the chamber where her maid was waiting. The two of them began unlacing the gown, loosing the wig and freeing Cassandra's own hair.

'Wear this,' Lucia bundled her into a plain wrapper and began scrubbing at her face with a thick cream. 'Here, take the rest of the pot and this linen to apply it, check carefully in a good light that there is no paint left around your eyes and hairline. Now go!'

Propelled into the chilly dawn light of the courtyard, Cassandra stopped, looking round wildly. How was she to get into her own *palazzo*? Then she saw the door standing ajar: Lucia's influence no doubt. She ran up the steps, then paused, one hand on the heavy iron ring, and looked back. Behind the lighted window, Nicholas's shadow crossed and recrossed the room: he was becoming impatient.

Fear lent wings to her feet as she sped towards her chamber. Candles burned on the dressing table in front of the mirror and she stooped to scrutinise her face as she scrubbed the linen over the last remnants of kohl under her lashes. Dragging of the wrapper, she bundled it into the clothes press and kicked the slippers out of sight.

The water in the pitcher on the washstand was cold but Cassandra splashed it over her neck and breast to wash away the lingering scent of sandalwood, replacing it with a splash of her usual innocuous rosewater.

The jewel! It still hung around her neck. Her fingers were fumbling with the unfamiliar clasp when the front door crashed shut with the force of a thunderclap echoing around the marble halls.

Cassandra whisked into bed, dragging the covers up to her chin, then lay back on the pillows steadying her breathing. Nicholas wouldn't come to her room—why should he? It was only her guilty conscience that prompted the fear.

As she closed her eyes, she heard him enter his chamber, shutting the door with slightly less vehemence this time, no doubt to avoid waking her. She could chart his progress around the room by his footsteps and the sound of drawers being opened and closed, his shoes being kicked across the floor with a muttered imprecation: then there was silence.

Cassandra had just started to relax when the connecting door eased open. She caught her breath, then forced herself to breathe deeply and slowly. Between slitted lids, she watched Nicholas in his brocade robe standing on the threshold regarding her. She turned slightly on the pillows to watch him more easily and muttered as though restless in her sleep.

How long he stood there she had no idea, although it seemed long minutes rather than seconds, but he made no move to come further into the room or to speak to her.

In the end, it was her own guilty conscience that made her feign waking. 'Nicholas?' She injected as much sleepy puzzlement as she could into her voice. 'What's wrong? What time is it?'

He hesitated, one hand on the edge of the door. 'Nothing, nothing's the matter. Don't worry. I'm sorry I woke you.' But he did not go back through the open door. Instead he moved slowly to sit on the end of her bed, his eyes steady on her face.

After a moment, he said, 'You look tired, Cassie.'

'I am. I haven't slept much.' She looked at him, seeing how the excitements and disappointments of the night had left him drained. 'Are you all right? You look ill.'

'I will survive.' He smiled wryly. 'Like you, I have had no sleep.'

He fell silent again, and once more it was Cassandra who spoke. 'Why are you here, Nicholas?'

'I felt the need to see you, but I didn't intend to disturb you. Cassie, I'm sorry. . . I felt, I feel. . . I should never have shouted at you, never have struck you. I had neglected you, no wonder you felt rebellious. . .'

'Nicholas, there is no need for this.' If he felt guilty, Cassandra felt a thousand times worse. His anger had turned to remorse, but she could feel no satisfaction at his apology. She put out a tentative hand and he took it gently.

'Coming to Venice was a mistake, I should never have brought you here. It was selfish of me.' He was patting her hand in a way totally removed from the caresses of an hour ago. 'Sleep now, we will make more plans tomorrow.'

When he had gone, she let out her breath in a huge sigh of relief. She did not deserve to have escaped the night's wild masquerade without discovery, she knew that. But she knew also that her heart would never escape the pain of unrequited love. Her fingers touched the jewelled snake and she sat up and unclasped it. The clasp unlatched easily now there was no need for haste.

The gold pooled into a supple coil in her palm and she stirred the jewel with her finger, evoking the touch of Nicholas's finger on her skin. No, she had not escaped unscathed: she was no longer the innocent girl who had set out on this mad masquerade six weeks before. Love hurt.

It was two heavy-eyed and silent people who sat down to break their fast at ten o'clock that morning. The servants, used to the effects of Venetian entertainments on visiting foreign guests, moved with unobtrusive silence around the table, then melted away discreetly.

Nicholas regarded Cassandra over the rim of his cup. She looked drawn and tired and he cursed himself for having woken her in the early hours. But the overwhelming need to look at her had drawn him to her door.

After letting himself be so thoroughly duped by the artful mock innocence of the young courtesan, he had had to reassure himself what true innocence really was. Cassandra must be about the same age as Antoinette, he supposed, although it was hard to believe as she sat there in prim black suiting, her face scrubbed and her hair tied back in a queue. What a contrast with that silken creature last night. And what a contrast with the scene he interrupted when he had gone looking for Antoinette! The ageing diplomat, flushed and dishevelled, ridiculous in his passion... Nicholas shuddered fastidiously.

Cassandra glanced up from the roll she was crumbling and caught his thoughtful regard.

'Don't look at me like that, Cassie! I'm not angry with you—I told you I was sorry I was so harsh with you.' Colour flooded her cheeks, and seeing it he spoke again, more gently. 'I was only angry because I was frightened for you. You don't know how dangerous this place can be; you are too innocent to even guess at the viciousness beneath the surface glamour.'

'No, of course, I'm not afraid of you, Nicholas,' Cassandra said briskly, pushing back her chair and getting up. 'You said we were leaving, shall I go and direct that our bags are packed?' He was becoming too kind for comfort!

'I have already told Antonio to prepare for our departure.' He, too, stood. 'Now I am going out to arrange for our travel papers. Do you wish to come with me? It will be a long and tedious business, I fear.'

'No, thank you. I would rather pack my own things myself.' If Nicholas was to be gone all morning, it would give her the chance to slip across to Lucia's house and return the wrapper and slippers. And satisfy her curiosity as to what had transformed Nicholas from lover to penitent.

When he had gone, Cassandra went back to her chamber, folded the slippers and jar of salve into a neat parcel inside the wrapper and tucked the whole under her arm. She was just descending the stairs when she heard Nicholas talking to the major domo in the hall below.

'Tell me, who is the occupant of the *palazzo* opposite?'

'La Puttana.'

'The whore?' Nicholas translated.

'A very great and powerful lady,' Antonio said drily. 'And a dangerous one. She is said to have the. . .ear, shall we say, of our most powerful senators. Few dare to cross her, for she has influence with many of the diplomats and ambassadors, and acts herself as their agent.'

'I see,' Nicholas said slowly. 'Perhaps I have an enemy I am unaware of. . .' He caught himself thinking aloud and added more briskly, 'I am not certain when I shall return, Antonio, but make sure all is ready for an early departure tomorrow.'

'As you command, milord.' Antonio bowed the Earl through the doors and vanished into the salon, leaving the way clear for Cassandra to flit down the stairs.

Once more the door into Lucia's *palazzo* opened as if by magic. Cassandra wondered if the little maidservant was in truth a mute as she gestured her towards the stairs.

The courtesan was in bed, sitting up sipping a cup of chocolate. She looked tired, and for the first time since Cassandra had met her, she realised that Lucia was not in the first flush of youth.

Her skin, now bare of maquillage, was smooth but there were fine lines at the corners of her eyes. Her hair had been captured into a long plait over one shoulder and the severity of the style emphasised the intelligence and experience in her face.

Cassandra could well believe that she was in the presence of a powerful and influential woman and wondered again at Lucia's background and parentage.

'Well, little one? How is your Niccolo this morning?'

Cassandra grimaced. 'Subdued. Very out of character: I'm not used to him like this. Why, he apologised for being so angry with me.'

Lucia smiled, and it was not a pleasant expression. 'And that does not make you happy that he is no longer cross?'

'No, it doesn't! I am sorry to seem ungrateful, Lucia, but I should never have done it, never agreed to such a deception.'

'It will do you no harm to realise early what hypocrites men are,' Lucia remarked coldly. 'And your Niccolo is no exception.'

'But what happened last night when I had left?' Cassandra perched on the end of the bed. 'I expected him to be angry, but he seemed chastened.'

'A man like that is not used to rejection.' She laughed shortly. 'And he came across Sir Humphrey and myself: trust me when I tell you that Sir Humphrey was nothing if not ridiculous! Your Niccolo has the intelligence to see that what is exciting and romantic when you are young and dashing and firm-fleshed, is ludicrous and sordid when one is flabby and ageing.'

Cassandra was taken aback by the vehemence and contempt in Lucia's voice. She experienced a flash of pity for Sir Humphrey—and to her surprise—for Lucia, too.

So, that explained Nicholas's revulsion. Suddenly she wanted to be in the fresh air, away from the cloying scents and veiled intrigue.

'I came to return these.' She laid her bundle on the bottom of the bed. 'And to say *adieu*, we leave early tomorrow.'

'Goodbye, little sister.' The courtesan's hard face softened. 'Do not despair: if you want him enough, you will get your Niccolo. Keep on loving him and one day he will realise he loves you, too.'

Cassandra shook her head sadly. 'No, I do not think he will ever love me. Perhaps you are right and he wants me, but that is not enough. Goodbye, Lucia—and thank you for trying to help.' She crossed and hugged the older woman, surprised at the sentiment in her eyes.

'Write and tell me what befalls!' Lucia called after her as Cassandra descended the stairs.

Cassandra spent the rest of the day alone in her chamber, trying to convince herself she had made the right decision.

Nicholas returned late in the afternoon, a fat portfolio of visas and passes to show for his pains. His encounters with bureaucracy had not, as Cassandra expected, fatigued and irritated him. Instead he seemed stimulated, once more the self-assured Earl of Lydford.

'It amazes me that we do not require permits to breathe in this city,' he exclaimed, tossing down the papers for her to peruse.

'How very impressive!' Cassandra ran a finger over one embossed and self-important document in Italian. 'What is this?'

'A certificate stating that neither of us has the pox,' Nicholas supplied wryly. 'That cost me more than any others—I had to bribe the doctor not to examine you.'

'Examine me?' Cassie cringed inwardly at the thought of such an indelicate procedure—to say nothing of the scandal. 'Thank goodness everyone in this city has their price! And this?' She held up a scroll.

'Our permission to leave the Venetian Empire. It is rather easier to get in than to get out. At least, once having secured your person they demand a high price for your freedom.'

Antonio brought in wine and salted almonds. 'The packing is complete, my lord. Do you dine at home?'

'Yes, we do,' Nicholas rejoined, with feeling. 'And an early night!'

'Now this looks like a *proper* passport!' Cassandra exclaimed, examining a leather-bound document the size of a small book.

'Indeed, it is. That is our entry into the Austrian Empire: once we enter Trieste, it will be the only document we need until we reach Vienna. And that,' he added with feeling, 'cannot come soon enough for me.'

Cassandra bit her lip. 'I *am* sorry, Nicholas. I know I have ruined your Tour. You haven't seen Rome or Florence or any of the great buildings and treasures you must have planned on visiting.'

'Never mind, brat: it wasn't your fault.' Nicholas smiled at her as he poured himself some wine. 'I cannot deny I shall be more relieved than I have ever been in my life when I hand you safe over to my mother's care, but mad as it sounds, I have enjoyed this journey.'

'You have? Why, you've been embarrassed in front of your friends, near drowned in the Rhône, attacked by bandits, bitten by every flea in North Italy and last night. . .' Hastily Cassandra shut her mouth, almost betrayed into indiscretion.

'Last night?' Nicholas's eyebrows shot up. 'What about last night?'

'Well, you obviously didn't have a very nice time,' she said feebly.

'No, I didn't have a very nice time,' he agreed with a grimace. 'But that was my own stupidity.' There was a pause before he continued. 'I have enjoyed your company, brat.' He raised his glass to toast her. 'And you have been a good influence on me. No doubt my mother will say it was time I assumed responsibility for something other than my own pleasures.'

'I am sure Godmama will say it is high time you were married,' Cassandra riposted tartly.

'No doubt.' He poured her a small glass of wine and pushed it across the table. 'Within hours of my arrival, she will have a bevy of eligible young women ready for my approval. The only consolation is that she has better taste than my Aunt Augusta.'

Emboldened by the wine Cassandra asked, 'Do you not want to get married?'

'I know I must marry. There's the title and the estates to consider. But I want more than an alliance, more than a social arrangement.' He twisted the stem of the glass between finger and thumb. Cassandra held her breath and sat still: it was almost as though he were thinking aloud to himself. 'To me, marriage should be more than that. I want a wife with character and a lively mind, not some little mouse who acquiesces because I am her husband.'

'Surely there are young ladies in the Marriage Mart who would fit the bill?'

'I have yet to encounter one!' He pitched his voice into a mocking falsetto. 'Yes, my lord, anything you say, my lord. Of course, the moon is made of green cheese, Lord Lydford, if you say so.'

Cassandra laughed at him. 'Surely they are not all such silly ninnies.'

'Of course they are not—until their mamas school them in the ways of husband catching. No, what I really need is a wife like you.'

She went very still. There was a ringing in her ears as her pulse raced and she realised her fingers were cramped on the arms of her chair. 'Me?' she croaked.

'Not *you*, of course, but there must be one of them with a sense of fun! Someone with your resourcefulness and spirit. But I expect yours will disappear when you climb into petticoats again, more's the pity.'

Clocks struck seven throughout the house and Nicholas drained his wine. 'We must dress for dinner: I will tell you then my plans for the journey.'

Cassandra glared at his retreating back, fighting down the urge to throw something at him. Not *her*, of course! Miss Cassandra Weston was *quite* unsuitable!

Why, she had a sense of fun, and resourcefulness and spirit, so he said. There were even moments when he found her attractive, however hard he tried to forget it. But was he so obtuse that he could not put these ingredients together and recognise that she would be the ideal partner for him? Or was it that

Miss Cassandra Weston was not good enough for the arrogant Earl of Lydford and therefore beyond consideration?

'Oh. . .!' She kicked the tableleg, wishing it were Nicholas's well-muscled calf. Just let him wait until they reached Vienna—she'd show him she was the same person in petticoats or in breeches!

# CHAPTER ELEVEN

'I CANNOT believe it is but two months since I left Ware,' Cassandra marvelled out loud as their carriage threaded its way along a highway lined with heavily imposing palaces and town houses, the Imperial splendour a world away from the sedate buildings and maltings of her home town.

'It seems like six,' Nicholas replied repressively. He regarded her sombrely from the opposite corner of the carriage, 'You are going to have to behave yourself here, brat: this isn't Venice!'

'What do you mean?' Cassandra asked, her eyes on a magnificent team of horses pulling a carriage, its door emblazoned with a coat of arms, every panel glinting in the sunlight.

'For one thing, the city is full of diplomats and their wives from every corner of Europe. If you make a scandal, there will be nowhere to retreat to and no corner where your business will not be known. As I said, this is not Venice: here, Society is regulated and regimented. If it is discovered that you had spent just one night in my company, no allowance will be made for the predicament you found yourself in. One slip of the tongue and you will be ruined.'

Cassandra contemplated him thoughtfully from under her lashes, her excitement quite gone. If she was ruined, what would the scandal do to her Godmama and Nicholas? His words chilled her: for the first time in many weeks, she was afraid. Both she and Nicholas had concentrated on attaining the goal of reaching Vienna and his mother, without thought of how their unexpected appearance could be presented to Society.

And for the first time doubts bubbled up in Cassandra about Godmama's attitude to her flight from Lord Offley and her home. What if Godmama agreed with Papa? If she thought Cassandra wilful and disobedient in not going through with the marriage? And what if she blamed Cassandra for compromising Nicholas and blighting his chances of a good alliance? The thought of him marrying anyone else but herself was agony, but she knew it must happen.

It was a very subdued and nervous Miss Weston who finally climbed down from the carriage in the courtyard of the English Ambassador's residence, a voluminous cloak concealing her valet's clothes, the collar turned up around her face.

Seven weeks in Nicholas's company had made her sensitive to every nuance of his voice and, through her own distress, she recognised the tension underlying his apparent composure as he dispatched the major domo to announce his arrival to the Dowager Countess.

'Stand over there,' Nicholas hissed to Cassandra, gesturing to a more shadowy corner of the sunlit room while he paced restlessly over the Turkey carpet.

Minutes later the servant reappeared and bade them follow him to Lady Lydford's suite.

'Are the Ambassador and my uncle, Sir Marcus Camberley, at home?' Nicholas enquired, engaging the man's attention as Cassandra followed quietly in their wake. 'It is several weeks since I read a newspaper, but I imagine they are very much occupied with the Treaty.'

'There are still many negotiations in progress, my lord. Although the Congress has long ended, there is much business to attend to. However, we expect both His Excellency and Sir Marcus to return for dinner.'

The major domo flung open the double doors into the Countess's salon and announced, 'The Earl of Lydford, milady.'

As the doors closed behind them and Nicholas strode forward, Cassandra shrank back against the gilded panels, wishing she could melt into them and vanish.

The Dowager Countess was seated on a bergere armchair, a white Persian cat on her lap and a most becoming lace cap on her dark curls. From the drift of paper at her feet and the gilded chocolate cup at her side, it was evident her Ladyship had been engaged in perusing her morning's correspondence when the news of her son's unexpected arrival had been brought to her.

'Nicholas! Darling!' She extended both hands in greeting, the heavy lace on her morning gown falling back to reveal smooth white arms. The movement sent the cat jumping to the floor, its plumy tail waving in irritation.

'Mama!' Nicholas stooped to kiss her on both cheeks, then stepped back to regard her. 'You look even more ravishing than the last time I saw you, how do you manage it?'

'I do, don't I,' she riposted with a twinkle in her dark eyes, so like her son's. 'I was stifling in London with those boring matrons with their boring little daughters. No conversation, no intrigue. . .and the fashions!' She shrugged delicately, 'What could I do? Your uncle needed me—at least, so I told him.'

She regarded her tall son shrewdly, and Cassandra saw the sharp intelligence behind the coquettish pose. 'Sit down, Nicholas, and tell me why I have the unexpected pleasure of your company. I am, of course, delighted to see you, but why are you not in Florence admiring the frescoes, as my reckoning tells me you should be?'

There was a silence while Nicholas took his time settling in a chair. He crossed one long, booted leg over the other and brushed an invisible speck of dust from the knee of his breeches.

'It's a long story, Mama. . .'

Cassandra held her breath, catching her lower lip between her teeth with the tension of the moment. Unnoticed, the white cat stalked over to where she stood and showed its displeasure at being neglected by sinking its claws into her stockinged ankle.

Cassandra let out a shriek of pain and clutched her leg. Lady Lydford's sharp gaze moved rapidly from her son's face to the slight figure by the door, apparently noticing it for the first time.

'You! Boy! Come here and stop provoking my cat.' The summons was sharp. Lady Lydford had obviously sensed her son's reticence and was becoming suspicious.

Cassandra obeyed, limping over until she stood directly in front of her godmother. She waited, eyes cast down, fingers twisting in the cord of her cloak.

'Take off that cloak,' Lady Lydford ordered quietly.

Swallowing hard, Cassandra let it drop and stood revealed in breeches, waistcoat and shirtsleeves.

'Lydford,' the Dowager began frostily, after one comprehensive look at the shivering figure, 'what leads you to believe that bringing your *fille de joie* into the Ambassador's Residence—into my rooms—is acceptable behaviour?' Her small figure seemed to grow by degrees as indignation filled her. 'In what way did I fail in your upbringing that you believed I would be complaisant? Or did you merely assume my eyesight was failing?'

'Mama, this is not a *fille de joie*,' he said firmly.

'Godmama,' Cassandra interjected, falling on her knees beside the outraged Lady Lydford, her cheeks burning with mortification. 'He hasn't. . .I mean. . .I'm not. . .' Her voice faltered, she was so overcome with nerves and emotion.

'Cassandra?' Lady Lydford uttered in a voice of rising incredulity. 'Can it really be you? Here? Dressed like this?' There was real anger in her eyes as she turned to confront her son. 'Lydford, what is the meaning of this. . .outrage!'

'Godmama, don't blame Nicholas. It is not his fault.' Cassandra pleaded.

'Hold your tongue, Cassandra,' Nicholas commanded brusquely. 'Mother, this is not how it looks. Can we all sit down and I will explain everything: it is a long story.'

There was a long, considering pause, before his mother replied evenly, 'Very well.' Thankfully, Cassandra sank into a bergere armchair next to Nicholas. Beside her, she heard him draw a deep breath, but his voice was steady when he began the tale of their adventure.

'Seven weeks ago Cassandra came to the London house seeking you. It was a foolish thing to do, but when I tell you that her father was coercing her to marry Lord Offley, you will see what desperate straits she was in.'

'Offley!' The Dowager shuddered. 'He must be mad: that man is no suitable bridegroom for a gently reared young girl.'

'Exactly. Cassandra was desperate and lacking all female friends, she had no one to turn to but yourself.'

'I disguised myself as a boy and took the stage to London. It never once occurred to me you might not be at home,' Cassandra burst out, lifting her hot face to her godmother's cool scrutiny.

'My poor child.' Lady Lydford reached out and gently touched the soft cheek. 'What a terrible position to find yourself in.' Her tender tone became barbed. 'And, of course, my intelligent and resourceful son could find no better way to settle the crisis than to drag you across Europe dressed like that?'

'It seemed like a good idea at the time,' Nicholas said firmly. 'At first I was going to leave her with the housekeeper: then Aunt Augusta turned up and my valet broke his leg.'

'Oh, stop rambling Lydford! What has my sister to do with your valet breaking his leg?' She broke off and regarded him through narrowed eyes. 'Did you say *seven weeks* ago? Am I to understand that for all that time you have had this child in your company, unchaperoned and dressed like this?'

'It seems like seven years, I have to confess, Mama!'

He flashed a teasing smile at Cassandra as she glared indignantly at him. 'But when we got to Paris. . .'

'Paris! Why were you in Paris?'

'I thought you were still there. I was going to leave Cassandra with you and continue my Grand Tour. . .'

'As if nothing had happened, I suppose,' his mother finished drily. 'There are moments when you remind me so much of your dear father. *If* you had troubled to read my last two letters to you, you would have been aware of your Uncle Marcus's posting to Vienna, and my intention to accompany him. But in any case, it does not take over a month to travel from Paris to Vienna.' Her dark brows rose interrogatively.

'We went via Lyons, Nice and Venice,' Nicholas admitted.

'And then there was the accident on the Rhône and the footpads on the coast road,' Cassandra added helpfully.

A delicate shudder passed through the Dowager's frame. 'I think we will save the detail for later. Nicholas—go away. I am quite out of patience with you. And remember: you have no valet and you have not seen my god-daughter for ten years. I don't want to see you until dinner. Cassandra, stay with me.'

After the door had closed behind Nicholas, Cassandra turned imploringly to Lady Lydford, 'Please don't blame Nicholas, Godmama, he had little choice.'

'Nonsense,' the Dowager responded robustly. 'I can think of at least two perfectly sensible courses of action.' Then she smiled. 'So like his dear father, so impetuous.' She drew Cassandra down to sit beside her. 'I suppose he took off without a thought to the practicalities of the situation. You have been travelling as his valet, I apprehend: that would necessitate a degree of intimacy I assume?'

Cassandra blushed fiery red remembering the kiss in Paris, sleeping in his arms in Nice, the heat of his passion in Venice. 'We had to share a bedchamber on occasion—but Nicholas was always, I mean, he never . . .there was always a screen around my bed.'

'And nobody penetrated your disguise?' Lady Lydford's eyebrows rose in surprise. 'For myself, I knew as soon as I saw you that you were no boy.'

'Peacock, your butler knows. And after I fell in the Rhône, and nearly drowned, the keeper of the inn—a French gentlewoman—she knew my secret. And in Venice, the major domo of the *palazzo* where we stayed: he knew, but he assumed we were. . .' She couldn't complete the sentence under that critical gaze.

'Quite. But, of course, no such thought entered either of your heads.'

'Of course not!' Cassandra protested, trusting her averted gaze would be mistaken for modest shock, not a guilty conscience.

'And you would have me believe that my short-tempered, self-centred, pleasure-seeking son remained equable and considerate throughout this escapade? You have had a thoroughly pleasant time in his company?'

'He was frequently very angry with me. I talk too much, you see, and I wanted to see the sights, and I answer back too much for a valet. But I did enjoy it— apart from the fleas, and nearly being drowned, and when I thought Nicholas was dead and I had to shoot the footpad.'

The Dowager rolled her eyes upwards. 'You have your dear mama's spirit, I see. Tell me no more now, that is all behind you. As for your being here, I think I can see how we may contrive to account for your sudden appearance. But, for now, we must get you out of those clothes before anyone in the household sees you. And you need a bath.'

The Dowager rang for her dresser, explained the situation to that formidable female in a few well chosen words and sent Cassandra off in her charge to bathe and rest. As she glanced back at the door, she saw her Godmama deep in thought, her firm little chin sunk in one palm, the merest frown shadowing her brow.

That evening Cassandra sat in the window seat in her room in the wing of the Embassy occupied by Sir Marcus Camberley and his sister. The street below was bustling with the fashionable life of the city. Society was making its way to dinner parties and soirées before the curtain went up in the theatres and opera houses for which Vienna was famed.

If only she had her boy's clothes again, she could have slipped out and joined the throng in the City of Music. But her godmother had ordered them removed and, Cassandra strongly suspected, burned.

It was strange how, now she had achieved the long-desired sanctuary and her tale was told, she was not as elated as she had expected. True, the worry that her godmother was going to send her packing back to her father had proved unfounded. She should be thankful, but surprisingly she was not: the freedom and independence she had enjoyed for the past two months were now at an end. Once more she would have to conform to the strictures of Society which ruled and regulated the existence of every well-bred unmarried girl.

And her closeness to Nicholas, to the man she loved, would be the first sacrifice she'd have to make. He would become as remote as any other gentleman to her: this was the price she must pay for her reputation. Already she was realising what a high price that was. Over those past few weeks they had been closer than many a married couple in so many ways.

There was a tightness that was almost pain around her heart at the thought that she would never share that closeness again, see his quick grin as they shared a secret jest, feel his warm skin beneath her fingertips, burn to the pressure of his lips on hers. Now he was in Vienna, he would soon forget her. Godmama would see to it that he was introduced to all the right people: his sense of duty would do the rest.

The scene outside blurred as unshed tears gathered at the back of her eyes and she was rubbing them angrily when the door opened and her godmama swept in, followed by a petite, sombrely dressed woman of middle years.

'Araminta, my goddaughter, Cassandra Weston. Cassandra, Miss Araminta Fox, my cousin.'

Cassandra got up hastily and bobbed a curtsey, stumbling slightly over her unaccustomed skirts.

Miss Fox held out a well-tended hand and nodded gravely, 'Miss Weston, I am very pleased to make your acquaintance.'

Cassandra glanced at her godmother, uncertain how much this lady knew of her predicament.

'Araminta is the only person in whom I have confided,' Lady Lydford remarked, gesturing to them to seat themselves. 'She has been lately acting as companion and housekeeper to her brother, the Bishop of Arundel, but following his recent marriage, she finds herself free to travel and I invited her to join me. It is our great good fortune that she arrived, unexpectedly early, two days ago.'

Miss Fox took up the tale. 'And as I was feeling rather indisposed after the journey, I have not been out into Society. For all anyone knows, you and I arrived together yesterday, having travelled in each others' company from England.'

'After all,' Lady Lydford finished triumphantly, 'who could be a more respectable chaperone than the sister of a bishop, and my own cousin?'

'But how could you have known of my predicament?' Cassandra felt slightly breathless. This upright spinster seemed to be entering into a scandalous intrigue with all the evident enjoyment of an actress!

'Why, I am sure you would have been in correspondence with me, Cassandra,' Lady Lydford said carefully. 'We would have been exchanging letters for some time, and as soon as I heard of Lord Offley's disgusting pretentions, I enlisted the aid of my trusted cousin.'

'Of course, even in the Bishop's Palace, we had heard whisperings of Lord Offley's reputation. Rest assured that had I heard of your predicament, I would have done all in my power to assist you, so no-one would doubt the truth of this story for a moment.'

Cassandra's brain whirled at the facility these two respectable ladies were showing for intrigue. 'But would no one have met us on our journey?' she enquired dazedly.

'Certainly not,' Miss Fox rejoined stoutly. 'My brother always insists I travel in a private carriage and stay in only the most select inns, avoiding English tourists.'

Cassandra could not doubt it. 'How will all this be explained, though? Surely it is not a tale we can recount openly?'

'Indeed not,' her godmother agreed. 'Leave that to me and to gossip. Tomorrow morning, the dressmaker and hairdresser will call. In the afternoon, I will hold a small tea party for a few select friends.'

'Only those of the utmost discretion, my dear Sophia!' said Miss Fox, with a wicked twinkle.

'But, of course,' her cousin assured her with mock gravity, 'I am counting upon it.'

Cassandra closed her eyes and leaned her slightly aching head back on the cushions. How could she have doubted her godmama for an instant?

'Sophia, my dear, this is a most select and mysterious gathering you have invited me to!' Through the hinge-crack in the painted Chinese screen, Cassandra could see the Ambassador's wife settling herself by the fireside. 'I am quite agog—you have preciscly the air of mischief you had about you when you were engaged in one of your pranks at Miss Lucas's Academy.'

'My dear Dorothea, that was quite thirty years ago—and just as I did then, I rely upon you now for your support and good sense, just as I do with Araminta.'

'But tell me the secret...' She broke off as the major domo flung open the double doors into the salon and announced,

'Lady Hartley.'

The Naval Attache's wife, resplendent in purple, swept into the room, greeting her hostess warmly. Cassandra felt confused, as she was followed rapidly by a group of four ladies of similar age and bearing, all equally agog to hear the reason for this intriguing summons.

Cassandra took advantage of the noise of greetings and the rustle of silk gowns to seat herself more comfortably in her hiding place. Godmama had suggested she observe the beginning of the tea party to ensure their stories matched. It would also be far less intimidating to meet these influential ladies, all pillars of the English community in Vienna, after observing them for a while without being observed herself.

Once the introductions to Miss Fox had been made and the tea tray brought in, Lady Lydford cut across the individual murmurs of conversation. 'Ladies, I have to confess I have asked you here with an ulterior motive.'

'We suspected as much.' The oldest lady present, Mrs Spencer, wagged her folded fan in a knowing way. 'Your note contained such a hint of mystery I immediately cancelled an engagement at a picnic.'

'You may have been surprised that my cousin, Miss Fox, has not been out in Society since her arrival last week.'

'We assumed you were indisposed by the journey,

my dear Miss Fox,' the Ambassador's wife remarked. 'Personally, I am always prostrated by the shortest journey: you are quite a heroine to set forth on such an arduous journey alone.'

'Ah, but I was not alone,' said Araminta primly, looking down at her hands folded in her lap.

There was a moment's silence, but Cassandra could almost feel the suppressed excitement in the high-ceilinged salon. Now, they were thinking, now we come to the scandal.

'Some of you may be acquainted with Lord Offley, or at least know of his reputation,' Lady Lydford dropped the words quietly into the silence. The result was as if she had said 'Fox!' to a flock of hens.

'*Lord Offley*!' exclaimed Lady Hartley in awful tones. 'That libertine rake! What connexion has he with you, Miss Fox?'

'Absolutely none, I am glad to say,' Miss Fox responded roundly, her back becoming, if possible, even more stiff. 'At the Bishop's Palace, however, we are not unaware of the opprobrium which attaches to that individual: I hesitate to call him a gentleman.'

'And knowing of that reputation, my sweet cousin did not hesitate to come to my aid when I apprised her of the crisis.' Lady Lydford paused, and gestured towards Mrs Spencer's cup. 'A little more tea? Or perhaps a macaroon?'

Cassandra marvelled at the skilful orchestration of the group: the ladies were hanging on every word, tea cups quite forgotten as they anticipated an awful revelation.

'No, no, thank you, Lady Lydford, I have quite

sufficient.' Mrs Spencer could bear it not longer, 'What crisis?'

The Dowager put her own cup down on the piecrust table beside her with deliberate care, and leaned forward in a confiding manner. Like marionettes on strings, the assembled ladies leaned forward, too.

'I have a goddaughter,' she began, low-voiced. 'She is just eighteen, and has spent her entire life on her father's estate in Hertfordshire, quite secluded. The poor child is motherless; her father, I must tell you, is a scholar of most eccentric habits.'

Knowing looks passed between the ladies at this point, and behind her screen, Cassandra smiled at this masterful understatement.

'Contemplating matrimony on his own behalf, her father has contracted her in marriage to Lord Offley.' Ignoring the sharp intake of breath around the tea table, Lady Lydford pressed on. 'This sweet child, who is not yet out, and who knows nothing of the ways of the world, is, as you may have guessed, a considerable heiress.'

Heads nodded. 'Nothing short of a fortune would tempt *that man* to forsake his bachelorhood for a respectable marriage,' Lady Hartley opined. 'Why, I heard the other day that he had formed a connexion with *both* daughters of a wealthy cit and was found. . .' At this point her voice dropped to a whisper, and strain as she might, Cassandra could hear nothing but the gasps and exclamations of horror which swept the little group.

'Exactly so,' remarked Miss Fox, leaning back once more in her chair. 'You may readily understand, dear ladies, why, when I received a letter from Sophie telling me of her goddaughter's predicament and entreating my aid, I lent myself to a scheme that under other circumstances, I would not have countenanced.'

The ladies could hardly contain their excitement at these horrid revelations. Lady Lydford inflamed them further by saying in a voice of quivering intensity, 'I know, dear friends, that I may rely on you all for the utmost discretion and support.'

There was a chorus of murmured assent around the little circle, and she continued. 'I arranged for Cassandra to slip away—with her maid, of course— and meet my cousin in London. From there, they set forth on their journey to Vienna for my god-daughter to seek sanctuary at my side.'

'And not a mile too far from the influence of such a man!' added the Ambassador's wife. Seeing the most influential lady present had endorsed the plan, the others lost no time in adding their voices in support.

'But are you certain she was not seen on her journey? What if he has hastened after her?' enquired Mrs Spencer, anxiously.

'I am quite certain,' said Miss Fox, straight-faced, 'that she was not seen in my company on the journey.'

Cassandra smiled wryly at the skill of the two ladies in manipulating the conversation. Miss Fox's obvious utter respectability and Lady Lydford's scandalous revelations combined to make a most titillating tea party.

'Now Cassandra is off his hands, her father will not concern himself further with her. I intend to bring her out myself, and, of course, present her at Court when we return to London—once mourning for Princess Charlotte is over.'

'A large fortune, you said?' ventured one of the ladies, as if it were a mere detail.

Lady Lydford tilted the heavy teapot on its stand and replenished a cup. 'Oh, more than respectable,' she rejoined, equally casually.

Watching through the gap in the screen, Cassandra admired her godmother's skilled manipulation of her audience, then found her admiration replaced by a small frisson of apprehension. If Lady Lydford was as intelligent as she appeared, it was going to be very difficult to keep secrets from her. How could she hide the way she felt for Nicholas from his mother?

She was jerked out of her brown study by Miss Fox enquiring if she should fetch Miss Weston from her room.

'If you would be so kind, Araminta.' Lady Lydford turned to her guests. 'I am sure our friends will be sensible of a young girl's feelings and not allude, in any way, to the distressing circumstances. . .'

Cassandra picked up her skirts and tiptoed out of the door behind the screen. She found Miss Fox waiting for her at the head of the grand staircase which swept up in a double curve from the ballroom.

'Could you hear all that passed?' Miss Fox enquired, pausing to tease out one of Cassandra's newly dressed curls high on her forehead. 'You look quite charming, my dear,' she added, nodding with aprobation at the high-waisted, high-necked sprigged muslin gown. 'Just arrange your shawl a little lower on your arms. There, that should have given the old pussies time to smooth down their fur before your appearance.'

Seeing Cassandra's look of astonishment at her frankness, she added drily, 'If you had spent as many hours in the company of clerical wives as I have, my dear, you, too, would be an expert on gossiping middle-aged ladies!'

Cassandra's heart was thumping uncomfortably by the time she was ushered into the salon by Miss Fox, and she felt her colour rise under the scrutiny of the assembled ladies.

Her embarrassment and the effort of remembering not to stride in her unaccustomed skirts kept her almost tongue-tied as the presentations were made, and she sank down gratefully at her godmother's side and accepted a cup of tea.

'...from Ware in Hertfordshire, ma'am,' she was replying to the Naval Attache's wife, while trying not to listen to Mrs Spencer whispering to her neighbour.

'Such a pretty child, and quite nice style.'

She caught her godmother's eye and received a small nod of approval, which gave her the courage to respond quietly and calmly to the unexceptionable questions the ladies were asking her.

She was just asking her godmother's permission to join a party driving into the country the next day, when the major domo announced, 'The Earl of Lydford, my lady.'

Cassandra knew the blood had been driven from her cheeks by Nicholas's unexpected arrival, but fortunately the ladies were far more interested in the eligible Earl of Lydford than in her reaction to him.

He stood just inside the room, self-assured and extremely handsome in a coat of deep blue broadcloth, his long legs encased in a pair of white trousers which Cassandra knew were new. His waistcoat was pale yellow silk with a broad grey stripe that she had helped him choose in Lyons, and at his throat, the snowy folds of his cravat were impeccable.

He strolled across to bend over his mother's hand, calmly ignoring the frigid glint in her eye. 'Mama, if I had any inkling you were entertaining so many charming ladies, I would have hurried home sooner.' He began to bow to the ladies in turn. 'Mrs Spencer, it must be at least two years since I had the pleasure; Lady Hartley, I trust I find you in good health. Miss Fox, I was sorry to miss you at breakfast. I must admit to rising late after yesterday's journey.'

Cassandra watched him making his rounds of the room, leaving the ladies flushed and fluttering in his wake. His technique, she realised, was to make each and every one of them believe that were it not for the inconvenient existence of their husbands, he would be slain by their charms.

'Mountebank!' she hissed at him as, finally, he stopped before her, eyes twinkling and bent low over her hand.

'At last, Miss Weston! Or may I call you Cassandra, for we are as good as cousins? Last time we met, I was in a ditch rescuing your puppy, was I not?'

'Up a tree, and it was my kitten,' Cassandra replied tightly.

'Of course, it was. May I sit here?' Not receiving a reply, he sat down anyway, accepting a cup of tea from his mother while assiduously avoiding her eye. 'Even at the tender age of fifteen, I was your devoted slave.' Nicholas gave her a sudden grin which made her heart lurch.

'So far from being my slave,' she rejoined with spirit,

'you did nothing but pull my pigtails and twit me about my freckles!'

The ladies laughed approvingly at these childish reminiscences, but Lady Lydford cut in hastily. 'Enough of this, Nicholas, you must not tease Cassandra! You forget, she is no longer a child of eight.'

'There is no danger of that, Mama,' he said smoothly, turning his attention to Miss Fox as the colour rose hectically in Cassandra's cheek.

The infuriating man! Cassandra set down her cup with a sharp click, and schooled her face so as not to scowl. What game was he playing? He had obviously not been expected at this afternoon's tea party, that much was obvious from Lady Lydford's mien, however well she covered up her irritation.

But if she thought Nicholas had done with his sparring, she was mistaken. 'Another macaroon, Cassandra?' He offered her the plate with a warm smile.

'Thank you, no,' Cassandra replied coolly, trying to think of a safe, neutral topic of conversation. Finding none, she lapsed into silence.

'Forgive me,' he said in a slightly lowered voice. 'My teasing has discommoded you.'

'Not at all, my lord.' She was pleased at the indifference in her tone. 'I am sure you were only humouring me, for you think of me as a child—one who was an inconvenient brat in the past, perhaps?'

'My dear Cassandra, now you are threatening to discommode *me*!' She had certainly succeeding in disturbing some of his air of assurance; there was a glint in his eye that was not all amusement, and one finger tapped the arm of the sofa.

'Oh, no, my lord!' Cassandra protested sweetly. 'Why, I declare nothing could discommode you—not raging torrents, nor foreign footpads.'

'Touché, Cassandra,' he whispered. 'Changing from breeches into skirts has done nothing to improve your temperament.'

Their secret squabble was interrupted by the Ambassador's wife rising to her feet, apparently a signal to the lesser ladies to take their leave, also.

In the flurry of goodbyes, Cassandra received several promises of future invitations. Lady Hartley said that her daughters would be charmed to take her about with them. 'I expect you, Lydford, will have many calls on your time,' she remarked archly as he bowed her out.

As soon as the door closed behind the last guest he collapsed gracefully into a chair, legs stretched out on the carpet. 'Mother, I congratulate you. A more worthy collection of influential gabblemongers you would be hard put to meet anywhere. And if I recollect, only Lady Hartley has daughters to dispose of.'

'You are out of touch, Nicholas. The elder is betrothed to Sommerson, and the younger is the reigning beauty in Vienna. She has no need to fear competition.' Lady Lydford dismissed the Marriage Mart and turned to her son in renewed irritation. 'What were you about, Lydford? You nearly ruined my entire strategy, arriving like that. Why, you might have put Cassandra completely out of countenance with your foolery.'

Nicholas snorted inelegantly. 'Ha! Nothing puts

Cassandra out of countenance, as I have found to my cost these last seven weeks. Why, if someone particularly disturbs her, she takes a pistol to them.'

Stung, Cassandra protested. 'Nicholas, that isn't fair! I thought he had killed you!' Her throat tightened with hurt. 'I didn't *want* to shoot anybody.'

'Lydford!' his mother began, but Nicholas had already jumped to his feet and taken one of Cassandra's hands in his.

'I'm sorry Cassie, that was unworthy of me. You were wonderful.'

Time seemed to stand still as she let her hand rest in his, and their eyes locked and held. Then Lady Lydford cleared her throat, and the moment was gone, but not before the Dowager had seen Cassandra's face, and the suspicion which had been growing all day, crystallised in her mind.

# CHAPTER TWELVE

'CASSANDRA!' Miss Fox hissed in reproof.

Hastily Cassandra roused herself from her day-dream and resignedly waited for the criticism that was surely to follow. She glanced down to check that her skirts were modestly arranged and that her satin slippers were still on the picnic rug and not on the springy woodland turf.

But no doubt Miss Fox was about to point out—as she had been doing all week—that Cassandra had once more committed some error of deportment or etiquette.

'The chicken leg,' Miss Fox continued, low-voiced. 'Do not gnaw it!'

She was not aware she had been: but weeks of pretending to be a boy, staying in wayside inns where daintiness would have betrayed her, had made settling back to being a demure young lady extremely difficult. Her sheltered homelife was no help, either. Cassandra soon discovered she had absolutely no talent for social small talk. Papa believed one should only open one's mouth when one had something worth saying, and gossip about gowns, affaires of the heart and the weather were outside her experience.

Sighing, she dropped the well-nibbled bones back on her plate, and dutifully turned her attention to the conversation of the other two young ladies sharing the rug with her and Miss Fox.

Lady Hartley had been as good as her word, and had arranged this picnic outing to the woods to introduce Cassandra to her daughters' circle of female friends. The elder daughter, Charlotte, secure in her new status as affianced bride, was holding court to a little gaggle of confidantes, all agog to hear of her bride clothes and wedding plans.

Lucy, the younger and more beautiful, caught Cassandra's eye and giggled. The two girls next to Cassandra had filled the past twenty minutes with an impassioned discussion on the relative merits of smocked or ruched edgings for a new gown, and Cassandra smiled ruefully back at Lucy.

'Will you not walk a while, Miss Weston?' Lucy called, already getting gracefully to her feet.

With hardly a glance at Miss Fox for permission, Cassandra scrambled to her feet, managing not to catch her toe in her hem as she was wont to do, and joined her new friend.

'May I call you Cassandra?' Miss Hartley asked. She slipped her hand through Cassandra's arm, as they gained the gravel path encircling the ornamental lake, which made this such a popular picnic spot.

'I wish you would,' Cassandra confessed frankly. 'I find all this formality rather daunting.'

'And you must call me Lucy.' They strolled on in companionable silence for a few minutes, then, when they paused to admire some ornamental waterfowl, Lucy continued, 'I believe Miss Fox said you have not been much in Society? That you have lived quietly in the country with your father? I do envy you. We scarce see anything of dear Papa these days, he is always so engrossed in diplomatic affairs.'

Cassandra smiled wryly. 'It certainly affords the opportunity to study the character of one's parent,' she said ambiguously.

'Indeed, it must.' Lucy took the comment at face value. 'I understand he is quite a noted Classical scholar? And you yourself, I think, are quite an accomplished student.'

Oh, dear. Cassandra groaned inwardly. That would be another black mark from Miss Fox, who had impressed on her vigorously the absolute necessity of avoiding the label of 'blue stocking'.

'It would quite ruin your chances if the gentlemen thought you *scholarly*,' she had said forcefully. 'Your little. . .' Miss Fox paused with a shudder, '. . .jest last night about the relative characters of Napoleon and Julius Caesar, while no doubt very clever, is precisely the thing to avoid.'

'Oh, no,' Cassandra denied hastily. 'I'm no scholar, although I can read some Greek and Latin. It does make it more interesting when one visits antique sites.'

'You have travelled then?'

'No. . .not yet, but I hope to, if Godmama is so kind.' Every conversation was fraught with traps! Cassandra was finding guarding her tongue every second very tiresome, even with someone as pleasant as Lucy.

'I do think your Godmama splendid,' Lucy said enthusiastically. 'I am so looking forward to her party tomorrow evening.' She paused, and added, not quite casually enough, 'Is the Earl intending to be there?'

'I presume so, I scarcely see him,' Cassandra admitted truthfully. It was almost as if he were avoiding her: but that was silly. After all, he had his own life to lead, why should he concern himself with a debutante his mother happened to be launching into Society? Everything was different now—she was hardly the Cassie with whom he had shared those weeks on the road. By the time Godmama and Miss Fox had finished with her, she'd be just another insipid young lady!

'Oh,' Lucy appeared disappointed. 'I was looking forward to renewing my acquaintance with him—we all were,' she added rather quickly.

'He has been out a great deal meeting his friends since he arrived. And I belive he has been seeing his tailor.' And, no doubt, attending the Opera and ballet and less reputable entertainments! Cassandra stifled the thought of opera dancers and actresses, and added, 'And, of course, Godmama has been taking me about so much to visit and to the *modiste*. I hardly see Ni . . . the Earl.'

'He is a very fine man, is he not,' said Lucy, quite failing to sound uninterested. 'So handsome, so well-dressed.'

'And so eligible,' Cassandra finished, rather drily. Thinking about Nicholas and actresses was doing nothing to improve her frayed nerves.

'Indeed, yes!' Miss Hartley's blue eyes were sparkling. Cassandra looked at the piquant little face and the artlessly arranged ash blonde curls and wondered just how well Nicholas knew her. What was it like to be fragile and dainty and so beautiful it took men's breath away? To be fair, she had to admit that Lucy seemed quite unaffected by her own loveliness, quite unconscious of the effect she produced.

Combined with her friendly charm and lively wit, Cassandra could quite understand why Lucy was the reigning beauty. And if Nicholas was a good catch, then so, too, was the well-connected, well-dowered Miss Hartley. Perhaps Godmama and Lady Hartley were even now planning to bring them together.

It was a painful thought, but not quite as difficult to face as the thought of Nicholas allied with one of the silly peahens they had left behind in the glade just now.

'Nicholas!' Lady Lydford fixed her only son with a cold eye as he strolled into the dining-room the next evening. 'Where do you think you are going in those clothes?'

Startled, the Earl glanced down at his irreproachably tailored trousers and evening coat and replied simply, 'Out—why?'

There was a slight pause while he took his seat and the soup was served. Across the polished expanse of walnut, Cassandra caught her godmother's eye and raised her own brows in response.

'You cannot have forgotten that tonight is the party I am giving for Cassandra. Why are you not wearing knee breeches?'

Nicholas put down his spoon. 'Oh, lord, I had forgotten. I'm engaged to play cards with Morton this evening.'

'Send a note: you can go on later.' His mother was crisp. 'I want you here to greet our guests. It is very important that you are here to lend Cassandra your support at her first soirée.'

'I'm sorry, Cass,' he began. 'Of course, I'll be there...'

'Don't call her Cass!' his mother wailed despairingly.

'How will I ever get her launched successfully if you don't watch your tongue?'

Cassandra and Nicholas ate lamb cutlets in attentive silence, while Lady Lydford rehearsed the guest list. It appeared to her goddaughter that the guests had been chosen with two purposes in mind: to launch her, certainly, but also to introduce Nicholas to as many eligible young women as possible. And, of course, he already knew Miss Lucy Hartley. . .

At the end of the meal, Nicholas vanished to change into satin knee breeches and evening coat. Cassandra, too, went up to her room for her abigail to tidy her hair and adjust her dress.

Godmama had decreed that a cream voile dress was entirely suitable for a first party dress. Looking in the long pier glass Cassandra had to agree it made the most of her rather unconventional looks.

With her chestnut hair and brows, debutante white would have looked insipid while the modestly scooped neck and high waist made the most of her height and slight figure.

In the hands of a skilful hairdresser, Cassandra's boyish curls had been transformed into a modish crop set off by a simple tiara and Godmama had presented her with a pair of simple pearl drop earrings.

'My dear, you look simply charming,' Godmama said from the doorway. In her hands she was carrying a pair of kid evening gloves. 'Here you are, Cassandra, let me help you with the buttons.'

Cassandra smoothed on her first pair of grown up evening gloves with a shiver of almost sensual pleasure at the smoothness of the fine leather. Then the pleasure turned to apprehension at the daunting thought of being the centre of attention at her first real party.

'Don't worry, Cassandra.' Godmama tipped up her chin very gently and looked into the intelligent, troubled dark eyes. 'I'll be there, and so will Nicholas.' She made no comment at the sudden flush that tinged Cassandra's cheeks and added, 'I know this week has been a difficult one for you, but you are quite ready to go into Society now. Forget your worries and enjoy tonight.'

An hour later, Cassandra realised, to her own amazement, that she was having fun. She had bobbed curtseys to all the formidable chaperones and heard many of them complimenting her to her godmother. Their charges were all girls she had already met, and suddenly small talk and chatter came easily.

It was exciting to meet so many pleasant young men, and flattering to observe their open admiration, as they competed to fill her dance card. Lady Lydford had engaged a string quartet to play country dances and had invited enough young people to make up twenty couples, but as she had said to Cassandra, 'No waltzes, we will save those for your ball.'

Godmama had opened up the Large Salon for the dancing, and arranged for card tables in the library for the older guests. As the dowagers soon became engrossed in their whist, the younger party were able to enjoy themselves without the close supervision of their elders.

Even so, Cassandra knew she must not dance more than two dances with any one gentleman, and was laughingly resisting the blandishments of Christopher

Hartley to join him in just one more set, when Nicholas strode over.

'My dance, I think, Miss Weston.' The smile he bestowed on Mr Hartley was perfectly pleasant, but the young man hastily relinquished all claims and retreated.

'Nicholas!' she protested as they took their places in the set. 'This isn't your dance and you were very short with Mr Hartley.'

'Well, you shouldn't flirt,' he said with no sign of teasing.

'I wasn't.' Cassandra said, as they joined hands and parted again.

'You'd danced with him twice already.'

'There's nothing wrong with that, and I wasn't going to dance with him again. I was telling him so when you interrupted.' It was very difficult having a satisfactory quarrel in the middle of a country dance. 'And in any case, why are you counting? You're not my chaperone!'

The music was ending with a scrape of violins and Cassandra dropped a cursory curtsey, raising her eyes, sparkling with indignation, to meet his.

There was an expression on his face she could not recognise. Despite all the moods she had seen in Nicholas over the past weeks, she had never experienced this one. 'Are you cross with me?' she hazarded, her indignation overtaken by puzzlement.

He seemed about to reply when Lord Stewart appeared by her side, claiming the next dance as his. 'Sorry, Lydford,' he said heartlessly, 'the lady's mine!'

Lord Stewart, against whose frivolous high spirits she had been warned by Miss Fox, proved to be a thoroughly entertaining partner. He was witty and amusing and his flirtatious sallies, while quite unthreatening, were flattering in the extreme. Cassandra found herself laughing up at him, completely captivated by his easy charm.

Lady Lydford emerged from the card room to find her son, arms folded, glowering at the sight of her laughing goddaughter.

'Ah, Nicholas! There you are. Doesn't Cassandra look charming this evening? And young Stewart is obviously captivated. You know,' she said, lowering her voice and leaning towards him confidingly, 'I have great hopes of that particular connexion. He might be only the second son, but his grand-uncle left him his entire fortune and Sir Marcus speaks very highly of him for the Foreign Office.'

Nicholas snorted inelegantly. 'Popinjay!'

'Nonsense, dear, he is merely high spirited. I think they look charmingly together. Oh, see now,' she added, apparently unheeding of the effect this conversation was having on her son, 'he's making Cassandra blush!'

Nicholas did not reply immediately, but followed the couple's progess with his eyes. 'I would have a care, Mama,' he said eventually, turning to face her. 'I would not place too many hopes on securing Stewart: he has a reputation as an accomplished flirt.'

'Like you, Nicholas, dear?'

'Just like me, Mama! And it is just as futile for you to strew my path with all these hopeful young ladies. Now I must join Morton's party.' He bowed gratefully over his mother's hand and left, unaware that Cassandra's eyes followed him from the room.

They were not the only eyes that followed the tall, lithe figure. Cassandra saw Lucy Hartley's concentration falter momentarily before she danced on. Well, that was one consolation. Nicholas might, for some reason she didn't understand, be out of charity with her, but he had paid her more attention than he had any of the other young ladies present.

She recognised a small flame of hope and ruthlessly suppressed it. Nicholas was not for her, she had to resign herself to that. But, enjoy the company of other men as she might, it was Nicholas she loved and wanted—and always would.

'May I escort you to supper?' Lord Stewart was at her side.

'Yes, please.' Cassandra rewarded him with a smile and allowed herself to be led away. A breaking heart was no excuse for bad manners, she told herself firmly.

The next morning, Cassandra came across the jewelled snake necklace coiled at the bottom of a drawer. She stared at it, suddenly cold, remembering Venice, remembering how close she had come to betraying both herself and her love for Nicholas.

It was too dangerous to keep; both for itself and for the memories it evoked. And if she found a respectable jeweller and sold it, she would have a little money of her own for emergencies. Cassandra slipped the jewel into her reticule and went downstairs thoughtfully.

She had the breakfast room to herself. Godmama, as usual, was partaking of chocolate and sweet rolls in her room and Miss Fox, according to the butler, had gone out for a walk.

'And Lord Lydford?' Cassandra enquired casually, toying with a little thin ham.

'He was up early this morning, Miss. He went out about eight o'clock, intending to ride.'

The butler bowed himself out. Left alone, Cassandra regarded the breakfast table. The ham was excellent. She helped herself to another slice and buttered some bread. She sipped her coffee and contemplated Nicholas's puzzling behaviour. What had put him so out of sorts? He had acted like an elder brother, and a particularly proprietorial one at that.

She was still musing when the door opened and the object of her thoughts strode in, banging it shut behind him. He was looking pale and fatigued and thoroughly out of temper at finding the breakfast room occupied.

'Coffee, Nicholas?' Cassandra enquired sweetly.

'Thank you,' he replied curtly, jerking the chair opposite her away from the table and slouching in it, long booted legs thrust out.

'Have you had a nice ride?' Now she had him alone, perhaps she could provoke him into revealing what was wrong.

'Not particularly,' Nicholas was obviously disinclined for conversation. He took the proffered cup and unfolded a newspaper with an irritable snap.

'I didn't realise you read German,' Cassandra remarked, peering across at the heavy Gothic script.

'I don't. I was merely trying to indicate—tactfully, I thought—that I would prefer to eat my breakfast in peace and quiet.'

'Well, have some ham, then,' she suggested helpfully. 'You know you're always irritable in the morning until you've had something to eat.'

There was a deadly silence while Nicholas lowered the paper and regarded her with hard green eyes. 'I suggest you watch your tongue, Cassandra. My mood early in the morning should be quite outside your experience—do not forget our acquaintance is supposed to be of a week's duration. Mama can scheme to her heart's content, but it will all come to nothing if you cannot curb your prattle.'

Cassandra counted up to ten in Greek beneath her breath, very slowly. 'It is excellent ham,' she said out loud.

'Damn the ham!' he exploded, jumping up from the chair, which fell back on the polished boards with a clatter.

'Nicholas!' Cassandra assumed an expression of outrage. 'You should not use such language in front of me—it is most improper.' She knew she was goading him, but here he could not threaten to send her packing back to her father, or put her over his knee as he had in Venice.

'Why, I must congratulate Mama on the transformation she has wrought,' he said slowly, his face hardening as he eyed the slim figure in the demure sprigged muslin gown. 'No-one would recognise Cass the valet now—or a certain young lady in a Paris bedroom.'

Cassandra gasped, the flush rising hectically to her face. How could he remind her of that! She was half on her feet when he rounded the table and sat on the edge, so close she was forced to sit down again. He seemed to tower over her.

'That wasn't fair,' she said in a voice that shook, and not only with indignation.

'If you want me to forget those weeks we spent together, Cassandra, you must stop invoking the memories,' he said, in a reasonable voice that still retained the hard edge of anger. 'Now you want to be treated like a young lady. You want insipid compliments and well-turned phrases. You want nice safe flirtations and gestures from your pack of young admirers. Like this.'

He picked up her hand in his. Her fingers felt suddenly cold against the enveloping warmth of his, still slightly roughened from the reins. He bent his head and brushed the briefest of touches across her knuckles, then surrendered her hand with a flourish.

'Well, Miss Weston? Will that suffice? It will have to, won't it? One step out of line, one indication of your impetuous nature, and the carefully woven illusion is shattered.'

'Oh, no, my lord,' Cassandra countered furiously. 'Lord Stewart, to take but one example, is considerably more ardent in his attentions. And, I may say, he is considerably more gallant than you; he says my natural high spirits are charming!'

'Stewart will never make you a declaration,' he said contemptuously. 'It is known he is hanging out for a wife with good connexions.'

'I know that; I am not as gullible as you seem to think. Don't forget, Nicholas, I have just spent seven weeks in the company of just such another gentleman! But Lord Stewart is witty and he is fun to be with— two qualities you are singularly lacking this morning!'

She stood up, galvanised by irritation and found herself standing so close to him her face was almost touching his neckcloth. The familiar scent of him, his warmth, filled her nostrils and seemed to take all power of movement from her.

The room was very still, the only sounds were of Nicholas's breathing, and the steady tick of the clock echoing her own heartbeat. Cassandra stood, fighting the urge to wrap her arms around him, bury her face in his chest and never let him go.

Nicholas did not move, and slowly she raised her head to look at him. He was regarding her steadily with hooded eyes, the trace of a smile touching his lips. 'It is very unfair, Cassandra,' he said softly, 'but well-bred young ladies can't expect to have fun.'

He kissed her then, before she had a chance to move her face away. The kiss echoed his voice, cool and sardonic, devoid of emotion or passion, but none the less thorough for that.

Cassandra jerked away angrily, face aflame. 'How dare you! I did nothing to warrant such behaviour from you! And you have the effrontery to warn me against Lord Stewart...why you. . .' She stuttered to a halt, lost for words.

Nicholas stood up quite calmly. 'But that is my point, Cassandra. Lord Stewart is *exactly* like me: and if you behave as recklessly with him, you may expect the same response—but considerably less discretion.'

Cassandra swung away from him, trying to hide the tears that welled in her eyes. Goading him had worked only too well: he was saying things she didn't want to hear, things that hurt because she loved him. 'Oh, damn it, Cassie, I didn't mean to make you cry!' There was an exasperated tenderness in his voice that made her heart thump. 'Come here.' Nicholas pulled her into the comfort of his arms, in an embrace so different from what had just passed between them, he could have been a different man.

'I'm not crying,' she protested unconvincingly.

'Then you obviously have something in your eye,' he said, humouring her. 'Have you a handkerchief?'

He was already reaching for her reticule as she stammered, 'No!'

He pulled the protruding corner of white linen. With horrible inevitability, the snake necklace uncoiled itself and lay gleaming in a shaft of sunlight.

Her sharp intake of breath was the only sound in the room as Nicholas stooped and picked up the jewel, letting it run between his fingers.

'How did you. . .' he began slowly, then as he looked at her betraying face, realisation dawned. 'It was you! You connived with that wh. . .' He bit back the word, his fingers white on the metal coils. 'Why, Cassandra? To get back at me because I had been angry with you? It must have seemed very amusing to humiliate me.'

'I didn't mean to. . .' she began.

'To let it go so far?' he queried dangerously. 'I am sure you didn't! I hadn't thought you would be so spiteful.' He looked at her through narrowed eyes, recollection blazing. 'Nor would I have suspected you capable of such seductive wiles.'

Cassandra felt the fiery blush rising as she recalled just how willingly her body had answered his. His face changed, hardened. 'What a fool I've been, worrying about your chastity all those weeks, when you knew full well how to rouse a man. Where did you practice, Miss Weston?' he sneered. 'With your father's ploughboys? Or the stableboy who was so willing to lend you his clothes?' If he had struck her, the shock could not have been greater. She expected—deserved—his anger. His contempt burned like acid. But how could she tell him that her responses had been instinctive, driven by her love for him? He would think it a lie, a subterfuge to extricate herself.

'Still no excuses? No convenient story to account for it? No, I suppose even your fertile imagination baulks at explaining this away.' The necklace swung from his fingers, mocking her.

'Nicholas. . .I. . .'

'No more, Cassandra,' he said icily.

The necklace moved in the sunlight, stabbing her eyes. 'Here.' He held it out. 'Take your whore's device. You can always sell it. Or you may have need of it again.' He smiled humourlessly at her. 'Why, I almost find it in me to feel sorry for Lord Stewart.'

Cassandra snatched it from his hand and ran from the room. At the foot of the stairs she paused. Her heart thudded and she felt sick with the force of Nicholas's attack. Yet she could not cry.

Fortunately, no one was about. She needed fresh air, to get away from these enclosed, silent rooms, the corrosion of Nicholas's contempt. On an impulse, she tugged the bell-pull in her room and summoned her maid.

Five minutes later, in bonnet and pelisse, Maria dutifully at her heels, Cassandra was strolling heedlessly down one of the wide promenades, in company with a throng of fashionably dressed people. She soon found herself in the Prat, which Godmama had mentioned to her as being an unexceptionable place to walk.

As she walked, she brooded on Nicholas's reaction.

She could not blame him for his anger, nor for the conclusions he had drawn from her behaviour. At that moment, if the pavements of the Prat had opened and swallowed her, she would have been grateful for it. But she had to think about it: she would have to face him again, behave as if nothing had happened, knowing that every time he looked at her, he would recall her body quivering against his.

With her maid silent beside her, Cassandra walked on, deep in thought. After a while, Maria, who had been wondering what could have upset her mistress so, noticed that the set, frozen look relaxed and a touch of colour came back into Cassandra's cheeks.

Lucia's words at that first meeting in Venice had returned to her; Lucia saying that, if Nicholas had been indifferent, he wouldn't become so angry with her. Anyone would have condemned her for her behaviour—she condemned herself—but would someone who was uncaring have reacted so bitterly, have thrown such wild and wounding accusations at her?

And if he cared for her, that explained his actions last night, and his bad temper this morning: he was jealous of the attention shown her by other men. The thought was so startling, Cassandra halted in her tracks, causing Maria to trip over the edge of her pelisse.

When she thought of him with other women, it made her feel hurt and angry—and thoroughly unreasonable. Could it be that seeing Cassandra as the centre of attention, especially from his friend Stewart, was arousing jealousy in Nicholas? But he couldn't be in love with her, or surely he would have said something. . .

Cassandra wandered on, her frown of concentration making her look fierce enough to discourage the young bucks, who were out to ogle the passing young ladies.

Perhaps he hadn't realised how he felt. In novels, so she had heard, men were notoriously slow in recognising a dawning *tendresse* for the heroine. Well, if he hadn't realised, she would make him! There was no point in flirting with the younger men; Nicholas had already dismissed them as puppies. But Lord Stewart was different. His mild attentions last night had already roused Nicholas to a display of bad temper. . . if she really tried to attach Stewart, there was no knowing what he would do.

Cassandra had a momentary qualm about toying with Lord Stewart's affections, then concluded that if he were dangling after a well-connected wife, she was hardly likely to break his heart. She turned on her heel and began to walk home. If challenged now, all Nicholas would admit to was a brotherly desire to keep her out of the clutches of a well-known roué. It was up to her to make him see things differently.

That afternoon, she sat in the Blue Salon with her godmother, writing out the gold-edged invitations, while Lady Lydford reviewed the prospective guests for the ball she intended to give in honour of her goddaughter's come-out.

'I suppose I must invite Regina Cooper and that bracket-faced daughter of hers.' She paused, adding, 'I always wished for a daughter, my dear. I *am* enjoying this!'

Cassandra smiled at her. 'I fear I am very expensive, Godmama!'

'Fiddlesticks, child. I love the excuse to spend money on clothes, and I am enjoying your company. Your mind is as sharp as your mother's, and I have missed my dearest friend.' She gave herself a little shake. 'I shall be getting sentimental, and we must press on with this list. A week is short notice, but I doubt if we will be short of company.'

The pile of invitations grew steadily. Cassandra had just paused to sharpen the point of her quill when the butler announced, 'Miss Hartley, Miss Lucy Hartley, my lady.'

'Charlotte, Lucy...what a pleasure. You will stay for tea? Hector, the tea tray in twenty minutes.'

'We have come with a note from Mama and to thank you for the party last night,' Charlotte said. 'Are you sure we are not interrupting?'

'Not at all, sit down, both of you, and I will tell you my plans for Cassandra's coming-out ball.'

The ladies were cosily involved in a discussion of the relative merits of a string ensemble or a military band for the music, when the butler reappeared, with the tea tray and the announcement, 'Lord Stewart, my lady.'

Even Miss Hartley, newly affianced as she was, paused to pat a curl into place. Lord Stewart entered with his customary ease, despite the handicap of two large bouquets, which he presented to his hostess and Cassandra.

'With thanks for an enchanting evening, ma'am,' he swept a bow to the Dowager. 'And the enchanting company,' he added, with a warm glance at Cassandra.

She accepted the flowers with blushing confusion, not entirely unaware of the envy she was arousing in

Miss Lucy's breast. Lord Stewart cut a magnificent figure with his slim, blond elegance and the faint military air which still hung about him, although he had resigned his commission the previous year.

As he sat down beside her, crossing one elegantly booted leg over the other, Cassandra reflected that if one's heart wasn't given to an infuriating, green-eyed, bad tempered Earl, one could very easily fall under the spell of this man.

Lord Stewart soon had the ladies' attention with his amusing description of the antics of his eccentric Austrian valet. He had just accepted a second cup of tea when he saw a small ink spot on Cassandra's hand and broke off to tease her about the dangers of working too hard.

It could not have been better contrived, Cassandra reflected afterwards, that Lord Stewart had taken her hand to examine the mark, just as Nicholas came into the Blue Salon. Lord Stewart retained her hand while he nodded amiably to his friend, but Cassandra laughingly withdrew her fingers.

'Tea, Nicholas?' his mother asked, as he took the seat between the two Misses Hartley.

Really, there couldn't be a better opportunity to put her plan into operation, Cassandra thought, turning with a brilliant smile to Lord Stewart. 'Do you ride much in Vienna, my lord?'

Five minutes later, while she was laughingly accepting his offer to take her riding and to lend her a horse, she risked a glance under her lashes at Nicholas.

Charlotte Hartley was deep in discussion of bride clothes with Lady Lydford, leaving Miss Lucy to Nicholas's undivided attention. Charming in peach muslin, which showed off to perfection her rounded figure and delicately flushed complexion, she was all attention as Nicholas chatted easily to her.

He was showing no interest whatsoever in Lord Stewart's attentions to Cassandra, and swallowing her chagrin, she had to admit Miss Lucy was enough to distract any man. And, of course, he must have known her in London.

It would be easier if she could dislike the young woman, but Lucy's good nature and bright intelligence had endeared her to Cassandra very quickly. She saw Lady Lydford watching the couple with an indulgent smile touching her lips, and her heart sank. Lucy Hartley, well-bred, well-behaved and exceedingly well-dowered, was every mama's dream for her son.

Beside her, Lord Stewart was describing delightful rides in the Viennese countryside and she responded with every appearance of interest, while inside her heart felt like lead. She must have been insane to have deluded herself that Nicholas felt anything for her. His behaviour last night was simply that of a rather over zealous cousin, concerned to protect the reputation of an inexperienced girl.

And his anger this morning, she thought miserably, stemmed from the discovery of her wanton behaviour, her apparent spiteful desire for revenge.

'Lydford, why do we not make up a riding party tomorrow, if the weather is good, and take the ladies to see that wonderful view you get from the western hills? Miss Hartley, Miss Lucy, would you accompany us?'

Lady Lydford added her approbation of the scheme, and suggested Miss Fox as a chaperone.

'Splendid idea, Stewart,' Nicholas agreed. 'But if I may suggest, rather than all go on horseback, it would be an excellent opportunity to give you that driving lesson I have been promising you, Miss Lucy. Come now, say you will.' His voice was warmly persuasive and Miss Lucy showed no inclination to resist.

'If mama permits,' she dimpled prettily, 'I would love to—if you think me strong enough to control your horses.'

'Don't be afraid, I'll be there all the time,' Nicholas assured her.

Cassandra ungritted her teeth with an effort: the mental picture of Miss Lucy in a dashing riding habit with the Earl's strong hands enveloping her tiny gloved ones on the reins was too much to bear.

'Unfortunately, I do not possess a riding habit,' Cassandra said tightly.

'Oh, what a pity,' Nicholas replied carelessly. 'Never mind, I expect you and Stewart can join us on another occasion.'

'Nonsense, she can borrow my habit,' Lady Lydford said cheerfully, as the young ladies rose to make their farewells.

When their guests had left, the Dowager regarded her son and goddaughter with complacency. 'Well, what a splendid afternoon we have had. Almost all the invitations are written, Nicholas—and did you see the lovely flowers Lord Stewart brought Cassandra?'

'Very handsome,' he remarked lightly. 'Perhaps I have misjudged him. Should I enquire what his intentions are towards Cassandra, Mama?'

'A little premature, I think, but I will not deny I

have hopes. Now, don't blush so, Cassandra, you seem to have quite a partiality for his lordship.'

Having effectively rendered her goddaughter speechless, she turned once more to her son. 'And as for you, Nicholas, I really am most pleased with you, I have had great hopes of your finding a suitable wife in Vienna. Miss Lucy Hartley would be ideal.'

'I will do my best not to disappoint you, Mama,' he said smoothly, opening the door to allow the Dowager to leave.

'Nicholas. . .'

He turned to Cassandra, his eyes as hard as emeralds and held up a hand. 'No, don't say anything. I have no wish to cause my mother pain, so I have decided we will say no more about Venice or what happened this morning. As far as I am concerned, the subject is closed.' The door closed behind him with the thud of finality.

# CHAPTER THIRTEEN

THE Embassy ballroom blazed with light from the hundreds of candles fixed in branched wall sconces, and the great chandeliers hanging at intervals down its length. It had taken a team of workmen most of the week to lower them, polish each lustre, and hoist the great weight up again.

At the far end, chairs and music stands were being set out for the orchestra and beyond that, the double doors stood open into the long drawing-room, where supper would be set out. The Ambassador had granted permission to use the Embassy plate, as well as the ballroom and his servants, and the overall effect, Cassandra thought, was as grand as a palace.

She had slipped in on her way down to dinner for a last look at the flower arrangements she had been helping with all afternoon, and had stopped in amazement at the transformation. With the dust covers removed, the lights ablaze, and watering cans and flowerstems tidied away, the room was magical.

'It looks very fine,' said the Ambassador behind her, causing her to jump. 'I'm sorry, my dear, didn't mean to startle you.'

Cassandra bobbed a quick curtsey. 'Not at all, sir, and I must thank you for letting Godmama have the ballroom and all the servants this evening. It must have put you to a great deal of inconvenience.'

The Ambassador, a man normally unmoved by the

rather vapid charms of most debutantes, found himself smiling paternally down at this one. A taking young woman, he thought. Not conventionally pretty, but handsome, with a lively mind. She seemed to him an interesting mix of innocence and common sense, and he detected an intriguing whiff of mystery about her.

He was, by profession, too discreet to ask questions, but he pinched her cheek and told her she was looking 'very pretty, indeed.' He consulted his pocket watch, then offered her his arm. 'Time to be gathering for dinner. Will you do me the honour?'

Sweeping into the reception room on the Ambassador's arm, to be presented to the minor royal who was the guest of honour, Cassandra had to pinch herself to bring her feet back to earth. Could it truly only be ten weeks ago that she had climbed out of her bedroom window and down the apple tree to escape Lord Offley?

Never, in her wildest imaginings, had she dreamed of a night such as this, held just for her. Whatever happened in the future, whatever became of her and Nicholas, tonight would be a special memory to treasure always.

Having made her curtsey without a stumble, and exchanged stilted conversation with the somewhat plain Grand Duchess, Cassandra thanked the Ambassador and slipped away to join her godmother.

'Come and stand quietly with me, child,' Lady Lydford said kindly. 'Let me look at you.'

Her gown, her first ever silk gown, was not in white or pink like most of the debutantes, but a deep cream, trimmed with old lace around the deeply flounced hem. The bodice and tiny puffed sleeves were smocked and caught with gold knots and the high waist caught with a broad golden ribbon which matched the tiara in her hair.

Godmama's hairdresser had pomaded her chestnut curls until they gleamed and clustered around her head and, as a finishing touch, Godmama had given her a pair of gold drop earrings.

Cassandra pointed one toe to admire her new satin slippers, then smiled at her godmother who smiled back. 'You look a picture, my dear. Every man at the ball will fall in love with you!'

Cassandra was laughing off the compliment when Nicholas arrived, impeccable in knee breeches and swallow tail coat, a filigree holder of dark yellow roses in his hand. She had scarcely seen him during the last week, since the outing to the western hills with Lord Stewart and the Hartley sisters.

He had been cold, distantly polite, but she would not let herself give up hope that his behaviour proved that he cared for her. Looking at him critically, she thought he looked pale, and his face, handsome as ever, showed signs of strain.

Having kissed his mother, he turned to Cassandra with a slight bow. For one wild moment, she believed he was about to offer her the roses, they went so perfectly with her gown.

'Nicholas. . .how lovely!' she began impetuously, stepping forward, smiling, her hand already outstretched to take the flowers.

He raised a brow in apparent surprise, took the proffered hand and bowed over it, kissing the air a good half inch above her fingers. Then he turned and made his way across the salon to where Lucy Hartley stood. She blushed prettily as Nicholas bowed over her hand and presented the flowers.

Cassandra stood cringing with embarrassment, convinced everyone in the room had witnessed the rebuff. Then the butler came in to announce that her ladyship was served.

The ball might be her come-out, but as a very junior debutante, Cassandra found herself seated well down the table, between the Ambassador's nephew and someone's aide de camp. Neither of them seemed greatly inclined to conversation, allowing Cassandra ample opportunity to watch Nicholas.

He was seated next to the Grand Duchess, nodding gravely at appropriate moments in the conversation she was dividing between him and Sir Marcus. He appeared to be managing Royalty with aplomb, but the Grand Duchess had neither the charm nor the looks to engage his total concentration.

Their eyes met as he glanced down the long polished table, and without thinking Cassandra gave him a small, conspiratorial smile. To her joy he returned it, suddenly the old Nicholas again, sharing a secret joke in some wayside inn. Then he turned back to his duty, leaving Cassandra glowing with an unexpected hope.

It was almost half past ten when the dinner party made its way through to the glittering ballroom. Cassandra took her place between Godmama and Sir Marcus at the head of the sweeping double staircase, and the next hour passed in a blur of compliments, bobbed curtseys and unfamiliar faces. Sir Marcus's diplomatic connexions and Lady Lydford's social circle had combined to produce a dazzling assembly of notabilities. Lady Lydford intended to make this ball the talking point of the Season, and already she recognised, with satisfaction, the heady buzz of a truly successful occasion.

When the receiving line thinned to a trickle, Lady Lydford dismissed Cassandra. 'Off you go into the ballroom now, child; dance with your beaux!' She looked at her goddaughter with pleasure, 'Enjoy yourself.'

Cassandra stepped into the ballroom with some trepidation: it seemed so full of unknown faces as the mass of dancers passed by in a swirl of coloured silks, a confusion of dress uniforms, and the dark elegance of male evening attire.

Then the music stopped and as couples came back to the gilt seats around the walls, she began to recognise faces. Soon she was the centre of a cluster of eager young male admirers, all clamouring for a place on her dance card. Laughing, she pencilled in names, trying to save space for Nicholas.

Surely he would come and ask her to dance soon? Surely that shared, secret smile meant something? She was clutching at straws, but to give up would break her heart. Cassandra looked around, hoping to see him, but could only catch a glimpse of the back of his head, bent to listen to a group of young ladies across the room.

'Dare I hope you are looking for me?' Lord Stewart was at her side, having displaced, with no apparent effort, a number of less effective young men.

Cassandra, her heart already engaged, was able to admire him dispassionately and realise that she was an object of considerable envy by many of the debutantes present. Anthony, Lord Stewart, was as blond as

Nicholas was dark and nearly as tall. He carried himself with a careless elegance that drew the eye to the sombre magnificence of his evening attire, moulding the breadth of his shoulders and the length of his well-muscled legs.

The arrangement of dark Palma violets in a filigree holder his messenger had brought earlier was a perfect complement to the cream of her gown and Cassandra thanked him warmly, holding the fragrant posy up to her nose to inhale the rich scent. Across the room, she saw Nicholas watching the little scene. He gave a slightly mocking bow, as if in reference to his jibe that she was trying to ensnare Lord Stewart.

Cassandra allowed herself to be swept into the next dance by Lord Stewart. Perhaps her wild plan, that she might pique Nicholas into recognising feelings for her he would not admit to, could yet succeed.

As they passed Nicholas and his partner on the floor Cassandra was laughingly protesting, 'But Lord Stewart, I could not possibly call you Anthony! That would be most improper. . .'.

For a moment, she thought Nicholas was going to ignore the provocation, then as she glanced out of the corner of her eye, he bent towards her and whispered in her ear, 'Minx!' Before she could make a rejoinder to this almost affectionate scold, the movement of the dance separated the two couples again.

'Can I hope you will be remaining in Vienna for the whole Season?' Anthony Stewart enquired, as he escorted her back to her seat against the cream and gold pilasters.

'I am entirely at Godmama's disposal,' Cassandra responded demurely. 'Do you intend to remain here, too, my lord? I felt sure I had heard Nicholas say you intended to leave next week.'

'So I did,' he responded easily. 'But then Fate took a hand, and I find my plans changed.' The look he gave her was warm and full of meaning.

'How inconvenient for you,' Cassandra murmured, as she sat down and unfurled her fan.

'May I?' He sat beside her taking the fan from her hand and began to wave it gently to and fro. 'I do not find it particularly inconvenient: perhaps you can guess why?'

This was going too fast for Cassandra. If he were in earnest—and he was too accomplished a flirt for her to tell—she could not risk wounding his feelings. Loving Nicholas as she did, it would be dishonourable to accept any other gentleman's suit without telling him why she could not return his regard. And, equally, she should not be encouraging a warm flirtation from a man such as this.

The young men of her own age were safe. They were too young yet to fix their interest and think of marriage, and a flirtation was safe and enjoyable for both parties. But Lord Stewart, like Nicholas, was too old and experienced to be taken lightly.

Flustered, she moved involuntarily and the heel of her slipper caught in the lace flounces at her hem with an audible rip.

'Oh, dear!' she exclaimed, twisting to look at the damage. 'I had better go and pin it up before it tears further. If you will excuse me, my lord?'

Some of the smaller rooms off the ballroom had been set aside for just such an emergency, and Cassandra slipped quickly through the throng, holding up her skirt carefully to avoid further damage. She remembered Godmama ordering one of the ladies' maids to remain in the smaller room with pin cushion and sal volatile to attend to whatever emergency might arise, and she pushed open the door, confidently expecting to find the woman in attendance.

A screen had been set just inside the door to afford privacy to the ladies and Cassandra was just about to slip round it when she heard voices.

Lucy Hartley was saying in a voice breathless with excitement, 'But, of course, I promise! I won't breathe a word!'

Blushing with confusion to have so nearly interrupted an intimate conversation—perhaps even a declaration—Cassandra was gathering up her skirts and preparing to back silently out when she was arrested by Lucy's next words.

'Oh, Nicholas, I am so happy!'

Cassandra felt as if her heart had stopped in her chest, and she reached out blindly to grip the door frame for support. Nicholas! Nicholas and Lucy Hartley! Her worst fears had come true. . .

But there was still hope, she realised dazedly. The man had not yet spoken. . . Nicholas was not an uncommon name. Perhaps it was another man and not her Nicholas.

Between the leaves of the screen was a narrow gap. Holding her breath, Cassandra put her eye to it just as Nicholas—her Nicholas—said, 'Lucy, you *are* a darling! What you tell me makes me so happy: you cannot believe the torment I have been through.' Through the crack, all Cassandra could see was the dark head bent towards the blonde and Lucy's white arm coming up as she reached up to his shoulder to draw down his face to hers.

Cassandra choked down a shattering sob and backed away from the screen in desperate silence. To be discovered there, to have those two feel sorry for her, pity her, was a humiliation she could never tolerate.

Every foolish hope, every foolish dream she had ever harboured, that Nicholas could feel for her as she did for him, lay shattered at her feet. All that mattered now was to escape undetected, her dignity intact. Now he was engaged to another woman, he must never guess how she felt about him. No wonder he was unwilling to talk further about Venice! What did it matter to a man who was in love, and was loved in return, by a beautiful young debutante?

Cassandra found sanctuary in the retiring room next door and sat shivering with reaction, unheeding of the abigail who pinned up the torn flounce. I must have been mad, she thought, her thoughts chasing round like a rat in a cage. How could I have mistaken his careless kindness, his protective anger, even the fleeting moments of passion for love?

How am I going to get through the coming weeks of betrothal celebrations and wedding preparations? Lucy would expect her new friend to rejoice with her and share in her plans. But what alternative was there for her now? To throw herself at Lord Stewart's head? Cassandra sensed that if she gave him enough encouragement, he would declare himself. But she could not do that to him, she liked him too well to hurt him. And to marry him without love would be to dishonour both of them.

'Miss. . .miss. . .I've finished.' The maid had obviously been trying to attract her attention for some moments. Absently, Cassandra thanked the girl and stood up. Opposite, a mirror showed her her own reflection, her eyes glistening with tears she was determined not to shed tonight. She smoothed down the cool silk of her skirts, remembering the hope with which she had dressed, then straightened her shoulders, took a deep breath and opened the door.

The first person she encountered as she crossed the passage to the ballroom was the languid figure of the Comte de Courcelles. As she stood there, unable to believe her eyes, she saw first puzzlement, then dawning recognition cross his features.

For one desperate moment, she believed he had not recognised her, then he stepped forward with both hands outstretched. 'Can it be? *Mon Dieu*, what a transformation from Paris! Just as I suspected—Cass the valet makes a very beautiful young woman.'

It was useless to deny it: speculation and mischief lit up his face. 'Guy. . .what are you doing here, of all places?'

'Why, I have just arrived in Vienna and I make it my business to have an entreé to all the most interesting entertainments. And you,' he gestured to her finery, 'you look beautiful! What a change from fustian and breeches. What are you doing here?'

'Ssh! Say nothing about that! It is my come-out.' Cassandra put her hand on his arm and drew him back into the ballroom. 'Lady Lydford is my godmama.'

'But, of course, I remember from our conversation in the library in Paris.' There was a pause. Cassandra was aware of his scrutiny. 'You are sad, little one. Why so, on your big night?'

'It is nothing I can talk about, and in any case, it is all my own silly fault.' She gave him a watery smile. 'You are kind, Guy, but there is nothing you can do to help.'

The Count shrugged, 'Perhaps it will seem better tomorrow. . .'

He broke off as Cassandra gasped at the sight of a beautiful woman waltzing past in the arms of a cavalry officer. 'But. . .that was Mariette!' The spiteful card-player from the Paris party was unmistakable. 'What is she doing here?'

'I made the mistake of offering her escort from Paris.' He shook his head. 'She is as sharp as a needle. . .'

Cassandra could see the woman's gaze riveted on them now. There was recognition and malicious speculation on her kittenish face. The look boded trouble.

'Ah, Miss Weston. We have missed you, I am quite pining away, I assure you!'

Anyone less in danger of pining away than Lord Stewart wold be hard to find, Cassandra reflected. She saw, with slight alarm, the steely glint in his eye as he glanced at Guy's hand resting over hers.

'Lord Stewart. . .that silly girl took such an age to do my hem. And on my way back I met the Count. . .' Her voice trailed away. How was she to explain her familiarity with the Frenchman when she supposedly had only just come out into Society?

'An old friend of the family,' Guy supplied easily. 'Guy de Montpensier, Comte de Courcelles, at your service, *monsieur*.'

'Lord Anthony Stewart.' The two exchanged formal bows. 'Miss Weston, I came to claim my dance—I am on your card, I believe?'

'I think not, my lord,' said Cassandra, composedly. 'I have already stood up with you twice, which some might think very forward. I dare not do so again.'

'Excellent,' the Count exclaimed. 'So that means this dance is free? Please do me the honour.'

It was a waltz. Although the Count had not been presented to her as an approved partner for this daring dance, Cassandra was beyond caring. Perhaps Godmama would not notice. . .

Guy encircled her waist lightly and as the music began asked, 'Is that the one who is breaking your heart?'

'No!' Cassandra was taken aback by his perspicacity. 'I mean, no-one. . .' Across the ballroom she saw Nicholas, his face suddenly arrested as he saw her dancing past with the Count.

'Nonsense! Do you expect me to believe that? Tell me who it is and I will run him through for you.'

Cassandra could not suppress a somewhat shaky giggle.

'That is better. Now, tell me how I can help you.'

Cassandra circled in his arms, her eyes fixed on the solitaire diamond in his cravat and wished she could pour out the story to him as easily as she had told the tale of her flight, that night in the library in Paris.

'Truly, Guy, no-one can help me.' She looked up into the sympathetic brown eyes and the attractive, ugly face. 'Not even you. I have been foolish, and it hurts, but I must live with that.'

As they left the dance floor, Anthony Stewart appeared at their side as if by magic.

'You may not feel able to dance with me, Miss Weston, but surely I may claim you for supper?' He extended his arm to her, with a challenging glance at Guy.

'But surely, Cassandra, you will not abandon an old friend on his first night in Vienna?' the Count pressed in his turn.

Cassandra looked from one to the other and felt herself wilting with the heat and tension. 'Gentlemen, you must both forgive me, but the heat. . .'

'My dear Miss Weston, allow me to take you to the terrace.' Guy saw her doubtful look and hastened to reassure her. 'Several of the chaperones are already out there, and some other parties have taken their supper outside.'

'That would be wonderful.' Suddenly the hectic colour and the noise of the ballroom on top of the shocks of the evening struck a discordant note; fresh air and the cool flagstones of the terrace would be soothing.

The Count propelled her gently towards the French windows. 'Out you go, *ma petite*, and we,' he cast a resigned look at Lord Stewart, who was obviously not going to give ground, 'will fetch you some supper and a little champagne.'

The cool air struck the heated skin at her breast and forehead as Cassandra wandered slowly across the terrace to a pillared belvedere which stood empty, looking out across the gardens. She rested her brow against a fluted column for a moment and let her mind empty. Tomorrow she would have to think, to plan, but tonight that was beyond her.

'Oh, Nicholas. . .' she whispered against the cold stone.

'Cassandra.' His voice behind her came so prompt on her words, she thought for one mad moment she had conjured him up out of her imagination

'Nicholas?' She turned and saw him, unmistakably real, the moonlight striking dark lights from his hair. She knew she had gone pale, but he did not seem to notice.

'I thought I was never going to get you alone.' He took her by the elbow and steered her further into the shadows, his voice low and serious. 'I must speak to you.'

# CHAPTER FOURTEEN

'No, NICHOLAS, you have said quite enough,' Cassandra began, certain he was about to confide the news of his betrothal to Lucy to her. She needed at least a night to compose herself to hear that news with anything like an appearance of complacency. She lifted her skirts and tried to brush past him.

'Wait, please hear me out.' He took her by the shoulders, holding her back against the pillar.

Cassandra shivered as the stone struck cold through the thin silk and instinctively Nicholas drew her closer to his warmth. 'Don't be frightened of me, Cassandra—I know I've been short tempered and difficult to be with. . .' He broke off, running one hand through his hair distractedly. 'No, damn it, I've been harsh and unfair. . .'

'I understand.' And she thought she did. He must have been on tenterhooks, worried that his suit with Lucy Hartley would not prosper. It was enough to make any man short tempered, and then to discover her deceit in Venice would have been the last straw.

Nicholas stroked the back of one hand lingeringly down her cheek. 'We have both behaved badly, there are things I regret. . .'

'There is no need. The regrets are all mine,' she said thinly.

'You don't seem to realise the position we find ourselves in. I had not intended to say anything of this to you tonight, but now that Guy and that little witch Mariette are here, everything is changed.'

'But why?' Cassandra was confused. 'He was so pleased to see me, he is our friend.'

'So he is, and an indiscreet mischief-maker when he chooses, although Guy's capacity for trouble is nothing as compared to Mariette's! She bears me a grudge. One word that they met you in Paris disguised as a boy, and you are hopelessly compromised. . .ruined.'

'But Guy wouldn't betray me,' she protested indignantly. 'And surely Mariette cannot be that wicked?'

'I cannot take the risk.' He broke off and regarded her with exasperation. 'This is not at all what I intended. Please, listen to me, Cassandra, and for once in your life, don't interrupt!'

Cassandra fell silent, watching his face in the moonlight. No doubt he was irritated that he had had to take time from his newly-betrothed to speak to her.

'What I am trying to say, Cassandra, is, will you marry me?'

Cassandra stared at him, lips parted in stunned amazement. When she could find words, she stammered, 'Marry? Me—marry you? But. . .Lucy. . .'

'So you know I've spoken to her? Don't worry, Cassandra, no-one else knows, and Lucy will understand, she is entirely in my confidence.'

'Understand!' What could he say, what could any honourable gentleman say, to explain why he was breaking an engagement only hours after making it?

'I will explain everything to her. But, Cassandra, never mind about Lucy, what is your answer?'

What could she answer to a man whose lunatic concept of honour would lead him to jilt one young lady in order to protect the reputation of another he did not love!

'I thought I had seen you at your worst, Nicholas!' She stepped free of his arms, drawing herself up, anger shaking every word. 'But I did not think I would live to be so insulted by you, or to see you behave so dishonourably!' Her fury burned away every tender feeling she had ever had for him. 'Now I see how you can behave. . .'

'Cassandra, you cannot have understood me. I repeat, I wish you to become my wife—why are you acting as if I had offered you a *carte blanche*?'

'Sir, I consider your behaviour as dishonourable as if you had asked me to become your mistress! Now, let me go!' She spat the last words at him and ran across the terrace, tears burning at the back of her throat.

She managed to evade Nicholas in the maze of small passages that led off the ballroom, but one pursuer found her as she threw herself onto a heap of cushions in the window seat of the small salon, and finally burst into tears.

Someone gathered her up; for a moment, she struggled, then she saw it was Guy, not Nicholas, and capitulated, sobbing bitterly into his shirt front.

He waited patiently until the tears subsided, then found her a handkerchief and sat her back in the cushions. 'Now, do not tell me there is nothing I can do to help. I can at least listen. Speak to me, Cassandra.' Once again she found herself pouring out her story to him.

When the whole sorry tale was told, Guy was silent for several minutes. Cassandra sat staring blankly at a vase of flowers which swam in and out of focus before her tired eyes. Confiding everything to Guy had left her drained.

'Of course,' he said thoughtfully, 'if it were only myself involved, I would go to Nicholas and assure him my lips were sealed. But there is Mariette...if I appeal to her good nature—which does not exist—she will know there is a scandal to be made. Yet if I say nothing, we can still be certain she will make trouble. She has no love for Nicholas: he has repulsed her too often; what he said to you shows he is aware of that danger.'

He fell back into thought. His solution, when it came, was so startling, Cassandra was jerked back to reality with a vengeance.

'You could always marry me.'

Cassandra stared at him incredulously, scarcely able to credit what she had heard. 'What? You mean elope? Guy—you don't want to marry me, how would that help either of us?'

He shrugged insouciantly. 'I have been thinking lately that perhaps I should marry, settle down. Domesticity has its charms!' He smiled at her. 'It might suit both of us very well, but, of course, I do not press you if you are unwilling. *Naturellement*, you would stay with my housekeeper and I will stay at an inn, so you can feel quite comfortable. We will announce our engagement: there will be some talk, but with my reputation...*c'est le vie*. That will convince Nicholas that he is free to do the honourable thing by Miss Lucy. And if you decide afterwards you do not wish to marry me, we can quietly break off the engagement.'

Cassandra rubbed one hand across her eyes, wondering if she were asleep and dreaming. She could never marry him, as he was so light-heartedly suggesting, but he was right, this would offer her a breathing space. And, more importantly, it would force Nicholas's hand.

'Do not worry, *ma petite*. You can trust me, you know.'

'I don't doubt that for a moment,' Cassandra assured him. He may be a rake, but he was a gentleman.

'So why do you hesitate?' He shrugged, 'We are friends, are we not? After a good night's sleep, this will all seem simpler. Tomorrow is another day.'

Cassandra couldn't believe she was even considering his offer. 'Guy, I can't do it! What of your reputation?'

Guy laughed. 'It could only be enhanced by your company.'

'No,' Cassandra stood up. 'I am sorry, Guy, but I cannot accept your offer, it would not be fair of me, nor honourable.' She looked up and caught his wry smile. 'But we can still be friends—can't we? You are the only one I can talk to. . .'

'Ah, *ma petite*, of course. And I will not accept this as final—my offer still stands if you change your mind.'

'I must go and find Nicholas and make sure he says nothing to Lucy to break their engagment.' She shook her head in bewilderment. 'I do not know what he was thinking of, to behave so dishourably.'

'Do not judge him too harshly. He is worred about you and he did not take the time to think this thing through. I have a reputation as an *intrigant*, but he should know I would never risk the reputation of a lady.' He raised her hand to her lips, then gave her a gentle push towards the ballroom.

Godmama and Miss Fox were sitting, heads together, on a satin covered banquette just inside the door, talking animatedly. Cassandra paused to make sure they didn't see her as she slipped past and remark her reddened eyes, then was caught by what they were saying.

'My dear Sophia,' Miss Fox exclaimed, with unusual animation. 'I do congratulate you! What an excellent match, what a charming daughter-in-law she will make.'

'Well, I must admit to some anxiety, my dear Araminta. He seemed so slow to recognise what was perfectly plain to me—that he was in love with the girl. But men can be so dense!' For a few seconds, the two ladies contemplated the frailties of the male sex, then Lady Lydford added, 'It will be such a suitable match, she has the looks, the charm, the character, to make him happy. When he told me he was going to ask her this evening, I was overjoyed—I do wish he would come and tell me he has been accepted. Where *is* he?'

As the two ladies scanned the dance floor, Cassandra slipped past behind a column and began her own search. So he had told his mother about Lucy! It was even more important now to make sure he did nothing to break the betrothal.

She found him at last on the terrace, but to her horror, not alone. Lucy Hartley sat by his side, one hand confidingly on his sleeve while she listened intently to his words. It was impossible to hear what he was saying, but the effect was clear to see.

Lucy's expression changed from concentration to one of shock and dismay. Then she fumbled in her reticule and dabbed her eyes with a delicate handkerchief, her face averted from Nicholas.

Cassandra did not wait to see anything else. It was too late to stop him now, but if she was out of the way, already ruined by some other action, then there was nothing to stop him marrying Lucy. And if she acted now, quickly, before the broken engagement became a public scandal, perhaps the gentle Miss Hartley might forgive him and take him back.

Lucy was not the sort of person who would blurt out the news of her jilting in public—she would have too much pride and sense of decorum. Cassandra thought she had until tomorrow morning at most to put things right, but she must act now and find Guy.

He was where she had left him. One look at her face as she entered the room brought him to his feet, his hands outstretched to her.

'It's too late, Guy, he's already broken off the engagement.'

'*Sacre bleu*!' Guy swore. 'So, what do you want to do now, Cassandra?'

'I don't know, I just do not know,' she cried. 'Loving Nicholas as I do, I cannot allow him to ruin his life!'

'Then come away with me,' Guy urged. 'Whatever madness is possessing him at the moment, he is an honourable man. He cannot marry both of you: by coming with me, you free him for Lucy.'

Cassandra stopped her agitated pacing in front of

him and stood looking deep into his eyes. She saw the concern there, and knew she could trust him, however madcap and unconventional he seemed.

'I'll do it,' she said resolutely. 'I'll come with you, Guy.'

# CHAPTER FIFTEEN

Guy took her hand and squeezed it encouragingly. 'Don't worry, things will work out.' He sounded very light-hearted about the whole business, Cassandra thought. She only wished she could share his optimism.

'I will come with you. I love Nicholas: if I cannot marry him, I will marry no-one. For his sake, he must marry Lucy, and you are right. If I am apparently engaged to you, he will believe himself free of his obligation and can follow his heart.'

Guy glanced at the determined, intelligent face. 'What is it? You have had an idea?'

'Yes! As soon as Nicholas is convinced of our intentions and the marriage to Lucy is announced, I will throw myself on Miss Fox's mercy. She will find me an eligible situation.'

It sounded a neat solution, but she had an uneasy feeling that in reality, things would not fall out so easily. That did not matter now—the important thing was to convince Nicholas she had gone beyond his reach.

As she had come to expect, Guy raised none of the objections she was so uneasily aware of. 'Very well, then, it will be as you say.'

'We must think what to do now,' Cassandra said. Having made the momentous decision to flee with Guy, she now felt stronger. 'We must act quickly so Nicholas has a chance of retrieving matters with

Lucy—and I must leave a note for Godmama telling her I am going to marry you. She wishes Nicholas to marry Lucy, so she will do everything to promote the match.'

'Is there a room where you can write without being interrupted?'

'My room would be best,' Cassandra decided quickly. 'No-one would expect to find me there now. Come,' she took him by the hand and led him through the maze of passages to her deserted bedroom.

Once she had begun to write, the words came easily from her pen. She explained that she had met the Count in Paris and fallen in love and now they had met again and seized their chance of happiness. Godmama would be deeply shocked, and the thought pained her, but at least the Dowager would feel free to wash her hands of such an erring goddaughter.

She pressed a wafer over the folded paper to seal it and slipped quietly along to Lady Lydford's bedchamber. The bed was already turned down, ready for when the Dowager finally came to bed. Cassandra heard the chime of the little clock as she laid the letter on the lace-trimmed pillow. She hesitated for a moment beside the bed, hoping her godmother would forgive her.

Once she had gone with Guy, there would be no turning back, Nicholas would be lost to her forever. Then she remembered Lucy's white arms encircling his neck so lovingly, and hardened her resolution: he was already lost.

Four o'clock already. Soon the ball would be over, carriages were even now collecting weary revellers, and the street outside was growing noisy with the

rumble of coachwheels and the cries of porters sum-
moning coachmen.

Back in her chamber, Cassandra pulled a small
valise from a cupboard. 'What shall I take?' she asked.

'I know nothing about the etiquette of elopement,'
Guy said drily. 'Surprisingly, given my reputation, this
is not something I have undertaken before, even in
pretence.' He paused, consideringly. 'It must look
convincing... Your hairbrush and so forth,' He dismissed feminine toiletries with a wave of his hand.
'And a gown suitable for travelling.'

'Shall I change now?'

'No. If you leave here in a day dress, it will be
remarked upon by the servants. In a balldress with an
evening cloak and the hood pulled over your face, you
will be in no way remarkable.'

He was right. Cassandra, her heart in her mouth,
slipped through the throng of guests, flushed and
laughing as they waited in the hall for their carriages
to arrive at the front doors. No-one noticed her small,
cloaked figure as she followed the Count's broad back
as he made his way out.

'I will not risk drawing attention by calling my
carriage. Come,' he slipped his hand under her arm.
'We will go round to the mews and find it there.'

Minutes later, they were bowling down the wide
boulevard away from the Embassy towards the house
on the outskirts of the city which Guy had taken for
his stay in Vienna.

Cassandra sat in the shadowed coach, stealing sideways glances at the man beside her. He was not conventionally good-looking; his nose was too prominent, his
expression too quizzical and sardonic, his hair unruly

despite his barber's best efforts. But his personality was so warm, his infectious enthusiasm so charming, that Cassandra felt she could trust him completely. And despite his devil-may-care reputation, she believed him when he said he would look after her.

Now the excitement of the actual escape was ebbing, she felt again the cold knot of misery in her stomach. She remembered Nicholas and their journey; the moments of tenderness, of passion, of joy and laughter. They could have been so happy together—friends as well as lovers.

She knew more about him than any respectable woman should. She knew he was bad tempered in the morning and that he did not snore. She was really most improperly acquainted with the Earl and his tastes. Despite her misery, a small snort of remembered amusement escaped her lips.

'Is that amusement or hysteria?' Guy asked wryly.

'Amusement, I think. No doubt I should be having hysterics, but I seem to have lost the capacity for vapours.'

'Believe me, Cassandra,' he said with feeling, 'I would never have carried you off if I thought you were prone to the vapours!'

The sound of the wheels changed as the carriage drew off the highway into a flagged courtyard. Guy helped Cassandra down and glanced up at his coachman. 'You have not seen this lady tonight, Jacques.'

'*Bien sur, monsieur.*' The man shook the reins and drove the team on round the corner of the house towards the stables.

A sleepy porter opened the door and was swiftly dismissed with an order to send for the count's valet.

'You can sleep here,' Guy pushed open a bedchamber door. 'It is my room; if you need anything, I will be in the dressing room next door, changing into riding clothes. I will go to an inn tonight as soon as I have spoken to the housekeeper about you.'

'Yes, of course,' Cassandra said thankfully, looking at the bed. How wonderful just to climb in and sleep for hours, forget all that had happened tonight.

As soon as the door closed behind him, Cassandra peeled off her long gloves, tossed her reticule onto the bed and began, with difficulty, to unhook her dress.

Lady Lydford reached her bedroom at four thirty and sank gratefully into a chair as her dresser unfastened her jewellery, then knelt to unlace her shoe ribbons.

'Good heavens, Siddons, I am quite exhausted, I must be getting old.'

'Not you, my lady,' the dresser said comfortably. 'Did you enjoy your evening? I hear we may be expecting happy news in the household. . .'

Siddons had been with the Dowager for many years and, while discreet, was not above enjoying a little gossip with her mistress when they were alone.

'Well, I hope so, Siddons.' The Dowager stood to let the gown fall to her feet. 'But I haven't seen my son for hours—it is too bad of him to keep me in suspense. But then,' she added thoughtfully, 'I have not seen Miss Weston for some time either. It is most improper if they are off somewhere holding hands, but then, if they are engaged, I suppose there's no harm. Besides, I'm too weary to chase after young people at this time in the morning.'

'My lady.' Siddons turned from the bed, a puzzled expression on her face, a folded paper in her hand.

'What on earth?' Lady Lydford broke the seal and scanned the contents swiftly, with a sharp intake of breath. She read it a second time, more slowly, then snapped, 'My robe, quickly. And, Siddons, not a word of this to anyone, but Miss Weston has run away.'

As Siddons helped her mistress into her robe, she said quietly, 'With your permission, I will find Miss Weston's maid and tell her to say nothing. If anyone should ask we could say she is too exhausted after the ball to leave her room.'

Lady Lydford nodded her thanks and hurried out, her long skirts sweeping behind her. She flung her son's bedroom door open even as she knocked and, to her relief, found him, apparently just retiring.

'Mother! What is wrong?'

'Read this.' She thrust the letter into his hand and waited impatiently while he read it.

Nicholas swore, then pulled on his coat again. 'The little fool! I don't believe a word of this. Although why she...' He broke off with a taut smile for his mother. 'Don't worry, Mama, go to bed. I will bring her back.'

'But, Nicholas, whatever did you do to drive her away and into the arms of this Comte de Courcelles, or whatever his name is?'

'I don't know, but there is some misunderstanding here,' he said grimly. 'I will get precisely what I deserve if she does marry him. Try not to worry, she may be safer than you fear: Guy is not the reprobate he likes to be thought. Or perhaps I am comforting myself. . . But there is no time for speculation now. I will bring her back.'

As he strode to the door, the Countess called, 'But how will you find him?'

'He will have signed the Embassy guest book with his name and direction. I will start there. I cannot believe she intended this madness from the start, therefore they will have to make some preparation.'

He was gone before his mother could respond and it seemed only minutes later when she heard the sound of hooves on the cobbles as he cantered off into the night.

After a considerable time, Cassandra had finally managed to free herself from her ballgown and was perched on the edge of Guy's bed, unlacing her shoe ribbons.

She sat wriggling her aching toes, almost too weary to make the effort to roll into bed. Without warning, the quiet of the mansion was shattered by a thunderous knocking at the front door, and the sound of raised voices.

'Milord! Stop! You cannot. . .my master is not receiving.'

'The devil he's not! Stand aside.'

Heavy footsteps pounded up the stairs. Guy, in his shirt sleeves and breeches, flung open the dividing door from the dressing room.

'What is happening?'

'It's Nicholas!'

'*Mon Dieu!* Events are moving faster than I thought.' He strode over and put a protective arm around her shoulders as she sat on the bed. 'Your godmother must have found your letter at once. Your Nicholas, unless I am much mistaken, is out for my blood.'

'Oh, Guy,' Cassandra clutched his hand, terrified of what Nicholas would do when he found them like this. She was acutely aware of her bare legs and shoulders, of her flimsy petticoats and Guy's own half-dressed state.

The chamber door opened with almost maddening slowness to reveal the Earl of Lydford, his face taut with anger. Through her fears, Cassandra felt her heart surge with joy at the sight of him. He was here and, for whatever motive, it seemed he cared enough to come after her.

'A very touching scene,' Nicholas remarked, eyeing the pair of them as they sat on the edge of the bed.

'Nicholas—it's not what it seems. . .' Cassandra began.

'That I can well believe,' he retorted. 'I suggest you take your arms from around Miss Weston, Count. This farce has gone quite far enough.'

'I have no intention of leaving the side of my affianced wife,' Guy said, with some panache. 'Leave my house immediately, you are distressing Miss Weston.'

'If Miss Weston is distressed, it is entirely her own fault. Cassandra, put on some clothes and wait downstairs. I will come and take you home in a minute.'

'No! I won't leave Guy! You'll challenge him to a duel or something dreadful and one of you will be killed. . .'

'Probably me,' Guy muttered, *sotto voce*.

'Undoubtedly you,' Nicholas remarked. 'Cassandra, will you do what you're told?'

'I think perhaps the time has come to tell him the truth.' Guy got off the bed and moved with studied casualness to a position nearer the dressing room door.

'How can you suggest that?' Cassandra said reproachfully. 'You know why I can't.'

'One of you had better tell me, or I will have to extract the information some other way.' Nicholas leaned one shoulder against a massive armoire. 'And my patience is not unlimited.'

Cassandra felt herself go pale. She couldn't let Nicholas fight Guy, yet nor could she betray whatever hopes there were of his honourably marrying Lucy.

Guy, however, had other ideas. 'No, really, *mon ami*. You cannot be considering fisticuffs? This evening suit has suffered enough, what with being wept down. . .'

Nicholas grinned. 'You have my sympathy.'

'Oh, stop it! Stop it, both of you!' Cassandra could stand it no longer. 'This isn't a joke. Nicholas, Guy was only trying to help. I came away with him so you would be free. . .free to marry Lucy.' There was a surprising lack of response from Nicholas, but she stumbled on. 'How could you hurt her by jilting her when you love her so? I saw you together kissing. . . how could you make her cry like that?'

Nicholas straightened up slowly, his eyes on her face. She had all his attention now, and the tolerant amusement had vanished.

'What is this about Lucy Hartley? I can make neither head nor tail of it. What has she to do with any of this? You can't have run away because the girl kissed me on the cheek, for heaven's sake! Why should I have to marry her?'

He seemed entirely sincere. Cassandra shook her head in confusion. 'But I overheard you in the retiring room. You were making a declaration, you made her promise not to tell anyone. And then you proposed to me out of some misplaced fear you have compromised me, and say Lucy will understand. No wonder she was in tears on the terrace.'

There was a long silence while Nicholas digested this outburst, then Guy said wearily, 'I confess I do not understand how you English manage to make simple matters of the heart into such dramas. It is a wonder any of you marry at all. And if you would stop regarding me with that sinister look in your eye, I will assure you that not one word of Miss Weston's escapades in Paris or here will ever cross my lips.'

Nicholas glanced at him. 'I will take your word for it. But why you felt it necessary to interfere, and why you had to descend on us with that minx Mariette in tow...'

'You've spoken to her?' Guy waved a hand. 'But surely you see, one word from her and Cassandra's reputation would be ashes.'

'Ah, but she now knows I can spoil her chances here in Vienna, just as effectively as she could damage Cassandra's good name. She will keep her mouth shut.'

Nicholas looked at Cassandra. There was an expression in his eyes she had never seen before, and when he spoke, it was as though he had forgotten Guy. 'Is this all true? That you fled because you thought I was proposing to you only out of a sense of duty—and for no other reason?'

She nodded dumbly.

Nicholas turned to Guy. 'You are decidedly *de trop*, my friend. Might I suggest you leave us?'

'With pleasure, Nicholas.' He slipped from the room, closing the door silently behind him.

'Now, let us be clear. On seeing Guy and Mariette, I am supposed to have decided to jilt Lucy, and offer for you, to save your reputation?'

Cassandra nodded. 'Well, didn't you?'

'No. What you overheard was me telling Lucy of my intention to propose—not to her, but to you, Cassandra. I wanted to propose to you tomorrow, when everything was quiet and we could be alone. Then, when I saw Guy and Mariette, I felt I had to establish your position at once, beyond any doubt. But I handled it badly, my love. I am not surprised you misunderstood.

'As for Lucy, knowing how close you had become over the last few weeks, I thought she might give me some clue as to how you would receive me. Lucy is a friendly soul, I've known her for years. People keep suggesting we should marry,' he added ironically, 'and perhaps we would have done. But neither of us truly loved each other that way, and mercifully, we are friends enough to admit it. What you saw was Lucy giving me her approval with a kiss. Then when I told her how coldly you had rejected me, she was upset: hence the tears.'

Cassandra stood staring at the man she loved, wondering at how this tangle had come about, then the import of what he had said dawned on her. 'You were

going to propose to me, anyway? Before you saw
Guy? But why?'

He moved slowly towards her, the tension easing
slowly from his face to be replaced by a wry smile.
'Can't you guess, brat?'

'But you don't love me,' she said shakily. This
couldn't be happening.

'Don't I?' He was very close to her now, but still he
did not touch her. 'Oh, but I do, Miss Weston. I think
I've loved you ever since you braved Aunt Augusta
with that pile of shirts. I just didn't realise it.'

'But why not?' she whispered, looking up into the
green eyes, too afraid to believe this could be true,
and not a cruel joke.

'First of all, because I thought you were a child, and
I felt thoroughly guilty about the way you made me
feel.' His hand came up to cup her chin gently. 'And
you made me feel so very. . .' He broke off at the
blush staining her cheeks.

'And when I discovered the truth about your age, I
was so confused by the responsibility I felt for you,
and my regret at dragging you half way across Europe,
and the sheer irritation you invoked in me every time
I started to feel fond of you. . .'

'Ha!' Cassandra exclaimed, suddenly, miraculously,
enjoying herself. It was all going to be all right: he
loved her, he had always loved her! 'I was never as
irritating as you were!'

'You were enough to try the patience of a saint.' He
smiled down at her. 'You still are. Cassandra. . .do you
think, just possibly, you could. . .'

'Love you? Is this a declaration, my lord?'

Cassandra feigned coyness. She hated to see Nicholas, her Nicholas, deprived of his usual self-assurance.

He raked his hands through his hair. 'Yes, of course it is, you provoking woman. I love you. Do you love me? Will you marry me? Is that plain enough for you?'

She opened her mouth to say yes, then was struck by a cold fear. 'Even after what I did in Venice?'

He didn't reply, but took her hand and led her to a chaise longue. Seated beside her, he gathered up both hands in his and said quietly, 'Tell me why.'

Cassandra looked into the strong, tender face she loved so much and struggled to find the right words. 'I wanted you to see me as a woman, not a silly, trouble-some girl who had spoilt your Tour. I wanted you to see that those moments when you'd seemed to want me, meant something, that we were right for each other.'

'But you could have told me.'

'I didn't think you would understand, seeing me as you did, a mixture of a boy and a child. But I loved you as a woman, although I didn't understand what that meant until that moment in Lucia's bedroom...'

'That woman! She led you astray. What can one expect from a...'

'No, that is not fair. She wanted to help me; she made me see that perhaps you cared for me. I was wrong to accept her solution.'

'Why did you run away having come so far?' he queried gently.

'I had no idea it would be like that, that I would feel so overwhelmed. I was frightened and then, I realised it would be wrong to do something that would dishonour both of us.' She lifted troubled eyes to his, 'Can you understand?'

Nicholas put his arm around her shoulder, pulling her hard against his chest. 'Why couldn't you tell me?'

Cassandra kept her face hidden in his shirtfront: the smell of clean linen and the warmth of him was achingly familiar. 'I knew you'd be angry. I couldn't bear you to think less of me. And I was afraid, I couldn't control what I had incited in you. . .'

'You have no need to be frightened, Cassie: next time it will be different, I promise you.' His voice was very husky against her hair.

'But not too different,' she ventured, daringly.

Nicholas laughed, and tipped up her chin. 'Minx! We are getting very solemn here, but while we are, let me say I never meant any of those things I said to you the other morning when I found the necklace. I was hurt and I struck out: I should have trusted my feelings for you.'

Cassandra twisted free from his arms and looked at him directly. 'Why did you not tell me how you felt when we reached Vienna?'

'Because I thought you had had enough of me!' he said wryly. 'I had scolded you, walloped you, lectured you, nearly got you drowned. You'd seen my bad temper. . . How could that compare with being courted by the likes of Lord Stewart or a horde of well-bred, amiable young men?'

'What could Lord Stewart give me that could compare with being attacked by brigands, bitten by fleas, poisoned by disgusting food and entertained by the Bulstrodes?' She regarded him from under her lashes.

'I think you must agree, Nicholas, that either I'm in love with you, or I am fit only for Bedlam.'

'I think we're both mad,' he said, with a smile. 'But tell me you love me, and will marry me.'

Cassandra looked at him, the happiness welling up inside her so she could hardly speak. 'Yes, Nicholas, I love you. I think I have loved you for years, but I only realised what it was in Nice. I will marry you, it's all I ever dreamed of. I only ran away with Guy because I saw no future without you—and I wanted you to be happy. I would never have married him—nor anyone else.'

'Little fool,' he said huskily, pulling her against his chest and kissing her with a passionate, possessive intensity. With a sigh of surrender, Cassandra responded, melting into his embrace. For the first time, she could express all the love she felt for him without reserve, without fear.

How long they would have stayed there locked in each other's arms she had no way of knowing. All she knew was that Guy tapped on the door and strolled in, a bottle of champagne in one hand, three glasses in the other.

'It seems I must play the chaperon tonight, my friends. Not a role I am used to, but then, tonight has been full of new experiences.'

Nicholas turned to him challengingly. 'How could you play such a trick on me, after all the years we have been friends?'

The Count was concentrating on setting the glasses down safely. 'I guessed Cassandra might be wrong, and if that was the case, I was sure you would come for her, as indeed you did. If I had been wrong, well, I would have done my best to help her.' He sketched a small bow, 'I am entirely at your service, my friends, and you see what risks to life and limb I am prepared to run for you!'

There was a short silence while both Nicholas and Cassandra regarded the Count, then Nicholas laughed, hugging Cassandra against his side possessively. 'It seems we must both thank you. Will you come to the wedding?'

The Count de Courcelles popped the cork and filled the glasses. 'Your health!' He raised his wine. 'To the Earl and Countess of Lydford!'

# MILLS & BOON®

## *Makes any time special*

### Enjoy a romantic novel from
### *Mills & Boon®*

*Presents...*    *Enchanted*™    TEMPTATION.

*Historical Romance*™    ♥MEDICAL
ROMANCE®

THE
# Regency
COLLECTION

*Where rogues find romance*

**Look out for the eleventh volume in this limited
collection of Regency Romances from
Mills & Boon® in March 2000.**

## Featuring:

*Not Quite a Gentleman*
**by Paula Marshall**

and

*A Lady of Independent Means*
**by Sarah Westleigh**

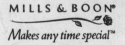

**Still only £4.99**

MILLS & BOON®

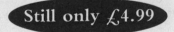

*Makes any time special*™

*Available at most branches of WH Smith, Tesco, Martins,
Borders, Easons, Volume One/James Thin
and most good paperback bookshops*